No One Dies

By Annie Pearson

Chaos House

Restoration Rules
Number One

No One Dies

Annie Pearson

Copyright © 2020 by Annie Pearson

Print ISBN: 9781939423979

Published by Jūgum Press
505 Broadway East #237
Seattle, Washington U.S.A.
www.jugumpress.net

Cover design by Jacyn Stewart

For Waverly, who remains my guide to True North.

Contents

Silvy, Silvy, all on one day,
She dressed herself in man's array,
A sword and pistol all by her side,
To meet her true love she did ride.
She met her true love all in the plain.
'Stand and deliver, kind sir,' she said,
'Stand and deliver, kind sir,' said she,
'Or else this moment you shall die.'

"The Female Highwayman"
Traditional ballad

—

But I prithee sweet wag, shall there be gallows standing in
England when thou art king?

— *Henry IV, Part 1*
William Shakespeare

Milestones:
The Foxes of Marborne Parish

1650: Samuel Foxe leads local royalists in Civil War
   Commonwealth & Interregnum, 1649–1660

1655: Samuel Foxe is 15th Earl of Marborne
   Oliver Cromwell is Lord Protector

1660: Foxe cousins born, 1659–1661
   Restoration; Charles II, 1660–1685

1665: Foxe cousins orphaned
   London Plague and Great Fire

1670: Foxe cousins at Revelstone House
   Test Act, 1673

1675: Ysabel serves Mary Stuart; Rowland in Paris
   Mary Stuart marries William of Orange, 1677

1680: Ysabel and Rowland in Amsterdam
   Charles II repeatedly dissolves Parliament

1685: Ysabel at home, February
   James II, 1685–1688
   Duke of Monmouth rebellion, June
   ...
   James deposed, 1688
   Mary II & William III, 1689–1702

No One Dies

CAMBRIDGESHIRE
JULY 31, 1685

1

Buccaneers of the Cam Tributaries

THE BRIGHT WHISTLE of a black-tailed godwit—*toe-wit toe-wit*—warned all in the woodland to be wary.

From behind a large oak, Tamsin Foxe signaled to her comrades with a godwit song. When she first chose that signal, they all declared it a good one—if you didn't know this little vale, its brook wending to the River Cam, was too far from the fens for even one lost godwit, much less four "birds" calling to each other beneath the trees.

The real birds and crickets stopped singing when Tamsin and her comrades arrived, but soon recommenced lazily calling to each other. The oak tree that shaded Tamsin had already been enormous a hundred years ago, when Elizabeth reigned and when the earls of Marborne kept the forests of this parish free of brigands and desperados. As children, Tamsin and her cousins played Highwayman and Cavalier along these trails.

While waiting, Tamsin's heart calmed on the promise of imminent success. Every aspect of life had been in turmoil for days, but here in the forest, the world remained fresh as God made it. Crickets fiddled, singing their summer song. Sunlight filtered through the leaves where a faint breeze whispered secrets, with each shrub, tree, and stone a gift from the Divine, as if Marborne parish had retained a portion of the lost Garden.

Tamsin intended to keep it that way. It was her duty, what she'd been born to do.

She touched the tiny goat-skin pouch that hung from a cord around her neck. She'd fingered the antique coin inside so often that she could trace through the leather to feel the coin's dragon and the Archangel Michael. That coin was the only relic from her mother, who'd tucked it into Tamsin's cradle days before she died. ("To bring wealth to her baby girl," as Mrs. Bell, their housekeeper, repeated the story.) The Archangel had never performed any such magic, but Tamsin touched it to tuck away fears she didn't have time to consider. And wishing she and her friends would not come to harm or be exposed.

Tamsin felt the thump of hoofbeats. She wiped a damp palm on her breeches, to better grip her grandfather's pistol, the one with the rusted wheel-lock found in an old tack box. She'd given Camilla her good pistol.

"You are my heart's root." Tamsin heard that in a song and felt, like when lightning strikes, that it meant Camilla Fairchild. Not because of Camilla's mischievous smile whenever Tamsin proposed an adventure. Not because she coaxed Tamsin into laughter on days when never-ending work dampened Tamsin's spirits. Not warm words, soft caresses, the chance to feel Camilla's heartbeat when they found a bower in which to hide. Not even the honey tones of Camilla's voice. Just "my heart's root," without any courtly vows about having been made for each other.

Which meant that beyond attending to every minute detail amid the dangers of a restoration, Tamsin intended to protect Camilla. She'd tried to forbid her participation in this family-only enterprise. But forbidding Camilla anything she wanted badly was impossible, and so today she had Tamsin's good pistol.

From the edge of the wood came a greenfinch's rising twitter-and-wheeze. Her cousin Ned's "be ready now" signal. His sister Lizzie, hidden across the road, responded with the godwit song. Another song came ten yards away, from Camilla.

Tamsin whistled her answer to the birdsongs. Time to stand.

That's what Uncle Absolom said yesterday morning. "It's time to stand together, like brothers at arms. Learn how the Earl of Hawksmoor has cheated us, so you can save Marborne."

Now the dear man was cooling in his coffin at home, freed at last from suffering. On this bright summer morning, four hours remained until Absolom's funeral. But to advance the rebuilding of the Marborne villages, Tamsin and her comrades came to this seldom-travelled lane.

Late last winter, on her twenty-fourth birthday, Tamsin had to assume the role of family protector, because her twin brother Tom was laid up ill. Tall for a woman and sharing the same nose, heart-shaped face, and brown eyes as her brother, she'd let down her hair and tied it back in the fashion Tom wore, slipped into breeches, and became Tom. Then she campaigned with her cousins to advance their restoration endeavors.

The first carriage driver that Tamsin-as-Tom begged for help was the craggy-faced Osmund Warboys, known to be as fearless as any fen man. In his young and wild days, during Tamsin's grandfather's time, Mr. Warboys ran with the Fen Tigers, smashing new drainage works, torching half-built pump mills. "Mr. Warboys," she'd said when she asked his help, "we shall take only from those who robbed our villages. Never innocents. Never women. We seek justice."

Mr. Warboys laughed. "Ye shall be our Robin Hood, Tom?"

"Aye, Mr. Warboys. We're forced by Fate to take back what's due the parish." Mr. Warboys only begged that they stop his carriage no more than twice a year, to protect his honest name.

At dawn this day, disguised again as Tom, Tamsin ran to the local villages with the sad news that Absolom Foxe of Marborne parish, and Doctor of Divinity at Trinity College, had passed beyond the veil. When she'd paused at the Phoenix and Swan Inn, the toothless old Mr. Warboys tapped his nose, bragging that he'd been hired to deliver Lord Hawksmoor to his home, since the earl's own driver had fallen ill.

Mr. Warboys whispered, "You might be interested. Hawksmoor has been visiting his business man in London. They say the earl carries gold home with him."

As a consequence, Tamsin and her comrades felt compelled to seize this opportunity. Exhausted after a day and a night keeping vigil at Uncle Absolom's bedside, they'd made a hasty plan, intending to seize Hawksmoor's own coin to pay that quarter's mortgage dues—the mortgage they'd paid to him for twenty years—so that people could farm and live in the parish, without fear that the law or a new lord might dispossess them.

She'd spoken with Mr. Warboys at five o'clock that morning, and now at nine o'clock, Tamsin slipped a scarlet kerchief over her face and tugged her tall Puritan hat down to hide her eyes.

When the carriage came into view, the Hawksmoor crest gleaming on its door, Ned shouted, his deep voice thundering.

"Stand and deliver!"

Tamsin stepped into the small clearing. Her comrades appeared too, all brandishing pistols and thick disguises.

Her cousin Lizzie wore a farmer's cap over her raven hair, and a velvet mask veiled her face. She manifested beauty in shape and movement, but this disguise rendered her invisible.

Ned, Lizzie's half-brother, hunched as if infirm, concealing his gangly scarecrow form, which anyone in the parish would recognize. He wore both a wool stocking and black felt hat to hide his bone-white hair.

Camilla had over-dressed in Tom's blue velvet jacket and second-best tricorn hat. Her honey-gold hair, too thick to tuck under the hat, had been tied and tucked inside the jacket. A scarlet scarf, holes cut for the eyes, hid her face.

"I say stand!" Ned barked again.

The carriage brakes screeched, grabbing the wheels. Hawksmoor's carriage halted at the bottom of the narrow vale, where the summer-dry brook trickled across the trail. The carriage sported well-sprung wheels, windows with waxed linen shades, and shiny black paint, but it was too heavy for a narrow lane like this one.

One side brushed against the spiny hawthorns that edged the trail. Four horses cried in fear. Tamsin pushed against sad regrets for the animals, but in an instant, the horses settled, nickering softly when Mr. Warboys called, "No fear, my sweet bairns. Daddy is here for you."

Ned bounded up the ladder at the back of the carriage while cautioning Mr. Warboys in a bad French accent. "Do not risk your life, monsieur, for those who have no care for yours."

He grabbed Mr. Warboys' ancient Dutch thunder-gun and hurled it into the hawthorn and gooseberry undergrowth.

"True more, you clog-pated frogman!" Mr. Warboys cried out in his thick country accent, jabbing a rude two-finger salute at Tamsin. "Not the proper day for this!"

True more...more than what? Tamsin wanted to call her question but was stopped by their rule: *Only Ned speaks.*

"What is it, man?" Lord Hawksmoor shouted from inside the carriage, his voice rattling like a bushel of stones hauled over rough ground.

"Shut your beak!" Ned clapped his hands harshly, which resounded through the forest as if he'd struck Mr. Warboys.

Ned handed down a handsome pair of banded boxes. Lizzie pounced on those boxes and dashed for a trail hidden in the undergrowth. That was the plan: seize boxes quickly, jab a shard of icy fear in heartless old Lord Hawksmoor, and disappear into the woodland. But even in a laborer's linsey-woolsey tunic and leggings, Lizzie moved too much like an elegant courtier. Tamsin resolved to teach her to run, despairing that her cousin didn't have natural good sense outside a royal court.

However, Lord Hawksmoor was as nearsighted as Bartimaeus of Jericho before Jesus healed him. If Hawksmoor saw anything, it'd be a blue-velvet dandy, a crookback, and a pair of ragged, itinerant laborers.

Ned heaved a larger chest down from the carriage, which Camilla rummaged through, it being was too heavy for her to carry away. Camilla insisted from the very first restoration that she be accepted as their comrade, promising that she wasn't playing a romantic charade, that she understood the Foxe cousins' need to preserve the Marborne village and farms.

"God keep my giddy cat! Can you believe this?" Camilla gripped whatever she found in that chest, waved it, then crushed it in her hands.

Tamsin, gloved hand on her lips, gestured for silence. Camilla glanced around and darted into the underbrush, headed toward the foot-trail that led to the Fairchild house. Tamsin loved every precise thing about Camilla, especially her ability to join bold adventure and to run properly when fleeing a restoration.

"Now, mon ami!" Ned's voice echoed from deep inside his otherwise thin chest, calling to the carriage's passenger. "Toss out what's in your pockets."

Mr. Warboys growled. "True more, you fool. With a lead fire stick to shove up your bum!"

Behind her scarlet kerchief, Tamsin's lips twitched while Mr. Warboys played his part, berating the faux bandits.

"Heed me!" The nearly toothless Mr. Warboys shrieked at them. "The king's men are like to hang you before the sun sets."

"They're all out chasing the Duke of Monmouth's rebels." Ned hung off the side of the carriage, near the one door that it was possible to open, given how the carriage was wedged against the undergrowth. His voice roared through his knitted mask. "Come, mon ami! Toss us your purse and pockets."

The carriage's veneered door creaked open near Ned, who leaped down, doubled nearly in half to maintain his crookback ruse. Ned stepped behind Tamsin when a satin shoe and voluminous skirts appeared from the carriage.

Which was not the plan.

Yet no one, Tamsin vowed privately, would see her fright. Because they all relied on Tamsin, and she refused to fail them.

"Now, mademoiselle. Let me help you from your royal coach." As Tamsin spoke, she grasped the woman's forearm and jerked.

Out tumbled a remarkably tall lady, her face hidden behind layers of black veil.

Ned tried to peer past the woman into the carriage, but the tall woman flashed a pistol, distracting him. Tamsin batted the pistol into the same tangled undergrowth that held Mr. Warboys' blunderbuss, bruising her forearm with the effort.

This was not Hawksmoor's diminutive, new wife.

"Now, now, sweet madam," Ned cautioned from behind Tamsin. "Ye shall be safe and on your way in an instant. It's your lord's purse and jewels we care to see."

The woman trembled, whimpering behind her veil. She held out a brooch from her cloak, but Tamsin didn't reach for it. They were robbing Lord Hawksmoor. This woman was merely swept along. Tamsin was not about to break one of their rules: *Never rob a woman*. Ned, however, must have forgotten that rule. He pocketed the brooch.

"True, I say!" Mr. Warboys shouted again, furiously gesturing with two fingers, as if signaling the devil.

Behind the veiled woman, a booted foot showed at the carriage door. Not the earl. Rather, a massive, muscled man in well-worn black leather held a long hackbut, his yellow hair run wild.

Tamsin recognized him. The same Goliath that she'd shot in Holland last winter, his ice-blue eyes glinting now like they had that chaotic day.

Two more! That's what the toothless Mr. Warboys shouted.

Not the plan.

Tamsin whistled, a shrieking eagle's call: *Take cover!*

No time to plan. She hurled her rusted pistol, aiming for the giant's head. When he ducked, she kicked out, knocking the two-foot-long gun from the giant's hand and striking him in the ribs.

Then she scrambled up from the dirt and ran.

The way you must run to escape the devil.

The earl's gravelly voice rang from the carriage. "I'll have the king's men after you! You shall be gallows bait!"

Ned ran north, where Lizzie had already scurried up the trail. Tamsin, the fastest runner in the parish, smothered her fear of that giant and sprinted for the least-used trail on this side of the marshes, each step sending up a funk of summer dust and forest duff. She was soon out of that vale to an opening in the copse where the sun reflected from the church towers in Cambridge, far across the distant fields.

Before Tamsin's own village church came into view, a single pistol shot rang in the neighborhood of Camilla's house.

Not the plan.

She ran with one hand pressing her Archangel pouch. No time for fear.

2

The Crested Coach

"HOLD THIS." PERRY handed Rowland a pistol retrieved from the weeds along the side of the lane.

"It's dirtying my gloves, Mr. Frake."

Readjusting that blasted veil and brushing dust from his tortuous array of black silk skirts, Rowland pitched his voice for the sake of the lord inside the carriage. To stave off jitters from that pitiful encounter with ragged thieves, Rowland slipped the gold angel from his glove and rolled the coin across his knuckles, a trick that children viewed as magic, but Perry called a bad habit.

"The wheel-lock on that thief's dag is so rusted, our Blessed Savior Himself couldn't raise a miracle to fire it." Perry stamped, sending up a cloud of dust to show his disgust. He brushed his long, straw locks back under his hat. Tall and quick, he resembled a marble-faced statue from a Continental garden, with chiseled cheekbones and a projecting Roman nose (broken only once).

Rowland stepped closer to where Perry searched the thorn hedge, far enough from the carriage that the driver and other passenger couldn't hear them. "'What fools we mortals be.'"

"This is the moment you choose to quote your infernal Shakespeare to me, Lieutenant? After that humiliation? Knocked in the ribs by inept bandits? My middle hurts as if the devil's own horse kicked me."

"We are braving the wilds of Cambridgeshire in hopes of making the world a better place." Rowland hoped to amuse Perry with this claim.

"A bennish belief, sir." Peregrine Frake had an odd Yorkshire phrase for all occasions, and even here in the back county, he deferred to Rowland's rank, though after eight years working together, Perry knew Rowland's heart and mind well. "We fools stand here maftin' in the sun…"

"Your granddam's word for hot and sweltering?"

"Aye." Perry found his hackbut and gave it to Rowland to hold while he continued to search the thorn hedge, his speech in harsh undertones. "I shall boldly declare that we are here, sweat rotting our privates, only because you long to be the romantical rescuing hero for a woman who hasn't spoken to you since Twelfth Night."

"A rank falsehood, Perry. I cannot afford to be in love." Rowland had no expectation of gaining sufficient coin for either love or a better home than a barracks. "A romantical gentleman requires a title or at least gold to buy a real officer's commission."

"And I can't afford new boots," Perry complained, "but here I am, my nether bits dripping in the summer heat, my skills as a man at arms insulted by ragged road agents, all for the sake of a lady who—admit it, Rollo—does not return your love in kind."

"That's not why we are here, Perry."

"Oddsfish!" The beak-nosed Earl of Hawksmoor, his cheeks and nose red with rage, emerged from the carriage long after the rag-tag highwaymen had disappeared. "I apologize for this outrage. Tell me you are well, madam."

"I am fine, your lordship." To maintain his masquerade, Rowland resumed his false accent. And slipped his lucky gold angel back into his right glove. "No harm done."

The earl continued to rant. "I promised on my honor to keep you safe on the road from London. After the torments you suffered in your country, I'm ashamed of this, Senorita Taresa."

Rowland returned to the carriage, rearranging his veil and lifting his skirts to climb up, finding his nether regions boosted by the elderly earl, who'd been trying to get his hands up those black silk skirts since they'd left London. Behind them Perry undoubtedly only pretended to cough and instead had seized up with laughter.

Days before, Rowland had put on that black silk gown and a veil to avoid enemies pursuing them from Amsterdam. However, because he'd strayed so far from the path of righteousness, he was now mauled by a roguish earl and robbed by inept thieves in a quaint English copse.

"In my country, a widow such as myself is called *senora*, your lordship." Rowland employed the accent he'd learned while gambling with a Catalan viscount in Paris.

Lord Hawksmoor didn't seem to hear. "Shall we inspect your baggage, senorita? To learn what those scoundrels stole?"

"We should continue our travels, your lordship. I shall make do with what the Good Lord preserved for me." Rowland owned little and wore everything he valued close to his skin. The bandits merely made off with his last change of fresh linen.

Hawksmoor continued to fret. "I swear on my father's head, I'll have the king's men on those scoundrels. The magistrate and constable shall hang the brutes."

A mottled red flame blotched the old man's cheeks and thick, aging nose. His lips were bloodless.

(Hold on! Those bandits had frightened the randy earl.)

Rowland might be stirred to pity the poor fellow, except he and Perry had followed the earl because—like other men they hunted—the man might have participated in a swindle that harmed others.

"It's not necessary to raise such an alarm, senor." Rowland didn't relish the idea of any militia men laughing themselves into an early grave, learning that he and Perry hadn't defeated the ragtag highwaymen. "Those men were the wretched of the earth. They didn't even have a horse."

"But your jewels were taken, Senorita Taresa! A cruel theft, after all you've suffered!"

"I never wear my best while traveling, dear Lord Hawksmoor. With all my adventures in Spain and France, it has long been my pleasure to cheat thieves." And Taresa's jewels were as false as Rowland in black silk skirts.

While Rowland watched from the carriage, Perry again rubbed his sore belly where a thief kicked him (or perhaps he'd cracked a rib while silently laughing at Rowland in skirts). His face twisted with disgust, Perry handed the driver his long Dutch gun, and then once more cast an evil eye at Rowland for having dragged him into the wilds of Cambridgeshire.

"Senorita, you have a rational sense I've never known in a lady." Hawksmoor drummed his fingers on the carriage's window ledge for two moments before he gave loud voice to his impatience. "Driver, what is the problem? It's Mr. Warboys, isn't it? We should be on our way, Mr. Warboys."

"I'm closing up your chest, your lordship." The elderly driver chomped toothlessly on his words. "And that foreign fellow is searching out the lady's pistol. I need his help to restore your chest atop the coach."

Perry passed that pistol in through the carriage window. Rowland tucked it away. Then the carriage rocked when a chest thudded onto the roof and again with the weight of the driver climbing back onto his seat.

Before they veered into this detour, Perry had nagged that this side project Rowland had undertaken would cause them to fail their paid work in London. ("We'll still be hunting these rogues when we're old men, slobbering in our ale.") Yet there remained no reason to *not* take this detour, since the man they'd been tasked to hunt was gone from London for a week or more.

"Here, dear lady, let me open the door for your guard."

The old gentleman found another excuse for brushing the senora's silk-clad knees.

"Senorita, ah, senora. Please let your cavalier understand that he has my gratitude for frightening off those brigands."

Perry twitched a smile as he folded into the smallest space possible for a big man. He gazed out the window, disregarding the other passengers, his shaggy hair hiding any expression.

Hawksmoor tugged at his ear, then his hands twitched in his lap, over-stimulated from that escapade. He had thick, blunt fingers like a working man's hands. Except soft as a woman's. The earl rubbed at the bags under his rheumy eyes. Likely the man sneezed all summer.

When the carriage got underway, Hawksmoor busily arranged his coat's cuffs and skirts. Although his family had risen in the county as austere Protestants, the current Earl of Hawksmoor wore a long coat with lavish skirts and cuffs deep enough to hide a small rabbit or a young weasel. The coat's buff silk wasn't suited to travel. Gold thread binding the buttonholes showed grime and wear.

"Ah, senora. My heart is still twitterpating, while you remain so calm. After how handily your cavalier handled those fen-bog thieves, I'm sure you think me a fool for having promised you safe passage."

"Nonsense, Lord Hawksmoor. You became my hero in London moments after you heard that my destination was Cambridge." Rowland, playing Taresa, laid it on thickly, like a pound of butter spread over sweet spoonbread.

Hawksmoor's hands braced his companion as the carriage lurched onward. "Steady, senora." His arms once more resting on his embroidered vest, the earl regarded his veiled companion. He began to speak three times but stopped.

Time to play the game to win.

Rowland placed his gloved hand on the earl's knee. "My dear lord, you can trust me with your own tale, as I've trusted you with mine. We shall be a comfort to each other."

The Earl of Hawksmoor opened his arms, as if opening his whole self to this new friend.

"Indeed, senora. I am at a loss, because my world has turned upside down." Hawksmoor glanced at Perry, who sat as still and as deaf as a stone. "You are such a good creature. I feel in my heart that I can tell you all of my sorrows."

Because the senora wore a dense, dark veil, the earl could not see eyes flash a warning against laughter to the other passenger.

3

Revelstone House

STILL RATTLED FROM hearing a pistol shot and breathless from running, Ned encountered Tamsin near Solicitor Fairchild's house, Camilla's home since marrying Fairchild's son a few months ago.

"I came to find Camilla," Ned said. They stood in the bracken, observing the house. Like Tamsin, he searched all the windows for Camilla's honey-gold hair, seeing no sign of her there or in the front garden. "And I expected to see you here. What was Camilla carrying when she ran off?"

"That pistol shot? Who was it?" Tamsin didn't answer his question, twitching like a trapped rabbit, her face pale as the gypsum Ned ground in mineral spirits, the color he used to paint lace. And snow. Camilla's absence worried Ned too, especially since that morning had delivered more jeopardy than most men could bear. But not more than he believed Tamsin could bear. She was the Rock, for all of them.

"Most likely, it was a poacher." Ned didn't know words to calm Tamsin. Camilla did. She needed to show herself...if only so Tamsin might find peace for five minutes.

"Shooting guns in the heat of summer? People trap or use arrows. A pistol shot draws attention." Tamsin kicked at the dirt on the edge of the trail. "We make plans to ensure nothing draws attention to our doings."

"We didn't have the best plan today," Ned said. "We'd better have stayed home and mourned Absolom the way enlightened people would."

*Enlightened people would...*that's how Absolom admonished better behavior among the orphans under his care. Each time Ned thought about Absolom, his throat caught on what felt to be a loss too great to face just then. He'd find consolation once he spent a day painting in his workshop. But then, Absolom would never again step into Ned's workshop in the evening to comment on the progress Ned had made that day.

"We can't knock on the Fairchilds' door while dressed like Dutch boomkens." Ned stated the obvious. "And Tom Foxe cannot call on Camilla the day our family buries our uncle."

Without another word, Tamsin piked off, speeding along the trail that led home. Ned hurried to catch up.

Back at the Revelstone great barn, they still hadn't discussed the morning's catastrophe. Ned stripped off his highwayman garments and hid them with his flintlock in an old salt bin. He wore only his thin linsey-woolsey shirt and breeches.

Tamsin stashed her jerkin, scarf, and hat at the bottom of a tack box, then pulled on Tom's old barn coat. Her brown hair was tied back, like how Tom wore his hair. They shared a classic, innocent visage, each with that perpetually questioning arch of one brow. It's a wonder she fooled the entire parish. She was far too serious to be anyone but Tamsin, while the real Tom, even bedridden, remained forever spritely.

"Where's your pistol?" Ned asked.

"I threw it at the giant when I whistled for you to run."

"We'd best wait until tomorrow to search for it."

"True." Tamsin offered her uncle's riding horse an early-ripe apple from a basket by the barn door. "I'm still worried about Camilla."

As if Ned couldn't guess that Camilla consumed Tamsin's thoughts. "And I'm still worried about those extra passengers in Hawksmoor's carriage."

"Hawksmoor traveling with a woman!" Tamsin exclaimed. "And it wasn't his wife."

"What happened? You said Mr. Warboys had only one passenger. We were supposed to be robbing Lord Hawksmoor." That attempted restoration represented justice. The earl had been stealing from them for years through unfair mortgage dues.

Ned leaned on a post by the stall, his thin shirt sweated through from sprinting in the summer heat. A barn cat leaped onto his shoulder, rubbing along his neck. He pulled the cat into his arms and stroked its bright orange fur.

"Don't glare at me, Ned. Yes, I was too eager today. And I didn't understand when Mr. Warboys warned us." She gnawed her lip, the way she did when she worried. "But, Ned, you failed to clear the carriage. That's your job."

"I deserve to be chastised. However, you halted as if you saw a ghost. Which scared me." Ned scooted the cat away.

"I did see a ghost. That Goliath?" Tamsin caught her breath, as if again seeing a ghost. "It's the rogue who tried to stop us when we fetched Lizzie from Holland."

"Then you aren't a despicable, wretched murderer after all?" Ned tried the light, bright tone he'd learned from Absolom, offering humor amid a morning gone to Hades. "That shall be today's good news, Tamsin."

"You can't make me laugh, Ned. I felt the same jolt of fear as in Rotterdam, when my pistol misfired. Did he track us here?"

"Half a year later? And here to guard Hawksmoor? Not possible." Ned kept his voice low as they crossed to the house. "It's a coincidence."

"He looked me right in the eye, Ned. Did he recognize me?"

"No one can see our eyes when we dress for a restoration. Perhaps you should've shot him again."

"I did kick him in the ribs. And don't try to make me laugh about it. My belly has been twisted in anguish this half year, believing I killed a man. That's another reason why we must follow our rules."

"Yes, Rule One: 'No one dies.'" Ned had joined Tamsin and Tom to create the rules that governed their restorations, adhering to the moral principles Absolom taught, while forced by circumstances to take a detour around English law.

Their discussion ended when they came through the kitchen door. Ned hailed Mrs. Bell, the housekeeper, a small woman with steel in her slim bones and steel-grey hair bound up in a lace cap.

"Any cackle-berries about the house, kind mistress? I was roused from my crib to undertake travails without the fortification of even one breakfast."

Mrs. Bell sliced cheese at the kitchen table. Just the kind of cozy and homely scene Ned liked to paint: a good woman at work. "You'll find boiled eggs in the buttery. We're too busy to wait on you, Master Eduard. Every man, woman, and child in the house is busy wrapping mourners' loaves. Or down in the cellar shifting ale casks. Or busy preparing the great hall for the averil."

"I take your meaning, Mrs. Bell. I'd best go do my part." Ned fetched two eggs, then whispered to Tamsin, "But first, I'm off to see what Lizzie snatched from Hawksmoor's carriage."

Tamsin whispered too. "You broke Rule Number Two: '*Never steal from a woman.*'"

"We can't give it back now, can we?" If Tamsin was trying to make him feel guilty, Ned couldn't find a lick of remorse in his body or soul.

— TAMSIN —

MRS. BELL HAD A Scots mother and, in her old-fashioned way, had taught them all to say *averil* instead of funeral repast. Tamsin and Lizzie let her dictate all that must be done to honor Uncle Absolom, because they had no idea what to do or how to do it. They'd all lost their parents in the London plague and so had no traditions for family funerals. What they had now was only tears, and little time for that.

The kitchen odors offered Tamsin a degree of comfort. Baking bread, burnt sugar, sizzling fat caught in the pans below the roasts turning over the fire. Absolom claimed that Mrs. Bell ran the kitchen and the household with the same efficiency as forty years before, when she'd governed the field-kitchen for Captain Samuel Foxe's Royalist militia.

"Now then, Master Thomas, did you deliver invitations across the neighborhood?"

"Yes, Mrs. Bell. I'm sure word has reached as far as Cambridge. With the promise of a funeral repast, they'll pack themselves into carriages as tightly as when Uncle Absolom last invited them for Twelfth Night."

Mrs. Bell always treated Tamsin in disguise as if she were Tom, but was not deceived, having cared for them as infants. She'd helped perpetuate the fiction that it was Thomasine who lay ill upstairs while Tom, the Master of Revelstone, attended to business. Mrs. Bell agreed with Absolom that "Thomas Foxe" needed to appear at the Cambridge assizes and go with Lizzie to beg the king of England to restore the title, the Earl of Marborne, to the Foxe family.

"My dear Master Thomas, I don't know how you managed to run so far. But we must all do our best, what with Doctor Foxe insisting we bury him the day he died. Now, I was out early, telling the bees that our master is gone. You need not take on that chore or worry yourself that the bees might leave us."

Telling the bees?

Ah, to ensure the bees wouldn't die of grief or desert the hives. Mrs. Bell had gone to tell the bees about Absolom to avert tragedy. That is, any further tragedy.

"That was kind, Mrs. Bell. Thank you. And you were kind to stay up all night to help us."

"I must warn you. The averil will strip our larder. It's taken all the turbinado sugar." She finished arranging the cheese on a platter, a stern look daring any piece to wiggle out of its place. "And this day's repast will finish off our wet-cured ham stores from last season."

"Yet we can do no less, Mrs. Bell."

"Indeed so. If any man deserves honor when he knocks on heaven's door, it's Doctor Foxe."

Tamsin's attention was caught by the creak of the kitchen's sole innovation in the last hundred years, a treadmill fixed to the wall near the fire. A small, long-eared pooch trotted, turning the spit for the roasts.

"Mrs. Bell, I must beg you not to enslave Caesar."

"We are short on boys, Master Thomas. Caesar must help us avoid shame. If we don't serve hot meats, the gossips will say we're as poor as shabby peasants from the marshes."

Except they were as penniless as marsh peasants. But Tamsin didn't say it aloud.

Tamsin removed Caesar from the spit-turning contraption.

He wagged his shaggy tail, expecting a treat. She sat on a three-legged stool and took up the dog's chore, turning the spit. Her right hand, the one that took a grievous injury when her pistol misfired in Rotterdam, was whole now, but not strong. During the morning's restoration, she'd held a pistol again, but without the strength to fire it (even if it weren't fouled with rust). Her writing remained frightful. And she had to look forward to a day spent shaking dozens upon dozens of hands in greeting, and so could expect several days of shooting aches and numbness. Turning the spit was a chore she could manage.

Caesar attempted two leaps before the third landed him in Tamsin's lap. A little squirming and many sighs later, the dog was snoring. "You've worn Caesar to a nub, Mrs. Bell."

The housekeeper, now busy wrapping mourners' loaves, didn't respond to that complaint. Instead, she said, "Mrs. Fairchild sent a boy with a message, to say that the Honorable Mr. Fairchild has not yet returned from London and so begs you to excuse him. She hopes you will freely ask her help if she can be of use in any way."

"Camilla?" If Camilla had sent a message, then she'd made it safely to the Fairchilds' house. But had there been time...

"No, I mean the elder Mrs. Fairchild. The solicitor's saintly wife." The housekeeper pursed her lips, as if stopping words she longed to say.

Tamsin and Camilla had played together since they were little girls, when Mrs. Bell disapproved of Camilla's carefree ways ("that hoyting girl"). Nor did she approve last winter when Camilla Candecote, a baronet's daughter, suddenly married Solicitor Fairchild's son. Unhappy under her father's roof, Camilla had fled into a marriage that resulted in worse than she'd endured living with her stepmother. Tamsin had no idea how Camilla's stepmother and mother-in-law could endeavor to thwart and punish Camilla at every turn—unless evil is forced to combat goodness. Because Camilla incarnated goodness, or whatever amount of goodness Heaven allowed to seep into Tamsin's life.

Then again, Mrs. Bell deeply disapproved of the elder Mrs. Fairchild. ("She married above her place, then came into our parish with her nose in the air.") Only three years in the parish meant the Fairchilds were newcomers. Until last autumn, her son Leighton had been living in London, so no one in the parish knew the man. Tamsin had skirmished with Leighton since the day Camilla married him, and had also resented Mrs. Fairchild for being cold and critical of her new daughter-in-law.

If only Fate might do the just thing, and tip Camilla into Tamsin's arms. Tamsin longed to rescue her from that new sad life. To shelter her. She wanted to say, "You are my heart's root," but whispering such words would be futile. Amid this year's chaos, Camilla never believed that her tribulations could be overcome.

"We can manage on our own, can't we, Mrs. Bell? We don't need Mrs. Fairchild." Tamsin stroked the dog with one hand and turned the spit with the other. "She'll only mutter, 'Shame. Too few servants.' She'll make us sadder than we'd be if left alone."

"With God's help, Master Thomas, we shall get on as best we can. We don't need charity. If indeed charity is what our good neighbor offered."

Having expressed her quiet resentment, Mrs. Bell stepped into the buttery. When she reappeared, she said, "My dear, you left this on the table last night when we prepared Doctor Foxe for eternity. Best keep it with you."

She handed Tamsin the amethyst ring her uncle always wore, which he'd had from his mother. Tamsin slipped it onto her thumb, wondering who should have it. Lizzie, perhaps.

Mrs. Bell was still chatting. "And we found this paper lost in the floorboards when we swept Doctor Foxe's room. You shall judge for yourself how best to preserve it."

Then Mrs. Bell did go, leaving Tamsin to read the tiny, meticulous hand in which her uncle wrote:

A History of Chaos and Renewal
On the Turmoil of the Commons in the Age of Restoration

Caesar stirred awake in her lap.

"Oh, poor puppy. Our Uncle Absolom is gone and he's not coming back."

Caesar licked her hand, looked up expecting—what? She stroked his head. Her sniffs threatened a torrent of tears if she didn't get hold of both memory and imagination.

No time for that.

She tucked the paper up her sleeve, saving it to share later with Lizzie and Ned and her brother Tom. Then she fingered the pouch that contained her Archangel coin, seeking ideas about what to do to make up for today's failed restoration. At summer's end, the taxes and mortgage dues would demand every coin they could earn or gain through a roadside restoration. What Tamsin wanted, beside the comfort of Camilla close by, was the liberation of the house and villages from endless, abject poverty.

And justice. Tamsin longed for justice. Injustice had gnawed a hole in her soul. The Marborne title had been suspended under the Commonwealth, because their Foxe forefathers fought for the Royalist cause. At the Restoration of Charles, the king had immediately granted all the lands to Lizzie's grandfather. Yet before the king and Committee for Privileges and Conduct restored the title, their grandfathers and fathers had died in the plague, leaving Absolom to hold the unentailed land and house, but with the title still in abeyance.

As soon as this dreadful day ended, Tamsin had to figure how to unwind the legal tangles, pay the current taxes and mortgage dues, and—for Lizzie's sake—persuade the king to restore the title of Earl of Marborne to their family. Then Tom would be earl. Only the return of the title would give the Foxe family power to fully protect the villages and farms. And, if Tamsin's suspicions were true, restoration of the title would help Lizzie make the kind of noble marriage that'd allow her to return to Princess Mary's court. Lizzie seemed to live in a haze since she'd returned home, deeply missing her former life.

"Finished with your mulligrubs, Master Thomas?" Mrs. Bell called out from the buttery. "Those roasts are done. You'd best dress for our guests. The averil begins at one o'clock, but Doctor Foxe's many friends are bound to arrive early, looking to sup our ale and gobble our cakes."

Tamsin roused Caesar and urged him down to the floor gently, the way one does with an elderly dog.

"Master Thomas, please carry this posset up to our invalid. It's cooling of a summer's day. And good for healing, I warrant."

4

Prowlers

IN THE SWELTERING carriage, Rowland roasted like an Easter lamb, which left him wondering if science might one day discover how fine English ladies survive a summer's day in so many layers of clothing. He longed to roll his lucky coin as he turned over in his mind how to convince Lord Hawksmoor to open his heart to the charming senora.

Hawksmoor said, "When we met in London, senora, I was thinking only of my own business in those offices. Our meeting was, as you say, Divine Providence."

Providence? After the Duke of Monmouth's failed uprising against King James, certain men were curious about what happened to funds committed to the venture but that had never reached the rebellious duke. Providence had led those curious men to Rowland, who'd been a subaltern in Monmouth's militia in Holland (though he and Perry didn't join the invasion, having pretended camp fever). Rowland knew the watchwords, hand signs, and code words among Monmouth's supporters. Hence, he and Perry had been engaged for the summer in the hunt to uncover the secret committees supporting Monmouth's rebellion. Rowland's taskmasters wanted all the lost funds found.

The night before Providence had led Lord Hawksmoor to meet Senora Taresa, Rowland and Perry broke into and prowled the offices of the last man they'd been pursuing, but that work didn't profit. The next morning they'd visited the man's offices, with Rowland as a wealthy foreign senora and Perry as her stiff and silent guard. The clerks reported that their master was gone on business in the countryside until the next Monday.

Having failed to advance their hunt, the two of them stood in the shade of the portico next door to the man's offices. It was brutally hot that day. Perry said, "This stalled hunt sticks in my craw. Why can't this fellow leave unlocked boxes and letters around, like the other men we hunted? We need to finish this adventure."

"Since we have no proof that he either raised funds for Monmouth or stole them," Rowland said, "we need to pull this man into a gambol, like we learned to do in Holland."

"What kind of gambol?" Perry's hands tapped impatience and doubt on the sleeve of his leather coat. "We aren't prepared to gull the men we're hunting into buying stolen Venetian glass, like we did in Amsterdam. We know no one in London who will lend us even a single piece of Ravenscroft's crystal to use as bait."

Rowland said, "We'll ask the man to help us create an investment syndicate. He'll introduce us to other investors. We ask for proof that he can manage syndicates. He'll show us his business, which is when we uncover how he's hiding funds intended for Monmouth."

"Invest in what? Our taskmaster won't lend us gold for such a gambol."

"Did you see all the paintings in the man's office? He's surely hiding profits in that art. We'll propose an investment to acquire, say, Italian art. Several rich men in Amsterdam are mad for it. Likely here in London—"

"You astound me, Rollo, with your ability to make a simple task complicated. We wait for the man to return to London and then take the first chance to pick his coat pockets. Since we didn't find any record of his sins in his offices, I wager that the man keeps all his sins inside his vest or down his pantaloons."

He and Perry hadn't yet agreed on a plan when the Earl of Hawksmoor passed them on the street and went into the offices of the man they hunted. Rowland, recognizing the earl, clutched Perry's shoulder. "Divine Providence calls. That man is the key to the other task I'm asked to undertake in England."

"Providence? Will that old man tell us how to find the man we're hunting?"

Instead of answering, Rowland (as the senora) walked back into the office and stood near the earl while asking a clerk how to travel to Cambridge, where a dear cousin had invited her to visit.

From the ruddy color Perry turned, he nearly exploded like a tossed grenade at Rowland's sudden foray into a new jig. However, the charming Senora Taresa snagged an invitation from the earl to join him on the journey to Cambridge.

Waiting with their scant baggage for the earl to fetch them in his carriage, Rowland convinced Perry that a journey to Cambridge was a good idea. "Come, Perry. The rogue we're paid to seek is out touring the countryside. While we wait for him to return to London, we'll pursue Lord Hawksmoor for the sake of the other project I had intended to undertake in England."

"It's not Providence," Perry said. "Mere coincidence."

"Fate looks on us fondly. You and I have profited from coincidence more than once in this life."

"Aye, Rollo. I was gut-shot last winter because of a coincidence. However, I fear that today's new coincidence will bring you close once more to that woman, who is likely breaking hearts here in England without a thought of your tender organ."

Rowland was not provoked into arguing about his Dark Lady's kindness. Instead, for a heartbeat, he remembered her whispers and laughter when they traded jests amid the commotion of Amsterdam. ("You make me laugh, Rollo. You are the cure, lambkin, for the 'vexation of the mind, and damn'd despair' of court life.") Rowland had been satisfied with curing his Dark Lady's vexations and being her pet. With no title and no future, Rowland governed his heart more strictly than any Stuart king had ever governed England. Perry was wrong to claim otherwise.

Perry had taken to pacing, never able to wait patiently for more than a few moments. "Mayhap messing about for a few days in the country can be no worse than kicking pebbles in London while waiting for the man we're hunting to return." Just as the earl's carriage appeared, Perry said, "If your Lord Hawksmoor was in the office of the man we're hunting, might he also be invested in the Duke of Monmouth's scheme?"

"God blind me! That'd be a hucker-mucker. The men who sent us to hunt in London would have to double our reward."

Now, two days later, the earl was being convinced to take Taresa de Flores into his confidence while the carriage lurched toward Cambridge.

"Was your business in London satisfactory, your lordship?"

"Senora, I learned that…" The earl took a breath, his voice and hands shaking. "Some of my New World investments have gone astray and…no, forgive me, I can't speak of it."

"Your secrets are safe with me, your lordship."

Safe as hens with foxes. Safe as the secrets Rowland learned while gambling in Holland with officers in the Duke of Monmouth's militia.

Instead of sharing secrets, the earl pointed out the window. "Senora, here is my house. It's an old one, but a good one."

"Exquisite, Lord Hawksmoor!"

"Please take my hand, senora, as you descend. The gravel can be rough on ladies' soft shoes. Will your cavalier come share our refreshments?"

"I believe Senor Peregrine wishes to stretch his legs after our travels and travails."

Inside the house, Hawksmoor led his guest to his study and called for a servant to bring wine for refreshment. "Excuse me a moment, senora, while I seek my wife."

Time to go to work. He trusted that Perry was prepared for more breaking, entering, and prowling for proof of the earl's sins.

5

Doctors of Differing Kinds

NED SWATTED AT a buff-tailed bee which then bumbled and buzzed against the window in Tom's room. The late-morning sun shone on Tom, propped in his bed. Winwood Oakes, Tom's physician, bent over his pocket watch while holding Tom's wrist. A mild-featured man with an aristocratic nose, Winwood Oakes wore his hair long in tawny curls. When Tom caught his eye and grinned, Ned sighed, having been holding his breath, a habit from months of wondering whether his cousin would live out the day.

Tom lay back. Ned's sister Lizzie gently bathed his head with a linen cloth. Preferring not to be corralled into nursing Tom, Ned instead rummaged through the boxes that Lizzie had taken from the morning's restoration. He examined what must be a gentleman's linen and shirts.

"It's a happy thing for you, Winwood," Tom's voice lilted high, preparing one of his jests, which came more frequently of late, "that my cousins didn't leave me on the wharf in Harwich when I fainted. Otherwise, you wouldn't be free to practice your experiments in modern medicine on me."

"We never would leave you," Lizzie said. "Don't tease, dear heart." She tapped Tom's skull, as if scolding him. Ned let his hopes for Tom rise, seeing Lizzie less worried than she had been for so long.

"We just didn't notice you'd fallen behind, coz," Ned said, feeling called upon to tease Tom as a cover for how much Lizzie and Tamsin worried, "until the silence was deafening."

While bringing Lizzie home last February, they'd met Winwood Oakes on the ship from Rotterdam, an apprenticed physician traveling to tend an ailing aunt in London. Onboard, he treated Tamsin's hand, which was badly mangled when her pistol had misfired. Arriving at Harwich, all of them seasick and cold, they were quarantined because Tom had caught a spotted fever. Winwood declared it chicken pox, not smallpox. Once they were freed from quarantine, the doctor stayed with Tom. Lizzie took Ned with her to finish a chore in London, while Tamsin stayed in Harwich to share company with Tom and the doctor.

Tom survived. Then Winwood had a message from his aunt that she was well and not in need of him. Tamsin invited him to Revelstone (it was just like her to think of that), where he tended to Tom through pneumonia, a violent infection, and in June, a new problem with his kidneys. Winwood saved Tom, preserved Tamsin's infected hand, and did his best for Absolom in his last days.

Ned said, "If I am not mistaken, Tom seems to be on the verge of surviving today."

Winwood said, "It's two weeks now without a fever. I very much hope—"

"I'm convalescent, Winwood. No longer an invalid." Tom rested his hand on the doctor's. "Tell my cousins to let me back into their games. Especially today."

"I have real hope. But you must give my new physick another week." After months of practice, Winwood had perfected a coaxing tone with Tom.

"Your new physick tastes like ox piss caught in a jar." Tom's return to his jolly ways gave Ned more hope than he'd allowed himself since late winter. "You shall not succeed, Winwood, when you try to peddle it at village fairs."

Lizzie opened the window to let that noisy bee escape. "We must get more than beef broth and gruel into you, cousin."

"See how I'm recovered? I can swallow again." Tom coughed. Ned flinched at the sound, however much Winwood reassured them: Tom had suffered from what he called pneumonia. Not a wasting consumption. "That's why I can choke down Winwood's ox-whiz concoction. Though I advise a few drops of port to improve the taste."

The doctor said, "We must let you rest, Tom."

"Go, Winwood. You will want to dress properly for our guests." Tom laughed, which again made him cough. "Here you are, a learned man in shirt-sleeves and vest. It must be near on to noon, and you're still wasting time with me."

"First, let me see you swallow today's second dose." Winwood poured liquid from a flask into a tin cup.

After Winwood departed the room, closing the door behind him, Tom ceased jesting and squirmed in bed. "I owe Winwood my life. If he hadn't stayed with me, I'd be—"

"Dead. More than once." Ned offered a fact they all knew, having lived through many long nights in fear of losing him. Ned had too often pondered deep in the night how he'd ever endure losing Tom, who served as a brother to him.

Gleeful again, Tom said, "Then you'd have had to host an averil for me. And I'd be unfairly forced to miss that one too."

— TAMSIN —

WHEN SHE ENTERED the room, Tom smiled brightly, despite all that he had to complain of. Tamsin grinned too, hiding how badly she wished to see his face as a twin of her own again, with the dark slash of arched brow, impertinent nose, and lips to make a woman love him. The pock marks from last winter had healed. His lung fever had subsided. But a new infection left him sallow and itchy again. Lizzie kept Tom's dark brown hair trimmed to a tidy fringe, so Tom most resembled a wan urchin.

Tamsin's smile came from a deep desire that Tom might never see how fear for his well-being clutched at her. Since Tom always managed cheer, she had to perform as well as he did.

"Caesar followed me from the kitchen." Tamsin set the mug of posset on a side table, doubting whether Tom could consume such rich food. "Do you want his company?"

"You know I do." Tom patted a place at his side. Tamsin lifted the old dog to cuddle beside her brother. "Winwood says I'm quite well and can come to the averil today."

Lizzie knocked Tom's skull with her knuckle. "That is not what the doctor said."

"Tom isn't better?" Tamsin had immense hopes—along with worries about how they'd ever repay Winwood. Lodging and food didn't seem the proper currency. Winwood altered his life to remain with Tom, for no discernible reason other than the doctor was a profoundly good man.

"He's very much better," Lizzie said. "But he's commanded to rest and take his medicine."

Ned said, "I believe that I might want this." He held up a white linen shirt from a box Lizzie liberated in the restoration, his bone-white hair brighter than the fresh linen when caught in a stray sunbeam

"It might fit," Tom said, "except you're bone-thin. You could hide behind a shepherd's crook. Tell me about the restoration that brought this shirt to our house."

Ned began to spin a tale for Tom about the morning's adventure, falsely claiming success.

"Tamsin," Tom spoke up when Ned's story trailed off, "we rely on you too much. You don't have to do it all."

Lizzie said, "Yet we are lucky Tamsin can perform the tasks Absolom gave her. While the rest of us—"

"Pretty much let Absolom down." Tom's false bonhomie didn't match his words. "Can you remember Absolom that day he assigned our futures? What age were we? Ten?"

"Twelve. I was thirteen." Lizzie took up his false brightness. "Absolom pointed the stem of his clay pipe at each of us as he spoke. 'Lizzie, who's the oldest, must serve a queen, to prove Foxes are loyal.'"

"Is that what you want, Lizzie?" Tamsin asked, because Lizzie had been distracted and distant since returning from Princess Mary's court in Amsterdam. Tamsin loved having her home again but felt sure that Lizzie wished herself elsewhere.

"When the proper time comes." Lizzie pressed her lips as if stopping herself from saying more.

Tom's eyes darkened. "Here's the failure. 'Tom shall study under a great barrister, to bring the law into service for us all.'"

To draw Tom away from dark thoughts, Lizzie finished quoting Absolom. "'And our Tamsin shall save the house and all the villages.' Now, we're all grown up. You'll be twenty-five at your next birth date. And—"

At the sound of her voice, Tom's attention drifted. "How are you always beautiful, Lizzie?"

"Mmm. I've been made hideous by our morning jaunt."

Lizzie had become her lovely self again, dressed now in a made-over black silk gown, its starched white lace collar stark against her warm-brown face, her raven hair bound up in a black net hood. She tucked her mother's handkerchief up her sleeve, as she always did. Today, however, she'd likely need it.

How was Lizzie always so divinely beautiful, even with the strain from weeks of tending Absolom? And fortunate to have run off before that day's restoration became a wracking failure.

"Rather than do like the poet and 'languish, sigh, and die,' we must look our best today. Tamsin, take one of those cravats to wear." Lizzie pointed to the liberated boxes. "That lady in the veil must have a husband awaiting her. She conveyed a man's linen in her baggage."

That lady...all the prickly fear from the morning's failure haunted Tamsin again. She seized a shirt spread across one box, longing to wear such thin, fine linen on what promised to be a hot and endless summer day.

"Too big for Tom. Not big enough for Lord Hawksmoor or that lady's giant guard." Ned took the shirt and headed for the door. "Just right for me."

"Button up your vest properly, Ned." Lizzie wagged a cautioning finger. "So that its owner won't recognize the shirt. I don't have time today to alter it."

They stood together, brother and sister who shared only the same mother. Pale, white-haired Ned got his gangly build, thin lips, and long, pointed nose from his Dutch father. Lizzie got that dark Spanish coloring and those exquisite features from her father, Samuel, whose mother's people came to England with Catherine of Aragon. In Absolom's stories, Samuel Foxe famously helped Charles, Prince of Wales, escape England during the first civil war, but no one had yet written that part of history.

In Absolom's stories… Come winter, they'd no longer sit by a fire while Absolom told stories about lost generations of Foxes, from Absolom's father to his three brothers, and then those brothers' sons, whose children Absolom inherited after the Great Plague in London claimed his brothers and nephews.

Now, how could they get on without Absolom?

After Ned left to dress for the averil, Tamsin wiggled out of her breeches and shirt in the dressing alcove. She chose Tom's seldom-worn black silk suit from the clothes-press, along with his best linen shirt. While still hidden from the others, she again dragged the cord of her Archangel pouch over her head, letting it dangle between her breasts. After Lizzie's help with fresh bindings and tying a cravat, Tamsin was ready to appear as the Foxes' eldest male heir, to accept mourners' condolences.

"You're such a handsome man." Lizzie brushed Tom's coat, then settled it on Tamsin's shoulders. "Do you think it changes you? I mean the real you—to dress and act as someone else."

Tamsin said, "The freedom to move might go to my head. But any joy from that is stopped by my moustache."

Lizzie tied Tom's best periwig on Tamsin's head, then began to affix a thin moustache to Tamsin's upper lip, for the second time that day.

"It was bad enough this morning, now your glue will melt in this heat." Tom's once-fine brown eyes were dulling with fatigue.

He rubbed at his arm, cotton gloves keeping him from scratching too hard.

"Warn me if need be, Lizzie." Even after months of disguise, Tamsin feared discovery when she had to meet more than people from the village or the inhabitants of Revelstone House.

"No fears, dear heart. I shall be at your side."

"I wish Camilla were here. I'm worried after this morning's failed restoration." Tamsin loved Camilla, body and soul, and if anything had happened, it'd be because Tamsin had allowed Camilla to join that day's adventure.

"She'll be here." Lizzie bent close to examine her moustache artistry. "You know that Leighton always arrives late and leaves early, no matter the occasion."

"Camilla might tell her scoundrel of a husband Leighton to go home without her," Tom said. "If you allow me out of bed, I can tell him for her. Or for your sake."

Tamsin resisted saying that the day would be unbearable without Camilla, who made Tamsin laugh, who consoled Tamsin with soft kisses. Who sought refuge with Tamsin whenever she could after Camilla's own mother died.

"Perhaps I will say it." Lizzie's smile twitched, which Tamsin always took as a sign that Lizzie wanted to be reassuring but might be offering a false hope. "Oh, good lord. That bee is back."

Lizzie swatted at the bee that bumbled against a window in the sunny room, waving it toward the open window.

"It worked," Tamsin murmured. The bumbling bee had not actually departed, but Tamsin meant that Mrs. Bell's talking to the bees worked, that the bees had been reassured about the loss of Absolom, that all would be well. Tamsin, however, did not feel any assurance.

"Agnes will sit with you through the afternoon," Lizzie said. Tamsin liked Agnes, one of Mrs. Bell's girls, because she took great care with Tom, who liked Agnes because she was funny.

Lizzie kissed Tom farewell. Tamsin had to preserve her delicate facial hair and therefore couldn't kiss her brother. She laid

Absolom's ring on the table and tugged on goatskin gloves. Lizzie had padded the right-hand glove, to protect Tamsin's weakness after the injury in Holland.

"Once more," Tom spoke slowly, with increasing effort, "into the breach, dear friends."

"Oh, Tom. Mrs. Bell found the last essay Uncle Absolom was working on. I shall leave it here. Agnes can read it to you if you grow too tired to read it yourself."

"I'm convalescent, not invalid. Please let Caesar stay."

"Rest, Tom."

Tamsin left Caesar with him, carrying away only the burden of secrets Absolom had left in her care. In the flash of sunlight before she closed the door, Tamsin imagined Absolom seated beside Tom, preparing to read, the same way he had since February, saying, "What shall it be, lad? Poetry? Philosophy? Shakespeare?"

"Whatever pleases you," Tom murmured.

—

A History of Chaos and Renewal
By Absolom Caius Foxe
Trinity College, Cambridge University
On the Turmoil of the Commons
in the Age of Restoration:
A Discourse in Three Parts
Part I: Modern Chaos

After one hundred fifty years of purifying campaigns and civil wars, England has now found itself tired to the bone, weary of deadly quarrels among Catholic zealots and Reformation dogmatists, exhausted from the hunting and burning of heretics, witches, and recusant and equivocating priests, and worn down by the legacy of spies and pursuivants paid to hunt dissidents and disbelievers.

This collective fatigue follows on the regicide of Charles I, two bouts of civil war among Royalists and Cromwell's Roundheads, an impotent protectorate in the interregnum

(Cromwell and his followers not being up to managing a nation), wars in the Low Countries, the restoration of the monarchy, and then fierce revenge for regicide, all supplemented by a series of failed or false conspiracies.

When the second Charles Stuart was restored as king in 1660, most of England welcomed the revels. Many overlooked the corruption, enjoying new wealth delivered by way of the New World colonies and East India trade.

However, with the recent coronation of James II, a committed Roman Catholic, many fear a return to old troubles. In Summer 1685, some men conspired for the throne to be assumed by the Duke of Monmouth, the natural son of Charles II, who calls himself James Fitzroy. Some waited for a future with Protestant rulers, that is, Mary Stuart, the presumed heir, and her husband William of Orange, who governs the Dutch Republic in the Low Countries.

And yet others in England, those with no political power, continue to yearn for the restoration of pasture and forest land stolen from them across years of civil war and betrayal. Because the Restoration courts often dealt in revenge disguised as justice, many villages have had no choice but to find their own paths to restoration.

The history of Marborne parish in Cambridgeshire shall serve as our example of the commons in turmoil. We care most about such cases because, after all, it is for the sake of common women and men that each village commons must continue to thrive.

—

Tamsin believed that the Foxe cousins weren't prepared to learn what Absolom told her the previous morning when she sat beside her dying uncle.

Absolom's voice had become a rasp while he lay ill. "Remember last month, when we went to London?"

Yes, she remembered. In past years, Absolom traveled twice a year to endeavor with an attorney (who'd read with him as a Fellow at Cambridge) to resolve the problems left after his brothers and nephews had all perished, with all records about their deaths subsequently lost in the Great Fire. Each year Absolom and his attorney chase the quest for the title and unentailed property from Chancery Court to the Committee for Privileges and Conduct. And the next year, they'd chase it back again. But last winter, that attorney died. The partner who took up their case wanted greater fees than they could afford. So, the cousins decided to appeal for an audience with the king as a last resort. Each trip to London was painful and unforgettable. Her uncle had been silent throughout that last journey.

He said, "Whilst you and Lizzie once more sought an audience with the king, I went to visit a man. Solicitor Fairchild had told me that Lord Hawksmoor sold our mortgages and sent me to the London agent who brokered the sale."

"Sold the mortgages?" She repeated the words, as if she were slow-witted.

"It's often done, Fairchild says. I went to that agent in London, carrying my copies of the original papers and receipts showing that we are done. Free at last of those endless payments. It was to be my surprise to you all."

"Oh, uncle. I am so happy we are done."

"No, another story arose. The agent showed me the papers he'd received from Hawksmoor, who sold to a blind syndicate."

"A blind...what?"

"It's a committee of investors who keep their names secret, leaving no way to know who makes up the syndicate. The papers he showed me indicate that we are to pay that syndicate for ten more years."

"Who is this agent?"

"One of Sir Charles Duncombe's men, he who makes every man in London as rich as a Spanish grandee. Except his agent is helping others to rob us."

"How can we proceed, uncle?"

"I went to Lord Hawksmoor, but he insists he'd washed his hands of those liens. I was so angry, I'd have struck the man. But his brother, the Viscount Heydon, made peace for the moment, suggesting I take action through the courts."

"Can you? Oh uncle, we must!"

"Of course. I then asked the magistrate how to bring action for us. But he says we need a legal man who hasn't previously been involved in this business. And it will be costly. But I am willing to pay any price."

The Foxe family did not possess the wherewithal to pay *any price*. Yet Tamsin said, "You are right to proceed."

Absolom didn't seem to hear her, intent on explaining his story to the plaster ceiling over his bed. "When I opened my satchel to show the magistrate our case, it was empty. Who do you suppose stole my proof about those mortgages? Was it the London agent? Hawksmoor? Fairchild?"

"What can I do?" Fear tingling in her fingers, Tamsin jumped up, as if she could run to fix this catastrophe at that moment.

"The magistrate guessed what could happen. With those papers missing, I cannot prove right of possession from the original royal grant of title. If those who bought the mortgage can forge those papers, what stops them from forging a Crown grant? Or from foreclosing through the courts?"

"Good stars, uncle!"

But Absolom had not finished his litany of despair. "Even if that syndicate does not take any tragic action, I've lost the papers we need to petition the Crown for the return of the title. I am the last tenant-in-possession of both the entailed and unentailed parts of Marborne. My brothers took all the Foxe family records—marriage, births, baptisms—to London to plead with King Charles to restore the title. Those are lost too, since nothing came home after they all perished in the plague."

"What shall we do?" Tamsin jumped up. As was her nature, she could not listen to calamity without thinking immediately of what action to take next.

"Sit, child. I've engaged the best intelligencer, who shall discover the fraud by Hawksmoor and that blind syndicate. Theo Gamlingay can help my intelligencer to comb through the parish records, to create a new pedigree to show the king."

"What can I do, uncle? You know I'll do whatever it takes to protect Marborne and our family.

"Just please, if I never rise from this bed, you must all stand together, like brothers at arms. Take what our intelligencer learns and then do whatever you can to get justice, to save Marborne."

When leaving Tom with Agnes and Caesar, Tamsin decided that the day of the averil wasn't the best time to tell the others about Absolom's final burden, heartbroken and ill from worry. Each of them already worked hard to help pay the quarter's taxes and mortgage dues. They didn't need to hear today, on the worst day of their lives, that the draining mortgage payments would go on for another decade. That unknown men could dispossess them of their land and their hopes for a restored title.

First, she had to figure out what to do about Lord Hawksmoor, who'd broken Absolom's spirit. The earl had inherited his title from his father, a new-made earl under Cromwell's protectorate. The earl held much more grazable land than Marborne; therefore, instead of generations of service to the land and its people, pure luck made Hawksmoor wealthy after forty years of civil unrest. It was the current earl's father who had offered the immense mortgages that Absolom's brothers were forced to take when bad harvests brought famine to the villages. Absolom had managed as best he could for the last twenty years. But the greatest barrier? That the Marborne title wasn't restored to the family upon the restoration of the king.

Tamsin tasted grief on her tongue. It might drive her to her knees, as if her veins were overfull, so she might leak grief if she moved or if she spoke. They might lose everything. As foolish as it was, she touched the Archangel in the pouch under her shirt, because she needed to hold all those sentiments for later.

Right then, she needed to be as strong as Absolom believed her to be.

And she needed Tom to be well, so he could help.

She needed Lizzie to shake off the blue haze in which she lived, which seemed to arise from despair about the title.

"We don't have time for despair." Tamsin repeated it every single day to Lizzie and Tom and Ned. Tomorrow—or perhaps Sunday—they'd be ready to hear Absolom's secret. Then Tamsin wouldn't be carrying that burden alone.

What else could they do but fight the way Absolom asked? Go to the colonies like haughty Puritans or prisoners of the Crown? No, they'd keep striving until this parish once again had enough pasture and good harvests to last the winter. With children living long enough to be sent to the parish infants' school. Everyone getting on with their lives. No more chaos.

That's all she wanted on this earth. Besides the improbable wish that Camilla live at Revelstone with her.

To do all that, she'd have to…take the next logical action. And then the next one. Just like every ordinary day. Absolom had offered only one saving hint: "I've engaged the best intelligencer…" But what amount of gold or silver had he promised? How to find more funds to pay an expert? Would it cost even more than that attorney wanted Absolom to pay?

Shaking her mind free for the moment, Tamsin prepared to walk out and accept the neighbors' condolences, delaying again her hopes for sufficient time alone to mourn.

6

Lady Hawksmoor's Parlor

LEFT ALONE IN Hawksmoor's study, Rowland opened a window and then closed the study door before crossing the hall to peek into the parlor. Lord Hawksmoor had an expensive wife.

Gold brocade on the walls.

Rose-colored velvet chairs and settees.

Glistening paint on the wainscot.

A gallery of Dutch and Italian paintings.

"Ah, please excuse me." A deep, mellow voice from memory, though Rowland couldn't connect a name. "I didn't see that my brother had company. Welcome, madam. I'm Poynter, the Viscount Heydon."

Rowland, as the black-clad Catalan lady, managed a curtsy in that cruel ocean of silk skirts. "Charmed, your lordship. I am Taresa de Flores."

"You're not English." Heydon seemed surprised.

"No, your lordship. The earl rescued me in London, carrying me to join my cousin in Cambridgeshire. I believe he's now in search of his wife."

"She's not at home."

Heydon was about thirty-five years old, at least twenty years younger than his brother. With hooded eyes and a long aquiline nose, he was more falcon-like than the earl with his eagle-beak. Well-preened in grey brocade and white lace, he'd had his suit cut to fit his narrow figure, without fashionable swishing skirts. A diamond pin set in gold sparkled in his cravat, the sole immodest display of wealth in his dress. Heydon wore his oak-brown hair tied back with a ribbon, without powder or wig. He had a subtle way of asserting power, even though he stood a head shorter than Rowland.

"You must be fatigued from travel, madam. What might I fetch for you? You have only to ask."

"You are kind, your lordship, but I am well. You can, if you would, show me these paintings. They are as fine as any I've seen in Paris or Madrid. His lordship has quite a fortune invested in these wonders."

"They belong to Helen...I mean to say, Lady Hawksmoor." Heydon offered his arm as escort to show his guest the paintings. "My brother hopes that his heirs shall do very well with this legacy, if and when such heirs come into being. I'm not an expert, but I shall do my best to remember the pictures' provenances."

"I'm grateful." And inventive. Rowland rustled the wretched silk skirts. "My father has a collection, which he has begged my brother to sell, though it will break my heart. Such beauty is of greater value than gold."

"You must be a great aesthete, madam. Now, please forgive my curiosity. Are you come to England from Paris?"

"Most recently, yes. My home is...was in Catalonia."

"Alas, I haven't visited there. But I should like to hear from you that Paris is as beautiful and exciting as when I left it."

Paris? That's where Rowland had heard that voice and when he last saw Heydon. ("'Tis in my memory lock'd," as the Bard said. What key can unlock what I once knew?)

"Paris is always beautiful, sir. But, as I have learned today, so is Cambridgeshire."

"It is, isn't it?" Heydon stepped a hand's breadth closer, his eyes flashing like a hawk diving on prey. "Who is the cousin you've come to visit? It's a small neighborhood. We all know each other."

For the first time in months, Rowland spoke the name of his own Dark Lady aloud, since he didn't know anyone else in Cambridgeshire to cite. "Do you know her, your lordship?"

"Yes, but I've been at court this last half year and haven't had sufficient opportunity to resume our acquaintance since she returned to England. I'm intrigued to learn she has cousins on the Continent."

"When we met in Amsterdam," Rowland continued, being good at spinning falsehoods, "we discovered that we are third cousins. Our great-grandfathers were brothers. My brother—"

"Who is your brother? I have a large acquaintance in Paris, perhaps we've encountered each other."

God blind me! Rowland was himself being interrogated.

"Orlando, Viscount de Flores. Our father is also called Orlando. Distressing times caused us to leave home. We are intending now to settle in England."

"And you met my brother Monck in London? What a coincidence. I am happy that we shall be neighbors in Cambridgeshire while you visit. Did you share the same inn?"

"We met in the offices of Lord Hawksmoor's business man, where I was seeking an agent to hold our funds safely."

Heydon's face darkened. "How did Fate lead you to that particular agent?"

Rowland's interest was piqued by Heydon's dark response to the mention of that London business man. Was Hawksmoor or Heydon—or both—involved with that agent's investment in the Duke of Monmouth's schemes? However, at that moment, what Rowland most needed was a quick falsehood.

"My brother sent me, senor, on recommendation of a friend in Paris. And my own good luck led me to meet his lordship the earl in London."

"Such a fateful coincidence." Heydon clutched Rowland's elbow, tight as a hawk's claw. "Now that we are a little acquainted, madam, I am compelled to be forward with you. My brother has been known to fall prey to grasping and flattering women. The nature of your meeting gives me pause."

Behind Heydon, Rowland spied Perry slipping out of the earl's study. Time to be on the road. And away from Heydon's inquisition.

"How charming, your lordship, that you care so for your brother's well-being. As I do my own brother."

"I also care for the well-being of all that the Earl of Hawksmoor is responsible for. Villages, cottagers, the parish curate. I will do anything to protect him, and to ensure his estate passes whole and healthy to his heir. I do what I must to be sure he's not a plum to be picked."

His heir? But Hawksmoor had no children. Heydon was his heir. That had been known throughout Cambridgeshire, even long ago when Rowland lived in England.

"Such care for your brother is charming. But please understand, I have my own title. And my own wealth. And more to the point, his lordship has a wife. It's indecent, an abomination, to come between a man and his wife."

Rowland removed Heydon's hand the way he'd seen his own Dark Lady escape a too-familiar hand in a crowd of courtiers. The two glared at each other until the earl's voice interrupted.

"Alas, Senora Taresa, my wife left on a morning call with Sir Isaiah and Lady Candecote." Hawksmoor seemed pleasantly surprised to see his brother. "Ah, Poynter, hello. You've met my esteemed guest." Then to Taresa, "I regret that it shall be another day until I can introduce my dear wife to you."

"I long to meet her, senor. From this lovely parlor, I aver she must be a delightful lady."

Hawksmoor glanced around the room, as if never before seeing it. "Aye. This room has all the fine qualities of my dear wife."

Heydon still stared at their guest. "It's one entire ship's fortune of tapestry and gilded furniture."

"Ah, Helen is worth every farthing," Hawksmoor said. "She launched the enthusiasm in this neighborhood for paintings as a good investment."

"I worry," Heydon said, "that it's an ostentatious and unreliable way to save for a rainy day."

Instead of answering that, Hawksmoor said, "Oddsfish, Poynter, you did not offer our guest a chair. Let me pour you a sip of cordial, senora."

A rift existed among these two brothers and the absent wife, who must be one of the grasping women that preyed on the earl.

"Please, senor, allow me to sip your cordial while standing. It's been a long morning, and I shall have to return to the heat of the carriage soon."

They chatted about the weather, with the brothers suggesting sights to see while visiting. "The colleges and their chapels are not to be missed. Cambridge is a pretty market town. And you must see the cathedral at Ely, though repairs are still underway."

Rowland set down his glass of too-sweet cordial on a table that held baubles: ceramic dogs, shiny stones, a dried flower. "Sir, is there a retiring room where I might freshen up before the next stage of my journey?"

"Pray forgive my inattention to your needs, senora." The earl pointed to an alcove near the front door. Then he sent a servant to fetch Mr. Warboys, who was taking refreshment in the kitchen.

With no time to strip and pour an ewer of water over his entire carcass, Rowland made do by dabbing exposed bits of flesh. He longed like a heretic in an inquisitor's oubliette to be free of all that stiff silk. Then Lord Hawksmoor's gravelly voice carried from the foyer into the retiring room.

"My agent's clerks in London confirmed it. I'm as skint as any beggar in the parish. I'm done up, Poynter."

Heydon said, "Let me help you, like I did when you needed to dispose of those mortgages. You have unentailed land you can mortgage and—"

"Absolutely not!" The earl's voice rose. "A mortgage is the road straight to perdition. We learned that from our neighbors."

Heydon answered, which Rowland very much wanted to hear, but Heydon's words didn't carry.

"I don't see an honest way out, Poynter, except to sell land."

"No, brother," Heydon said. "Do not sell a single fistful of dirt or stone. Let me help to set your ship right again."

"Will you ever understand how I loathe the idea of debt?"

"I do understand. That's why I made you sell those mortgages. It's as painful to hold a mortgage as it is to pay one."

"What else can I do, Poynter? I have nothing except land."

"Sell me those paintings, Monck. You can leave them hanging in your parlor. Your wife need never know."

"I can't...perhaps I can. It's a good idea. What must I promise you in return, Poynter?"

"Nothing. Except you must restrain your wife's profligate ways, until we can regain your fortune."

"Then is it true, Poynter, as she says? That you had a *tendre* for my wife before she chose me?"

"No, Monck, that's nonsense. Her heart was always set on you as the greatest man in the shire. Now, to do this business, we shall create a syndicate, like men of wealth do. But it will be only you and me putting money in and taking money out."

Rowland had now gained useful tidbits about the earl's business by eavesdropping. When he emerged from the retiring room, the front door stood open. Outside, Perry crossed the yard, stopping to stretch. A finger to his lip, Heydon watched Perry walk to the carriage, ignoring his brother and the foreign guest.

That intimate gesture, the focused gaze. Rowland now recalled the ambassador's Paris salon, where Heydon bent to speak with a young lieutenant, the prettiest man in the room.

If only he could remember which lieutenant that was.

7

The Averil

"COME, LIZZIE." TAMSIN tucked her cousin's hand into the crook of her elbow, the way a man guides a woman. "We'll stand at the front door, the way we did at the Easter open house."

The trestle tables in the Revelstone great hall were covered with linen, using most of the cloth in the house. Mrs. Bell gave Lizzie mourners' ribbons for any who might need them.

"Lizzie…" Tamsin struggled with the knot in her throat that refused to go away. "Remember how Absolom said to laugh, no matter how difficult the chore?"

"The first time I remember came with a command to shell walnuts one Christmas." Lizzie wrinkled her nose. "I was six. There were hundreds of walnuts. Thousands."

"Today, when I press your hand, it shall stand for laughing in the midst of endless dreary tasks and dreadful moments."

Tamsin and Lizzie, laughing despite the gloom, pushed open the front door of Revelstone House. In the yard, Ned instructed the boys about where carriages should be left, the younger boys having been freed from great-room chores to help with the horses. Ned presented a tall, commanding figure in a brown linen-and-wool suit, the one he wore only when on business in London. He'd been jollying the harried boys into making a game of their tasks.

"You shall have cake at the end of the day." Ned, hand on his chest, swore on his honor. "Together with Absolom's special cider, which he asked me to save specially for you lads."

"Can Ned ever do as I ask?" Lizzie waved a finger, indicating how her half-brother's creatively tied cravat exposed his liberated linen shirt. "He'd put me in a passion, if I expected better."

"Scolding doesn't become you, Lizzie. And you tied me up in another of the liberated cravats from—"

The sound of horses echoed up the lane. When the riders rounded the bend into the yard, it proved to be a half-dozen of the king's men, their horses' hooves drumming like the devil on the thin skin of a bad conscience.

"God's bodkins!" Tamsin's belly lurched, and she cried out for God's help the way Mrs. Bell did when upset. "Did Lord Hawksmoor call out the militia after the highwaymen?"

Lizzie clutched Tamsin's bruised forearm. Tamsin removed Lizzie's hold and stepped into the yard to greet their visitors, showing bravado she did not own in her bones.

"Good day. It's Captain Starbuck, isn't it?" They'd met when the regiment first quartered in Cambridge a week earlier, having come in pursuit of the Duke of Monmouth's rebels. Though her mouth felt full of wet wool, Tamsin forced out the proper words. "We are surprised to see you, Captain, on this day of all days."

The captain dismounted, removed his feathered tricorn hat, bowed to Lizzie, and shook Tamsin's hand. Her hand ached when the officer released her gloved fist.

"It is a hot day, isn't it?" Captain Starbuck was a pleasant man with fine manners and a formal posture that suited his slim frame. He stood out from the militia he led, with a well-groomed Van Dyck beard, natural golden-brown locks, and a fresh face that might be considered pretty. "I had a message this morning, and therefore we came over immediately."

"Thank you. How kind of you to come." Relief flooded her veins. This visit was about Absolom, not highwaymen! Tamsin could have embraced the captain if she gave in to impulse. She glanced at Lizzie, who kept her head high. Tamsin had to invite them, there being no way out of it. "Won't you and your men step inside for a cup of averil ale and a piece of shortbread?"

"Averil?" Captain Starbuck puzzled over the word, as if he didn't know its meaning.

"It's Doctor Absolom Foxe's funeral today. We lost him to heaven last night."

"Forgive me, Mr. Foxe. I had no idea." The captain blushed a brighter red than his coat. He glanced around, seeing the crowd of boys gathered around Ned, people busy in the great hall, black ribbons around each person's arm. "Please accept my sincere condolences. Our business shall wait for a better moment."

"Your business?" Tamsin asked, curious, yet also satisfied that no Foxe brigands were to be arrested just then.

"I understand that Lieutenant Rowland Foxe is your cousin." Captain Starbuck shifted his hat from under one arm to the other. "We came to inquire after him."

"Rowland Foxe?" Her relief tilted to dismay.

This captain sought their cousin, who'd either gone mad or bad on the Continent, so that it shouldn't have been an earthshaking surprise he turned traitor last winter, becoming an officer in the Duke of Monmouth's militia. Tamsin's face burned hot, fiercely angry that Rowland brought the danger of the king's men to Revelstone.

Controlling of all those emotions, Tamsin said, "Our cousin has been gone from England these ten years."

"Yes, I know." Captain Starbuck mounted his horse. "We shall visit when your household isn't in distress. Again, my condolences, Mr. Foxe. And I beg your pardon, Miss Foxe, for stirring up all this dust."

The mounted men disappeared to the south, past the village. Moments later, carriages began to arrive.

"I've feared all year that Rowland might cause trouble." Lizzie leaned one hand on the entry door post, as if weak with relief. "Since Monmouth has been defeated and hung, men like that captain are hunting fools like our cousin."

"Yes, but…" Tamsin touched her Archangel pouch. "I shall drop with apoplexy if that captain returns."

"I think Captain Starbuck likes you." Lizzie teased, seeming less frayed by the militia than Tamsin had been. "He appears to be frightened to death of me. Too bad you cannot meet him as Thomasine Foxe. He may be eligible."

"Aye, a captain in need of an impoverished, dispossessed woman who plays desperado to—"

"Hush. Here comes the first of Absolom's Cambridge colleagues. Don't make me laugh when any scholar misbehaves."

"I can't laugh with my heart caught in my throat, Lizzie. The king's men discomfited me so."

People were exiting their carriages. Ned left off instructing the boys, dusted his breeches, and joined Tamsin and Lizzie at the door to Revelstone House.

"Ned," Lizzie admonished, "so much paint on your hands. Put on gloves like a gentleman."

"It's just stains from my honest work, not dirt. What did the captain want?" Sounding unbothered by the visitors, he donned the white gloves Lizzie offered him.

"Our cousin Rollo." Lizzie answered, her voice shaking. "It's a wonder Captain Starbuck didn't ride straight to our door when he first came to hunt rebels in Cambridgeshire."

"Then we aren't hanged today?" Ned laughed, but if you knew him, you saw him wincing at the truth. After Lizzie tied a black ribbon around his sleeve, he joined them at the front door, offering tin cups of ale to each guest who mounted the steps to condole with the Foxe cousins.

"Not hanged, but under siege." Ned pointed to where the three most disagreeable women in the county were crossing the yard, led by Mrs. Fairchild. "They didn't bring Camilla?"

Getting through today without Camilla would be unbearable. Tamsin touched her Archangel pouch, preparing to greet those women, holding out her gloved hand, wishing she had Camilla's sweetness to temper her own bitterness.

8

Funeral Clothes

— NED —

ALWAYS UNCOMFORTABLE IN a crowd, Ned longed to be painting, not serving ale. And he wanted to paint portraits instead of dogs and flowers, though those sell better. Yet how could he secure portrait commissions if no one knew "Eduard Wijck" as an accomplished painter? London people only saw the quaint farm scenes and bowls of flowers painted for ready money. Just like Lizzie-as-a-seamstress and Tamsin-dressed-as-Tom, Ned had to continue the mundane businesses that kept them afloat, with no way to quit the restorations and disguises.

Tamsin held out her hand in greeting. "Lady Hawksmoor! Lady Candecote! Mrs. Fairchild! You are so kind to come today."

Three striking figures arrived in the crowd of mourners, women he'd rather paint than having to bear their judgment while he offered ale and cake. Like three ill-matched Medici porcelain figures, they each strove to dress more fashionably than other women in the county—in inappropriately shiny threads. The other mourners all followed custom: no shiny garments at a funeral. Except these three, who flaunted expensive raiments.

And, as usual, they didn't notice Ned. When he offered mugs of ale, they saw the tray, not the bearer. Fine. He'd learned long ago that he was free to gawp at people while invisible, to assess how he might paint them.

Lady Hawksmoor, of small stature and a soft build, had large, wet eyes, as if ready to release tears at any moment, matched by her tear-shaped gold locket and earrings.

Sir Isaiah's stick-thin, auburn-haired young wife (Camilla's stepmother, though they were the same age) had delicate features, like a too-precious-to-play doll. She wore an elaborate, overwhelming necklace, with beads crowding a single sapphire that'd show better as its own pendant.

White-haired Mrs. Fairchild (Camilla's mother-in-law) was tallest and at least fifteen years older than the other two women. She wore a silver starburst brooch, like a militia man's campaign badge, but which drew attention to her (intimidating) bosom. Her commanding ways overwhelmed her friends, especially Lady Candecote. As usual, Mrs. Fairchild's large nose was up in the air (as Mrs. Bell liked to say).

After Lady Hawksmoor released Tamsin's hand, the other two women offered their own limp hands to Tamsin and then to Lizzie. They each raised a handkerchief to catch tears, all three in metallic tones that flashed in the sunlight.

Hawksmoor's wife wore gold brocade with a richly embroidered bodice and gold threads woven through the fabric. A wide length of lace traced the seam where the skirt met the bodice, with cobwebby white sleeves and a lace shawl around her shoulders caught in a gold brooch that matched her pendant and earrings. He liked to paint wispy lace but had too few opportunities. He could try that new compound he found in London, to paint a flashy dress without wasting gold flakes.

Lady Candecote's gown was blue silk, dark as midnight with silver threads. Her stomacher covered most of her fine linen shift, except for the extravagant cream lace across her shoulders and chest. The midnight-blue would be a delight to paint, with all the silver highlights in the folds. But the blue of her dress was too dark for her cultured-cream complexion, so Lady Candecote's goggly eyes filled her delicate face.

If he painted the truth, there'd be unhappiness. A lead-oxide would not flatter such a face. But that blue silk called out for the New World indigo he'd wanted to put to good use.

The stark-white threads woven in Mrs. Fairchild's dark grey silk dress served to highlight her whitening hair. The gown resembled a style Lizzie drew for Camilla last Easter, a new creation she'd seen in Mary's court, with layers of grey wrapped around waist and hips, then left to drape over her arm, like an old statue in one of Absolom's books. The palette challenge would be to balance colors for the lead-white of that woman's hair. And the brush challenge? To be patient, to not reveal that termagant's true nature.

"Oh Mrs. Fairchild!" Lizzie said. "It is good of you to come. But where is—"

"Sir Isaiah?" Lady Candecote, the baronet's wife, suggested. "He is in the yard. Gossiping, I aver. Men say they never gossip, but we know they do."

Camilla. That's who Lizzie meant to ask about. Ned glanced at Tamsin. Her clenched fists, arms stiff at her sides, meant that she had her impatience well in hand.

"We are so sorry for your loss." Lady Hawksmoor spoke in a grating Norfolk accent.

While playing Tom perfectly, Tamsin said, "You are kind to say so. Lady Hawksmoor, you've been introduced to my cousin, Miss Ysabel Foxe? You haven't had good opportunities to know each other since she returned home from service to Princess Mary in Holland."

It wasn't nice of Tamsin to make it plain that these women owed Lizzie deference. Or at least respect. It wasn't nice, but Ned rejoiced that Tamsin said it.

"Charmed, my dear." Lady Hawksmoor's fluty voice grated. "Aren't you a lovely creature in black silk?"

"Yes, Miss Foxe is always lovely." Tamsin-as-Tom smiled, but Ned guessed she was fuming, because he was. Lizzie wore black silk solely to honor Absolom.

Lady Hawksmoor continued to appraise Lizzie's beauty.

"Such a smooth complexion for one so dark! Are you one of those mulattos from the sugar plantations?"

A barb, spoken with English charm.

"No, my lady." Lizzie smiled, because she claimed to have a special skill, knowing how to hide her emotions, a skill Tamsin and Ned hadn't mastered. "My people were exiled from Spain for joining the Reformation. They served Queen Elizabeth, which earned a barony for my father's great-grandfather. Since then, all daughters are named for the Good Queen."

"How sweet," Lady Hawksmoor cooed.

The women left, likely to torture someone else in the parish.

Ned discarded any idea of painting those three terrors. His father had warned him that portrait work requires more hours with the subject than one spends with a lover. He'd rather paint Lizzie or Camilla in such rich dresses. Yet he kept seeking more glimpses of that midnight-blue silk with cream lace.

How in this life was he ever to prove that he could paint dark silk folds and pale dolls' faces better than any man in England?

9

Hide Your Eyes

— ROLLO —

EXAGGERATING HIS FALSE Catalan accent, Rowland said, "You have been so kind, Lord Hawksmoor. And I'm very pleased to have made your acquaintance, Lord Heydon."

Heydon's curt nod indicated that he did not return the warm sentiment.

Out in the yard, the earl again watched his guest shake out skirts and straighten veils, preparing to travel. He seemed struck by emotion while saying good-bye.

Oh God in heaven! Was the earl going to embrace the senora? No, Heydon diverted his brother. Perhaps there *is* a Divine Being who answers prayer.

Hawksmoor helped the senora into the carriage. "We shall see each other again while you abide with your cousin. I should like to meet your brother when he joins you."

"You cannot estimate, your lordship, how I treasure your friendship in my heart."

"Ah, here's your cavalier."

The carriage rocked when Perry climbed in. Hawksmoor closed the door, crying farewell and shouting to Mr. Warboys to take care of his friends. The carriage wheels scratched in the gravel, then settled into unpredictable thumps after returning to the country lane. Sun flashed through the carriage window, alternating with shade from oak and beech trees.

Perry exploded as soon as they were away from the house. "That raggedy brigand jammed his boot into the same rib I broke in Rotterdam. And now I must endure another overheated jerry-cummumble ride in this blasted carriage."

"You are unhappy? Is it because the varlet who struck you wore a Puritan's tall hat?"

"Highwaymen shoot you. They don't break bones. Did you see any faces? What I viewed out the carriage window were tatty beggars. One was hunchback, who I shall recognize if I ever see him again. One wore blue velvet. What did you see?"

"Too little through this veil."

Rowland fetched his gold angel from its hiding place, blessing his own good luck that the highwaymen had missed it. He rolled it over his fingers, having foregone that comfort over the past days spent as Senora Taresa.

"Perry, I mean to put your manly form to use. You can easily beguile the Viscount Heydon. He's a viscount in his own right, you know. It's not just a courtesy title."

"I shall not, whether he possesses his own title or not. False seduction is an abomination before men and angels. Do it yourself if you want to play that bluff. I cast no lures save for a man who beguiles *me*." Perry sat folded up in his corner of the carriage, rigidly decisive. Then his curiosity got to him. "Why beguile the viscount?"

"He guides Hawksmoor's money. I suspect the brother, not the earl, is the nemesis my uncle seeks. And I have identified the viscount's weak point."

"It pleases me that you think I might be a man's weak point." Perry held up a finger, indicating that he meant the opposite. "However, my entire physical corpus declines to be exploited for whatever connivance you are considering."

"Fine, Perry. I'll find another way to approach Heydon. Since greed is the original sin against those we serve in this adventure, the punishment must involve wealth."

"Whatever rig you are planning, I don't have wealth to lend to its success. And that will not improve while we are on this detour into the realm of your inamorata."

"I swear, we aren't on this detour because of a woman. She hasn't sent one message since we nearly drowned on her behalf in Holland. I'm done with heroics for her sake."

"No. Now you're in love with memories of your precious childhood. Ever since that letter came last week, begging your help, I've had to listen to stories whenever we're drinking wine in the gloaming. Can we go back to our real work? I've said since we set off for Cambridgeshire, whatever you think you are asked to do on this detour, it will not bring us glory."

Once again, Rowland said, "After we uncover Heydon's scheme, we'll return to hunting Monmouth's financiers. Now, what did you discover in the earl's study?"

"You discover. I merely prowl." Perry wrinkled his nose, which meant he'd been successful.

"Prowling. Like a cat seeking the best prey. Please reveal all, Mr. Frake."

"It's as the old gentleman hinted. The earl is as skinned as a poached hare." Perry handed over a clutch of papers from inside his shirt. "But I found no sign of the mortgages you wanted to see. He made a large investment in sugar cane and indigo."

Rowland shuffled through the papers. "Behold! As I conjectured. Listen to this." He read one paper to Perry.

> My dear Monck: As your brother and friend, I beg you to let me take those mortgages off your hands. I'll take them to Sir Duncombe, my agent in London, and return the proceeds to you. It is past time that you free yourself from this burden. I would be honored if you would let me help you.

"You see, Perry? This detour might be resolved quickly. We already know more than we did in London."

"Far be it from me to caution you, Rollo, but it wasn't at Sir Charles Duncombe's office where Senora Taresa met the earl."

"True. In the office where we met, the earl had come for the sake of an investment from which he appears to have suffered a cold dunking."

"I wager that ships with Hawksmoor's cargo have all been lost at sea."

"Most likely. That agent's business saw many cargoes lost this year. It's one reason why we were sent to see what that business man has been up to." Rowland rolled his coin, thinking. "How does Hawksmoor keep an expensive wife without a feather to fly? I wager she'll bolt."

"After we meet the earl's wife, I can speculate whether she'll bolt in the face of poverty."

"Perry, I've invented details about Senora Taresa's brother, the Viscount Orlando. You need to know, for the next gambol. We aren't introducing your lieutenant to the rustics of Cambridgeshire."

"You are giving up skirts, Rollo? You have a great talent for inventing crinkum-crankum on the fly." Perry steepled his fingers, as if preparing to recite from a catechism. "All I know about your brother, senora, is the sticky pudding you ladled on the earl in his carriage. For my part, I only met Senor Orlando for a trice when he hired me to guard his dear sister while he searches for a house in the city."

"He's a brilliant business man, is my brother Orlando. He's rescuing our fortune after our father fell out with the Spanish government and his Catalan neighbors. As for me, my wealth is tied up in an inheritance dispute over my dead husband's lands in Catalonia."

"You, a widow, show great courage through all of this, with your life a farrago. I admire you greatly, senora."

"Thank you, Mr. Frake. You are kind to say so."

They jolted along in silence for a bit. Then Rowland asked, "What do you most desire, Peregrine Frake?"

"To stay alive, whatever the assignment. To avoid hunger. To have a bit of coin to send to my mother at each half year. To stave off death from boredom and bad carriage rides." Perry rubbed at his sore ribs. "No one in your country gambol will ask what I desire, my friend. What do *you* want?"

"Justice. A proper place in the world. Now, please hide your eyes while I change my habiliment. I need to become Orlando."

"Hide my eyes? I stole the gown and then helped you wiggle into it every morning for the past week. I've often seen you as bare as when God dropped you on this earth."

"Pretend, Perry. It's what we do."

"Fine, I shall pretend modesty. But what you're missing is the dignity you lost while the earl fondled your boney knees."

The carriage driver called out, "We are here, madam, sir."

Rowland said, "Will you please distract the driver while I exit the carriage? He has already seen the last of Taresa de Flores."

"As you wish. He's one of those old-time, woman-hating fellows. Mr. Warboys didn't like the idea when the earl declared that Senora Taresa was to ride in his carriage."

"You must be wrong, Perry. Everyone likes me. It's the foundation upon which all my work is built."

"As you say. No one, save me, knows your heart." Perry was then out of the carriage and hailing Mr. Warboys.

Rowland had five days' practice with that gown, which he now shed. Unfortunately, his satin court suit was just as uncomfortably hot as that wretched silk gown.

The Viscount Orlando de Flores prepared to emerge from the crested carriage. He rolled that gold coin across his knuckles one more time for luck.

A woman's voice carried from just outside the carriage. "Why isn't it a scandal? They say she was a slave to Princess Anne, brought from Barbados."

"No, my dear. Your sources are wrong." The gossiping woman who replied spoke in a mercantile Norfolk accent. "Her grandmother's family came from Spain generations ago. She's been in Mary Stuart's court for a decade." The woman dropped her voice. "She is so dark. And such a gilflurt."

Rowland's hand stiffened on the carriage door latch. ("My mistress' eyes are raven black..." Do they malign my own Dark Lady?)

The first evil gossip spoke again. "Indeed. So posh, so vain. At least she stays out of the sun, so she's only brown as a nut, not worse. Oh la. There's my husband. Let's talk in the arbor, away from all this dust."

Furious over strangers' insults, Rowland slammed open the carriage door, stepping out into the middle of a dozen people, with two dozen more behind them.

"God blind me! What are all these people doing at Revelstone House?"

10

Condolences

— TAMSIN —

WHILE STRIVING TO remember each mourner's name, Tamsin had to chase away memories of Absolom's gossip about his Cambridge colleagues ("...called the butler of his house a turd in his teeth... sued by a housemaid for unpaid wages...abuses his horse..."), while reciting the appropriate response to condolences. She lost count after the first three dozen.

The magistrate arrived with his wife, who took greater pride in her husband's knighthood than he did. They crossed the yard from their carriage, wearing sad faces in preparation for offering condolences. The magistrate held out his hand.

"Please accept our deepest sympathy, Mr. Foxe."

His wife greeted Lizzie. "Miss Foxe, we grieve with you."

Tamsin shook hands and offered the appropriate response, made herself look the magistrate in the eye, even though she'd led a restoration just hours earlier. She glanced into the yard, wishing Providence—or even Leighton Fairchild—might deliver Camilla to the averil. Licking her lips, dying for posset or ale or just water, Tamsin sensed a hair on her tongue. She worried about the moustache melting off her face almost as much as she worried about that visit from the king's men. Or about the Goliath who appeared at the morning's failed restoration. Or about her own loneliness and worry at Camilla's absence. At least nothing worse could happen that day.

She only had to say over and over again, "Doctor Foxe would rejoice to know you came today…Please have a portion of shortbread…"

"God blind me!" A man's voice whirred nearby. "What are all these people doing at Revelstone House?"

Tamsin faced the surprised-sounding man, who was tall and impressive in a copper-colored satin court suit. A distinctly Continental visage, with a long face, sharp bones, and pointed chin. Utterly unsuitable for a funeral, he dressed as a dandified cavalier, lace dripping from his cuffs and collar, his unpowdered white wig falling in court-style curls to his shoulders.

Rowland Foxe. Here! In the flesh. The faithless courtly mercenary.

He mirrored her surprise and cried, "Tom!"

"Why are you here, you—you scullion! You rampallian!"

Her hands scrunched into fists, unbidden; anger heated her veins. His name had brought the king's men to Revelstone.

"You're quoting Shakespeare to me?" Rowland stepped close, eyes burning with devil's fire, as the devil she believed him to be, given that he'd turned traitor in Holland. "I'm here, Tom, because Absolom wrote that I must come join in your battle."

"What can you do, Rollo?" Tamsin said. "You've been gone ten years. We don't know you."

— ROLLO —

"IT'S GOOD TO see you, Tom." Rowland offered his hand, but his cousin Tom ignored it. "Absolom begged me to help discover his enemies, for which I have a particular talent."

"You…you…Captain Sharp?" Tom choked, his eyes stabbing Spanish daggers, which Rowland parried with a smile.

"Is there a grievous sin that I don't remember the pleasure of committing?" Rowland had expected to be welcomed home, but instead Tom was cold and cross. Worse, Lizzie, his own Dark Lady, glared at him while remaining as beautiful as ever.

"You missed meeting the king's men, Rollo." Lizzie crossed her arms over her heart, as if defending from him. "They rode here moments ago, asking for you."

Then…Lizzie's heart didn't burst from happiness at seeing him again. His own heart became unexpectedly fragile, cracking open to reveal the secret hope he carried for their reunion.

He knew better. (Yet, as the Bard also knew, "…the miserable have no other medicine, but only hope.")

"The king's men came here," Tom repeated, scowling. "The militia that's scouring the countryside for Monmouth's rebels."

"Three men know I'm in England, and two of us are here." Rowland laughed, which earned deeper scowls from his cousins. Their fury must be catching, like a summer ague, because Ned, busy serving guests cups of ale, also had nothing for Rowland but dark looks. "Must I ask again, Tom? Why all these people?"

"We lost Uncle Absolom to heaven yesterday." Lizzie's voice broke. No, it shattered. "This is an averil in his honor."

"To heaven?" Rowland stopped, feeling smashed with a brick, blinking several times, his voice breathless. "To heaven?"

"Yes, where we all hope to go when we die." Tom dropped his voice to a furious whisper. "Except, perhaps, you, Rollo."

"Absolom gone?" How could Tom be so cold? Long ago, they'd been a band of brothers and Absolom their king. "Why harass me, Tom? Can we please weep together?"

"We wept all of last night." Tom's words are as cold as Amstel ice in winter. His eyes had lost the waggish sparkle he and his twin Tamsin always shared.

Tom adjusted his lace cuffs, shaking them loose, as if to add space between them. But then Tom quivered like a kicked dog when Perry came through the door and rested his hand on Rowland's shoulder.

— TAMSIN —

GULPING PURE FEAR, Tamsin wanted to run away, when she saw the glint in Goliath's eye. No, his eyes scanned past her to Lizzie. A smile twitched at the corners of his mouth. He squeezed Rowland's shoulder. His eyes rested on Ned.

Then Rowland traveled with that Goliath, likely in Rotterdam and…now…She cast aside fear to form a clear thought.

That woman in a black veil, riding in Hawksmoor's carriage. Good stars! It had not been a woman but Rowland.

"Tom, Lizzie, may I introduce my associate, Mr. Peregrine Frake? Perry, this is my cousin, Mr. Thomas Foxe. And you may recognize Miss Ysabel Foxe from Amsterdam."

Lizzie said, "I believe we met upon occasion in Holland, Mr. Frake. You often served as guard for visiting diplomats, if I'm not mistaken." She offered Perry her gloved hand with her usual graciousness. But then, Lizzie hadn't seen Goliath in Rotterdam or on the trail that morning. "Won't you take some ale in our uncle's memory? We have fruit and cake and cheese and…meats in the great hall."

Tamsin did not hold out her hand to Perry, but he grabbed it and squeezed, offering a bare-tooth grin and a grip that could have brought Tamsin to her knees.

"Aye, we shall be grand friends now, Mr. Foxe. You may call me Perry." He slammed Tamsin's shoulder hard enough to knock her down, grinning all the while. Then he bowed to Lizzie again and accepted the ale Ned offered. "Rollo has persuaded me to forget the mistakes of that foul day in Rotterdam. We misapprehended each other, when we all sought to save Miss Foxe."

Perhaps she'd burst into flames right there, burning with the wildfire Rowland had ignited. They'd all hang, because Rowland led the king's men here, to tie nooses around the necks of highwaymen. She bit back on vitriol, choosing less violent words, but then found a moustache hair on her tongue again. She couldn't speak her enraged mind until the crowd departed, leaving the Foxe cousins, nose to nose.

Traitor to the Crown.

Beggarly bravo.

Cockish cobweb cheat.

Tamsin *would* allow herself free rein for one moment in this life, to spit Shakespeare at him, the way he'd begun quoting the Bard when he was ten. A line formed on her tongue, along with that stray hair. (As one of Shakespeare's women said, "Thou art unfit for any place but hell.")

"How is your poor sister, Mr. Foxe?" Mrs. Fairchild reappeared, asserting her way into the conversation. "It is such a shame. And, for pity sake, I continue to pray each day for dear Miss Thomasine's recovery."

— ROLLO —

HIS THOUGHTS FOUNDERED in a deep cave, as if Rowland had uncovered only dark emptiness by coming here. Tamsin ill? Absolom had said nothing in his letter. But that, perhaps, explained why Tamsin ceased writing her own letters to him.

The intruding grey-haired woman had a frosty military manner to match the ridiculous silver star on her bosom, jewelry designed to make its center diamond seem larger than it was. If it was a real diamond.

Lizzie took the woman's hand, giving that woman all the attention Rowland had hoped for. "You are kind to inquire, Mrs. Fairchild. She is better some days. Thomasine is unhappy that she's not sufficiently strong today to be here to honor our Uncle Absolom."

Fairchild? The solicitor's name on papers Perry had found at Hawksmoor's house. Rowland marked her face for later discovery, too distressed about Tamsin to act right then.

"What does Dr. Oakes say?" The intrusive Mrs. Fairchild persisted, though Lizzie and Tom obviously sought to change the subject. Rowland also wanted to know about Tamsin.

"Madam." A man manifested at the woman's side, taking her gloved hand in greeting. He flaunted a mane of tawny curls, with hazel eyes. "Excuse me for overhearing my name."

"I was about to say, Dr. Oakes," Mrs. Fairchild stepped closer to the doctor, "that we are so fortunate you came into the parish. What hope do you hold for poor Miss Thomasine?"

"I'm flattered by your confidence in me as a physician." The man spoke in a low voice. Rowland strained to hear. "It has been a hard case, but I have new hope that we can now do more than merely keep our patient comfortable."

Tamsin gravely ill. Absolom gone. Rude greetings from each cousin, even Lizzie. What had Rowland come home to?

"I'm beyond sorry that I could not do more to save your uncle." Dr. Oakes grasped Tom's elbow and then offered a firm handshake, different from other greetings Rowland had seen, indicating a strong bond between the two men. "Please allow me to offer my deepest condolences."

After the doctor and Mrs. Fairchild retreated, Rowland asked Lizzie, "Tamsin is ill? Can I see her?"

"Tamsin declines visitors." Tom folded his arms, as if he meant to be intimidating, but the shoulders of his coat rose up inelegantly. "She had the pox."

"As did I." Rowland masked his irritation, that Tom denied him the chance to visit Tamsin. "Half the Continent and most of England carry smallpox marks."

"Not smallpox," Lizzie said. "Chicken pox. And then there was the pneumonia and an infection which left..." Her eyes shifted. "Which left our cousin in a decline."

Tom shifted and regripped his forearms. "I'll carry your message to her, sir."

"*Sir?* It's me. Rollo. Let me see Tamsin. She's almost a sister, and the only one among you besides Absolom who wrote to me."

Lizzie grasped Rowland's cuff again and tied a black ribbon on his arm. "We shall talk after our guests have departed. Now, go sup your averil ale, Rollo. Eat a cake."

11

An Introduction

— NED —

"IT'S AN ARRESTING thought, Mr. Wijck. Is it not?" The magistrate waylaid Ned for a second mug of ale. "Doctor Foxe in heaven, while we hang here on earth. My condolences."

Arresting. Hang.

Ned's attention had been deeply engaged elsewhere, so those words caught him unawares. The tray shook in Ned's hands. The magistrate drifted away to speak with a group of Cambridge men quaffing averil ale. Ned managed to steady the tray and offer mugs to mourners while again absorbed in observing that so-tall man who'd arrived with Rowland. He was called Perry, and surely there's no other man like him in England. Ice-blue eyes with sun-streaked, straw hair. The prominent bridge of his eagle-like nose. More muscle than a laborer at harvest time.

Ned's fingers itched to paint the planes of the man's face. It'd require more than color and motion to capture the alert flash of his eyes and the worldly knowledge etched on his visage. No, he'd have to try porcelain, not paint. And he'd use bare fingers since no intermediating tool, even the finest badger-hair brush, could replicate the harsh curves of that man's face.

But the man seemed to have disappeared. Ned scanned the averil crowd, seeking the tallest man there, yet not finding even a gleam of sun-blond hair. He only wanted to shake the man's hand and introduce himself. Nothing more than that.

"Ah, I see you are the kind of man," Perry's voice startled him, "who never stops inspecting the world around him. I wager that you see a great deal with those haunting silver eyes."

Ned jittered. This man, who'd wielded a pistol and a knife earlier that day, seemed to be flirting. Before this day, Ned's flirtations (only in London, never in the parish) had been insignificant events, raising no more ripples than Marborne brook in late summer. This moment, the man's breath so close to Ned's ear, felt like the lower Thames at high tide.

"How do you do, sir. It's Mr. Frake, isn't it?" Ned pretended to be his natural self and held out his hand for the introduction he'd wanted. "I'm Eduard Wijck, Miss Foxe's brother."

"I aver, Mr. Wijck," Frake kept hold of Ned's hand too long, peered too closely into his soul, "your Creator endowed you with eyes the color of a silvery winter sky, just before it snows."

"It takes a good arsenic white to make silver."

Zooterkins, what did he just say to the man? Fortunately, Mr. Frake pretended he didn't just meet the parish goose-cap.

"You are a painter, Mr. Wijck? Rollo never mentioned it. And I'm surprised—though that's not to say I'm displeased—about how much you differ from your sister."

"Half-sister. Do you have sisters? Brothers?" Ned did not like the sensation that he was a clever man made stupid by an attractive man standing so near.

"Five brothers. All still living. And all much younger. So, you see, Mr. Wijck," Perry touched Ned's shoulder, sending a shock through his frame, "I need to earn a good living."

"Then what are you doing here, Mr. Frake? Marborne is stark broke. Neither fate nor kings have treated us well."

"Be comforted. Rollo says that Fate may yet restore your fortunes, my friend. I hope we shall be friends, at the very least."

Comforted? With that man close by, Ned had seldom felt so uneasy, so backfooted. And he found little comfort in the idea that they might be rescued by Rollo. May Jupiter preserve their entire band of comrades.

12

Commendations

"GO SUP YOUR averil ale, Rollo. Eat a cake."

Rowland couldn't speak for a moment, disconcerted by Lizzie's abrupt dismissal. She'd graced him with a few quick smiles, up until he'd asked to see Tamsin.

He strengthened the guard on his heart, because he had three days to do what he could here, then they needed to be back hunting that man in London. Yet Fate had proved fickle so far that day. First, that assault by land pirates had roiled his gut; he was a soldier, not a gull for cloddish ruffians, but Taresa's shoes and veil had hobbled him. And too many strangers milled about here (some of them busy insulting Lizzie), so he had no opportunity to speak forthright with his cousins.

Ned thrust a tray of ale cups at Rowland while his pale eyes stabbed at him like icicles under a cold winter sun. Yet when Ned offered ale to Perry, sparks flew. Although the two men had never met, you could kindle a coal fire with that heat.

Tom glowered, marring his good looks. He seemed to be wearing a padded coat. The dark brows, the full lips and too-snub nose. Brown eyes and long dusky lashes, which were fine for his twin Tamsin, but Tom resembled one of King Charles's famous spaniels.

And Tom's anger about the king's men asking for Rowland seemed thin sauce. In his letters home, Rowland had always been guarded about his employment. And now they believed he'd turned traitor. Well then, he must douse Tom's fire and thaw Lizzie's ice. They had work to do and needed to do it together.

"Come, cousin." Rowland clutched Lizzie's elbow.

He half-pointed, half-dragged her into the alcove near the front door. He held back the tapestry that hung in its archway while beckoning Tom to follow. With the three of them crowded into the narrow space, he dropped the tapestry.

He held out open, apologetic palms.

"Think of me as King Hal with scaling ladders before the wall. We shall 'sheathe our swords for lack of argument!'"

He rested his hand on Tom's shoulder, taking a risk, hoping Tom wouldn't reject his friendship.

Yes, Tom's coat was padded.

— TAMSIN —

"HOW ARE YOU like King Henry in any way?" Tamsin so longed to put a cork in Rowland's arrogant flow of words. "Truly?"

"It was a good choice of words," Rowland said. "Just not the same context. When we were ten, you understood King Hal's notion of a band of brothers. Nothing is more sacred than the virtues Absolom taught us, so I came to help when he asked me."

Not swayed by the band-of-brothers gush, Tamsin said, "You came here when the king's men are seeking Monmouth's rebels?"

"They aren't hunting me." Rowland pretended to think, then heightened Tamsin's ire by teasing Lizzie. "Why are you rusticating here, Lizzie? Did Princess Mary command you to molder in the fens until you can regain the lost earldom? To help grow her band of loyal supporters in England?"

Lizzie flushed. "Rollo, why did you desert me...I mean, the Crown, by serving Monmouth?"

"You are unkind, Lizzie," Rowland said. "As unkind as a smizzling Dutch rain. That is nothing like the truth."

"They say you served Monmouth in Holland." Lizzie cast the darkest frown that Tamsin had ever seen from her.

Tamsin seethed, not daring to speak her own dark thoughts. The Foxe orphans weren't raised on Puritan notions of sin, yet

Absolom did teach that betraying the Crown ranks high in any notion of damnation.

"My dear cousins," Rowland scolded, "I am compelled by Absolom to help you, but I owe service elsewhere. Therefore, I do not have time for empty quarrels. I serve the Crown, not traitors. What do you think I've been doing for the past decade?"

Lizzie said, "Working as guard and messenger for diplomats. Until you turned traitor last winter."

Rowland laughed, then rubbed his face when he saw that Tamsin scowled and Lizzie just looked sad. "Yes, I served diplomats. But I also was assigned by King Charles's agents on the Continent to help protect Monmouth."

"Then, you miting betrayer, you...you..." Tamsin sputtered in disgust.

"You joined Monmouth's militia when he prepared to invade England." Lizzie shifted to a brave stance.

Rowland answered as if Lizzie were jesting. "You thought me a betrayer? Lizzie, did you and I not often whisper that we were better than others at court, because we live by Absolom's rules? Did you not laugh at that lord from Bath who complained when I refused a bribe to carry love letters to my master's wife? Now you think me a miting betrayer?"

"People at court said you were a traitor."

"People in Mary's court?" Rowland offered Lizzie a wry smile. "Remember when people at court whispered that William had a mistress? How did that turn out?"

Lizzie twisted away, as if uncomfortable. "It was a lie—one which I never believed. Mary had to dismiss almost everyone in her court."

A story of court politics Lizzie once described, like a tale from a distant continent. not anything Tamsin knew about.

Rowland said, "Then for shame, Lizzie, that you believed rumors about me. Before James Stuart became our new king, one of his agents spawned that lie about William having a mistress. And I helped to find that duplicitous agent, because..." Rowland spoke to Tamsin in a harsh whisper. "Because, Tom, I am an intelligencer for the English Crown."

"In...telli...gencer." She repeated the word slowly.

It nagged her soul that Absolom used the same word ("I've engaged the best intelligencer...") and assumed Tamsin knew he meant Rowland. What else had she missed? How was she going to protect them all if she did not understand clues or even direct words from Absolom?

13

The Most Reverend

— N E D —

HE SHUFFLED FRETFULLY, having been left alone to greet visitors while Tamsin and Lizzie harangued Rowland in the alcove near the front door.

Mrs. Bell brought Ned a new tray of ale cups. He enjoyed the relief of having her friendly face nearby while accepting the weight of the newly loaded tray. The giant, Mr. Frake, persisted in watching Ned, standing with his back against a pillar on the porch, an unreadable smile on his face.

"Do we have sufficient ale and posset?" Ned asked Mrs. Bell, keeping her near a tick longer. "Must we soon change to cider?"

"As we predicted, our guests are quaffing posset and wolfing cake like trolls," Mrs. Bell whispered. "But it's the cinnamon that is insufficient for the amount of posset they keep sipping. It's too late, I know, to find more. At least we have sufficient gloves and loaves for averil gifts."

The cinnamon came from a trove the cousins "found" when they liberated goods from a tradesman who'd cheated the whole village last summer, selling flour full of mealworms and sugar cut with talcum powder. A crate of white gloves had been liberated in that same restoration, which was how they could offer gloves to averil guests, each pair tied with a ribbon and a sprig of rosemary for remembrance.

Mrs. Bell hustled away after her chores. His cousins had not reappeared from their confabulation. The tall Mr. Frake shifted his stance, seeming to come closer. But (rejoice!) here was The Reverend Theophilus Gamlingay, who'd let Ned paint him last autumn, and whose conversation never frayed one's nerves. Ned painted him with a bushel of apples pouring across the table, a tankard of cider, and two cabbage moths. Gamlingay added a cat's skull to the collection, though Ned had no idea why. The other artifacts were symbolic of nothing, because Ned didn't subscribe to such notions. He just knew from paintings he saw in his agent's warehouse that such elements brought a better price.

The rector's voice was consoling, burbling like a brook, the kind that sends stones tumbling at high flood. "A sad day for the Foxe children, eh, Ned? And yet my old comrade, Absolom, is dancing in heaven now."

Ned said, "Absolom considered you the greatest of friends, sir. You know best our uncle's prospects for heaven."

A portly man, Mr. Gamlingay wore worsted wool, black and shiny with wear. His collar was clean, but old, more Puritan than most people wore these days, yet he hadn't cinched up his collar strings, so they dangled disreputably over his vest. His white cavalier's beard had caught a bit of egg below his lip. However, Ned couldn't think of a graceful way to caution him.

Mr. Gamlingay begged for a second cup of ale to tide him until he began the service. "Everything else about this day is hard to swallow." He pretended to laugh, but Ned detected a somber tone.

"My cousins would be happy to have you to Sunday supper, as we always do." Ned said it, thinking how lonely Mr. Gamlingay would be without his friend Absolom.

And yet, they'd all be so lonely at Sunday supper.

"Thank you, lad." Mr. Gamlingay grasped Ned's shoulders, as much as the old gentleman ever entered into an embrace, and then he wandered away, ale cup in hand, seeking shortbread in the great hall.

In the lull, when there were no new guests to greet, Mr. Frake peeled himself off the porch pillar and advanced on Ned, who held the tray as a barrier, not knowing what to expect.

"I've been thinking, Mr. Wijck, about you being a painter. Those I've met in the Low Countries all have paint on their shoes and shirts and fingers." He glanced down at Ned's boots, his best, which showed only flecks of yellow and green. "It should prove educational, both for the sake of science and the philosophy of aesthetics, to examine a painter's bare fingers. Will you have time today to remove your gloves?"

The ale cups rattled and sloshed on Ned's tray. "We are quite busy with our guests."

"Indeed." Perry brightened. "But there's tomorrow. We'll be here a day or two more. Tell me I'll have a chance."

Ned stopped a *yes* from escaping his mouth. Lizzie and Tamsin were still quarreling with Rollo in the alcove and…

"Mr. Ned?" One of Mrs. Bell's granddaughters tugged at his sleeve. "I'm to ask if you can help bear a new jug of posset up from the kitchen."

"Let me help." Perry snapped up as if to attention. "A man should always be useful, don't you think so, Mr. Wijck?"

With Perry gone, Ned was again free to eavesdrop while Rollo harassed Tamsin and Lizzie. Should he intervene, for his sister Lizzie's sake? No, both women would have his head off if Ned attempted to stop their argument.

Tamsin, especially, delighted in that kind of sparring.

14

An Intelligencer in the Parish

ALTHOUGH HE EXPECTED the word *intelligencer* to herald the dawn of understanding, Rowland heard Tom pronounce the word as if it were foreign while his expression turned darker.

"Anyone aligned with Monmouth," Rowland said, "is likely to use the word informant. Infiltrator. Spy. No true gentleman does what I do. But no diplomat's errand boy earns enough to keep a horse or private living quarters. I do it to survive in the royal courts that Absolom said I was born to serve."

He did his best to tell his own history briefly. When he'd arrived in Paris a decade ago, he secured a place as page to an English diplomat, where he showed aptitude and discretion. At seventeen, he served with the English ambassador's personal guards, where he met Perry. Their master led them into a new kind of service, using French words to describe that work: *surveillance, reconnaissance, espionnage.*

Or the English words: intelligencer, spy.

Captains for Charles II paid them to protect his natural son, the Duke of Monmouth, whenever Monmouth happened to be in Paris. When Monmouth moved to Holland, their master sent Perry and Rowland to new work under a spymaster for William of Orange, husband to Princess Mary, England's presumed heir. In Amsterdam, they again worked as couriers for English diplomats while also assigned to unearth secrets among Monmouth's entourage. And he lived like an exile, serving the king at a far lower status than his father and grandfather had.

Rowland said, "Perry claimed we should go to India. Or sail to the Americas. But I never have spare coin to go elsewhere. Hence, we spied on Monmouth, never believing he could amass an army sufficient to stake his claim to be king of England."

Lizzie's eyes brimmed. "And yet, lambkin, you never told me such secrets when we talked at court in Amsterdam."

Lambkin! Then he was her pet again!

"My visits with you were holidays from treachery, Lizzie. Was I mistaken to trust you?"

Lizzie didn't answer. A tear escaped, which she brushed away with her kerchief. Rowland had never seen her weep, and that tear of remorse brought him no joy. Why didn't he notice in Amsterdam that her trust was being beguiled away from him?

Tom interrupted the silence. "Rollo, you didn't tell us about your work in the letters you wrote."

"Didn't Absolom let you read his letters?"

"Yes. Or he read them to us."

"You are an educated man, Tom. Absolom and I used quotes from Shakespeare, so I didn't betray my work." Rowland made a wild guess, since Tom's face indicated he still puzzled over the idea of intelligencer. "You didn't see those lines? How Absolom and I traded lines from Shakespeare's spies? Reynaldo spying on Laertes. Polonius spying on Hamlet. Famous spies in Good Queen Bess's time."

Tom hadn't seen it. He went furiously red in the face, likely because of that lapse. Tom and Tamsin always sought to be the smartest among the cousins. Tom must have become more like Tamsin, furious about gaps in understanding. Too bad. In former times, Tom would jest about a mistake and serve himself up as the butt of his own joke.

Rowland touched the back of Lizzie's gloved hand. "Didn't Absolom correct you when you claimed I'd turned traitor?"

"I didn't want to blacken your name to him." Lizzie unfolded her hands, as if she'd stopped resisting him.

(We must be friends, Lizzie. Whatever happens, that must be preserved.)

"Absolom always spoke of your goodness, in service to the Crown," Tom said. "We didn't want to dissuade him."

"Lord keep us from adversity." Rowland raised his hands, pleading to heaven. "You preserved the tender sentiments of the one man who'd disabuse you of that lie? And you, Tom? The fire remains in your eyes. You still don't believe me?"

Producing a packet of letters from deep inside his copper-satin coat, Rowland took one page from the packet and held it out. "What does this say, Lizzie?"

Lizzie read in a whisper. "'I commend Lieutenant Rowland Matthew Foxe to any of the best colonels in England that might be in need of an officer who is steadfast and loyal to the Crown.'"

"Read the signature," Rowland said. "Because if you want to claim that I might have forged this—"

"God's wounds!" Lizzie exclaimed. "That seal belongs to William's spymaster. I know the handwriting, because..." She trailed off, didn't complete her thought.

"God blind me!" Rowland laughed, relieved. It was now clear. "You, dear Lizzie, carried a message to London with the same seal, believing I chased you across Holland because I was a traitor. While I was assigned to escort and protect you."

Lizzie's upper lip twitched. She handed him the letter and then folded her hands, as if contrite. "I repent that I believed a lie. However, I didn't know it was you who chased us in Holland."

Rowland took back his letter. "Perry heard you call for Tom on the wharf in Rotterdam, so we knew you were safe. And although Tom shot him, Perry's leather cuirass saved him. Now this time, we shall work together."

"Yes, lambkin." Lizzie dropped the angry glare with which she'd tortured him. "We can help each other, without misunderstandings."

"Misunderstanding?" Tom exclaimed. "I have believed this whole cursed year that I killed a man!"

SHE SPOKE SO loudly that the sound might have escaped the alcove. Tamsin dropped her voice to growl at him. "For months now, I thought I'd murdered a man. That I'd polluted my soul."

"Then seeing Perry today must have been a relief for you, Tom. He's healed quite well." Rowland was not teasing.

"My heart has not yet repaired itself from that shock." From Goliath pointing a pistol at her in the middle of a restoration. And from Camilla's continued absence. From the appearance of the king's men. Despite Rowland's confessions, Tamsin only pretended her usual calm. "And I am still grappling with your sudden appearance."

"And, of course, you want to know," Rowland said, "what Absolom wanted me to do for Marborne." He handed over a second letter from his packet.

"Read it, T–Tom." Lizzie stuttered, stopping herself just in time from saying Tamsin's name.

Tamsin began. "It says, 'Dear Sir Walsingham.' Who is that?"

"It's how I signed my letters to Absolom," Rowland said, "after Good Queen Bess's spymaster."

"Good stars! I thought it was a private jest you shared with Absolom. You never wrote it as one word. It was always 'Well Signed Hand.'"

"Tom, you must show a quicker wit in the work we are about to undertake together." Rowland produced a coin from nowhere and rolled it over his knuckles, like a juggler at a May-faire, showing impatience with his slow-witted cousins.

Tamsin skipped the sparse greetings and read the part that sounded exactly like Absolom, as if he were there.

> We are much beset by evil that rises from the Earl of Hawksmoor and the infernal mortgages my brothers took just before they died. Hawksmoor is my nemesis, the author of a cheat that threatens to undo our family. Please come and use your talents to uncover our enemies and defeat them. Help us carry on with grace and courage, as a band of brothers.

Fear not. You won't do this work alone, though the way
ahead is so jumble-gutted.

Her uncle's voice, which she'd never hear again. Which bashed
at the sore place behind her heart. She pressed at the Archangel
coin that lay under her shirt, then caught herself and whipped that
hand behind her.

"Absolom wants—wanted you to spy for us?" Lizzie asked.
"To discover and defeat our enemies the way Charles dealt with
the regicides? Or how King James is dealing with rebels?"

Rowland said, "Less dramatic than the king's current business.
I've been prowling to discover Absolom's nemesis. And I am
divining a scheme for—"

"Revenge?" Lizzie asked.

"Recompense," Rowland said. "As Absolom said more than
once, 'Revenge is not the way of enlightened people.'"

"You'll help bring our case before the law?" Tamsin asked.

"No. I know quicker, less costly ways," Rowland said. "And
it's not likely that English law can help Marborne. Unless King
James restores the title to our family—restores it to you, Tom."

"First," Tamsin said, "we need money for this quarter's taxes
and mortgage dues. Will you help with that? Or have you come
solely to defeat Hawksmoor?"

"Your cheating neighbor is Lord Heydon. Hawksmoor is pocket-
empty. He had Heydon sell the Marborne mortgages to a blind
syndicate, which is—"

Though surprised that he'd uncovered that part of Absolom's
secrets, Tamsin interrupted. "I know what a syndicate is. I know
the mortgages were sold."

Lizzie blinked, surprised. "You didn't tell me."

"I only learned it from Absolom yesterday. There hasn't been
time to tell you, Lizzie." And Tamsin had not envisioned Rowland
showing up and casually revealing secrets. "And Absolom was
adamant about who was involved. Hawksmoor, Solicitor Fairchild,
and the agent in Sir Charles Duncombe's office."

"It's Heydon," Rowland said. "I doubt Hawksmoor has the wit to organize his own breakfast."

"You've been gone too long from the neighborhood, lambkin. Heydon is no villain," Lizzie said.

"Besides, he's rich," Tamsin added. "Heydon has investments everywhere. Charleston. Barbados. Elizabethtown. What do we have that Heydon might want?"

Rowland frowned. "He could beg the king for the Marborne title, to become an earl without waiting for his brother to die."

Annoyance flitted over Lizzie face. "The heat has overcome your good sense, Rollo. Heydon is not our enemy."

Rowland persisted. "I'll prove it's Heydon who is cheating you. For now, to solve your dilemma, we shall launch a scheme that shall restore Marborne wealth."

"You intend to cheat Heydon?" Tamsin asked.

"Yes, to gain recompense for how Absolom was cheated."

Lizzie tapped his hand. "A scheme? Like that Dutch baron who cozened people into joining a syndicate and then disappeared into the wilds of—what was that savage place called?"

"Pennsylvania," Rowland said.

"Your work?" Tamsin asked because the expression on his face rather resembled an egg-sucking dog, proud of his theft.

"My work in Holland was to help Mary and William," Rowland said, not answering her question. "For Absolom's sake, we shall work a similar scheme that promises great wealth. And we'll invite Hawksmoor, Heydon, and the solicitor to join."

"How can you advance an investment scheme?" Lizzie asked. "I've heard no rumors from Holland that you're a rich man."

"Tom can help," Rowland said. "How much gold and silver are you holding for this quarter's taxes and mortgage dues? We can use it as bait, to gull our would-be investors."

"Good stars, Rollo!" Tamsin's belly lurched with renewed fears. "You cannot gamble with our money. Not one farthing."

"My juggles always work." Rowland bragged. "Without any need for me to run off to Pennsylvania."

"No," Tamsin said. "Lizzie, we must return to our guests." Half her fears had been quashed in previous moments, but Rowland roused new trepidations with each proposed idea. "We can't keep hiding in here."

"Yes." Rowland brightened. "Come, Lizzie. Introduce me to your neighbors, so we can find and defeat Absolom's nemesis. You do know them all, don't you?"

"T–Tom knows all of them, better than I do."

"Still, since I have only a few days free to solve your problems, let's get busy."

Lizzie said, "Fine. As the poet says, 'You have subdued my heart,' lambkin. However, I shall lovingly admonish you to soak your head if you do anything to humiliate us."

Rowland tucked Lizzie's hand into the crook of his elbow and pulled back the tapestry that hid the alcove. "I'm no scaramouch. I am your true hero, Lizzie."

At the front door, people from the villages and from the university stepped forward to shake hands and offer condolences. No one noticed that Tamsin's world had spun sideways. She had mourners to greet and no time for fear. She pressed at her moustache to ensure it remained reliable. Her injured right hand had begun to ache from the fatigue of shaking hands. Absolom had commanded her to take care of everyone. She must help Rowland, even though she preferred that he be snatched away by the devil, since his name had brought the king's men down on them just hours after that day's restoration. And Rowland had not proposed anything, so far, that removed her fear that the English courts might take Revelstone and everything else from them.

Or sentence them to hang as thieves.

Winwood touched her elbow just then, whispering in her ear that Tom was resting but refused to sleep. "Too much good gossip to overhear. Too hot if I close his window. Tom says this is the best day since Twelfth Night." Winwood paused. "Except for the overall sense of abject grief."

15

Meet the Neighbors

"TELL ME, MR. Wijck." Perry surprised Ned once more, speaking near his ear. "I've been meeting some of your guests, like that handsome doctor who lives at your house. It's charming how he is so in love with your brother Tom. He can't take his eyes away whenever Tom is near."

Ned glanced in the direction Perry gestured, where Tamsin and Winwood spoke, their heads tipped close together. "I have no brothers. Only my sister, and we have different fathers. Tom and I call each other cousin, because Tom is Lizzie's cousin. However, he's as close to me as a brother."

And Tamsin as good as a sister. Ned hoped she'd soon be free to be her true self. He needed to keep Perry, an outsider, from prying into their secrets.

"Ah. Do you mean to say that only Miss Ysabel Foxe is truly your relation? Then perhaps it doesn't matter to you that the doctor wants to own Tom Foxe's heart."

Tamsin and Winwood? No. Ned redirected the conversation, equivocating while unsure whether he was being teased. "T–Tom is married to Marborne."

"Oh," the big man said, "I think Tom's heart has room for more. He likes that the doctor adores him. He turns his head away, then looks back. They trade small gestures as if sharing a private language, the way would-be lovers do."

"I do not perceive what you claim. I do not have time to think of more than our guests." Ned fought the sensation of being swept away, as if pushed by a storm wind, while it was a hot summer day, the air hanging humid and still, made hotter by that man's heat when he stood so close.

Yet it wasn't just the flirting Ned resisted. Perry seemed to be wiggling into the Foxe cousins' private business.

"I might be wrong." Perry didn't sound like he was admitting to such. "I do believe that the doctor's quarry has never before been courted. Tom responds rather like an unbroken colt. Still and all, I believe the doctor's case is not hopeless."

When Winwood left off speaking with Tamsin, Perry peeled away from Ned's side, following Winwood into the crowd, leaving Ned free again to attend to his chores.

While repeatedly searching for the tallest man in the crowd.

– ROLLO –

ROWLAND GLANCED AROUND before speaking, in case Perry might be eavesdropping. "Lizzie, can we make each other laugh again, the way we did in Amsterdam?"

"Yes," Lizzie said. "But, lambkin, we can't be seen laughing at our neighbors."

Lambkin. Once more opening a deep shaft in his heart from which hope could be mined.

However, still not as forgiving as Rowland wished, or as Scripture taught that he should be, Tom said, "Please behave as an enlightened being."

"If you remember how," Lizzie said. She walked toward a knot of mourners. Rowland caught up and tucked her hand into his bent elbow again. Her dark hair shone in the sunlight, even with the black net holding it back. When he touched her arm, she pursed her lips but didn't scold him. They crossed to where Cambridgeshire's leaders gossiped in the yard. On the way, Lizzie paused to respond to greetings from a young woman, whom she addressed as Lady Hawksmoor.

Fate smiled on him! Here was the earl's lady.

He tucked his angel coin away, and inserted himself between Lizzie and the woman, who was as over-decorated as her parlor, and plump with small features like the embroidery on a child's doll. She kept fingering a pendant, a gold teardrop that hung from her neck against her gold silk gown? Lizzie must find the combination appalling.

"Madam, you are Lady Hawksmoor? Lord Monck Hawksmoor's bride?" Rowland exaggerated his faux-Catalan accent, didn't wait for her to answer. "His lordship the earl did our family a great honor, rescuing my sister Taresa in London."

"Indeed?" Curiosity overcame the lady's surprise at being addressed by a stranger. She spoke just that one word, but Rowland recognized her as one of the voices he'd overheard outside the carriage, insulting Lizzie. "Have we met, sir?"

"I am Viscount Orlando de Flores. My sister Taresa and I are cousins of Senorita Ysabel." Rowland seized Lizzie's hand to affirm their cousinly connection. Her gloved hand accepted his grasp. Then he bowed and took the Hawksmoor woman's hand in Paris court fashion. "But I shall allow your husband to tell you what a hero he proved to be."

As if a cloud covered the sun, Lizzie turned away. She had to answer a guest's condolences, so Rowland had no business feeling that she'd deserted him.

Besides, Lady Hawksmoor warmed to Lord Orlando, forgetting the solemnity of the day. She liked Orlando, who was more flirtatious than Rowland ever dared be in his own skin. He intended to amaze his cousins with how quickly his juggle succeeded.

"Oh my! You are from Madrid?"

"No, madam. Catalonia. However, my father is a diplomat, so we've known life in many lands. And I have this day arrived from London. Pray, consider me your humble servant."

"The way you cock your brow, your lordship, does it mean that are you a suspicious person?" She giggled. There was no other word for it.

Yes, he was suspicious. And also familiar with flirtatious lords' wives. "My face was made this way, kind lady."

"Ah. Perhaps you will not believe it of me, but I can tell men's fortunes with phisnomy. It is a true science. Shall I tell you the future written on your face?"

"Please, Lady Hawksmoor, I want to hear my fate."

"First," the woman preened, enjoying his attention, "that arching brow means you always question what others accept as truth."

"My nursemaid called it quizzical," Rowland said.

"Your sharp cheeks indicate an unsullied leader who shall endure fame and power. Your straight, narrow nose means wealth comes to you easily."

God had not set aside wealth for Rowland, and as for being a leader, even Perry wouldn't follow him any further than the next dice game. But he smiled at the woman's predictions.

"Now, my lord, your slim build and noble chin mean—"

"Please, no more." He held a hand up to stop her words. "I have a pleasant but forgettable face. And I must not stand here coaxing flattery from you." (And I cannot bear flirting with both the earl and his lady on the same day.)

Thankfully, Ned interrupted just then. "Lady Hawksmoor, may I offer you a cup of ale?"

Two other women joined her. When Ned greeted them, Rowland fixed their names to memory.

Lady Hawksmoor wore an outsized gold locket shaped like a giant's tear drop.

Lady Candecote, the baronet's whip-thin wife, wore a hideous sapphire necklace.

Mrs. Fairchild, wife of Absolom's solicitor, older than the other two, had a big nose and an ostentatious silver brooch. And when she spoke, Rowland recognized the second gossip who'd insulted Lizzie while he lingered in the carriage.

Ned offered the women hospitality. "Perhaps, my ladies, you might prefer a cool posset and shortbread in the great hall."

"Doctor Foxe would rejoice that you've come to honor him." Lizzie returned, murmuring a thank-you to those women, who again offered condolences. Though Rowland still could not guess Lizzie's sentiments, she no longer sent dark looks his way.

Lizzie and Tom turned their attention to a woman who approached, her arms open to offer condolences, then weeping copiously over Lizzie's hand. Rowland recognized the constable's wife, more worn than when he was a boy—and who gave no sign of recognizing the grown Rowland.

Tamsin ill. Absolom gone from this world. Tom now a martinet, as if he had to take Tamsin's place as their leader.

And no one knew him or cared to. Not even his cousins.

Rowland had to shut a door over grief and do the work Absolom asked of him. Those three judgmental women circumventing the great hall led his attention away from that morose pit.

"I overheard those women insulting you," he whispered to Lizzie when they were alone for two instants. "Besides what Absolom asked me to do, I shall also rescue you from your dreadful neighbors."

"They have good intentions." Lizzie's secret smile wasn't meant for that weak claim, because she tapped the back of his hand, the way she did in Mary's court, mock-scolding him for teasing.

He was back in her good graces. (*O Dark Lady:* "Torches are made to light, jewels to wear. Dainties to taste, fresh beauty for the use.")

Rowland laughed. "No, they don't. You, Lizzie, of all people, can recognize obsequious, vaunting ambition. You saw it every day in Princess Mary's court. Those creatures will pocket whatever your nemesis hasn't already stolen from you."

"And Absolom insisted our nemesis is Lord Hawksmoor." Tom appeared. Like one of King Charles's famous spaniels, he couldn't let an idea go once he got his teeth into it.

"I know you shall persevere until I prove you wrong." Rowland glanced around. "God blind me, are these people all here to drink Absolom's cellar dry?"

"Good stars! The ale is the last of our worries, Rollo." Behind his bad moustache, Tom couldn't spout an oath stronger than what a Puritan dowager might exclaim. "We can brew ale without coin or others' aid."

"That's a comfort." Yet Rowland saw in his cousins' faces that they'd been bankrupted of all comfort.

16

Absolom's Pipe

— TAMSIN —

SHE SQUIRMED INSIDE Tom's black suit. After the three Furies stepped into the great hall to harass other neighbors, Tamsin tugged at her cravat, then dropped her hand to avoid attention.

But that motion caught Rowland's eye. "Nice linen, Tom. Do you order from Holland?"

Lizzie grasped Rowland's dripping lace cuff again. "You weasel! When did I gain a cousin from Spain? With a sister?"

"Catalonia. We're third cousins, from brothers in Good Queen Bess's time. Lizzie, you purse your lips that way when you want to scold me."

"Why tell lies?"

"Because Rowland Foxe cannot do what Absolom wants— wanted. Please call me Orlando."

"My stars, it's hot in here." The Reverend Mr. Gamlingay stepped into the circle of cousins, not noticing that he interrupted them. He wiped his face with a kerchief.

"God bless you, senor." Rowland extended his hand to the rector, speaking with that false accent. "I'm Orlando de Flores. My family, we are cousins with Senorita Ysabel. Her grandfather married a niece of my great-grandfather."

Tamsin, astonished, governed her expression. A familiar twitch of calm control passed over Lizzie's face, though Tamsin couldn't tell if Lizzie suppressed laughter or a frown. The aged rector studied

Rowland as if he might know him, but then merely shook Rowland's hand and accepted a cup of ale from Ned.

"Shall we begin the services, sir?" Lizzie prompted Mr. Gamlingay, her hand on his elbow to guide him inside.

"Aye. Best begin before most of Cambridge and all of Marborne are too far gone with your ale and posset to mumble so much as an Our Father." Mr. Gamlingay left his empty cup on Ned's tray and stepped into the great room.

Tamsin punched Rowland's shoulder, furious again, hardly able to stop from thoroughly pummeling him. "You suborned us, Rollo. Made us complicit while you lied to Mr. Gamlingay."

"I shall repeat. 'Rollo' cannot do what Absolom asked. I have begun the work to address your problems. Now, join in, and please call me Orlando."

"You shall be in my prayers, *Or–lan–do*."

Tamsin turned away, her wit burned to a nub by the anger that flared when Rowland arrived. Absolom had called him home, to help them. Yet how much of Rowland's extravagant charade must she endure? She knew well that Fate wasn't fair and equitable. But the Catalan Viscount Orlando? Honestly!

And Lizzie seemed to have abandoned the unity with which they'd entered the averil together. She showed no sign of harsh feelings about Rowland and was now more playful with him than she'd behaved with any man since returning from Holland. Sadly, Rowland's presence revealed more than one gap in Tamsin's understanding. She didn't know what the dreamy and pliant Lizzie truly desired.

If Camilla were here, she'd calm Tamsin's frustration and anger; she'd see the toil this insufferable day had demanded. Tamsin pressed at her Archangel, hoping to wipe irritation with Rowland from her thoughts, from her posture, because she had to present the best face for Marborne. However, it remained her secret wish that the Archangel might free the dragon to bear her flamboyantly disguised cousin away.

She crossed the room to join the rector, hoping people saw her as Tom Foxe steeped in mourning, not worrying that Camilla had disappeared. That the militia might return and uncover their restoration activities. That the weight of English law might come down on all of them.

Taking a breath to speak in her deepest tones, Tamsin addressed the guests, her voice carrying across the great hall.

"We have lost the great Doctor Absolom Foxe, our uncle and friend, and known to many of you as a professor of moral philosophy at Trinity College. We are here to honor him, and The Reverend Mr. Gamlingay has come to comfort us with prayer. Let us begin with the Marborne tradition, sharing the Moment of Peace to remember our departed friend and uncle."

It wasn't a family tradition. Tamsin simply needed a moment of peace and, dressed as Tom, had the power to declare it.

— ROLLO —

THE GREAT ROOM wasn't silent, though no one spoke. People shuffled. And sighed. That trio of ill-mannered women, who seemed to believe they'd been sent to judge the quick and the dead, fanned themselves. Rowland stood still as a statue and used the moment of silence to study his cousins.

Lizzie, a favorite in the Princess Mary's court, shone amid threadbare villagers, like Persephone in the underworld.

Tom, that dulpickle, ought to give up that wispy moustache. Why didn't Lizzie make Tom shave it? It wasn't a proper style for the current world; it reeked of Puritanism. Tom was supposed to be the barrister who'd rescue the Foxe family title, but instead played Master of Revelstone.

Tom kept touching his chest, like a man with regrets. Or persistent belly pains. But best not to judge others harshly. Absolom had urged a kind heart on Rowland from infancy?

What hadn't happened? Inglorious work, spying for the Crown on the Continent. Striving to appear as a worthy Englishman in crowds of exiles and grovelers who toadied to anyone with any splash of Stuart royalty in their breeding lines. Then, assigned to seek traitors among men he'd gambled with.

Now, what to do about Tom, who said he accepted Rowland's truth about the past. But Tom did not yet trust him. It showed in his stiff posture, in how Tom maintained a stiff (moustached) lip, examining Rowland with that quizzical brow.

Rowland didn't find it pleasant having that shared Foxe trait, that quizzical brow, of—

"Dearly beloved." Mr. Gamlingay fumbled for his spectacles and then for his place in the prayer book, though it was a certainty that the man, who'd buried the parish's dead for fifty years, knew the words by heart. While rummaging and rattling the pages, the rector repeated, "Dearly beloved."

His cousins stayed beside the rector. Rowland drifted alone to stand nearby, not missing that Lizzie nestled Tom's hand in the folds of her black silk skirts. (Strike me blind, else tell me she did *not* leave life in Mary's court for an impoverished second cousin at the edge of the fens. No. Unbelievable.)

Meanwhile, instead of praying, Perry traded peeps with Ned, which left Rowland alone in the crowd, contemplating that he lived in a world which no longer included Uncle Absolom. No more stories. No more lines of poetry. ("Dear Sir Walsingham, How dost thou, sweet lord?...")

Mr. Gamlingay's voice rose, commanding the room in the same way he had in Rowland's childhood. "Whether we live or whether we die, we are brothers and sisters in the Lord."

In Rowland's memory, Theo Gamlingay didn't believe such pish-posh any more than did Absolom. Rowland once listened in the yard of a summer's night while Absolom and the rector enjoyed brandy and their clay pipes. "Oh, Absolom, this century's pother has led to regicide, civil battles, a thieving protectorate, new vain-glorious kings." And Absolom answering, "Theo, you and I have made our own equivocations many times before the Church of England. That's a grand word we learned from absconding Roman priests."

During the prayers, Rowland edged closer to an open window, seeking a gasp of air, finding one of Absolom's clay pipes on the ledge. No mistress had allowed pipes in the great hall, perhaps since Raleigh first brought the noxious weed to England. Rowland smelled the pipe's peaty odor, thinking of that time when Absolom caught him with it. Age five? A wee lad.

Gamlingay was intoning, "A man must find grace while enduring life this side of heaven."

What would Absolom think of Gamlingay's wheezing repetition of the Church's avowals on the nature of life and death?

Tom glanced back at Rowland. Such a shame Tom had grown up so poorly. That kind of charm would be fine for Tamsin. But Tom in his padded coat, like a swordsman's practice dummy? It was too much by half. If Tamsin were here, she'd see the value of Rowland's help. Unlike thick-headed Tom. Unfortunately, Rowland had to win back Tom's trust quickly, to gain what Absolom had promised in his letter: "You won't do this alone, though the way ahead is so jumble-gutted."

The rector's voice broke during the final prayer, which shook Rowland from his selfish introspection. That must be why the old gentleman read the service instead of reciting it. Head bent, Gamlingay consigned his best friend to heaven. Only someone standing as close as Rowland might see the trembling chin, eyes fighting tears.

From long habit, Rowland adopted the rector's posture of grief. Beseeching words welled up from within, offering comfort to others when the world offered none for him. Could he use this posture and resonance in a disguise? He dashed the idea as profane, even for him. He had work to do, with no time to be lost in grief. All he had was Absolom's admonition in that letter: "Help us carry on with grace and courage, as a band of brothers."

After the final amens, Ned stalked away to offer ale and cake to visitors. Perry stood in Ned's way, taking a piece of cake in one bite, eyes still on Ned. The two men seemed locked in wordless gawps. And God bless him, Ned seemed to be wearing Rowland's linen shirt. Revelstone folks must have stooped to buying stolen goods. That meant his cousins were acquainted with common thieves. Which might be useful in coming days.

Lizzie appeared. When she stopped to accept condolences from villagers, her perfume filled his senses.

No time for that.

17

Orlando in the Maelstrom

THE REVEREND MR. Gamlingay lingered with the constable and the magistrate. Ned offered the rector a cup of ale.

The magistrate accepted a second cup. "I say, Mr. Gamlingay, were you here last Twelfth Night? When Doctor Foxe took us out with lanterns to view what he called his Roman stones?"

Ned knew that place, a patch of tumbled stones on the west edge of the parish. Uncle Absolom insisted it was a Roman fort or a villa, though he never convinced any scholars to explore. Tom, Rowland, and Ned dug there, unearthing scraps of iron and pottery that Absolom gently cleaned and placed on a shelf in his room, declaring them "antique."

"Yes, indeed," Gamlingay said. "And didn't we all have a sore head to answer for it the next day?"

The magistrate said, "Wasn't Doctor Foxe famous for his antiquary ways?"

"Aye," Gamlingay said. "Doted on every piece of old paper he found. Preserved the libraries of his college against the iconoclasts and Puritans."

"And he loved to remind us all," the constable spoke at last, "how Marborne appears in the Domesday Book."

The magistrate said, "It's a shame, this house falling to ruin. Cromwell's war served to level, but not always in a useful way."

"Yet we survived those sad times," the magistrate said.

Ned offered a choice of posset or ale to Sir Isaiah (Camilla Candecote's father, who'd been made a baronet soon after the Restoration). He hung at the edge of the parish leaders, showing more interest in sipping posset than in conversation. Sir Isaiah was a crufty-beau with a painted face that emphasized his too-thin nose. His long, sandy hair, lightly powdered, waved softly as he moved, the sort of manicured hair possible only for a man who keeps a dresser or has a devoted wife. He habitually ran his fingers through the tresses hanging over his embroidered maroon coat, whose skirts flowed out widely, though the baronet was a skinny-rumped man with much less height than most men around him. Only the maroon-dyed ostrich plumes of his brimmed hat towered over others.

How to paint Sir Isaac? Ned's father warned him about mistakenly creating a caricature when painting a silly man.

While Ned served the baronet and the men close by him, new arrivals came on horseback. Lord Hawksmoor, Viscount Heydon, and a third man Ned didn't recognize. A City man with a furrowed brow and fleshy nose, wearing a velvet suit, violet with lemon-yellow piping at cuffs, collar, and button slashes. (Mrs. Bell would not approve of such flash at their averil.) The man had neither carriage nor countenance to make him interesting as a subject of portraiture.

With the new arrivals, the men in the yard resorted themselves, many clustering around Heydon. Rowland—Orlando—stepped up to join that knot of men. Ned wanted to watch what unfolded but had to refresh his ale cups as an excuse to move among those men (none of whom would greet or notice him except to beg more ale).

Where did Mr. Frake go? How does a man that tall disappear in a crowd like this?

— ROLLO —

ROWLAND PREPARED TO exude the bonhomie needed for his work, but had to wait, because it'd be rude to interrupt while Heydon held everyone's rapt attention.

Fate once more rewarded Rowland, as if choosing to play a beneficent role in the rig he'd planned. The averil had brought together most everyone that Rowland must inspect for perfidy against Absolom. He prepared to plunge into the work, happy to apply his skills for Absolom's sake, and for his cousins.

In the afternoon light, and without Taresa's veil, Rowland got a good look at Heydon. A face too long and too hawk-like for courtiers to consider him handsome, yet a commanding carriage and cool expression seemed to draw men to Heydon. Still clad in the grey brocade suit from earlier that day, with his diamond pin catching the sunlight, Heydon now wore a well-styled wig, a cascade of coffee-colored curls worthy of a Stuart king's court. Heydon folded his arms, one finger tapping his forearm like a tutor mid-lecture. "Our new king James has the west country under siege. The militia in Bristol hung twenty men last week. They left the bodies in the sun and put heads on pikes over the city gates. There's gore in the market squares of a dozen cities."

Rowland cast his eyes down, lest anyone peek into his soul. When he and Perry arrived in London, they'd heard about the king's revolting butchery. Worse, Rowland had blood on his hands. Last winter, Perry argued for leaving Benjamin Baird off their list of men committed to Monmouth: "Benjie is too easily gulled, but a good man. He detests army life and wants to go home. He doesn't need grief from his adventure in Holland."

Yet Rowland had argued for the principles their masters taught. "Corruption follows on omission of facts. Next, we'd be selling our discoveries like common street cheats. Our officers can decide what to do with the information we uncover."

Many of the rebels Rowland and Perry found in Holland were persuaded by William's spymaster that North America was safer than the Continent. He preferred schemes to bankrupt or transport any surviving rebels. But in England, the king and his advisors chose no such solutions. Instead, poor Benjie and his cousins and uncles were all dead.

The king had gone too far. People wanted peace, not heads on pikes. Transportation to the colonies would be sufficient to disperse rebels. Rowland shook away the memory, his periwig slapping at his eyes. He had to attend to Absolom's betrayers.

"Bloody fool!" Lord Hawksmoor barked his response to Heydon's tale. He fluffed the curls of his wig, his felted hat under one arm, its plume dangling at his side. His enormous lace collar floated over a sky-blue velvet coat with gold embroidery, three years out of style. While Rowland was estimating how much Hawksmoor might earn by pawning his buttons, the earl turned to Sir Isaiah. "Don't you agree, Sir Isaiah?"

"Who? Who's the fool?" Sir Isaiah asked, surprised by the earl's passionate response. Rowland hadn't recognized the baronet until someone called the man's name. Sir Isaiah had shrunken in size and aged a great deal over the last decade. And he'd become an outrageously painted beau who spoke as if he might be addle-pated, repeating himself as if his tongue twitched. Rowland matched Sir Isaiah with the top-lofty wife with the doll's face and the dreadful sapphire necklace.

"Our new King James is foolish," the earl said. "Oddsfish, the last thing England wants is brutality from a Catholic king."

Heydon tipped his head, thoughtful. "No, it's the Duke of Monmouth who played the fool, believing he had more support than England would give."

"Monmouth paid for that folly with his life. With his life." Sir Isaiah repeated words twice, like a man who wasn't used to being heard. His weak understanding of politics left him easily persuaded by Heydon and Hawksmoor.

"Monmouth's supporters in the west country also paid the full price." Heydon tapped a finger, maintaining his instructive posture. "Now we will pay surcharges on other men's folly."

"How so?" That curious question came from the third man who'd arrived with Hawksmoor. A fortyish fellow, his face past youth, coarsening.

And for one blink of a wary eye, Rowland caught Heydon watching him assess this third visitor.

Like bobbing birds on a fence rail, the other men nodded along when Heydon answered the question. "Since the battle at Sedgemoor, the king is wild to expand his standing army. He seized a windfall from Monmouth's supporters, but cannot count on future windfalls. Therefore, we can count on more taxes."

"The same way," Lizzie interrupted, surprising Rowland, since that wasn't her style in court, "we can also count on apples dropping in the orchard after an autumn storm."

Every man turned to Lizzie, like cattle called by a drover.

"Now, gentlemen," she said, "I shall not chide you for sinking into politics this afternoon. We live in difficult times."

While he'd been dressed as Taresa, Rowland had at times dangled for men's attention and yet never managed the grace with which Lizzie tipped her head to show each man favor, all the while smiling like a benevolent saint.

Every man fell under Lizzie's spell except Heydon, who observed the others like a university don waiting for his students to cease their stupidity.

"Please allow me..." Lizzie began. Those men took a collective breath, waiting to hear her wishes. "I want..."

(Please want me, Dark Lady.)

She said, "Lord Hawksmoor, please allow me to introduce my cousin, Viscount Orlando. He's just arrived from Paris." Lizzie's bones knew protocol. She placed the earl's hand on Rowland's, her hand covering both, like a blessing. "Lord Orlando and his sister are visiting at Revelstone while hunting a new home in England."

"My sister's hero? You are Lord Hawksmoor?" Rowland thickened his faux accent and bowed. "I am Senora Taresa's brother. A more grateful and humble servant you have never met, senor. Thank you for carrying my sister from London."

When they shook hands, Rowland touched Hawksmoor's arm, as if in mistaken familiarity. Yet the earl took no offense, and hence, Rowland proceeded to draw the earl into his trust.

A better position from which to find and conquer all who had cheated Absolom.

18

Marborne, Muddled

"VISCOUNT ORLANDO?" THE other man who'd arrived with Hawks-moor accosted Rowland, seeking to draw him away from the crowd. "I am Danvers Duncombe, your lordship. Forgive me for not seeking a formal introduction."

Rowland offered his sunniest, friendliest self, quickly masking his surprise. "I'm greatly pleased to meet you, sir. Are you Sir Charles Duncombe's agent?"

Fate rewards the diligent intelligencer! How convenient that the probable traitor he'd hunted in London came directly to him. He glanced around, seeking Perry, wanting his comrade's attention on this man.

"Sir Charles is a cousin," Duncombe said. "He has advised me considerably. But I have my own business in London."

About twenty years older than Rowland, Danvers Duncombe had a wide mouth, a fleshy nose, and a broad, furrowed forehead. His violet-and-yellow suit (tailored to disguise his belly) and grandiose manner would declare "London man of business" any-where in England. He had an unbalanced face, skewed, as if he spoke out of different sides of his mouth. Nothing indicated that (as Shakespeare's lady said) the milk of human kindness flowed in his veins. While he spoke, Duncombe ran his hand along the side of his velvet breeches, as if grasping for something invisible, either out of habit or palsy.

"Ah, how embarrassing." Rowland hoped he flushed red. "My sister met Lord Hawksmoor in your London offices. Though I'd instructed her to seek out Sir Charles."

Duncombe's mouth thinned. He squinted, his eyes expressing annoyance, despite his deferent manners.

Rowland pushed on, happily inspired to combine Absolom's task with his assignment for the Crown. "My sister's mistake is of no matter. I am pleased to meet you, Mr. Duncombe."

"Miss Foxe mentioned that you are considering certain investment decisions." Duncombe rubbed his velvet seams.

No Perry in sight. Tom remained trapped in the business of shaking mourners' hands. Lizzie was deep in conversation with that dubious and overly handsome doctor.

And hence, Rowland seized that opportunity to launch the scheme he'd discussed with Perry in London. He'd developed details during the grueling journey to Cambridge, and if he acted now, he could employ the same scheme to trap Absolom's enemies. Further, he decided in a flash that neither Tom nor Lizzie needed to know about his investigation into Mr. Duncombe. He proceeded immediately to draw Duncombe into a scheme that would provide a good view into the man's business.

"Si, senor. Miss Foxe's…uh, *mentor* presented an opportunity for a guaranteed investment."

Duncombe's eyes flashed a knowing glint, which indicated he'd heard Lizzie's history and assumed that mentor was Mary Stuart, the presumed heir.

Rowland continued. "A good deal of my own wealth is tied up until December. I therefore need ready money to purchase the house I found in London. This prospect with Miss Foxe promises significant and guaranteed returns. However, I need a business man's help to create a syndicate, so that my cousin and I can invest together."

"If you need such advice, I can offer my services. I am quite familiar with the mechanisms for creating investment syndics."

Duncombe's ears burned red. His hands again rubbed at the sides of his velvet pantaloons.

A bite! Rowland had baited the hook and now intended to reel in this rebel quickly. Further, Duncombe had manifested here with Hawksmoor and Heydon. The gifts of Fate were wondrous.

"I pray," Rowland reined in giddy joy at finding the rogue he and Perry pursued, "that we shall be better acquainted, sir. Are you staying in Cambridge, Mr. Duncombe? I'd like to learn more about how investment is conducted in England."

"Yes. I am visiting in search of property to purchase."

While he spoke, Duncombe's attention was captured by exclamations among the three most powerful men in the yard: Heydon, Hawksmoor, and Sir Isaiah. Then Duncombe's attention fixed on Lizzie. He left Rowland's side, calling, "May I offer my condolences, Miss Foxe?"

Once more, Rowland caught Heydon watching Orlando watching Duncombe chat with Miss Ysabel Foxe, whose own eyes kept wandering to Heydon.

Rowland couldn't guess what she was up to. (Ah, Lizzie! What poet said it? "A friend is one that...uh...understands where you have been, accepts what you have become, and still, gently allows.")

Two women deep in conversation stepped near Rowland to avoid the milling crowd. Lady Hawksmoor (clutching her golden tear-drop pendant) and Lady Candecote (of the frightful sapphire piece, as lovely as a pit-fighting dog's collar).

"But, Mariah, is Mr. Foxe really going to marry his cousin, like royals from the Continent? My brother is a better choice for her, don't you think?" The matchmaker's voice (which Rowland recognized from their introduction and his earlier accidental eavesdropping) was Lady Hawksmoor.

Matchmaking her brother-in-law Heydon with Lizzie? Deliver us from evil...

"She's a second cousin, they say." It was Lady Candecote being addressed as Mariah. She glanced around while choosing her words, not seeing Rowland nearby. "My husband insists that marriage

with Thomas Foxe makes sense. Miss Foxe is the presumed heir—
if the Marborne earldom is restored."

"You are misled, Mariah. Only a male in the direct line can
inherit that title."

Lady Candecote said, "A close connection with a title would
be the only reason an Englishman might choose such a dark bride.
Even her Spanish cousin isn't *that* dark. Though she is pretty, in a
foreign way."

"Since she won't inherit, perhaps it's best to dissuade my
brother from pursuing her. He could do so very much better for
himself than the impoverished Miss Foxe."

"He claims his heart is set on her, Helen."

God blind me! Heydon sought Lizzie. Did Heydon think he
could snare the Marborne title, with Lizzie as a pawn?

Rowland rubbed his hands, fixed the cuffs on his coat. He dis-
believed the preposterous notion that Tom had captured Lizzie's
affections. For Lizzie's sake, he restrained from scolding those
gossiping women. He lifted his shoulders within the sweat-dampened confines of his copper-satin court suit, to shrug off the distraction of nattering harridans.

— NED —

NED SHOOK HIS head at foolish impertinence. A dark angel must
have possessed that London business fellow, causing him to touch
Lizzie's arm.

In an instant, the London man (who seemed to be the gold-
never-brass sort) was missing a button on his deep cuff. You
couldn't see it happen, even if you knew to look.

Lizzie once described being pawed in Mary's court, saying, "If
a rich man trespasses against me, I lighten his pocket. And how
else am I, a helpless woman, to earn my pin money?"

The heat at Ned's back warned that Perry again hung close by.
Ned, who loomed a head above every man in the parish, was not
familiar with the sensation of someone whispering in his ear in the
midst of a crowd.

"Your sister is extraordinarily talented, Mr. Wijck, as well as beautiful." Perry's breath brushed his ear, warmer than the hot summer afternoon. "In Princess Mary's court, it's called courtly manners, and Miss Foxe incarnates its genius. Each gesture a masterpiece."

"You think so?" Ned suspected that Perry's praise for Lizzie was intended instead to flatter her brother. Him.

"Use your fine silvery eyes, man." Perry gently tipped Ned's head with one hot finger on his jaw. "That London fellow thinks he's making sweet time with your cousin. He thinks her smiles, her glances aside, express womanly modesty and gratitude for his attentions."

"He appears to be a wealthy man." Ned hedged an answer. He never could read Lizzie's face to know what she was thinking. "We've only seen this Mr. Duncombe for mere minutes today. Perhaps women often appreciate his conversation."

"You can spy the worth of a man. Mr. Duncombe doesn't walk among the demigods of Olympus. Your sister responds out of habit, as an exquisitely talented courtier who makes any fellow think he's the only man on earth."

While Lizzie seemed to attend to what the London man might be saying, her eyes flickered away to others in the averil crowd who called greetings. The London man touched her again. Her elbow this time. Ha! The fool was now missing another gold button.

"The poor man thinks he's a star rising in Miss Foxe's celestial heaven," Perry whispered. Yet Perry had missed seeing Lizzie attain her own justice. "But she offered the same attention to the old rector before the service. Come tomorrow morning, if your sister remembers this London fellow, I shall give you a farthing, the same sum as how much regard your sister has for that man."

"Truly?" Ned didn't want to commit to any ideas while his whole body hummed. Because Perry stood so close. Ned glanced sidewise at him, caught only a flash of ice-blue eyes under the shaggy, straw-colored hair.

"Aye. This London man will lay his head on his pillow tonight, dreaming he's been invited to court the goddess Ysabel."

"What does my sister think of him?" Ned wanted to hear Perry's impression, while he himself believed that Lizzie saw a rich man who trespassed against her and must be punished.

"Ah, the riddle of the ages! I warrant, Mr. Wijck, that she wants to scrape him off the soles of her velvet slippers. However, she's too well-mannered to let any of us know. Now other courtiers less talented than she is might take advantage of a foolish self-flatterer, likely leaving him naked in the wilderness. But not your sister. She's nice."

"Did you know her in Princess Mary's court?"

"I'm simply Rollo's comrade, observing from the shadows. Rollo, however, knows her, I wager, better than any man in Christendom."

"Has from the cradle." Ned wanted to move away from Perry's heat. Except he also wanted to stay. If nothing else, he wanted to understand what Perry meant about Lizzie and Rollo.

"Aye. And she knows Rollo is worth more than that London man, even if the fellow were dipped in gold."

"But Lizzie says Rollo is one of Monmouth's traitors."

"Oh, Mr. Wijck. You have a brilliant mind, too brilliant to be gulled by liars. Rollo is incapable of being a traitor."

"He's not a traitor?" Ned brightened. But of course! Rowland was as he always was, first among equal comrades, like the rest of them, just a step below Tamsin.

Perry tipped his head, seeing Ned's changed mood.

"You can see that Miss Foxe and your cousin Tom no longer believe that falsehood. If you ask Rollo, he'll tell you that we were both stolen from the cradle and dropped into the king's intelligencers on the Continent. Neither Rollo nor I ever had any choice but to serve the king."

How could Perry know what Tom believes? Oh—he meant Tamsin.

Perry glanced past him into to the averil crowd. "And look, your cousin Tom has yet another man pursuing him."

He tugged at Ned's sleeve, persuading him to turn and look, an astonishing sensation. And yet…

By Jupiter! It was one thing to be tricked into outrageous flirting, but Ned had allowed this stranger to pry into his cousins' business. There was no room at Revelstone, amid restorations and other business, for a stranger to be prying.

Especially a man who just proclaimed himself an intelligencer for the Crown.

— T A M S I N —

SWEAT TRICKLED FROM Tamsin's clavicle, down between her bound breasts. Rivulets streamed along the valley of her spine to be caught in the waistband of Tom's best breeches. She scanned the milling crowd, seeking Camilla, any glimpse of her bright golden-honey hair.

But Camilla would have sought Tamsin as soon as she arrived at Revelstone. Perhaps someone should be sent from the kitchen to the Fairchild house, to inquire after Camilla. She longed to know how Camilla fared after fleeing the restoration. To be scrupulously honest, she longed even more for her friend's company. If Camilla were here…

Tamsin sighed deeply, then worried she had disturbed her fragile moustache. She touched her Archangel pouch, saving fear for a future hour when she was free to think of more than enduring the averil.

"Gad's bobs! Where are you hiding my wife?"

An over-excited Leighton Fairchild jammed himself in front of Tamsin, snatching a cup of ale from Ned. His outlandish signet ring, a present from his mother upon his marriage, flashed in the sunlight. Thin as a willow switch, in black brocade and a starch-stiffened white shirt, Leighton dripped sweat that stunk of wine. His blond hair curled up into a damp, bushy crown.

Tamsin's knees locked, keeping her from running instantly in search of Camilla. The heat and weight of her coat kept her from squirming in desolate fear. If Camilla hadn't gone to her own home, then where…

"Leighton, you are so kind to join us in honoring Doctor Foxe." Tamsin attempted to turn away Leighton's passion, though she seethed, detesting the man. "But we haven't seen Camilla this afternoon."

"She walked over here yesterday, Tom, and we haven't seen her since." Leighton jabbed a finger at Tamsin's chest, poking so hard that Tamsin had to avoid wincing. "She came to nurse your sick sister, like Camilla does nearly every day."

Tamsin said, "Camilla stayed with Thomasine while we sat with Uncle Absolom in his final hours." Except for her ability to wear Tom's clothes, Tamsin wasn't good at falsehoods, but she'd had practice lying to Leighton about his wife. "Lizzie begged Camilla to sleep here, since it was too late to walk home. She sent a message to your house at supper time." Tamsin spoke truth but added a fabrication. "And she walked home at dawn. Because she loves the dew-time best."

"You didn't send her home in a carriage this morning? That's your way, Tom Foxe. No ability to take care of women. Did it occur to you what could happen to her along the way? She…she might have been shot by…by highwaymen." Leighton wrinkled his pointy nose, more angry than worried.

You'd think Leighton might recall that the indolent Camilla never rose before ten o'clock (unless Tamsin had an adventure afoot). Leighton continued to grouse, leaning close. The wine-stink on his breath revolted Tamsin, who let his insults roll on, the same way Tom would.

"My wife cares more for nursing your miserable sister than for her own home."

Tamsin needed to prevent an interruption of the day's solemnity as much as she worried about Camilla. "Leighton, you know Camilla loathes funerals. She is likely in her cozy garden nook, busy with her needlework, under the blooms of that Apothecary's Rose she planted."

"Perhaps you are right." Leighton still fumed—and didn't note that Camilla hated needlework. "Yet I worry. People were in a fuss at the Phoenix and Swan because Lord Hawksmoor's carriage was robbed this morning near the Cambridge road."

"Truly, Leighton?" Lizzie came up beside Tamsin.

"With highwaymen roaming the country, none of us can be safe. When I heard, I galloped to Cambridge to call the king's men." Leighton spoke breathlessly, proud of his adventure.

Tamsin coughed, disturbed once more, but then pretended to clear her throat. "What did they say?"

"They were abroad, but I left a message. You see, I insist on Camilla's safety, Tom." Leighton thumped Tamsin's chest again, sending shards of pains across her torso as he huffed wine-stink in her face. "It's not safe for Camilla to gad about. When I try to persuade her, she nods but her eyes drift away. No argument restrains my wife."

While Leighton ranted, Tamsin worried more for Camilla with each breath. Camilla who showed care for everyone Tamsin loved and never listened to caution from anyone. Further, Tamsin hadn't had so much as a sip of cider and so wasn't prepared for an averil-style brawl with Leighton, who'd attacked Tamsin-as-Tom in a drunken temper twice before.

At last, Ned came over to intercede. "Leighton, step out of the sun. Enjoy the averil repast in the great hall."

Rid of Leighton, Tamsin sighed, pressed at her wilting moustache to keep it in place. She stood rigidly straight, to keep from leaning on the door post out of despair, endeavoring to manage fearful worries over what had become of Camilla.

"Bless me, Tom. You're such a busy man." Rowland came up from behind, so Tamsin inhaled in surprise. "Camilla Candecote? The girl you proposed to when we were children? Now you entertain the married Camilla daily."

"Go stuff your head with cabbage, Rollo."

"Clever. That's what Tamsin said whenever she lost an argument. But please, call me Lord Orlando, since we are friends again."

19

The Churchyard

HE REGRETTED TEASING as soon as Tom stalked away. But how had Tom forgotten their childhood pledges of brotherhood? The unfortunate confusion in Rotterdam and Lizzie's false rumor had been put to rest. What still divided them?

Rowland saw that he'd best stop teasing Tom, who had appreciated every jest in the old days, but now was as bad as Tamsin used to be about resenting teasing jests. He'd best…

Gad, he kept pushing at despair blooming inside. True comradery had ruled his past life with his cousins. How to re-create that union, especially with Absolom gone? The only course was to be the hero Absolom asked him to be.

Hungry, Rowland surveyed the disappearing funeral repast. In addition to the averil food, his cousins had spared nothing in honor of Absolom when it came to the customs of funeral gifts. Women from the villages unfolded their shawls and tied them into carry-bags, loading their bags with rounds of cheese and packets of averil bread, which had all been neatly wrapped in white paper. More trays offered gloves tied with black ribbons. Lady Candecote, who'd quizzed Lizzie and Tom in the guise of condolences, slipped more cheese and bread into her shawl-satchel, glancing around before picking out three pairs of gloves.

Instead of resenting the avarice of averil-gift hoarders, Rowland decided to find it soothing that each guest carried away a reminder of his uncle, a man who taught the truth, even when the Roundheads pounded on the university doors. A man who kept his family's house united through years of war, chaotic rule, and famine. Who had sheltered orphans after the rest of his family perished. The balm of Absolom's kindness and guidance cooled Rowland's heated heart.

At the door, Lizzie tucked stiff cream-colored cards with black edges in among people's averil gifts as they passed. In the afternoon light, Rowland made out the words drawn in a familiar script on the card. She must have been awake all night, writing their uncle's name a hundred times.

> Absolom Caius Foxe
> b. 1602 d. 1685
> Requiescat in Pace

"Cousin. Senor Orlando."

Lizzie's voice drew Rowland from his reverie, her dark eyes piercing his soul. "Will you join in the lifting of the remains and the journey to the churchyard?"

"Yes, of course."

Rowland approached Absolom's eternity box. Carrying that box in this heat promised to destroy his last suit of court clothes. But then, the sight of the coffin poked at the shutter he'd closed over the hole in his heart. Easy enough to carry his uncle to the churchyard. Beyond that, Rowland had to carry forth his uncle's goodness. He needed to tuck his emotions away again, to prepare to do a decent job of uncovering Absolom's enemies.

"Let's go, bravo." Ned nudged Rowland's elbow. "While folks are sober enough to walk as far as the church."

"Bravo?" Rowland said. "I am not a heartless mercenary. I'm a respectable servant to the Crown."

Almost respectable.

Without seeming to care about having landed a wound, Ned left Rowland and took a place behind Tom, who stood at the middle of the coffin, opposite the man called Dr. Oakes. The doctor inspected Rowland with the careful mannerisms of a gamester rook in a Paris gambling hell. The guests at the door called him "doctor" because he was responsible for Tamsin's health, though young for that profession. Perhaps he was merely a gamester, whose game had yet to be discovered.

The magistrate took the place opposite Ned at the end of the box, which left Rowland to take the fore position, though Tom should claim that place, as the oldest male in the Foxe family. When the constable stepped up to take the remaining place, Rowland said, "Sir, it's good of you to honor my cousins' uncle. But please, let my brother do the heavy lifting."

The constable glanced at Rowland, not recognizing him, but yielded his place when Rowland motioned for Perry to take the opposite corner. Tom might offer thanks after Rowland and Perry lifted most of the weight off his shoulders.

Yet when the six men hoisted the coffin to bear it out of the great hall, they could have been lifting a mere child. Absolom was a small man, and this eternity box proved to be a weight only in Rowland's heart.

— TAMSIN —

WHEN TAMSIN AND the bearers departed the house, Lizzie stayed behind to offer cards and accept condolences as men followed the bearers to the church.

Mourners who had slipped outside after the prayers now meandered and chatted in the yard; they then began to gather behind the coffin-bearers to parade in a rag-tag fashion to the churchyard. Many mourners still carried their ale-cups, most men leaving their parcels of averil goods with their wives.

The bearers walked the trail leading from the yard to the village, under the line of tall oaks, their leaves drooping in the summer's heat like languishing ladies in layers of silk, their spreading branches protecting mourners from the sun. Four tall oaks, each planted by the last Earl of Marborne at the births of his sons and named by young Foxe cousins after their grandfathers and great-uncles. More than eighty years old, the trees' bark was nearly black and deeply fissured. Tamsin believed herself to be as anchored to this land as the great oaks overhead. When their uncle declared that the orphaned cousins must go out in the world to serve the family, she'd pleaded to remain here.

Absolom's kind voice rang in her memory: "You shall stay, Thomasine. One Foxe must remain to save us."

She glanced up into the deep shade of the branches, spying one plank. Then the next. All four planks still in place.

Eighteen years ago, when the barn loft's rotten floor was being repaired, the cousins had made off with four planks. And a rope. Then they collaborated to haul the planks into the upper branches, each declaring ownership of the oak named for their grandfathers and great-uncles.

Samuel, Lizzie's oak.

Walter, Tom's.

Josiah, Rowland's.

Absolom, Tamsin's.

Tamsin often shared a space on her plank with Ned, who paired with Lizzie on days when Camilla came to play. Each summer, the planks served as ships and castles, their owners ruling as admirals and generals.

Lizzie had insisted: "Elizabeth was queen. I can be an admiral or a general."

Rowland shouted: "I am captain of the buccaneers."

Tamsin called back to him: "If you're the captain, you have to save us all."

And Rowland always whistled with two fingers (which she never mastered) and said: "Absolom says that's your work on this earth, Tamsin."

She trusted Rowland back then, though she often modified his wildest schemes. Absolom still trusted him. And she must, also. Everything that afternoon seemed to prove that Rowland wanted to help out of respect for Absolom, and that he still loved this place. That was the foundation, for Tamsin. She had to concede that she must trust him because she needed his help—especially if he had a better idea of what to do than she did.

If only she also understood what was happening between Lizzie and Rowland, since they hadn't been separated for years like Tamsin had. At some point, she'd have to coax Lizzie into revealing her deepest thoughts and desires. And she'd have to be prepared to hear from Lizzie what she feared: Lizzie wanted to be gone from Revelstone, to be back in Mary's court.

For now, Tamsin prepared to go where she never could as Thomasine, to an internment inside the church. The absence of women, however, was simply a custom. No sins accrued for her appearing, respectfully, in Tom's clothes.

— NED —

FROM HIS PLACE at the end of the bearers, Ned kept his eyes on Tamsin, in case it was too much weight for her to bear. However, between Rowland at the front and Ned at the end of the box, they kept most of the weight off her shoulders. Then again, Absolom proved surprisingly light on the way to his final rest. Such a slender, elfish figure to have lived so large in their lives.

When Ned felt his eyes growing wet, he turned his attention to Perry Frake at the front of the bearers, chief among the surprises Rowland brought home to Revelstone. That majestically large man provoked Ned at every turn. How would all this unfold? Rollo was disturbing Tamsin and beguiling Lizzie, while Ned found his thoughts jumbled in every conversation that Perry launched.

When the bearers passed under the oaks, Rowland glanced overhead, which caused Perry to look up too, though Perry couldn't know what these oaks meant to the Foxe cousins years ago. Their fleet still sailed amid the clouds of oak leaves.

Once, at one of Absolom's midsummer celebrations, Rowland suggested they wreak revenge on the magistrate, who'd reported to Absolom that Hawksmoor's ranger found rabbit traps believed to be set by the Foxe kits. During the fête, each time the magistrate passed under their lofty fleet, the cousins beaned him. With pebbles, Rowland said when he explained the rig. Tom joined in immediately, but Tamsin insisted they use peas, which would be lost in the grass. Lizzie and Ned agreed to the lark once Tamsin and Camilla joined in. They'd enjoyed an afternoon's jest, until Rowland accidentally beaned the constable, causing Lizzie to laugh aloud when the man glanced around with a shrewd look, not bewildered like the magistrate. The constable lingered after other guests departed, then confronted them in the moonlight when the cousins descended from their fleet. Tamsin performed a kind of magic that let Camilla run home safely while the rest of them faced the constable. Absolom asked, mildly, why Tamsin hadn't kept the others in check, which crushed her spirit for days. Tom sought to argue their way out of punishment, like the man of law he intended to be, but he was sentenced to deliver the letters of apology that Lizzie and Ned had to write. Rowland, with a reputation as the spark of their larks, was sentenced to write out *Henry V* over a day spent alone in Absolom's room, with only plain bread and water.

However, Rowland emerged from his sentence exuberant, urging them back up to their fleet in the tall oaks, where he taught them the St Crispin's Day speech and made them declaim it on a hot summer day, dust in the air. Each of them had to take turns crying out quotation after quotation.

> From this day to the ending of the world,
> But we in it shall be remembered.
> We few, we happy few, we band of brothers;
> For he to-day that sheds his blood with me
> Shall be my brother...

Now Rowland was about to do it again, talking them all into a jig they might not escape safely. And he had that beautiful giant with him, to help coax them.

— ROLLO —

UNDER THE ENORMOUS shading oaks, Rowland smelled the England he remembered. For years, it had been so distant, though a tiding of magpies could fly from Cambridge to Amsterdam or Paris in a day. He glanced up into the tall oaks, seeking the one called *Josiah*, named after Rowland's grandfather. Holding forth on long summer days in his tree fortress—that must have been the last time Rowland was wholly captain of his fate.

No, that's a weepy and untrue exaggeration.

The cousins had practiced in their lofty fleet, elaborating on what they'd been taught from the cradle. They were bred to serve England, yet rueful that their parents' and grandparents' service had not been properly rewarded at Charles's Restoration.

> That England, being empty of defense,
> Hath shook and trembled at the ill neighborhood.

The sounds of England echoed up the path where it curved near the churchyard gate. The sexton was advising a shaggy black-and-white collie to finish herding sheep out from where they grazed among the tomb markers.

"Come, Jupiter. Our sad company is here. Coax your pets out to the commons, my lovely boy."

The fleeing sheep seemed bent on tripping Rowland. To avoid sheep—and sheep muck—Rowland kept his eyes on the pathway to be sure of his footing. Therefore, they'd stepped into the churchyard before he peered up at the church itself.

The back half had burned. The charred tower loomed like a bewitched skeleton over the lower roof.

"God blind me!"

Perry said, "The village too, Rollo. Look there."

Two more steps into the yard and Rowland saw what the taller Perry had spied. The timber houses closest to the church were now charcoal sticks. Other cottages further on bore the patchy remains of scorched thatching. On the tops of a pair of cottages, thatchers had abandoned their work for the day.

"Not as bad as London took it," Perry muttered.

"But as bad for these householders," Rowland said, "as for any Londoners."

Inside the church, which could accommodate only half the mourners, the floor vault had been opened. After everyone departed, the sexton would place blank squares of marble over the vault. Later that summer, a stonemason would carve a stone like the ones placed over Absolom's father and mother. The place smelled like a charcoal pit, with the afternoon sun angling to shine through the charred hole in the west wall.

Rowland sniffed charcoal along with his own sweat. Tom breathed in counter-tempo to the rector's prayers. Memories flowed, of the house, the commons, the forests.

Learning to count over games of backgammon.

Pretending to read when finally allowed to hold one of his uncle's books.

Walking together in the forest, repeating the names of trees and spring flowers.

What kind of philosopher makes time for children that anyone else would have left with nursemaids? The kind who'd pause to marvel at a sea of bluebells while insisting Rowland repeat his catechism. Not the catechism of the English Church. Nor a forbidden Catholic one. Rather, Absolom's set of unbreakable rules that separated enlightened people from savages, from the first, "*I keep my promises,*" to the last, "*I never fool an honest man.*"

Rowland privately laughed at that last rule, invented when Absolom taught him to win at cards without ever admitting to his own cozening. Absolom wasn't a puritanical uncle who'd torture a boy for the sin of laughing at a funeral. Truly, the old man had been an enigma as much as he'd been their savior.

And then Absolom asked Rowland to act as savior.

But Tamsin was always their savior. All Rowland had ever invented for his cousins was trouble.

This time, Rowland promised—upon Absolom's soul—that he'd step up and do what Absolom asked, to rescue them all. Likely Absolom had never envisioned Rowland creating a syndicate to snare enemies and empty their pockets. He felt confident about this, given experience with past schemes and the details he'd planned for this one.

Now, he'd have to convince his cousins to play their roles in his scheme, the same way they did in that fleet up in the tall oaks.

Though, unfortunately, Tamsin wasn't available to command them, so Rowland had to lead them to consensus about how they'd have to work together.

—

Doctor Foxe's Rules for Enlightened People
I keep my promises.
My family obligations are sacred.
I was born to help others.
The world improves from my toil.
I never fool an honest man.

20

After the Last Honors

ABSOLOM'S FINAL SERVICE ended with a chorus of funereal amens. Tamsin moved ahead of the rising tide of the crowd, the waves of which carried them back to the yard at Revelstone House. When she and Ned arrived at the house with the rector, Lizzie placed her hand at the crook of Mr. Gamlingay's elbow, guiding him to a bench under the shade of the oak trees.

The rector protested that he must be off to home. Tamsin offered him a small cask of ale. And Lizzie offered a cake wrapped in paper and tied up in a black ribbon with a sprig of rosemary.

Lizzie said, "We shall send a boy to carry these to your house, dear sir. We don't want you to bear a burden in this heat."

In the yard, all the proper funeral traditions of English villages continued. Still drinking a sea of Revelstone ale and posset, men were now quarrelling with anyone still standing. The trampling in the yard raised dust clouds. Tamsin fought an impulse to rip off her shoes and run barefoot in that hot summer dust, which would be mud again come the next soaking rain.

Yet people still wanted to shake hands with the Master of Revelstone. Tamsin repeated a thank-you for each condolence while remaining bereft, gaining no consolation, and the pain in her right hand had gone from dull to throbbing.

Ned couldn't leave Perry's side.

Lizzie stole glances at Heydon. And at Rowland.

Rowland smiling, as if this weren't a day of great heartbreak, and moving toward Hawksmoor and Heydon, whom he schemed against.

Tamsin, like a leaf caught in the whirl where Marborne brook fed the River Cam, drifted among the throng of condoling neighbors and Cambridge scholars.

— ROLLO —

WHEN HE CROSSED back under one of the great oak tree (*Samuel*, Lizzie's tree) to join Perry, Rowland heard a few of the quarrels among local villagers and farmers.

"My dogs harried your goose? No, your goose got out of its pen at dawn and stirred up my dogs." "You owe me those eggs."

"Your wife told mine that I'd got to be a tickle pitcher. I'll toss you over the Cam if she won't shut it." "You can't toss a stone over the River Cam to save yourself." "Tell your own homely witch to mind her tongue."

He stopped beside Perry, who observed from the edge of the yard. "Perry, have you met Mr. Duncombe yet?"

"Aye. And I congratulate you, Rollo. You've managed to have Fate bow before you.

"Did you notice how friendly Duncombe is with Hawksmoor and Heydon?"

"They drifted apart pretty quickly once they arrived at the averil." Perry looked around, seeming to seek Ned again. "Duncombe also introduced himself to Miss Foxe, though she didn't seem charmed by the new acquaintance. What else do you want me to see in this crowd?"

"Have you found that crookback and the other varlets who robbed us?"

"You were useless this morning, Rollo."

"That veil was like blinders on a horse."

Four score people milled in the yard, which kept Rowland from listening to a new exchange between Tom and Hawksmoor. The earl shook Tom's gloved hand and kissed Lizzie's offered hand. Meanwhile, several Cambridge dons lined up, hoping to be noticed by Lord Hawksmoor.

When Rowland tried to catch Lizzie's attention, she returned brief glances, a twitch of a familiar smile from when they secretly laughed at the preposterous and pretentious—and reminisced over the rules of enlightenment Absolom taught the orphans he'd salvaged. Here in Revelstone's yard, where she was too far away to tap his hand, to note the ridiculousness of the people around them, she tapped a finger in the air.

Perry gripped his shoulder. "I am distressed, Rollo, that you are distracted by your cousin. You promised that this detour was not undertaken to revive your angst for Miss Foxe."

"That's done and died, Perry. I'm merely observing who we must pursue. Especially Mr. Duncombe." Rowland glanced over his shoulder, expecting Perry might torture him, but Perry (arch hypocrite!) had already crossed the yard to be distracted by Ned.

Therefore, Rowland turned his attention to the people he must charm into joining his investment scheme. That meant the people closest to Heydon and Duncombe.

First, of course, was Hawksmoor, who enthusiastically offered his friendship to Orlando. And also his pert little wife with the gold tear-drop necklace, who liked that Orlando flirted with her.

Next, Sir Isaiah, who ignored his chittifaced wife's pleas to depart. Sir Isaiah earned a place on Rowland's list because his wife was reprehensible, and because his daughter had married Solicitor Fairchild's son. Rowland regarded such a close alliance with suspicion.

Sir Isaiah was pulled along by his peers, and Hawksmoor seemed to trust Mr. Duncombe. They'd follow him into Rowland's gambol.

The only difficult man to be engaged: Heydon.

Speaking in a low voice with Tom and the magistrate, Heydon motioned toward Hawksmoor's crested carriage across the yard. Heydon remained impervious to friendship with either Taresa or Orlando. Perhaps Tom or Lizzie might help snare Heydon into the gambol.

What joy he'd have, advancing his work for the Crown while on this detour. However, Rowland would have to explain the pleasures of this gambol later. Perry had refused to play more than

Taresa's private caballero, and now couldn't be moved more than ten feet from Ned's side.

"For shame. I tell you..." Mrs. Fairchild joined the gaggle that Rowland studied. Lady Hawksmoor and Lady Candecote left off begging their husbands' attention and joined Mrs. Fairchild for whatever dark news those gadding gossips desired to share.

"*Excusez-moi. Perdoni'm.*"

Offering Orlando's Continental niceties, Rowland edged his way through the crowd to reach Tom (under *Josiah*, Rowland's oak), wishing that Perry might leave off prowling Ned to join in the work they'd come here to do.

While dodging several drunken mourners, Rowland bumped shoulders with another man.

"Beg pardon, sir." Mr. Gamlingay stopped, smiled broadly. "Oh hallo, Rollo. Good to see you here. Come by before you leave the shire so we can sip a tot of brandy together. You're old enough for brandy now, aren't you?" He patted Rowland's shoulder and chuckled. "Viscount Orlando. Good lark, Rollo. Absolom is surely laughing in heaven. If there is such a place."

Then the rector meandered his way out of the crowd.

With the rector's recognition, an unexpected jolt of joy hit Rowland's heart. Someone here still knew him for who he was, and who he'd been in former times.

And the old gentleman invited Rowland for a drink instead of shouting "'Thou subtle, perjur'd, false man!'"

— NED —

NED WANTED NO greater consolation in this life than for this crowd to go home and leave the household to its forlorn sadness.

With the declining sun, the Revelstone yard was freed from the hellish glare, but the sticky heat remained. People clumped together under the lengthening shade of the trees, still eagerly gobbling ale and gossiping.

Dust puffed up in small clouds wherever people stepped off the grass and the gravel paths. Ned coughed, worried that the dust might raise an even greater demand for ale. Surely Mrs. Bell would soon announce that they must switch to cider.

Rowland, Tamsin, Lizzie, and Ned stood at the four corners of the yard, too far separated to call out to each other, and three of them were still jammed up in mourner-greeting duty.

Heydon engaged Lizzie's attention, the two in deep conversation near the climbing yellow rose beside the house.

Ned had used up a month's allowance of nickel titanium and gold ochre to paint those roses, but he'd earned more from the results than any other study the last two summers. It'd soon be time to paint fading-rose-of-summer studies, which should be worth more than a farthing in London.

Heydon plucked one of the roses. Thorns must have poked the man's fingers, because he glanced down, scowling. Lizzie relieved him of the rose, twirling it in her gloved hand as she talked with Heydon.

"I wonder what interesting thoughts Heydon and your sister found to explore together." Perry hummed in Ned's ear. Ned expected yet another impertinent remark, but Perry was silent.

Which forced Ned to ask outright, wondering whether Perry tricked him into expressing ideas he'd never in this life say aloud.

"Is Lord Heydon also pursuing my sister?"

"Nay, unless every conversation in the public square shall be called courtship." He took a cup from Ned's tray, wrinkling his nose, which likely indicated that the cellar crew was reaching the newest, bitterest barrels. "You and I know better."

Zooterkins! What did Perry and he *mutually* know? Every time Perry popped up, Ned ended up mazed, dizzy—and wanting more.

"But Heydon listens closely when my sister speaks. And she's attending to him. Nothing else steals away her attention."

"Has either person smiled at the other since they first said hello? Is Miss Foxe touching her hair or veil? Turning her head? Casting her eyes down?"

"No. She is definitely not flirting with him."

"He's a lucky man then. But consider. How can Lord Heydon be of use to her? How can he help her return to Mary's court?"

Ned disliked what he inferred from Perry's question, that he might not know his own sister's thoughts and desires. Everyone was happy to have Lizzie at home, which also gave Tamsin a confidante and partner for the burdens she carried. Yet Lizzie's doleful expression when she believed no one saw her? Perry might be right, that Lizzie yearned to be away from Revelstone.

"And yet, my sister is beautiful, and Heydon is touching the breast of his own jacket."

"You think he's offering her his heart?" Perry disdained the idea. "No, Heydon is not preening to draw Miss Foxe's attention. See how they stand at angles from each other. He's likely drawing attention to his diamond pin, reminding her he's a rich man."

Exasperated, Ned said, "This is beyond endurance, sir. All I see is two people talking to each other."

"Indeed. Mayhap you fail to see the small gestures of Miss Foxe's court manners."

"I've never seen her in a royal court." Ned hadn't seen any royal court, except from a porter's entry when delivering a painting from his workshop, feeling himself once more backfooted by Mr. Frake.

Perry waxed eloquent. "If such a conversation occurred in a royal court, one might notice that Miss Foxe considers herself to be Lord Heydon's equal. Which is true, is it not? Her father should have been the Earl of Marborne. Heydon is the brother of an earl. Mayhap she's being kind, rather than demanding that Heydon acknowledge she was born a step above him."

"A step above?" Ned seized another tray filled with ale mugs, intending to move among the guests and away from this maddening man. "No one has a station here. It was taken from the family when Cromwell's people cut off the king's head."

"But the viscount, in each gesture he makes while they speak together, treats Miss Foxe as a titled lady."

"He is *not* courting Lizzie."

"An astute observation, Mr. Wijck. Heydon is on the same path as the doctor, the path that leads to your cousin Tom. He's followed Tom through the crowd since he first rode into the Revelstone yard. Even your sister sees it. Look now. She tossed aside Heydon's yellow rose as soon as he left her side."

"I do not see it, Mr. Frake. Heydon does not pursue Tom."

"No? If you can see past the dark air of worry Tom Foxe carries on his padded shoulders, then you might say he is an attractive man. If that's your taste, Mr. Wijck. Though I very much hope it isn't."

— TAMSIN —

SHE FIXED A SMILE in place and thanked Lord Heydon when he offered greetings.

"My condolences, Tom. I haven't found space in the press of the crowd to speak with you."

Tamsin searched Heydon's face for evidence of what Rowland claimed, that this man was Absolom's nemesis. Perhaps she didn't have the skill to see evil on a man's face—though she'd been quick to identify that tradesman who'd cheated the village last summer. She had too much confidence in Absolom to believe he'd been blind to the possibility of Heydon as his nemesis.

"I know it's hard to live through." Heydon placed a hand on her shoulder in a brotherly sort of way. "I lost an elderly uncle of my mother's last year. It cuts the world from under your feet. The voice that's always been there, offering guidance, and then suddenly, God has him."

"Yes." Tamsin choked out the word, pushing back again at the grief that over-filled her veins.

"And Doctor Foxe has always been the wit and soul of our neighborhood." Heydon had a deep, musical voice, offering soothing sounds over the raucous noise of the crowd. Rowland must have gone lunatic, thinking this man was their enemy. "How long will it be until God sends us a replacement?"

Rowland headed her way, taller than most in the crowd, his white curls bobbing, the wig at least one pound sterling more expensive than other men's wigs.

"Your cousin seems an interesting fellow." Heydon had also spied Rowland in the crowd. He spoke with surprising intimacy, as if the two of them might conjecture together. She needed, badly, to consult with Tom to know more about his acquaintance with Heydon, whether he could be trusted.

"Lord Orlando is not my cousin, sir." She'd been suborned earlier and had no other choice, so she repeated Rowland's falsehood. "He's a distant relation of Miss Foxe's. I haven't had a moment to take his measure."

"And his sister, Senora Taresa? I met her this morning. A great adventurer and a rare bird, my brother Monck calls her."

"We haven't said more than hello." When she'd committed to collaborating with Rowland, she'd underestimated the mire of falsehoods she'd be forced to utter.

"But Miss Foxe trusts the pair of them?" Without waiting for an answer, Heydon spoke in her ear again. "Tom, please come see me. We haven't spent time together for months."

"Sir?" What would Tom say?

"Oh, I freely admit, the lapse is on my part. I've been at court since Charles died. But I'd like to talk business, before the chores of your estate overtake you. I'm staying at my house in Cambridge this fortnight. Come for supper tomorrow."

"Yes, thank you." She offered the affirmation she believed Tom would make.

Heydon retreated, Tamsin's curious attention following him. That supper invitation meant the opportunity to prove to Rowland that Heydon was not their villain. She again touched the gold Archangel hanging over her breastbone.

Rowland arrived at her side just then, his shameless smile in place, his white wig gleaming in the late afternoon sun, his copper-satin suit shining amid all the people in mourning weeds. He'd returned to lead her into a gambol again, like in the old days. She'd join in, as soon as she made sure the plan was safe. And that it abided by all their restoration rules.

21

Silvy, Silvy, All on One Day

— NED —

TALLER THAN ALL others, Ned and Perry surveyed the milling averil crowd. Each time Perry spoke, it was as if they'd sailed to a separate world, invisible to others around them. Ned breathed the rare atmosphere of that world, which held only two men on this long hot day.

"Can you sing?" Perry spoke so close to Ned's ear that his nose touched Ned's earlobe. "You look like a man who can sing. When you speak, your voice turns words into a melody. Singular. Remarkable. Especially for a Nederlandse man."

"My father was Dutch. I'm English."

"Now, Englishman, we must discover whether you can sing. I propose we get royally drunk and sing until our ears bleed. We shall want brandy for that exercise. Or brisk champagne. Your uncle's averil ale sits too heavy in the belly to allow a fellow to sing. Do you like champagne?"

"I've never had champagne." More words might be required, but Ned sunk into a quandary. He wasn't stupid. Or naïve. He flirted without knowing how to play his part, to indicate that he was *not* resisting the tempest in that separate world.

Ned wanted to sail straight into those high winds.

"No champagne? We must remedy that." Perry stepped behind Ned to let a trio of village women pass. He placed his hand on Ned's waist, perhaps to guide him out of the way, though that tempest might carry them both away. "What else have you never done that I might help with, Mr. Wijck?"

Ned wavered in the gale, uncertain.

Another duet of ladies passed.

"We cannot decently discuss that in this crowd, Mr. Frake."

"Oh, I am comforted. You are promising me a tomorrow? Singing, perhaps? Surely, you'll remove your gloves." Before Ned could answer, Perry had his hands on his hips, staring across the yard. "Now, who is Rollo following? It seems that your sister has managed to shake free of him for the moment."

— ROLLO —

AFTER THE DUST settled from the first departing carriages, Rowland saw Tom offer an ale cask to the for-hire drivers, advising that they might share it while waiting to carry their customers back to Cambridge. Then Tom paused to chat with the elderly driver Hawksmoor had hired at the inn. Hawksmoor's coachman had brought Mr. Warboys' for-hire carriage, to trade for the return of the earl's coach. That for-hire carriage could be useful for future escapes. Surely the old fellow wouldn't be robbed twice in a week.

Rowland once more scanned the crowd for Perry. Perhaps they'd find enough food among the repast leavings in the great hall, and perhaps he'd find a peaceful moment to assuage how the happenings at Revelstone roiled his innards. He waded through the crowd of villagers, not another soul recognizing him.

But his way was blocked before he reached Perry. The constable tugged at a drunken dandy, coaxing him away from the crowd. It proved to be the glimflashy fellow who'd quarreled with Tom earlier, a relative of the formidable Mrs. Fairchild.

"Come, Mr. Fairchild. You're done in by heat and ale."

"I'm done in by the two-faced Master of Revelstone."

"Our friend is in mourning." The constable pushed at the fellow's shoulder to stop his progress toward Tom. "Wait another day to quarrel."

The fellow doubled his fist and shook it, an impolitic thing to do when upbraided by a constable. Then he unwound his fist, twisting a signet ring that likely scratched his own palm. The bluster continued.

"I shall pull his cork if that cock-robin Tom Foxe continues to subvert my wife."

(Hello! I meant to tease Tom, not stick my finger in a wound.)

The slim coxcomb, worse for drink, straightened his cuffs and adjusted his cravat, both of which had been defeated in the day's heat. Across the way, Ned glanced at the fuddle-capped fellow, then returned his attention to Perry.

The constable gave a gentle shove to move the man away from Tom. "Odds bodkins! Mr. Foxe isn't after your wife."

A crowd of rowdies gathered, calling their opinions about the constable and the man he sought to divert. Many tugged at the dandified fellow and others backed the constable, though it was unclear who sought to part the quarrel and who wanted to get their own fair licks in. Now, if Absolom and Tamsin were here, they'd arbitrate this quarrel and restore peace quickly. Rowland had no business in this, other than to avoid the mêlée like an enlightened man and to judge whether that toss pot had any connection to the Foxes' legal affairs, since his name was Fairchild.

Rowland reached Perry at the edge of the crowd while the constable struggled with the inebriated fop. Perry's intelligent face had turned daft, as if he too were besotted—but with Ned, not strong drink. An orange cat resting on Ned's shoulder jumped onto Perry's. Coaxing the cat down to rest in the crook of his arm, Perry said, "I'll put a stop to the quarrel. People do what I ask when I merely loom over them."

"No, Mr. Frake. My people, my village. I'll stop it."

Perry shoved Ned's shoulder, but in a brotherly way. Their earlier exchanges had turned into a competition about good manners. "I have endured a day that's fried my gingamobs like goose eggs. Now you want to steal the best entertainment."

"Zooterkins!" Ned shoved back. His hand stuck as if glued on the mass of muscle below Perry's collarbone. "I am not the sort of man, Mr. Frake, who'd rob another man of a diverting spectacle.

Do you take me for a Puritan?" Rowland glanced at the crowd, curious to see who noticed that these two were about to set the shire afire. However, the constable and wet-head Fairchild held most everyone's attention.

Perry's finger traced Ned's hand where it rested on his chest. "Indeed, no, Mr. Wijck. I take you for—"

"*Aide-moi!*" A thin voice cried for help.

A wee man in blue velvet leaned on the churchyard gate, then staggered toward the yard at Revelstone. The blue coat had dark streaks down the front. The fellow was drained white, a color that meant he'd lost too much blood.

Tom rushed for the man. Ned deserted his squabble with Perry to join Tom. Lizzie ran off without finishing her good-bye waves to Lady Candecote and Sir Isaiah, who were departing.

"Winwood!" Tom shouted, his voice breaking as if he were fourteen years old. "Help us."

The so-called doctor with the tawny locks joined them, easing Tom away. He bent down to loosen the bleeding fellow's collar and inspect him in a way Rowland had seen among surgeons on the edge of a battlefield.

Rowland tried to hear, along with the seventy remaining mourners. Perry tapped his shoulder. "Since the constable's here, should we tell him that bleeding fellow is a highwayman?"

"One of those cheap thieves from this morning?"

"I'd swear to it, though I saw just a flash from the carriage of the fellow in blue velvet running away."

"I don't know." Rowland remembered the stupidity of their morning encounter. "I was blind behind that veil."

"…needs to be moved to the house." The doctor quietly delivered orders. "Best, to my own room."

"Ned and I will do it." Tom commanded a blanket from one of the carriages—the ancient driver from the inn again—and then quickly turned it into a stretcher, with Ned lifting the front and Tom the end by the brigand's feet.

"Thomas Foxe, the noble lordly hero!" That querulous dandy, further gone in drink than any other mourners, weaved toward Tom and Ned, the constable having failed to calm the man's ire. He swayed when he arrived too close to Tom, who stumbled, recovered, and jerked an elbow into the gentleman's mid-section. The fellow bent in two with pain.

"Step back, Leighton." Tom scowled, a fiercer glare than anything Rowland received that day.

As gone into his cups as he was, Leighton Fairchild caught sight of the figure on the make-do litter. He straightened up, choking with astonishment.

"Get my mother to help!"

The doctor, or the gamester-sharp or whatever he was, nudged Leighton. "Please move, sir. Let me do my work."

Lizzie followed close behind the doctor.

"Can I help?" Rowland came up behind Lizzie.

"No. This is not your affair."

Perry claimed the man in blue velvet must be one of the brigands who'd stolen Rowland's linen. However, when Rowland finally got a good look, the figure on the litter was Sir Isaiah's daughter, Camilla Candecote.

All grown up now, bleeding out her life's blood.

22

The Master's Dilemma

THREE THIN SCRATCHES, sealed with beads of dried blood, traced Camilla's face from cheekbone to chin. Tamsin yearned to wash that wound clean. She knelt by the bed. Camilla's eyes opened. Closed. Opened again. Deep blue in the candlelight.

Camilla gazed at Tamsin, who imagined that she smiled.

"What happened?" Tamsin whispered.

"Accident." Camilla sighed, as if speaking hurt her. "Wanted to shoot him."

"You tried to shoot Leighton? Why?" Every single day was a good day to shoot Leighton, but why now?

Camilla was sinking. "Letter drove me mad."

"Please send for Mrs. Bell." Winwood spoke quietly.

Ah, the very thing to do. Mrs. Bell was their best nurse.

"Is she all right?" Tamsin wanted to hear yes, nothing else.

"We shall see." Winwood peacefully called directions. "Lizzie— Miss Foxe, fetch your scissors so I can cut away these clothes. This accident happened a while ago. Much of the blood has dried."

Tamsin said, "I'll fetch your kit from T—the invalid's room."

Chaos was everywhere. In the hallway. In her head. In the room where Camilla lay, lost to the world. Voices rang from the great hall below and from the yard. "What happened?" "Who is it?" "Did you see who the fellow was?" "A poacher, you say?" "Or a highwayman?

132

Tamsin found Mrs. Bell and then carried Lizzie's scissors and the doctor's kit of tools back to where Camilla was being tended. Winwood cut open the coat and then cast it to the floor.

When Mrs. Bell arrived, hot water and linen in her hands, she pushed Tamsin out of the room. "Master Foxe, go reassure our guests. Thank them for coming and bid them all good night. For Doctor Foxe's sake."

When Tamsin resisted, Lizzie whispered, "*Tom* cannot help undress Leighton's wife. Go be the Master of Revelstone. Trust us to do our best."

Against every impulse in her belly and head, Tamsin pulled the door shut, closing her mind on the images there. A bloody coat in tatters. Camilla's slight, white torso, crusted with dark red. An inner voice kept chanting, in defiance of reason. *My fault. My bad plan.*

If not for Tamsin, Camilla would not have been shot while wearing Tom's second-best clothes. She wouldn't have a pistol to be fired, accident or no, except that Tamsin lured her into adventure. *My fault.*

Leighton and his mother were mounting the staircase. Ned came to Tamsin's side, so that together they barred the door. Tamsin used her deepest voice to reassure them.

"Dr. Oakes says she's not in danger." No, he hadn't said that. And no one wanted Leighton near Camilla.

"Pity's sake. Allow me to help." Mrs. Fairchild spoke in that way she had of ladling out kindness to bully others, so she'd get her way. Those tones always raised Tamsin's hackles, even under the padding of Tom's best coat. Camilla's whispers ("wanted to shoot him") inclined Tamsin to resist every request.

"Thank you. I'm sure Dr. Oakes will appreciate it, when he's ready." Tamsin turned to Ned. "Can you please show Mrs. Fairchild and Leighton to the yellow parlor? Make sure our friends have all comforts while waiting for news from Dr. Oakes."

She glared at Leighton, daring him to interfere with her again, but he was under his mother's control and meekly followed Ned downstairs.

Repeating words of reassurance when she felt none, Tamsin passed Tom's bedroom, longing to step inside to hide and whisper secrets with him, but instead scuffed behind the Fairchilds. She trudged down the main stairs, not remembering until halfway down the steps to release the stair-rail and hold herself upright like Tom.

Camilla bleeding. Perhaps dying.

That thought pierced Tamsin's belly like an arrow.

And it was Leighton's fault. *Not my fault.*

She reached the front door and began offering numb words to guests, not doing a good job of remembering who had departed and who remained. Ned appeared after one huddle of guests passed. He pushed a cup of cider on her.

"Drink this. Have you eaten a bite today? Here's a wedge of cheese. Our guests have gobbled up the roasted meats."

"I'm not hungry."

"Zooterkins! You are off your feet, cousin. No man or woman in England could manage what you have done today. Certainly not without food and water. Come, swallow more cider, please."

She sipped. "Thank goodness for Winwood."

"Yes." Ned's silver-grey eyes flashed. "Tamsin, do you think perhaps Winwood wants—"

"What? To not have to patch up a skulk of sodden-witted Foxe-kits? Or perhaps to live where the inhabitants possess a portion of sanity?"

"No, I mean, does Winwood want…"

But then a few of the remaining guests approached the Master of Revelstone, gloved hands reaching out, "So very sorry for your loss" painted on their faces with broad strokes.

23

Revelstone Secrets

IN THE GREAT HALL, after dipping the last of the posset into a tin mug, Rowland took a sip, then passed it to Perry. "Won't slake the day's dust. More punishment than refreshment."

After searching out any leavings from the repast, Rowland said, "We need to sally forth on an expedition of exploration in this house, like the first surveyors of the New World."

"You distress me, Rollo. Is it possible that things in this house are not as they seem?" Perry dropped his voice to a low growl. "The rear doors of this room are all locked."

"I shall obtain an invitation for us."

"Because your cousins welcomed you so warmly?"

"Because of how I cozen people so that they warm to me."

Perry groaned—and produced from one of his many pockets the lock-pick by which he'd proved his worth earlier that day. "Here's my swift invitation to exploration."

They disappeared from the great room, along with a shaded lantern from one of the tables.

The door Perry unlocked from the great room opened into a room that had been called the ladies' solar when Rowland roamed the house as a child. A hundred years before, the earl in the time of Elizabeth I built the house to serve the queen and the crowds of the royal progress. Likely this room held the plank trestle tables now set out in the great room for the funeral repast. In the current makeshift arrangement, boxes were pushed against the north windows that faced the garden.

The paperwork scattered across the boxes proved to be leaves of parchment from disassembled books. The books' boards had been stacked against another wall. On the opposite wall, where there were no windows, a narrow workbench held carpenters' tools. One task at that workbench was gilding a partially assembled frame.

The room smelled of old dust, musty paper, hide glue, and the remnants of recent joinery.

"This appears to be a factory." Perry stated the obvious.

"If I were to guess—no, I know—they are tearing apart the damaged books Absolom rescued when iconoclasts attacked the libraries at Cambridge."

"Why?"

"In Paris and Holland, the new-made English lords are mad to purchase their history from the ancient past. I wonder how my cousins dispose of their manufactured antiquities."

To his certain knowledge, none of his cousins would dare to harm a book. Therefore, his cousins must be butchering books with Absolom's knowledge, which meant the work was being done in desperation. Badly decayed pages—water damaged, singed, worm eaten—were in stacks beside the workbench. He shuffled through the unbound and rescued pages.

Gilded illustrations from an old prayer book, which would have been too papist to survive Cromwell's iconoclasts.

Odd pictures that seemed part medical, part fantasy.

The title page of Tyndale's New Testament, likely needing rescue from destruction when one clutch of Protestants disagreed with another.

Two fresh papers caught his eye, the kind of creamy linen paper that Absolom treasured when he could get it. "Perry, look at this. It's a piece of Absolom's writings."

Rowland handed Perry two papers, one in Absolom's tiny, even-handed Latin, the other a draft translation of the first. Perry read it, whispering the title: *Life Beyond the Fens: Part II. The Early History of Marborne Parish.*

"Scholars make it too complicated." Perry set the papers back where Rowland had found them. "Kings do what they will. The rest of us hunt for bread and cheese. And mutton, if we're lucky enough to get it."

"You, my friend, are what scholars call a cynic."

"Nay, Rollo. I have a simple life. I did not come to the edge of the fens to rescue a house and title, to sort who stole what. That's your burden."

"You aren't by any chance remaining here, Mr. Frake? Due to an unplanned fondness for—"

"Shut it, Rollo. Unless you shall first confess that it's your over-burdened heart that brought us here."

Perry had his hand out to open the next door, when men's voices drifted from the great room, the walls separated only by plastered lath, not stone.

It was Lord Heydon, upbraiding his brother. "Come, Monck. There's no more posset, and your wife is eager to be home."

"This house is a wreck, Poynter. That's why it's better to sell than mortgage." Hawksmoor slurred his words, sounding fuddle-capped. "We must not end up like Absolom's orphans."

"It's why you must *not* sell, dear brother. Marborne suffers because of the civil wars and the imbalance of Charles's Restoration. That's not the case for your estate. I can help you get right again, if you'll let me."

"Truly?"

"I always tell you the truth, Monck. For now, it is as they say, that the ale-wives of Marborne brew stronger ale than we are used to at Hawksmoor. It's time for home."

A voice called from farther across that room. "Your carriage waits, your lordship."

"I avow, Poynter. You should marry Absolom's nut-brown niece. The one that was a slave to Princess Mary."

"Do you think so? Come away, before your wife has cause to scold both of us."

Perry tilted his head, listening for whether the great hall was empty, then said, "Rollo, your voyages of discovery take the oddest turns. We set out seeking the Spice Islands but drift into the Barbary Coast. Your skills of discovery are uncanny."

"Fate delivered that discovery. Though you'll call it luck."

"It distresses me that you will not admit the obvious, that you rely almost wholly on luck."

Perry pushed at the next door to enter what had been a passage that allowed servants to circumvent the great hall privately. Opening the door unloosed the strong odor of mineral spirits. The tiled floor was covered in canvas cloths that bore splotches of brightly colored paint. Shelves held paintings, mostly elaborate studies of food, flowers, or women busy in their kitchens.

"Our diplomatic masters in Holland hang paintings like that in their houses," Perry said.

"Ned's father was Jan Wijck of Amsterdam." It quickly occurred to Rowland what he was seeing. "We were strictly commanded to keep out of his workshop. He trained in a famous studio but was captured in one the Anglo-Dutch wars. My uncle Samuel Foxe rescued him from among the prisoners digging ditches in the fens."

"Gad, what a story! I had no idea." Perry reached to touch one of the painting but stopped. "But these are fresh. Is he still living here and painting?"

"No. Absolom wrote to me when the elder Mr. Wijck died. I think it was two years ago."

"How is it Ned, a fair-haired son of a Dutchman, is brother to your cousin Lizzie?"

"The elder Mr. Wijck was painting Lizzie's mother's portrait when Samuel went to London to celebrate King Charles's restoration to the throne. We gained Ned as a playfellow. I didn't know he'd inherited his father's ability to paint in the style of a Dutch master. Rather, more than one master."

"I disappoint myself. I saw the paint stains on his shoes. He told me that he painted. But I never envisioned such as this."

"Ned's doing something more here. A few of these are Lizzie in old-fashioned court dress. It's as if—"

"As if he's preparing to pass new paintings off as old?"

Perry opened the next door, which the shaded lantern revealed to be a stitchery room. Garments, hanging on lines or laid out on shelves, were in various stages of disassembly and new construction.

Rowland whistled softly. "This must be Lizzie's factory."

"Half these are ancient. These gowns with embroidered pearls? Must have been your granddam's."

"I wager that Lizzie is reconstructing the contents of our parents' and grandparents' clothes-presses, making them new again. She is a genius with a needle." Rowland wanted to laugh, but then one idea caught him up. "Do you guess that I shall have to run a factory if I stay here, working like the devil's own serf?"

"What I shall guess, Rollo, is that you were hatched in a nest of natural born swindlers."

—

Life Beyond the Fens: Part II
The Early History of Marborne Parish

Marborne first appears in the Domesday Book, written twenty years after the Normans invaded and began to rule this island, which previously knew Angles, Saxons, and Danes as kings.

In the re-establishment of the parish after His Majesty Henry VIII brought the Reformation to England, the village name was attached to the broader lands under the Earl of Marborne, the Foxe family having been heir to that title since long before the Houses of Lancaster and York warred against each other.

In the peace under Queen Elizabeth, the Earl of Marborne built a new house, called Revelstone, where the queen paused on her royal progresses at least twice, as shown in the parish records.

The Reformation took hold in the parish, so strong that a vicar from Marborne parish was burned during Mary Tudor's reign, clinging to his Protestant faith to the end. The village proclaimed that vicar as the first martyr of Marborne. At the time of this writing, that vicar has remained the sole martyr.

Yet that event marks the beginning of perils in the parish, which had always enjoyed whatever peace and prosperity the reigning king of England could maintain. As we shall see, that is part and parcel of the fear and hope which arose across the parish commons for what might be either lost or restored under the new reign of James II.

24

Red Knight, Red Knight

— NED —

DESCENDING THE STAIRS with Lizzie and Tamsin, Ned spied Rowland and Perry lingering by the front door. The cousins aligned as if sides had been chosen for a game of Storm the Castle. *Red Knight, Red Knight, Storm the gate with all your might.*

Caesar wandered into the space between the lines of cousins, sniffing one set of boots and then another, finally settling near Perry. Ned wanted to follow Caesar but stayed by Lizzie's side.

"How does Miss Candecote fare?" Rowland sounded concerned instead of teasing.

"After a bullet tore her velvet coat?" Perry bent to scratch Caesar's ears, then grinned at Ned. "Mr. Wijck, your injured friend resembles one of the brigands who robbed us this morning. Did the king's men hunt down and shoot her?"

Tamsin bristled, as if she might fly at him. Lizzie intervened while Ned fumbled for the right words, knowing Perry meant to tease but had no knowledge that Tamsin was strung tight as a bow string, concerned about Camilla.

"No, Mr. Frake." Lizzie managed to answer calmly, or at least pretended to. "As Rowland can tell you, Camilla is Sir Isaiah's daughter, who recently became our solicitor's daughter-in-law."

"Dr. Oakes says it's not dire, if no infection creeps in." Tamsin answered Rowland, her face tight with worry. "He gave her brandy and Dr. Sydenham's tincture of opium."

"Who would shoot a baronet's daughter?" Rowland sounded truly concerned.

"She says it was Leighton. In an accident," Lizzie said.

Ned considered Leighton a waste of human flesh, but felt the man was too chicken-hearted to take a pistol to his wife.

"I wish only Winwood cared for her. Not Leighton or his mother." Tamsin made an obvious effort—everyone in the hallway must see that—to hide her deep fears for Camilla. "Anything can happen tonight, before Winwood goes to the Fairchilds' house tomorrow."

"Is that man truly a doctor?" Rowland asked. "Field-surgeon, yes. But physician to gentry?"

"Yes, he's a physician." Tamsin seemed indignant for Winwood's sake. "And a good one. But Mrs. Fairchild insists that Camilla go home to be cared for."

Carrying Camilla downstairs was Ned's job. He and the Fairchild coachman carried Camilla downstairs in a makeshift litter, while Tamsin waylaid Mrs. Fairchild, so that they didn't have that termagant on their heels. Outside, Ned found Perry holding open the carriage door.

"I should like to assist you, Mr. Wijck."

"I believe we have nearly achieved our goal, Mr. Frake." Ned wanted to say yes but was nagged by the sense that Tamsin wouldn't want a stranger inserted in her personal worries.

"Yet I can take the coachman's burden, so he can climb inside to receive her."

"The doctor warned to be gentle." Ned repeated Winwood's caution while too distracted by Perry to decide what was best.

Together they moved Camilla gently into place. The coachman went to find Mrs. Fairchild.

"What about the *borachio* that Mr. Tom Foxe says is her husband?" Perry again stood too close, speaking in Ned's ear.

"Leighton? I suppose we let him sleep and then send him home after breakfast."

"He's the sort you prefer to breakfast with?" Perry pursed his lips, as if disgusted.

"Do not insult me." Ned didn't think it worth even one shake of his head to deny that provocation.

"Then let us help the fellow to his mother's carriage. That way, he won't miss an extra minute with his wife. And we shall enjoy our breakfast without him."

Leighton was too lost in wine-weighted sleep to protest until they'd wrestled him downstairs and into the carriage.

"I cannot ride backward." Leighton threw off Ned's guiding arm. "I'll spew. It always happens."

"Mayhap, you'd best ride up top with the coachman," Perry suggested.

"We can't move Camilla." Ned repressed his usual desire: to punch Leighton a good hard one. "Dr. Oakes cautioned against jarring her."

"I can't spew with my mother onboard." Leighton shrugged away from Ned's help, ignoring Perry. "You don't know how she is. Camilla must move, or I shall—"

Perry slammed a fist into the side of Leighton's head. The man fell into Ned's arms.

"Up we go!" Perry did the greater work of shifting Leighton's position in the back-facing seat. "See? He folds in his arms, leaving more room for his mother, like a gentleman does."

When Perry emerged from the carriage, straightening his jacket, he beamed at Ned, like a man finishing a task who's pleased with the results.

"I should thank you," Ned searched for the right words, "for service to our friend Camilla." He couldn't wait to tell Tamsin this tale. And yet: Why had he never felt free to baste that beastly beau? Punching Leighton Fairchild was the obvious thing to do, for more occasions than this.

"Nonsense. The man begged for a thump."

"Aye, you've given me joy, Mr. Frake, and—"

"Pity sakes!" Mrs. Fairchild's inexcusably piercing voice interrupted. "This house needs more servants."

She peered into the carriage, inspecting her son. Perry firmly closed the door opposite her. The coachman helped her into the carriage, but then had to return to the house to fetch something the woman had forgotten.

"Be quick about it!" Mrs. Fairchild admonished her servant over her own mistakes.

Once they'd walked away from the carriage, Perry said, "I am eager to breakfast with you, Mr. Wijck. But can you point me to the kitchen now? I find myself gutfoundered. I shall perish if I'm forced to forego substance until the morrow."

"Take the hallway to the left and follow the steps down. You'll find food there, Mr. Frake."

"But you won't join me?"

"I have more chores with my cousins."

"Ah yes. The termagant called it a shame that you don't have servants." Perry lingered still. "*Goedenacht,* then. That's how the Dutch say it, do they not? I'd rather be saying *Goedemorgen,* because then it will be time to see you again."

"Good…" Ned felt breathless. "Good lord, stop teasing."

Perry pressed his hand over Ned's thumping heart. "Aye? Mayhap there's aught else I should stop?"

— TAMSIN —

SLIPPING INTO TOM'S room, Tamsin intended to relieve her brother's caretaker for a moment.

"Please take a rest from your duties, Agnes. I shall sit here," Tamsin said, "until our invalid sleeps."

She took the chair where Winwood usually sat when he read or played chess with Tom. Absolom's ring still lay on the table. Tamsin pulled off her goatskin gloves, stretched her sore hand, and then once more slipped the ring over her thumb.

The room was dimly lit by the fading light of a summer's eve. Tamsin sucked in a breath and rushed to tell the hardest part of the day. "Someone shot Camilla."

"Zounds! No! Did Leighton do it? That picaroon!"

Reliving the pain of it, Tamsin repeated what she'd seen, what she'd heard from the doctor, and what Camilla said, that Leighton tried to stop her from shooting him. She did not speak aloud the punishment Leighton deserved.

"Too bad she failed. Will she be well? Thank all the gods of Olympus that Winwood is here."

"He says she shall recover. We had Mrs. Fairchild haunting the house for a long hour, waiting to get her claws on Camilla."

"That froward nithing." He'd used that word before to describe the woman, liking the connotation of hatred and strife.

"She means well." Tamsin imitated one of Mrs. Bell's favorite falsehoods, which was meant to indicate that nothing could be done about the petty sins of one's neighbors.

Tom laughed again. "It's always, 'Shame this. Fie on that. Pity you're poor.' Dorcus Fairchild is odium incarnate. From the moment Camilla began that ill-conceived arrangement with Leighton, his mother has doubled the misery of her life."

"Mrs. Fairchild and her friends are not kindhearted."

"How can we protect Camilla?" Trust Tom to understand what Tamsin longed to be doing: serving as a barricade between Camilla and the Fairchilds.

"Don't know yet, Tom. But I vow to have an idea soon."

"And the averil—which you forced me to miss. How was it?"

"A good memorial. Many people spoke kind words—eagerly, but sadly—about Absolom."

"I shall wager that Mrs. Fairchild didn't weep."

"Aye. But Mr. Gamlingay did while he read the prayers."

"Poor old gentleman. Losing his best friend."

"Tom, Rollo is home and—

"Is that why the king's men came looking for him?" Tom pointed to the window. "I heard the thundering horses arrive in the yard. Now, where is Rollo? When can I see him?"

"Not yet. He's...he's...a sort of mad man." She found fresh cotton gloves and sat at the edge of Tom's bed to change the wrapping that kept him from scratching in his sleep. "Absolom wrote to Rollo, asking him to help find who cheated Marborne over those old mortgages."

"Then Lizzie was wrong? Rollo isn't one of the Duke of Monmouth's rebels? That's a blessing."

"He's an intelligencer for the Crown."

"No. You are funning me."

"Yes, and he says that Absolom knew." She gently tugged off one of Tom's cotton gloves, preparing to give him a new, clean pair. "Rollo is telling the entire parish that he's Viscount Orlando de Flores from Catalonia. He came in Lord Hawksmoor's coach, wearing a black silk gown, pretending to be Orlando's sister."

"He never did! What wicked pickthank gossip, Tamsin."

"It's true. Rollo must have that black gown in his baggage. I wonder where Mrs. Bell stashed it."

Tom laughed until he coughed. "That must be the box the boys banged up the stairs. I wish I'd seen Rollo dressed as a Spanish lady. What a famous adventure! But wait. Rollo was in the carriage you liberated this morning? You've had a day!"

"Yes, he came with that giant I killed in Rotterdam. Though I didn't kill him." She replaced the right glove with a fresh one. "That man—he's called Perry—has made Ned his great friend."

"And Rollo came home to pursue the evil Hawksmoor?"

"Except he says Heydon cheated us, not Hawksmoor."

"That's not right, Tamsin." Tom's distressed plea drew up bruised feelings from deep inside her, the same way his cough did. "Poynter had me to supper so many times while I was reading at Cambridge. We've spent hours talking about the duty a man owes to his family and that a lord owes his villages. At Twelfth Night, he offered to help think how we might restore the Marborne title."

"We need that as much as we need to pay the mortgage."

"Though I shall not make a useful Earl of Marborne."

"You'd be a fantastic earl," Tamsin said. "But one thing at a time. Heydon asked me to come for supper tomorrow. Should I be afraid, given Rollo's claims that he's our enemy?"

"No, have no fear. But this is too much on your shoulders. I should go to Poynter, since he's my friend." Tom endured the replacement of his left glove until his wrapped hands lay atop the coverlet. "Perhaps Winwood and I can go in the pony cart."

"Winwood is needed to attend Camilla."

"And yet, I shall beg him for more physick, to make me better faster. You must return to being Thomasine again."

"Soon enough. Now, you must tell the truth, Tom. How are you are faring?"

"I promise you, Tamsin, I am much mended. Winwood's new physick is a magic elixir. Though I believe he compounds it out of chicken droppings and tanner's sluice. I shall make Winwood confess it when he comes to me later."

25

The Highwaymen

– ROLLO –

IN THE KITCHEN, a dozen boys wolfed down scraps from the funeral repast while running riot, with no sign of their mothers or fathers or other responsible person. The older boys were drinking cider, which was never allowed when Rowland lived here. The odors of baking bread and roasted meat lingered, but chiefly the kitchen smelled of that piercing odor of young boys.

"Ease off and leave some for us!" Perry slipped into the riot, though he was twice the size of the tallest boy.

"There's only ham now, sir. The beef roasts are done for."

The boys opened up places around the big worktable, offering to share meat and bread from the ravaged trays. The boys stuffed themselves without pickle or relish to garnish their feast. Rowland poked about the buttery, seeking at least mustard.

"We have the last of the cider, sir!" a boy called after him.

"Is there one cup left for me?" Perry teased. "Will you force me to sip your dregs?"

Rowland emerged from the buttery with a pot of mustard, a dented tin dish serving as the pot's cover. He offered it to Perry.

"O my stars! How elegant!" Perry snatched the pot and used a wooden kitchen blade to scoop out deep yellow paste onto a sliver-thin piece of ham. "We shall eat like lords, even if none of us can claim to be one."

A boy piped up. "Mister Ned says we may have more averil cake than an earl could eat. That's a lot, isn't it, sir?"

"Aye. In my time," Perry said, "I did see an earl eat a whole cow at one sitting. And a duke what ate a meat pie big as a carriage wheel."

The boys all went slack mouthed with awe. "O sir, do you swear it is true?" one of them whispered.

It didn't seem fair, with Perry so large and commanding. "My friend Mr. Frake appears to be pulling your leg."

Three of the boys peeped under the table.

But Rowland didn't want to laugh at them, since they'd graciously shared their supper. "I mean to say, he is teasing you."

The oldest boy nodded solemnly. "I knew that, sir."

They all stuffed themselves with ham and averil cake. Rowland prowled in the buttery again but found neither wine nor brandy, which meant it had all been poured down the gullets of Absolom's mourners.

"Sir, is it true what they say?" A little boy gawked at Perry. "Are you Spanish buccaneers? Like Mr. Ned told us?"

"Aye, lad." But before Perry could say more, a noise rose in the yard. A carriage driver called out a caution, which drew all the boys out the back door.

"Mrs. Fairchild is leaving!" a high voice shouted. "We must wave, so she remembers how we helped."

"Aye! We came to her aid when she first arrived."

After quiet settled in the kitchen, Rowland said, "Tom is engrossed with Camilla Candecote. She made him promise to marry her when we were...I think eight? Nine?"

"Then why is she married to that *borachio* with a fiendish mother?"

"I don't believe it." Rowland slapped the table, frustrated with this puzzle.

"Everyone says Camilla is married to that fool."

"No. I don't believe the gossip I heard, that Lizzie is going to marry Tom. That makes no sense." He shoved away from the table. "Let's find our kip for the night."

"Mr. Warboys said he settled our baggage with the house-keeper." Perry rose, too. "Was that antique driver from the Phoenix and Swan in on the cheat with the highwaymen?"

"Could not possibly be. The innkeeper declared Mr. Warboys to be the most honest man in Marborne parish."

"Mayhap, 'most honest' is ranked just above the bottom, given the factories for forgery that we found off the great room."

They climbed the main stairs, turning east to Rowland's old room, which lay at the end of the long hall in that wing of the house. Rowland had his hand on the door to his room when three boys from the kitchen riot shoved past him, their high voices again screeching in excitement.

"Papa! Mama! Mrs. Fairchild gave us two half-pennies!"

"Two!" another cried. "That's like a whole penny. Just for keeping the horses quiet when she arrived this afternoon. She must be rich as a lord."

"And Mr. Ned asked Mrs. Bell to make sure we had two pieces of averil cake. Two for each of us!"

"That's when we saw Mrs. Bell put the buccaneer's bloody coat in the fire! Mrs. Fairchild took the buccaneer away with her."

"To be hanged!"

The younger voice exclaimed, "Mr. Ned gave us cider with our dinner. He called us good fellows because we worked so hard."

"Bless my bones!" A woman called from within. "Now you'll be silly until dawn and good for nothing on the morrow."

"You shall never guess. We met the queer viscount and his swashbuckler, them what come here from Spain."

A man's voice droned from deeper in the room, but his words weren't discernible.

The boys' voices dropped to a sensible range. "Yes, sir. We certainly shall."

Rowland backed away from the room, nearly stepping on Perry's boot. He closed the door.

The housekeeper appeared then, carrying a bundle of linen.

"Mrs. Bell, a dozen beggars are camped in my old room."

"Not beggars. One of the families from the village."

"Why are they in my room?"

"There's nowhere else to go since the village burned. We have six families here and several older widows. They cannot sleep rough until their cottages are repaired."

"How on God's green earth can we afford that?" Rowland heard "we" after the word was out of his mouth.

"They more than earn their keep." Mrs. Bell seemed intent on passing him by, to be on her way. "The boys brought your baggage to Doctor Foxe's room, to get it out of the way. You'd best take that room. Mr. Frake will be with you, since we don't have sufficient room for a magpie to take a leap in the dark."

"Thank you, Mrs. Bell. Is there hot water come morning?"

"In the kitchen, yes. And if you use the thunder-mug, you'll be the one to empty it. Best use the jakes."

Humbled by that scolding and distracted by the unfolding puzzle of Revelstone House, Rowland led Perry up another set of stairs. The banister under his hand rattled.

"This is a palace, Rollo, like you claimed." Perry didn't bother to whisper. "But like an old cavalry boot, down at the heels. Stripped bare in the war, you said. But it's forty years since the Roundheads killed Charles I and battled Royalist cavaliers. Yet this house hasn't recovered. It's clean and tidy, but so old that every worm-eaten board begs to be replaced."

Rowland didn't answer Perry's banter. After such a fatiguing day, he climbed to the upper floor as if he traversed a war-torn landscape. The day's generous funeral gifts didn't match such a shabby house.

"Natheless, Rollo, this day delivered up as much joy as a village fair. And tomorrow we shall discover who cheated your Foxe cousins, which shall play like a King's Company comedy." Perry paused. "Will we be asked to pay a farthing for hot water come morning?"

Irrationally irritated after Mrs. Bell's set-down, and without Absolom to castigate him about how an enlightened gentleman always keeps his temper, Rowland kicked open the door to his uncle's room. The door collided with their baggage, bouncing back to smash his knee, leaving him pained more by his foolish act than the bruise he'd earned.

"Watch your head, Perry." Rowland warned at the moment he remembered to duck. "These rooms weren't intended for tall men."

Rowland found Absolom's room as he remembered, with his uncle's prized antiquaries neatly lining the shelves. His three cousins were bent over Absolom's study table, the one where they'd all learned to read and do sums. His cousins glanced up, each face without expression. Lizzie sat on one side of the table, needlework in her lap. Ned sat beside Tom, opposite Lizzie, and was tallying on paper. They'd changed from their funeral finery into threadbare country clothes, like cottagers, not gentry. In his glossy court clothes, Rowland found himself to be a peacock among Aylesbury ducks.

Tom, pointing to a line in the ledger, wore Absolom's ancient amethyst ring. Which should be Lizzie's.

Meanwhile, Tom sat there dejected, indecently pretty for a man. Lizzie again took Tom's hand in warm sympathy.

He wanted to cry out, while breathing the Bard's "smoke made with the fume of sighs." (*I am here, Lizzie!*) Instead he said, "Now that we're all here, shall we get started on a plan?"

The room's familiar odors of tobacco and dusty books evoked more remembrances, the way Absolom had whispered in his imagination that day. He focused on the acrid odor of the tallow candles, so he didn't smell Lizzie's floral perfume. Meanwhile, she bent her head over the needlework in her lap, where she was stitching a gold thread up the center of a cravat, a Paris fashion from last year.

Tom pressed his fingers on that ridiculous moustache.

— NED —

"WHAT ARE YOU doing in here, Rollo?" Ned asked.

"Mrs. Bell says we're to doss here, Mr. Wijck." Perry leaned on the door frame, his eyes again shooting flaming darts at Ned. "As I understand this house, we must all do as Mrs. Bell says."

Perry tossed his long form down on Absolom's bed, kicked off his boots, and lay back, arms behind his head. Tamsin scowled, likely because of the impertinence of the man resting where they'd all knelt in grief the night before. However, Ned believed Perry must be innocent of transgression; when the man teased, it had a purpose beyond inadvertent barbs.

Rowland offered a warm smile and took the empty chair beside Lizzie and opposite Tamsin. "We met a few other guests on our way up. How many people live here? Fifty?"

"Only thirty-five, including all of us." Ned rendered a distracted answer, still regarding the recumbent Perry.

"How antique," Perry said. "Like how villages crowded into the castle when the ancient Normans attacked England."

"With all these guests, you'd think they'd help fix the house," Rowland said.

Ned said, "They're either in the field all day or at their trade or working to repair their own burned cottages."

"Why are you all up here?" Rowland said. "Did you give up your own beds to homeless villagers?"

Ned studied Rowland, hoping he could tell whether Rowland saw the jig Tamsin played, being Tom. But no. Both Rowland and Perry believed Tom Foxe sat here at Absolom's table. Yet no one who knew those twins would ever accuse Tom of being as resolutely serious as Tamsin.

Lizzie answered Rowland's question. "We spent the last two nights up here by Absolom's side. After today, it was the one place that's peaceful. We needed a few moments to think."

"If you're thinking about what to do to keep Marborne," Rowland said, "I shall help, as Absolom asked." Spying the ledger under Tamsin's hand, Rowland tugged it over and began to read. "Tom, 'This is very midsummer madness!' How do you all survive on so little?"

"There's bounty from our farms," Tamsin said. "Plus, the hives and honey works. We saved many firkins of ash from the village fire for a soapboiler enterprise after the harvest is done."

"We'll also have a jam factory in the autumn," Lizzie said.

"Truly, Lizzie? You must be excited."

Lizzie frowned (which Ned noticed seemed to disturb Rowland). "Yes. 'What wond'rous life in this I lead!' But, Rollo, what did you achieve this year?"

Rowland's eyes shot toward Perry, then returned to Lizzie. "When we worked for a merchant-master in Amsterdam, we identified the three servants who were thieving from his wine cellar."

"What say you, Mr. Wijck?" Perry drew attention away from Rowland and Lizzie. He moved from the bed to take a seat on a chest near Ned. "How are you helping to keep the family afloat?"

Ned guessed he was like the tinker who woke up on the moon. The entire day had tossed his soul like a ship in a storm. All their fears about Rowland had dropped away; he wasn't a traitor sought by the king's men. Moment by moment, Ned felt as if Perry peeled off the layers that wrapped his soul...nay, Perry stripped the veils off the world as Ned knew it, so that Ned wished to bare his soul.

Nothing was as it had seemed. Even Lizzie carried secrets, different from what Ned had believed about her.

All that left Ned torn (*"Red Knight, Red Knight!"*) between the loyalty he felt in his bones for Tamsin and Lizzie, and the extraordinary unknown that pulled him toward Perry.

Which also left Rowland in the middle, seeming to be as rational a voice as Tamsin ever was.

"We all do our chores," Ned said, not yet prepared to switch sides. "And hope for the best."

Perry waggled an admonishing figure at Ned while shaking his head, as if they shared a secret.

— ROLLO —

WHILE HE READ the ledger, Rowland untied his cravat. Though it was cooler with his shirt open, he smelled that he hadn't bathed since before leaving Rotterdam a week ago. Lizzie settled back in her chair and took up another piece of needlework from her lap, snipping at threads in a length of linen. He was struck once more by her beautiful face. If only she were that innocent.

Tom continued his inventory. "The sheep for wool and cheese. We tried making a poacher's cheese, which earns more, but we need to purchase more cattle if we want to make cow's cheese for market. We're repairing ditches along the water meadows. Come autumn, we'll have added pasture sufficient for a dozen more cattle. Though we shall have to barter for them."

"That will take care of people in the house." Rowland didn't want to quarrel with his cousins anymore and worried they'd take his questions as accusations. Tom's pronouncements served as decisions for all his cousins, as if Tom had taken the invalid Tamsin's place. "But how will you pay the mortgages? The taxes? You must be a bleeding magician, Tom."

"We are careful." Tom's expression was as closed as a gate-sentry examining soldiers' passes. "Also, we have the good luck that this is the best year in a decade for the price of victuals and grain people here must purchase."

"You are careful." Perry slapped his knee in answer to Tom's declaration. "Indeed, this is better than a village fair."

"Excuse me?" Tom exaggerated his indignation but had ceased with the dagger-eyes.

"Come, Tom," Rowland said. "We discovered your factories downstairs. I confess you all astonish me. What you've done is remarkable, but it won't free you from mortgages and taxes."

"I've a notion," Ned said, "for a new factory using old wood left from the burned cottages. My agent in London can find buyers for knights' painted shields, from generations before the great King Hal. Absolom has…had an antique book with images of those old arms."

Rowland didn't answer, distracted first by Lizzie snipping threads with her tiny gold scissors, and then by Perry.

"I aver, bantlings," Perry spoke cheerily. "Your strategy is better than that of the lady pirate in blue velvet we met today."

Tom bit his lip, like his sister Tamsin used to do when unwinding a puzzle. And Tom again pressed at his chest. Colic, perhaps? Something caused Tom pain that day besides Rowland's unexpected return.

"Are you well, Tom?"

"Of course. It's just that, I thought we'd made a decent plan. But Camilla can be impetuous."

"God blind me!" Rowland slapped his hand on the table. "You were playing at Highwayman and Cavalier with Hawksmoor's coach." He was slapping at an immense sadness that they hadn't trusted him to reveal it before now. His only choice was to treat the cockup as a jest. "I feel robbed yet again, but in a new way. You've robbed my soul, playing us for fools."

Tom grimaced.

"Which one were you, Mr. Wijck? The crookback, I'll wager." Perry shook a finger again, as if Ned had been naughty.

"I couldn't see while wearing that blasted veil." Rowland mused over what he'd missed that morning, aware now that his cousins had skills to be used in the scheme he was creating. "Tom, you're angry about the king's men coming, because they might seek you."

"It's you they asked for." Tom remained stubborn.

"Was today your first time?" Perry seemed intent on provoking Ned, his voice musical with a second meaning.

"No, not at all." Ned missed Perry's innuendo.

"You aren't especially good at it." Perry sounded kind.

"We've never failed before," Ned said.

"We do that work, disguised as highwaymen, in order to survive." Tom showed no sign of guilt or remorse. "Why were you disguised as a woman?"

"To get out of Holland when we were pursued. I found the costume useful for certain work in London."

"Who were you running from?" Tom pressed at his stupid moustache.

"Not your business, cousin." Rowland had revealed far more than any of his cousins had shared with him.

"It will be our business if any king's men again come in search of Rowland Foxe. Or the duplicitous Viscount Orlando."

Rowland took a breath, inhaling the odor of Absolom's dusty books and tobacco. "You worry about the king's men because of your jig as highwaymen. You must cease that career. We must advance our gambol without begging to dance at the gallows."

Ned fished inside his shirt and tossed a ragged leather purse on the table. "You'd best take back your baubles. They're as false as your Spanish lady."

"Catalan." Rowland said it, though that fiction didn't matter.

"I...I..." Lizzie held up the linen from her lap. "You'd best have your shirt back. We were going to sell it."

"Thank you." Rowland took it, seeing that she'd been picking the initials out of his last good shirt. "What did Camilla steal from Hawksmoor's chest? What did she shout?"

Tom said, "She cried, 'God keep my giddy cat,' which is what she says when she's excited."

"Whatever Camilla stole," Lizzie exhaled, a sigh to break a buccaneer's heart as she touched Tom's hand, sending a pang through Rowland's side, "Camilla didn't have it when we cut away her coat to dress her wound."

(Ah, Lizzie. You pierce my soul.)

Yet, Rowland consoled himself with one clear idea: Mary Stuart would never allow Lizzie to marry her threadbare and untitled cousin Tom. Whatever were Tom and Lizzie playing at?

— TAMSIN —

SHE HAD LET Camilla be carried away to an unfriendly house, where Leighton posed a danger to her friend's well-being. Distracted, Tamsin roused from those worries to find Lizzie arguing with Rowland.

"Lord Heydon cannot be our enemy," Lizzie said. "He's rich. He serves in the king's court."

"And why would he cheat us?" Tamsin wrestled with the burden of Absolom's secret about the falsified mortgages. Yet she wanted one more day before sharing that ill news, before adding to her cousins' grief.

"As I suggested earlier," Rowland said, "Heydon might long to become the Earl of Marborne."

"What a chuckleheaded notion, Rollo. Don't tease." Lizzie tapped his hand, admonished him with a wagging finger. "Heydon is twenty years younger than his brother, who has no children. Hawksmoor must be near sixty, so Heydon will be named Earl of Hawksmoor in his own right one day."

Rowland said, "I personally heard Hawksmoor say that his brother persuaded him to sell your mortgages. We need to proceed as if both men might be our enemy."

"That doesn't make Heydon the man who cheated Absolom."

"No?" Rowland said. "I heard Heydon say to his brother: 'I made you sell the Marborne liens.' See? He's the original author of that evil idea."

"I'm not satisfied that proves guilt," Tamsin said.

"No? Heydon also said, 'We shall create a syndicate, with only you and me putting money in and taking money out.' This time they prepared to cheat Hawksmoor's wife, not Absolom."

Lizzie said, "I need more than such thin soup to agree that Heydon is involved with cheating us."

Tamsin agreed. "While you've been gone, Heydon has been a friend..." She kept from blurting the truth: A friend to the real Tom.

"Here's what Perry uncovered in Hawksmoor's house." Rowland retrieved a letter from his pocket and read it to them.

> My dear brother, you and I know what happened when the repulsive affair with Samuel Foxe came to such a sad end. That burning ember in my soul led me to agree when you advised me to step out of that wretched business and rid myself of those liens. My hands are now clean. Thanks to you, I have made my peace with God, if not with Doctor Absolom Foxe.

"It only indicates that Hawksmoor sold those mortgages, not that Heydon was involved." Tamsin smothered relief about what Rowland's stolen letter revealed. She didn't have to be the one to tell her cousins about that part of Absolom's secret.

"What is the 'the repulsive affair' with my father?" Lizzie asked. "Our parents perished in the plague. Is that it?"

"I do not know," Rowland said. "But we must learn who helped Hawksmoor and Heydon in this affair, so we can pursue all who participated in swindling Absolom."

Lizzie wrenched her hands. "Please remember one of the restoration rules that protect us. *'Never cheat a neighbor.'*"

Rowland seemed to be confused by this particular appeal to their rules. "Then why, Lizzie, did you bandits set out to nick gold from Lord Hawksmoor on the highway?"

"We intended," Ned said, "to use it when we next paid the mortgage, in recompense for his years cheating Absolom. You, Rollo, stole the earl's papers outright."

"O ye bantling lamb." Perry settled his hand on Ned's shoulder. Ned accepted the weight, as if calmed by it, instead of shrugging away as Tamsin would. "We merely borrowed the earl's letters. I shall return them when I have a moment to trot over to his house. We are intelligencers, not common thieves."

"Are you calling us common thieves?" Tamsin felt her face tighten; her toes curled. She recognized that Perry was teasing, yet she pressed at her Archangel pouch, wishing to replace irritation with hope—that she could collaborate with Rowland and Perry to make their way through the mire of fraud and failure.

"Mr. Foxe," Perry knocked on his own chest as if in a solemn vow, "there is not one thing about any of you that could ever be called common."

"I shall for now," Tamsin said, "endeavor to accept your claim about Heydon. But you must prove more, before we draw him into your gambol."

"Now, tell us your plan, Rollo." Perry snapped his fingers. "Get on with it, ye booberkin."

Ned said, "It's not your quandary, Mr. Frake."

"Aye, dear Mr. Wijck. But I've been trapped all this long day in the moider of your family drama, which lacks a sword fight or a poison-in-the-ear murder to keep my interest."

"In our gambol," Rowland said, "Ned's pictures are the bait we'll use to trap the greedy. Lady Hawksmoor has a gallery of similar paintings, likely to hoard wealth without paying taxes." He pointed to four paintings hanging above the shelf that held Absolom's antiquities. "We can use those, too."

— NED —

"NO, ROLLO." NED stretched out his arms, wanting to protect those paintings. "These came from the workshop where my father trained. He brought them here a decade ago, after he visited his former master."

"All the better," Rowland said. "I won't risk your wealth or treasures. We need merely to uncover a few secrets about our enemies to undo them with my gambol."

"How quickly does your rig advance?" Perry asked. He had his eyes on Ned. "It grieves me to say it, but Rollo and I must return to our work in London soon."

Rowland said, "Today I laid a foundation. Hawksmoor, Heydon, and Duncombe have heard that I'm undertaking an investment with Lizzie to raise ready money."

"Good!" Lizzie said. "We need coin soon. But how?"

"I, the Viscount Orlando, am liquidating assets—that's what men of business call it—for ready money to buy property in London. I am selling my father's painting collection at handsome prices. I've just now sold a painting signed by Rembrandt van Rijn and—"

"No, don't say Rembrandt," Ned sat up, pleased he had wisdom to contribute. "Better to claim you owned a Velázquez or a Bernini or another Italian. Holland was ruined in the war with France, and the market for Dutch art was ruined, too. At best, you might get fifty pounds for a Rembrandt. If, that is, you have provenance. An Italian painting will bring three or five times that among wealthy Parisiennes."

"What is provenance?" Perry asked.

"Proof of authenticity and legal ownership," Ned said. "Very difficult to falsify."

"But you do it, Mr. Wijck?" Perry beamed with pleasure. "And never afeard of detection, I wager. I admire your courage as much as your talent."

Ned flushed under the compliment, so it took him a moment to see that Rowland appeared a bit stunned.

"Does Cambridgeshire know you as an expert, Ned?"

"No," Ned said. "My agent in London takes care of all my business. And no one in London knows I create what I sell."

"I shall repeat, my dear man." Perry poked Ned in the intimate way he'd adopted. "You must cease the dangerous land pirate business, to protect your hands for the truly wondrous work you do."

Ned protested. Tamsin interrupted. "Mr. Frake is correct. To save Marborne, we must endeavor to remain on the safe side of the river, near the forces of law and order."

"You mangled the Bard," Rowland said. "But I'm assuming you are ready to invest in my gambol."

"Those highway restorations are our one true joy." Ned supposed he was unreasonably disappointed.

"We shall have our frolics, Mr. Wijck." Perry slapped Ned's shoulder. "You shall enjoy the much finer games."

"And now, Lizzie, for your part," Rowland said. "You shall claim that Princess Mary told you privately that our King James is selling the art his brother Charles collected. Parliament made James wealthy, but he longs to buy a larger standing army."

"That all belongs to the Crown of England!" Ned exclaimed, at the same time Lizzie said, "Mary would never do that."

Rowland held up his hand for peace. "Mary has urged you to sell your paintings before the king causes values to fall. Like what happened to Dutch paintings."

"What paintings?" Lizzie puzzled.

Rowland pointed to those on the wall. "These."

"We can't sell these," Ned cried in a passion.

"We shall not," Rowland said.

Lizzie offered Rowland her purest smile. "Ah. Lord Orlando says my collection is worth no less than five hundred pounds. I shall ask our neighbors if they might choose to join my venture, so that we all get rich before the king spoils the world for us."

"If an authority verifies them as authentic," Rowland added.

"Ah, that's how your gambol shall work." Perry again turned to Ned. "I wager that's your part to play, Mr. Wijck. What a nice juggle this shall be!"

"As master of this gambol," Rowland said, "tomorrow morning I'll give you each your parts to play in the effort to gull Uncle Absolom's nemesis and any unkind neighbors who helped."

"Behold, 'how my passion does flow,'" Lizzie said.

"Truly, Lizzie." Rowland place his hand over his heart. "I am here to do what I've been trained to do."

Ned, however, saw Perry also had his hand over his heart, with his eyes again prying at the edges of Ned's soul.

26

The Tinkers' Oath

"You SHALL BE our hero." Lizzie grasped Rowland's collar, pulling him down to kiss his cheek. Tamsin did not miss Rowland's dark look after he turned away from Lizzie, yet she didn't understand it.

Rowland said, "You all must be fatigued after last night and then today. I need to finish planning our gambol, and so wish you a good night."

The three cousins lit candles to find their way through the house. In the hall, Lizzie clutched Tamsin's elbow and leaned her head on Tamsin's shoulder.

"Tell me we'll be all right," Lizzie said.

Before Tamsin could answer, and before Ned closed the door behind them, she again glimpsed Rowland, the bones of his long face as sharp as an imp carved on an old church, his amber eyes fixed on Lizzie.

"Oh, my stars." Tamsin should have seen it sooner. Rowland was in love with Lizzie. And jealous of Tom. "We'll come around right, Lizzie." She kissed Lizzie's cheek. "When this work is done, then you can return to Mary's court. I didn't understand until today, but that's what you desire most in this world, isn't it?"

She let Lizzie and Ned continue downstairs, then mumbled an excuse and tapped at Absolom's door. Her own greatest desire was to strip off her linsey-woolsey work clothes and climb into her own bed, to tear at her lip and pull off that wretched moustache.

But she needed one more word with Rowland.

Because she also wanted to see the Fairchilds punished for Camilla's sake, especially Leighton.

Because she needed someone's help, and Fate declared it must be Rowland. For his scheme and plans to work, he needed more information, such as Solicitor Fairchild's role in cheating Absolom. This required the day's...the week's...the year's biggest plunge into trust. More than she'd ever risked.

"Come." Rowland answered her knock.

Hesitating, she remained at the open door. Rowland put aside the papers he was reading, waved for her to enter.

"Rollo, in Holland, we misunderstood each other. And I—"

"Jove save me from this maelstrom!" Perry grabbed his boots. "I'm going to the jakes. Necessity saves me from more rumbling among Foxe cousins."

She stepped aside so Perry could pass. "Mr. Frake, I am sorry for what happened that day."

"I cannot express the profound consolation you bring me."

"I am sincere," Tamsin said. "And Fate punished me. My hand was injured when my pistol misfired."

"I am sorry that you took any hurt that day, Mr. Foxe, when the Fates flummoxed us all."

When the door closed behind Perry, Rowland relaxed, his arms open on the tabletop. "Sit with me, cousin. It's a bit of a tale if I tell it correctly." He described how he and Perry pursued Lizzie across Holland, to save her from what he believed were enemies intent on harming her. "We thought she'd been abducted by Monmouth's agents, while—"

"While Lizzie thought his rebels were chasing her." Tamsin sat at the table, her hands in her lap. "Lizzie apologized for her misunderstanding, but I have continued to doubt you, Rollo."

"I saw that today. You and I haven't spent time together for many years. We must learn Absolom's lessons again."

"But still." Tamsin gnawed on her lip. "I believe in my...my mother wit. In Holland, we were sure we were performing—"

"Heroic acts for Lizzie? Yes, Perry and I were also sure when we rode out of Amsterdam in pursuit."

"Then, Rollo, before we say goodnight, I want to ask if you remember the summer when Absolom invited traveling tinkers to camp on the edge of the commons."

"I remember that we learned to take our jumbles elsewhere after learning greater invectives and insults from the tinkers than we'd learned from Shakespeare."

"Remember when we climbed the church tower?"

"The morning before Lizzie left to serve in Princess Mary?"

"Aye. What did we say that day?"

Rowland closed his eyes, as if the memory had the solemnity of a prayer. "We swore a solemn tinkers' oath, on our ancestors' bones. To be true to each other, as brothers in arms, until either angels or demons take us from this green land."

"Can you swear it again? On Uncle Absolom's bones?"

"Yes, I swear. *'My family obligations are sacred.'* Truly."

"I shall swear the same to you. But I also came back just now to tell you what I haven't shared with the others. You need to know more about what prompted Absolom to write to you."

"He wrote because he believed Hawksmoor cheated him."

"It's worse." Everything was always worse. She shared the story Absolom told her on his last day.

How Absolom learned from Solicitor Fairchild that the mortgages on their unentailed land had been sold.

How Absolom had gone to London to discover who bought the mortgages.

How Sir Charles's agent showed Absolom forged papers that claimed the mortgages ran for another ten years.

How Absolom confronted Hawksmoor about the fraud, with Heydon seeking to make peace.

Rowland listened closely. "I must do whatever is possible to seize those mortgage papers."

"Let me finish, Rollo. Absolom came home to find his original mortgage papers had been stolen somewhere between Fairchild, Sir Charles's agent, and Hawksmoor. Our fate is…"

"…in the hands of a blind syndicate holding forged liens." Rowland didn't seem shocked, learning of this tragedy.

"Yes. He had no way to prove it. He also lost all the proof of the Foxe family claim to the Marborne title. I swear it led to his decline and death," she said.

"Your secret does tell me what to do, Tom. It is work with which I am familiar."

"What is that?"

"Preserving the Crown's secrets. You shall have to trust me, because we just swore on Absolom's bones. I remain confident it's the hawk-faced Heydon that we must pursue. And Mr. Danvers Duncombe may help us by persuading the others to join in our scheme to defeat those who cheated Absolom."

"That Mr. Duncombe we met today, who came with Lord Hawksmoor? Not Sir Charles Duncombe?"

Perry banged his way back into the room and sat on the bed to pull off his boots. "How refreshing. Walking a league in the dark to the jakes. Waking a dozen dogs and babies in the house."

"Welcome back." Rowland greeted Perry instead of answering Tamsin's question. "In your absence we have achieved peace among us."

"Jove bless me! The devil shall let us all sleep tonight?"

"It is to be hoped for, if not prayed for, Mr. Frake." Tamsin saw it'd take time for the two of them to know how to rub along. Half out the door, she stopped to ask one last question. "Rollo, how will it be with our friends and neighbors, when your scheme is done and you prove to be Rowland Foxe?"

"Honestly? I shan't be here the next day after finishing this work. Perry and I have an assignment to finish, and then we shall seek new service to the Crown."

"MY DEAR LORD Orlando, may I beseech your gracious lordship to snuff the candle and allow the lower orders to sleep?" Perry complained after Rowland closed the door.

"Like the Scottish lord, Heydon hath murdered sleep. I shall sleep no more."

"Bless me. Your cousins' playacting hath diseased your brilliant mind."

"I'll sleep in a bit, Perry. I want to study the papers you lifted from Hawksmoor's house."

"It distresses me, Rollo. You want an officer's commission, and yet the first opportunity you shall have to command more than one minion, it's to pitch your baffled cousins into your gambol. I aver, I never knew such innocents."

"Innocent?" Rowland said. "They are quick-witted and used to fooling gudgeons. We shall tutor them the same way our masters taught us."

"'How to spin falsehoods while uncovering a liar.'" Perry imitated the frog-bark of their first captain-tutor in Paris, ticking off items on his fingers. "Keep gazing into your target's eyes, but do not intimidate. A man blinks too often while uttering falsehoods. Or will glance away from your gaze."

Lizzie hadn't looked at Rowland, even while scolding him.

"Be open with your hands or keep them at your side." Perry repeated the item they'd practiced many times, learning to appear innocent. "A man often stands stiff as a guard and covers his vulnerable belly while uttering falsehoods. Or shuffles, ready to run away."

Ned was prepared to run away all day, hands over his belly like he had to protect from attack.

"A man," Perry intoned, "uttering falsehoods might cover his mouth, as if he's hiding the truth."

Tom pressed his moustache whenever challenged. Definitely hiding a secret.

"Perry, I declare, we have the best students. They are, as you say, natural born swindlers."

"And so, Lieutenant Foxe, shall I report what I uncovered in my prowls while you were making new friends today?"

"Is it possible to stop you?"

"Seldom. First, the doctor loves Tom. I cannot discover who it is that Tom loves, but I suspect it's the buccaneer lady."

"What does Ned say?"

"I regret to report that those beautiful silver eyes do not perceive everything around him. Now, whatever the doctor's intentions toward Tom might be, the denizens of the house and the village consider the man to be a god sent to heal mankind."

"Must be glorious for the doctor," Rowland said.

"Thou shalt not be bitter, my friend. Before we are done, they shall know your true glory and genius. Now, for all the doctor may be a god among men, everyone in the house speaks of your cousin Thomasine as if she's ready to meet Absolom at heaven's gates."

That disquieted Rowland more than any other news since arriving at Revelstone. "I must see her tomorrow."

"It's the third door on the left at the top of the first stairs."

"That's where Tom and Ned and I slept until we were…oh, seven, I suppose. What else?"

"Mr. Leighton Fairchild hates Tom but is too much the fool to notice that the entire parish—and especially his wife, the lady buccaneer—all loathe him as a drunkard and a fool."

"It's not very Christian to judge," Rowland said, "but Mr. Fairchild's whine does make one long to plant a facer."

"As to that, I couldn't resist while Ned and I hauled him into the carriage." Perry rubbed his knuckles.

"That might raise you in Tom's estimation. I swear, he's as much in love with Camilla as he was when I lived here."

"Could it be that Miss Candecote married Mr. Leighton because his family has more money than Tom?"

"What a desolate thought, Perry."

"I shall enquire tomorrow. Mrs. Bell carries a burden of grievance for the Fairchilds. She'll unload tales as if dropping a yoke of firewood if she has a sympathetic listener."

"Perry, don't ask more about Tamsin. I shall discover that puzzle for myself. And just so you know, Tom and I swore a famous oath to each other while you were out. You don't need to pry more into his business. What mysteries did you discover about Lizzie?"

"Our favorite lady? Perhaps, as with the invalid Miss Thomasine, you can learn more than it's possible for me to uncover. Lizzie and Tom share a silent language. Ned adores his sister but doesn't see the kind of creature she is, didn't understand her performance when she spoke with Heydon or with Mr. Duncombe."

"She spoke with both men?"

"She and Heydon seemed deep in business that I could not overhear. He treats her with great deference."

"And Mr. Danvers Duncombe?"

"That man doesn't know what Lizzie is. Whoever might be using Duncombe as an agent of business, it can't be any of the king's courtiers. The agent does not perceive how far out of his touch your Lizzie is."

"And I'm convinced she will remain so," Rowland said.

"Whatever is she doing here at the edge of the fens, Rollo?"

"I am puzzled. When I ask, she finds an interruption to wiggle away."

"It bears pondering, doesn't it? The week King Charles dies, your Miss Ysabel is sent away from Mary's court—secretly. She lives in a neighborhood where she shines like a diamond in fen waters. And she's gone to London at the first of each month since she came home. To succor a sick friend, Mrs. Bell tells me. But she takes Tom and Ned with her."

"Shall I guess, Perry? Mary sent Lizzie to reclaim the Marborne title. To secure alliances with whatever family Lizzie marries into, and any others she might befriend."

"And in London?"

"She's seeking audience with the king, to make a case for the earldom. While Ned the devil-drawer sells his forgeries."

"You have found the best romps for us, Senor Orlando."

"I try, Perry. Now, what about Ned? What secrets have you uncovered, besides our discovery that he's a genius forger?"

Perry took a long time to answer, turning twice in the bed. "Can we snuff the candle now, Rollo?"

"In a minute. Perry, I must remain at Revelstone for as long as it takes to save Marborne. If you want to return to London and wait for Duncombe to return to his offices—"

"Nay. I am loath to proceed without you."

"Then I must warn you, I'm losing faith in our endeavors to uncover rebels. Did you hear today about the king's butchery in Bristol? That's not how our spymaster in Holland handled rebels for William. He just worked schemes to seize their fortunes and send them into exile. That's all it takes. Not heads on pikes."

"It would be like me to say, 'It's the world we live in.' But, Rollo, do you see the other jeopardy in which we are enmired?"

"Aye, it destroys my peace. That picaroon Duncombe might have pulled Hawksmoor into treacherous investments. Therefore, he might have pulled the Foxes of Marborne unknowingly into treacherous business. Though, from what Absolom told Tom, it's Sir Charles's agent that holds the fraudulent mortgages."

"Jupiter forfend us! It shall not be pleasant if our prowls lead us into the den of so significant a man as Sir Charles."

"Yet another reason for you to return to London and not be entangled in all these double-dealings just because I am."

"Nay. I shall not for the world miss this gambol with your larcenous cousins."

"Then keep prowling in Mr. Duncombe's business."

"Aye. Now, the candle, Rollo?"

Rowland packed up the letters he was reading and blew out the candle.

After a moment of silence, Perry said, "He has provoking silver eyes, does Ned. And nice hands with streaks of blue paint on several fingers."

Perry spoke with a softness Rowland rarely heard from his friend. They both had more at stake than just uncovering any enemies of Absolom or the Crown.

27

Marborne Brook

BEFORE DAWN, ROWLAND intended to discover what lay behind one door in the house before its inhabitants spilled forth from their beds. Perry agreed to prowl the outbuildings and cellars, to assess the Foxe family's livestock and any stores that weren't recorded in the ledger. In the house and up the first stairs and down the hall, Rowland turned the door's latch.

"No candle, please!" The hoarse voice inside the deep-dark room whispered in near panic. Rowland complied, blowing out the taper he carried. "The doctor says the light can hurt my eyes."

"Tamsin, it's me. Rollo."

"I–I'm astonished."

"They didn't tell you I've come home?"

"No. Yes. T–Tom told me last night."

A thump on the floor indicated something had come off the bed. A dog sniffed at Rowland's feet, then whined, rubbed on Rowland's boot, begged attention.

"Caesar, leave our guest alone."

"Caesar? Our puppy?" Rowland bent to pick up the dog. "This can't be the same Caesar. He'd be a hundred years old."

"It is Caesar. And he smells like a hundred-year-old man."

Rowland scratched the dog's head, was nudged to do more, making it easy to find the right place to rub in the dark. "I'm beyond sorry to hear you haven't been well."

"Thank you. Winwood is a master. I am improving."

That wasn't what the doctor told those three impertinent ladies at the averil. Or what Ned had told Perry. But Rowland couldn't argue with the invalid.

"I've missed your company and your wisdom, Tamsin. We all missed you at the service."

"But I wager Mr. Gamlingay did us proud."

"Yes. As did our cousins and Mrs. Bell and people from the village. Mr. Gamlingay, though, suffers—"

"He's not ill?" That whisper rose in volume.

"No. But he suffers the loss of Absolom as much as we do. He wept through the prayers." Rowland's voice broke. He'd let his feelings show. It must be because he could trust Tamsin. The weight of the last day's disappointments were…not too much, just hard. Especially without Absolom and with Tamsin ill.

After a long silence, Tamsin whispered again. "We have much to do, our band of brothers."

Just like Tamsin did years before, the invalid offered comfort. And recalled what they swore to each other. Caesar nudged Rowland's hand, because he'd forgotten to attend to the old dog.

"That's why Absolom summoned me."

"Forgive me, Rollo. I didn't ask about you. How have you been?" The whisper brushed Rowland's ear like a ghost.

"Me? I'm always well, Tamsin. I do need a bath after traveling, and I'm warned it's not easy to beg hot water."

"It's summer. Try our favorite pool in Marborne brook." The whisper turned to a thin chuckle. "It will be almost warm by now. Rollo, do you remember the June day we stripped and dashed into that pool, surprised to find Theo Gamlingay floating there, naked as a baby hedgehog?"

"Aye. Instead of scolding, he dunked me. And Ned."

"And you shrieked blue devils because of how cold it was."

"Perhaps you'll hear me shriek later," Rowland said. "I do need a bath and can't wait for hot water."

The door opened. A voice called, "Are you well, my friend?"

"Yes, Winwood. It's my cousin Rollo, come to say hello."

Rowland didn't hear the doctor's reply. He stirred to depart. "I'd best say goodbye. Please allow me to visit you."

"We shall see what the doctor says. Rollo, please take Caesar to the kitchen. Mrs. Bell will soon have breakfast for him."

— TAMSIN —

IN THE AURORA light, the time of day when she was most grateful to be impersonating Tom, Tamsin ran her usual circuit in the parish. When she no longer needed to be seen as Master of Revelstone, she'd have to find a way to preserve this privilege.

At the Fairchild house, she stopped to beg water from the man who was filling the horse trough outside the small barn Mrs. Fairchild called a carriage house. He was a friend of Mr. Warboys and had been drinking ale with the other drivers at the averil when Camilla arrived, and who'd driven Camilla home when Mrs. Fairchild seized possession of her daughter-in-law.

"Is Mrs. Leighton doing well this morning?"

"Cannot say, Mr. Foxe. Her maid Jane is still upstairs and has never said a word except to beg for hot water."

"But she endured the travel home last night?"

"Yes, though you can imagine the uproar when we arrived. Mr. Fairchild came from London to find an empty house and deemed that he'd been done a bad turn by all of us going off to Doctor Foxe's averil."

"I'm sorry to hear that. We were humbled and grateful that your household came to honor my uncle." Tamsin couldn't think how to elicit more information about Camilla.

"Jane helped me take Mrs. Leighton up to her bed, so we escaped the scolding the others suffered upon returning home. Can I say again, Mr. Foxe, how deeply sorry we all are for your loss? Doctor Foxe was as fine a man as any in the parish."

"Thank you. And thank you for sharing your cup with me."

He called her back. "Mr. Leighton has a tremendous bruise from that man, Viscount Orlando's guard. Tell the fellow he got in a good hit."

"Excuse me?"

"When Mr. Leighton asked us to shift his wife so he could ride where we'd laid her, Mr. Ned refused. They argued. That big fellow thwacked Mr. Leighton a good one. Knocked him cold."

"Good stars! I apologize for our forward guest."

"No need. I suspect Mr. Leighton won't remember it."

Tamsin ran for home, knowing she couldn't learn more until Winwood called on his patient. She intended to accompany him. She didn't care for whatever else must be done that day, except to learn how Camilla fared.

Damp and vivified from her run through the parish, Tamsin ducked into the Revelstone great barn, intending a few private moments' consolation with the horses. The balm of the barn's smell, imbued in the wood after a hundred years of horses, dogs, and cattle, soothed her nose.

Perry had a cat curled in the crook of one arm. With the other hand, he scratched the ancient horse Thunder between his ears. "Good morning, Mr. Foxe. And a fine morning it is, giving us respite from yesterday's heat and turmoil."

"Hello, Mr. Frake. I've been to the Fairchilds' house. Their coachman says to tell you that Mr. Leighton Fairchild sprouted a great bruise he got from you."

"Truly?" Perry's face split with a huge grin. "We had so few joys yesterday, amid all the mourning and such."

"I congratulate you."

"Nay, you wish it was you that done it." Two more barn cats twined around Perry's ankles, seeking the affection the tabby in his arms received. "I'm happy to do such for you whenever you require that service."

"I don't usually strike my neighbors." She'd never struck anyone in her life, except for shooting Perry. She inhaled Thunder's sweet, musky odor.

"Yes, I see that, Mr. Foxe. You're a soft sort of man, the kind that must use his head instead of his hands to fight enemies."

"I suppose that's true." Tamsin determined to ask, instead of guessing the man's intensions. "Are we still at odds with each other, Mr. Frake?"

"No. We share the jumbled way ahead over the next days' work. I shall help as I best can, but you shall require a hard heart. The gambol that Rollo plans, it will harm some of your neighbors."

"We are taking back what was stolen from us."

"Aye," Perry said. "But I heard what you cried in that alcove with Rollo and Miss Foxe. 'I thought I murdered a man!' It pierced my heart to hear it, and I'm not any kind of soft man."

"I didn't intend to kill you then. My pistol misfired. And I didn't know you were Rollo's comrade."

"We all understand that now. What I mean to say," he pushed the tabby into Tamsin's arms and then scooped up the other two cats for their turn, his massive arms able to cuddle them both. "A man who lives like I do, ready for any kind of battle, has seen comrades and enemies dead in a ditch, whether it be their souls or bodies. We learn how to keep away from any mare's nest of bad memories and bad dreams."

"I think I understand your meaning."

"Do you, Mr. Foxe? What I see in you is a soft-hearted man managing huge burdens like a hard-headed man. Your uncle's eternity box was a light load. Getting the justice Doctor Foxe wanted, that's going to weigh a great deal more."

"What do you suggest?" She took a deep breath, inhaling the odors of dust and manure and tack soap and hay, and about to accept spiritual advice from a giant petting cats in a horse stall.

"Let Rollo—and me—carry the weight as we commit trespasses against your neighbors. Do not ponder the sins we must commit to gain justice. Do not take on needless blame, the way you did over the murder you never committed."

Ned called out from the open door of the barn. "Hello?" A clutch of boys pushed past him, having arrived to muck stalls before the day's heat set in.

"Ah, Mr. Wijck. Tom and I were just talking—may I call you Tom? Now that we're friends?"

Tamsin nodded, more abrupt than was proper, but perturbed about advice from someone who saw through her bravado. She needed to change out of damp clothes and wash and think about what it meant to let Rollo carry their sins in pursuit of justice. She stopped at the door, where Ned stepped aside for her. She said, "Mr. Frake—"

"Perry. Please consider me a friend.

"Perry, are you giving Miss Foxe this same advice?"

"Miss Ysabel Foxe? She did begin life with the rest of you nestlings, but she came of age doing battle in a royal court. She's seen plenty of souls dead in the ditch, their bodies still walking about. Might be she has put down some souls herself. She knows." Perry pointed at Tamsin. "You're a handsome man without that moustache, Tom. It suits you."

Tamsin, who habitually used her hard head to fight enemies, had forgotten the moustache when she dressed —An unthinking rebellion against the tasks she owed the family and the house. As the heat of summer bore down, she wanted to tear off the shell of Tom's clothes. She wanted to be free of it all, except for the sweet hour of dawn when she ran freely through the parish, fleeing her hard-headed thoughts, her heart and legs working while she gloried in the thrill of a good run, freed from worry and trepidation.

The boys took possession of the barn, urging Mr. Foxe, Mr. Ned, and Mr. Frake to depart so they could make the place clean and cozy for the beasts.

— ROLLO —

THAT BRIEF, ILLICIT visit with Tamsin lifted Rowland's spirits. A rosy dawn sprawled across the horizon when he left the house. He passed under the oaks named for their grandfathers, and again remembered the cousins' roles in their childhood romps.

Rowland, who prompted the rigs they ran on neighbors and villagers. Perhaps he'd begun his profession then, long before Paris and learning from ambassadors' intelligencers.

Tamsin, who cautiously judged the merits and perfected the methods of their frolics, or reined them in.

Lizzie, the encourager of the most fantastical ideas and the owner of the most innocent face.

Ned, the lookout for what might trip them up.

Tom, who invented the fictions for their excuses if they should be found out.

Now Tom had a burden to carry, taking a second role while Tamsin lay upstairs, an invalid.

His razor and soap in hand, Rowland tramped down to the place where the Marborne brook pooled, deep enough to swim. The brook had changed its banks, altered by flooding. The tall trees he and Tom and Ned jumped from in former times were now too far from the stream. He stripped, slipped into the pool, and washed away the last of Holland, the dash to London, and the hot and sticky ride to Cambridgeshire in Hawksmoor's carriage.

He shaved, wishing again for hot water, then he emerged from the pool clean, cold, and convinced that his former master in Amsterdam was correct: Rowland did poor intelligence work when his family was involved. After hearing his cousins' views of events, he had to admit his part in the failure in Rotterdam, his lack of discovery. And now, it had taken him far too long to reach a simple insight. Tamsin had never once in their entire childhood stripped to join the boys in that pool. Most certainly, the Reverend Mr. Gamlingay never dunked or splashed a naked Tamsin.

A brilliant, sunlit image from the previous day flooded his memory: Tom in a padded coat, pressing at that ridiculous moustache, mocking him.

He, meanwhile, had missed or misinterpreted half of what unfolded at that averil. Like the doctor's fancy for Tom.

Or when he insisted his cousins trust his help because he was England's best intelligencer.

"God blind me!" His shout scared the birds in the trees overhead and sent a creature scrambling away in the hedges. Yet he couldn't blame God for how blind he'd been to the work of a master trickster. And he couldn't be angry with Tamsin for pitching such a perfect gambol. He had to admire her.

And he owed her recompense, having teased about what he though was Tom's affection for Camilla. She must be wretched over Camilla's so-called accident. And he, Rowland, had compounded her hurt out of stupidity.

Rowland fished the gold angel from his pocket and rolled it over his knuckles while he returned to the house in his shirt and breeches. In the yard, women were building fires under the laundry kettles. He came in the door at the back of the house.

"Bless me, Doctor Foxe. You can't smoke in here." Mrs. Bell's voice carried down the hall. "You promised your mother and—God's wounds!" Her voice dropped and her next words ran rapidly and softly together. "May Our Father bring peace to our home."

Rowland entered the hallway.

"Oh, it's you, Mr. Rowland. I mean, Lord Orlando."

"Did I interrupt you, Mrs. Bell?" Rowland felt Absolom's presence in the house, but also knew it wasn't a ghost.

"No. A whiff of Doctor Foxe's old pipe fooled my memories. It takes one a bit to remember that them what was here yesterday are gone now." She carried a load of linen that reached her chin and muffled her words. "Master Thomas is in the dining hall. He asked after you."

"Thank you, Mrs. Bell. But first, you must let me help you." He reached to take that load from her. "I see you have the fires going already." She followed him out the door. He carefully set down the load where she indicated.

"I am obliged, Mr. Row—Lord Orlando."

"Not at all, Mrs. Bell. We are all obliged to you. Though I'm surprised to see a great washing undertaken on a Wednesday."

"It's just all this linen from the averil, sir. And in this weather, it shall all dry quickly."

Inside again, he overheard portentous words coming from the dining room.

"Does he know the truth?"

"No." Tom's voice—nay, Tamsin.

"You know I will move heaven and earth to help you. Speak just one word."

Rowland gave ever greater credence to the sensation that this house held many untold secrets. When he stepped into the room, the doctor with the auburn curls hastily released Tom's hand. Except Rowland now recognized Tamsin, her head bent close, listening to the handsome doctor's promises.

"Do we have to catch and kill our own food?" Rowland came in noisily, hoping he achieved a properly light tone. He had to help Tamsin out from under the burdens she carried for everyone. "Good morning, Tom. And good morning to you, Doctor...?"

"I'm Winwood Oakes." The man offered a strong grip, more like that of a field-surgeon than a ladies-parlor physician. "We weren't properly introduced yesterday, Lieutenant Foxe. Though Tom says that I am to call you Lord Orlando, is that correct?"

"Consider it an ancient soldier's *nom de guerre*." Rowland shook the man's hand, certain that the doctor served as a more-than-willing supporter of Tamsin's masquerade.

"You might be the youngest ancient soldier I've ever met." The doctor smiled at his own levity.

"But you *have* met many soldiers?" Rowland couldn't keep from prying.

The doctor's eyes drifted away, as if Rowland had unmasked him. Meanwhile, Rowland privately committed to not confronting Tamsin. He should wait until she chose to share more confidences with him. And he had to find a way to coax her into letting him carry part of the weight she bore, performing as both Tom and Tamsin for the entire parish.

28

Groundwork

— TAMSIN —

"THERE'S BREAD AND the last of the minced ham on the sideboard, Rollo." Tamsin hoped her welcome declared her belief that it was a new day and a new world where Rowland was a comrade, not an enemy. "There's breakfast cider. Mrs. Bell held some in reserve, though the ale is gone for the coming week."

"Goodness, Tom! You shaved!" Rowland touched his own upper lip. Tamsin resisted the impulse to touch her face. "That clean-shaven visage flatters you, Tom." He piled ham onto a piece of bread. "Are we off to visit Camilla today, Tom?"

"Yes. Though the Fairchild house is in chaos." Tamsin flinched each time Rowland said Tom's name. She tore at the crusts of her bread, dropping crumbs on the napkin spread on the table, her belly and heart torn to pieces from the slim news to be had about Camilla.

"Naturally they are upset," Winwood said. "The whole parish saw Camilla bleeding at the churchyard gate."

"Has the chaos in our house spread like an infection?" Rowland sipped his cider. "Though I understand Perry darkened Mr. Leighton's daylights in the carriage yesterday. That should warm hearts throughout the parish."

Tamsin bit her lip to keep from exclaiming how she wanted all the Fairchilds taken down in Rowland's scheme, for Camilla's sake. However, the cousins had a rule: *Reap justice, shun revenge.*

Instead, Tamsin repeated what she'd learned on her morning run. "Mr. Fairchild's sister put him in a stagecoach from London before dawn. He arrived home near midnight, unhappy to find the servants and his wife all gone to the averil. So, he wasn't there when Leighton shot Camilla."

"She said it was an accident," Winwood repeated.

Rowland set his mug down and, not commenting about Leighton, he changed the subject. "That's good gossip so early in the morning, Tom. From messenger pigeons?"

"Tom cannot sit still in the morning." Winwood regarded Tamsin with a wry expression. "He's run around most of the parish and heard all the servants' gossip before the rest of us rise from our slumbers. Fastest runner in the county, I'm told."

"I'd forgotten that about Tom," Rowland said. "But then, we were fifteen when we last saw each other. That's a third of a lifetime." He sipped more cider. "You have a handy talent. Like an intelligencer who collects secrets to use later."

"I–I hadn't thought of it that way." Tamsin hoped she didn't blush at Rowland's compliment.

"Can we speak freely about today's work?"

"Yes, but…" Tamsin glanced at Winwood.

"Excuse me. I must attend my patient." Winwood rose from his seat. "It's time for our invalid's dose of the physick I've prescribed. I believe it's having a positive effect."

After the doctor departed, Rowland asked, "Why did he leave?"

"Dr. Oakes is a discreet person who…" She paused. Yesterday in Tom's room, Winwood repeated that he preferred to keep a veil of innocence over all the Foxe machinations. "Who is a good friend to us. And unlike what your friend Perry hinted to Ned, Winwood is no one's paramour, nor is he—"

In the outer hall, Ned was saying, "Tell me, Mr. Frake, is Rollo your own…"

"Bless me, no!" Perry exclaimed. "He's baptized and confirmed in the petticoat persuasion. Now tell me, Mr. Wijck, who crowned your cousin Tom king of Revelstone?"

"Our Tom has the best ideas."

Sipping her ale to cover her smile, Tamsin enjoyed a flicker of pride. And (she hoped Perry noticed) she hadn't led her cousins into committing grievous and dark sins in pursuit of justice. Only a little highway robbery of the guilty.

— NED —

"GOOD MORNING, TOM. Rollo." Ned led Perry into the breakfast room, motioning where food could be found on the sideboard. "Or should I say Viscount Orlando?"

Tamsin and Rowland looked up at Ned. He felt their eyes prying, as if they too recognized that something extraordinary was unfolding amid his morning conversation with Perry. They'd better not ask him about it, because Ned did not yet understand what had suddenly happened to him.

"Give Rollo the message." Perry prodded Ned's elbow.

Ned held out a letter that had been folded and sealed with a wafer. "This came for Viscount Orlando, carried by one of the Fairchilds' servants, who is in the kitchen awaiting your answer."

Rowland broke the wafer, read the letter, and then held it aloft as if triumphant. "The gods of Olympus smile upon us!"

Lizzie came in, dressed in her gold-linen morning gown that Ned had painted last spring. Beautiful, as usual. Ned repressed a smile when Rowland sat up straight and stuttered a hello. Of all the possible ardor Perry had pointed out at the averil, the man had missed this one.

"Good morning, Lizzie," Tamsin said. "Rowland is about to share the details of his scheme."

"Aye. We begin our work this morning. Read this, Tom." Rowland handed Tamsin the letter, which she read aloud.

> To the Honorable Viscount Orlando de Flores.
> Felicitations. After our intriguing tête-à-tête yesterday, I have apprised my host, Mr. Sheldrake Fairchild, Esquire, and he too wishes to hear more. We beg you to join us today at Mr.

Fairchild's house. Is noon a satisfactory hour?
Your &c., Danvers Duncombe

"One cast of my fishing line into the pool, and I've already got a nibble." Rowland clapped his hands as if delighted.

Perry seemed pleased too, leaving Ned to ponder what else he and Rowland planned, while also wondering when the pair of worldly-wise intelligencers might recognize Tamsin's true self.

Lizzie said, "Come with us, Rollo, when the doctor visits Camilla. Perhaps we can ask Mr. Fairchild to explain the arrangements for the mortgage payments we've been making."

Tamsin agreed, but remained mute. Ned had to admire that she continued to play at being Tom so very well, with only Ned and Lizzie to see how she hid her fright over Camilla.

Ned said, "First, Mr. Fairchild should read Absolom's will and testament. Perhaps Absolom left us more commands about what we should do about Marborne."

"Aye, ye galloping Tartar hordes," Perry said. "You might be longing to take on too much of a single day."

Ned saw then that Perry's jests in fact offered care, as if he considered the Foxes his charges. Did Tamsin perceive that?

"Fine, Perry," Rowland said. "Toss a wash basin on our enthusiasm. For now, let's be sure each of you understands how we'll defeat our enemies."

"Without touching one farthing of our mortgage and taxes savings," Tamsin added.

"Indeed." Rowland then explained his plan and the role each of them was to play.

— TAMSIN —

ROWLAND'S PLAN WAS easy to understand. First, Lizzie must shyly present the opportunity to make a fortune selling her painting collection, using an art dealer introduced by the Princess Mary. Tamsin (as Tom) would be Doubting Thomas, complaining that the opportunity required haste and an initial investment.

Then Orlando would pounce on the idea, promising the dealer and his adept assessor would come to Cambridge tomorrow to value Lizzie's collection. The day's goal was to excite Mr. Duncombe and Mr. Fairchild, and to draw Hawksmoor and Sir Isaiah into joining the opportunity Lizzie presented.

"And tomorrow, what's the next step?" Tamsin asked.

Rowland said, "Do you remember, Tom, how you used to run a rig with Tamsin whenever Absolom invited his Cambridge colleagues to a fest? How you'd swap names, with you in skirts and Tamsin in pantaloons?"

"Oh, I love a masquerade," Perry said. Tamsin worried momentarily that she was found out, but Perry showed no sign of seeing her as she truly was.

Rowland's idea was that Ned and Tom play the "art dealer and his adept," who would offer Lizzie outrageous payment on the spot for one painting and make wild claims about the value of their neighbors' paintings.

"And in the end, Rollo, what happens?" Lizzie said.

"The dealer shall collect his fee in advance, and then pack up the paintings to take them to Paris."

"And never be seen again," Perry said.

"I like your plan," Tamsin said, "especially because it plays on their greed without stripping away *all* of our neighbors' wealth and dignity."

Perry frowned. "I am desolated. Stripping your enemies would add great jollification to our efforts."

Lizzie, ignoring Perry, expressed doubts. "Some of our neighbors might be swept up by mistake."

"We can identify our true enemies while the gambol is in progress," Rowland said.

Tamsin said, "We must restore investments to anyone who joins in error. For the sake of Absolom's honor." However, she intended secret revenge, for the sins against Camilla perpetuated by the Fairchilds and Lady Candecote. Ned and Tom would agree that they must be treated as enemies, even if they hadn't helped cheat Absolom.

Ned and Lizzie murmured agreement.

"But—" Perry began.

Tamsin held out her hand to silence him. "This work must be conducted under Absolom's rules and under our own rules for restorations. Now, how does this gambol ensnare and uncover our enemies?"

Rowland said, "The principals we want to join in this scheme are Hawksmoor, Sir Isaiah, Fairchild, and Heydon. I want to involve Mr. Duncombe…" He paused, which made Tamsin wonder what he was up to. "because I think he will persuade the others to join."

Tamsin said, "I overheard most of them at the last assizes discussing London investment ideas, especially ideas for ready money instead of two-year or four-year investments. And Sir Isaiah and Mr. Fairchild also own several paintings."

"Each canvas is worth more," Ned said, "than a solicitor or a baronet like Sir Isaiah should be able to afford."

Rowland said, "I overheard how Heydon intends to help his bankrupt brother by buying his paintings. This gambol will appeal to his need to gain from that investment."

"What role does Mr. Frake play?" Ned asked.

Perry said, "I shall be master of the secondary task of milking the pigeons. I shall discover the names of men in blind syndicates that hold your mortgages. Then—"

"What?" Ned and Lizzie asked at the same moment.

Ned puzzled more. "Blind syndicates?"

Tamsin startled. She'd kept Absolom's secret too long.

"T–Tom, I must tell the others." Rowland stared at her, as if demanding to speak. "As I told Tom last night, Perry and I have discovered that for the last two years, your payments have gone to a syndicate with secret investors who bought the mortgages. Further, the syndicate holds forged papers that claim the mortgages run another ten years."

"Ten years!" Lizzie exclaimed.

"It is a fraud. Which we shall uncover in days to come." Rowland said that while still staring at Tamsin. Then he nodded, having safely taken that revelation upon himself. She didn't have to confess to her cousins that she'd kept Absolom's secrets from them. She wasn't ashamed about keeping the secret, or annoyed that Rowland revealed it. Instead, she was simply relieved that Rowland was taking on part of her burden.

"How under heaven will you do that?" Ned asked. "How do you uncover a fraud?"

Perry said, "I shall find the mortgages and records in London. And when I discover who holds your fraudulent mortgages, you can be sure they will be brought to—"

"Justice," Lizzie said.

"You are so kind, mademoiselle." Perry kissed his hand in tribute to her. "I was about to say, 'brought to the gates of hell.'"

"Will you return to London today?" Tamsin asked. "If so, take one of our horses. Do you agree, Lizzie?"

"Yes." She turned to Rowland, clutching his sleeve. "You cannot go about as a tatterdemallion while pretending to be a man of wealth. There's a suit for you in my workroom."

Lizzie took Rowland away to dress him, with perhaps more pleasure shining from his face than he might care to reveal. Perry and Ned scavenged the remains of breakfast makings.

That left Tamsin a moment to reflect on Rowland's plan, through which a narrow stream of rational fairness flowed, like a narrow ditch in the fens. She'd have to explain to him why it was important to pursue the Fairchilds, for Camilla's safety and freedom, as well as to obtain justice for Marborne.

She pressed at her Archangel, grateful that at least she no longer carried Absolom's secret alone.

— NED —

WHILE WAITING FOR Tamsin, Ned wanted to ask about the notions Perry stirred up regarding Heydon and Lizzie. And about the doctor. After the others had departed, he had a query half formed, but

Perry clutched Ned's arm, holding him back where the morning sun illuminated the breakfast room.

"Mr. Wijck, my dear friend, today is the day you learn to be a significantly more artful thief. You shall open the way for me, as your first lesson."

"You're going to steal from the Fairchilds?" Ned couldn't hide his astonishment. "That's against our rules of restoration."

"I should like to hear those rules when we have time. The purpose of our gambol is to deprive enemies of what they've taken from you. For that, we need evidence." Perry came close enough to whisper. "Sweet chucking, we seek information, not to light-finger their silver and jewels."

"What shall I do?"

"I won't be joining your invasion of the Fairchild house. What you must do for me is open the window in your solicitor's office. And drop your kerchief outside the window, so that I can see which window is the one I should enter."

"How can you—you're a large man. It's a bright day. Someone will see you."

"No one ever sees me. Now, my dear friend, last night Rollo swore an oath to Tom." Perry again spoke intimately.

"What kind of oath?"

"He called it a tinkers' oath, and says he swore it on Doctor Absolom's bones. Do you know that oath? Aye, you do. Now, I shall make that pledge to you. Though I can swear only upon my own bones."

"Why?" Ned turned. The two men stood a hand's breadth apart, which mangled Ned's composure.

"Because I never met your Uncle Absolom—who, I believe, is not your blood-uncle, Mr. Wijck."

"I mean, Mr. Frake, why are you throwing your lot in with ours? You know we are threadbare."

"Because you have merry times, with your highway robbery and swindles." Perry grinned. "It will be a holiday, finding the cove that cheated Lizzie's family, after the time we've spent hunting Monmouth's supporters."

Ned's throat tightened in disappointment, yet unsure what he wanted Perry to say, since an oath should be enough.

"I was taught to believe it is an honor blessed by the angels when a man swears his faith and honesty."

"I suppose it is that." Perry brightened. "Yet what do I know? I've never sworn an oath beyond my own brothers before. Henceforth, you shall call me Perry and I shall call you Ned, because we will now work together as if we were—"

"Brothers at arms?" Ned offered, while considering what kind of oath he might offer in return.

"I wouldn't call it that. But I shall allow you a day and a night to think whether that's all you'd like it to be."

29

Borrowed Coats

"STOP FIDDLING WITH that coin, Rollo. Please hold still while I tie your cravat."

Lizzie's scolding added to the disturbance whirling in Rowland's belly from having her so near again. She adjusted his buttons and lace, combed and tied back his hair, touching him with her bare fingers.

(Calm my wild horses. More than the Bard might claim, my own Dark Lady smells like an English summer's day.)

"You look well, Duke Orlando."

"Viscount," Rowland said.

"As you say, your lordship. You were never a *beau coc* vainly amazing himself in Mary's court. But if you could afford the clothes, lambkin, you could readily play the part."

The suit Lizzie lent him did not resemble the satin finery of Rowland's own court suit and wig (unclaimed pawn purchased in Amsterdam), yet such a fine suit raised Lord Orlando to the level of wealthy Continental gentlefolk, a sensible man prepared to do business among the best of England.

One color carried through all the suit's pieces, called French mole in Paris, a grey-brown not too ostentatious for a gentleman at business. The silk overcoat had deep cuffs with brass buttons molded in the shape of acorn caps. The gold epaulets added to the suit's richness without shouting cockscomb any more than did the ocean of lace at his neck and cuffs. The slim pantaloons that buttoned below the knee and the light tweed weskit (the same length as the coat; the style both Charles II and Louis preferred in their courts) was lined with cream silk. Twenty useless buttons down each side of the coat, with the weskit boasting another dozen down each side.

"The silk stockings show my shapely calves to advantage."

Lizzie tapped her finger on his hand, acknowledge the jest, but refused to compliment him. "Please take care not to ruin those stockings. And you can wear this periwig. We liberated it in the same restoration. Never before worn, I'm sure."

Chestnut curls, the same color as his own hair, but cascading down past the frothy cravat. Parted and peaked at the crown—this year's favorite in Paris—so that even Perry would have to stretch to peer over the top of Rowland's wig-crowned head.

Perry caught Rowland when everyone prepared to walk to the Fairchild house. "A fine gentleman you make, Senor Orlando. A word, please, about a bit of learning from my prowls before breakfast. Tom and Lizzie sleep in the same room."

"I'm not surprised, given the vast multitudes living in the house." Rowland struggled not to laugh out loud. "But it means the same as you and me sleeping in the same room."

"And what meaning do you take?"

"That they are not going to marry each other."

"O how that assuages my distress. Now, given that Tom is not her *amour*, I also believe Miss Ysabel Foxe does *not* seek a love match with Heydon. From the exchange that Ned and I saw yesterday, your Lizzie seeks only a business arrangement with him."

Perry wandered away to once more latch onto Ned, leaving Rowland devastated, as if he'd been gutted with a dull blade. Though perhaps this time, Perry hadn't intended as much. Except the blasted man often as not said the opposite of what he meant. *Not* seeking a love match...only a business arrangement. How to learn more...what even could he ask without betraying himself?

Perry and Ned, now enjoying first-name familiarity, kept lagging behind while Ned explained where each trail and lane led, and the best ones used each season for crossing any portion of Marborne parish or for visiting neighbors. Ned's telling revived Rowland's memory of the Gordian knot of lanes and cow paths crossing the parish. Before trekking up a gradual rise to the Fairchild house, they crossed two ditches, both in better repair than Rowland remembered about local waterworks.

"How far are we walking?" Perry asked.

"The Fairchild house is nearer to Cambridge than is our house," Ned said.

"You'd think," Lizzie said, "the elder Mrs. Fairchild might have moved the whole household to London. She obviously longs for fine society."

"Camilla wouldn't like that," Tamsin said.

"Aye." Ned agreed. "That ladette is happy to play silk dress-up for a fête. But you can't keep a wild creature like Camilla in the city."

"Show me," Perry said, "the least observable path to your neighbor's house."

While Ned and Perry chatted, Lizzie walked at Rowland's side, her hand on his forearm, as graceful and courtly as ever. She squeezed Rowland's arm when the faux-Tom bent to retrieve a magpie feather from the path. Rowland wished that feather had been his to discover. Court lore in the Low Countries claimed the magpie as auspicious for new love.

That's why Rowland did not spy the feather first. He felt Lizzie squeezing his arm as a reminder that he must find hope and courage elsewhere.

Perry had warned him (many times before today). She's *not* seeking a love match—with any cousins or neighbors.

Given Perry's other reported discoveries, Rowland observed that Winwood's hand lingered on Tamsin's arm while they examined the magpie feather. Rowland intended to watch out for whatever scurvy sharp that doctor might be running on his clutch of Foxe cousins. But the doctor did indeed have a *tendre* for Tamsin.

"It's once again too warm too early in the day." Lizzie offered a commonplace remark, like one did when conversation was constrained in Mary's court.

"It pleases me that you speak as friend." Rowland offered a faint teasing note to cover his skittishness.

"Truly?"

"Yes. Yesterday we were at daggers with each other. Today, we can enjoy a walk in the English countryside. Because we've all found enemies greater than each other."

"But it is warm." Lizzie blushing? That wasn't her way. "Or perhaps I'd forgotten what an English summer is like."

Perry emerged from a hedge, Ned trailing behind him. "A half-dozen king's men are in the yard at the Fairchild house."

"The servants are offering them refreshments," Ned said, "while their captain is being entertained inside."

"Two are handsome specimens, with intelligent faces," Perry said. "The other four pistoleers must have been dragged up from the nether alleys of Southwark and loaned dead men's red wool coats to cover their naked selves."

Lizzie sighed.

Tamsin touched her vest as if in prayer.

Rowland prepared for more of her panic over the king's men.

— TAMSIN —

"LIZZIE, GO WITH Winwood to visit Camilla." Tamsin once more directed her cousins' actions, since Ned and Lizzie went ashen and froze on the trail. "Rollo and I shall join you after the Fairchilds' other visitors have departed."

"And Perry and...and me?" Ned spoke in a quieter voice than usual. He glanced from Perry to Tamsin, as if determining—what? Where his loyalties lay?

"You two shall continue as you'd planned," Tamsin said. "I trust Perry shall follow your guidance and take caution in a landscape unfamiliar to him."

Perry turned to Rowland. "You missed out this morning, Rollo, learning that your cousin has endowed me with his trust. He even allows that I may call him Tom."

Perry and Ned disappeared back through the hedge, while Lizzie and Winwood continued down the lane, Lizzie peering nervously over her shoulder three times before the pair of them passed out of sight.

"Shall we seek cover off the road?" Tamsin touched Rowland's arm, intending to guide him to Camilla's favorite oak.

"Hide? As if 'I am pigeon-liver'd and lack gall'?" Rowland teased, which she sensed he'd done more that morning than the previous day.

"We shall climb this tree, Prince Hamlet, for a view of the territory and for shade from the hot morning sun. Camilla can climb this tree in skirts, so you can too. Take care not to harm your exquisite suit before Lizzie can sell it. Else she'll have your head for it."

"You liberated this suit in a highway robbery? It's French, and it's never been worn."

"A lord cheated Ned's agent in London out of the price of one of his paintings. And we happened to be on the same empty road leaving London that evening."

"Ah. Recompense for a lost forgery."

"A restoration from a thief, as I see it."

They settled in the boughs where she and Camilla often met to trade...confidences. After many dry days, the tree smelled of sunburned dust and that sneezy odor of musty oak. The day's heat was gathering. It was too early for harvest activities, and animals had been driven to the commons much earlier, so no workers appeared in the local fields. Only the lace-web spiders spinning their webs had enough energy to do any work.

"I'm impressed," Rowland said, "that you recognize Shakespeare each time I quote the Bard. I learned by suffering long hours of punishment, inscribing whole acts of plays on cheap paper with a ragged quill that wouldn't mend."

"You forced a recitation on us, Rollo, each time you were released from your chastisement. That, and three different times you forced us to act out *Henry V* under your direction when we were snowed in, with no larger spaces for our endeavors than the great room and the barn."

"Yet I let Lizzie be Prince Hal the last time, while I played Pistol. 'To England will I steal, and there I'll steal.'" Rowland mused on that memory, sober faced. "The king's men aren't seeking me. Else they'd be at Revelstone."

"That's what you continue to claim, Rollo." She didn't want it to be Rowland they sought, but she (his own cousin) had thought him to be a traitor, so the king's men might also.

"Today they came seeking *you*. Because yesterday Mr. Leighton Fairchild rode to Cambridge to call the king's men to hunt the highwaymen who attacked Lord Hawksmoor. They've come now to hear Leighton's complaint."

While feeling she might catch fire and perish, Tamsin forced her most rational voice. "Leighton was not in Hawksmoor's carriage yesterday. He cannot know—"

"No, Leighton saw how his pistol-shot wife is playing dress-up. And he hates you. Be assured, Leighton will beg them to ask Mr. Warboys to describe his attackers, all the while hoping he can point their enquiry toward Tom Foxe."

"No one would think to attend to the ravings of a drunken man in the summer heat. Who shot his own wife. Accident or not, he will have to admit it eventually. As soon as Camilla is strong enough to tell her story." Tamsin's fury flared again, at what Camilla endured from Leighton.

"While that may be," Rowland said, "I'm seeking a way to help you out of your predicament. Until I do, you must trust that I can help you sail into calm waters."

Tamsin, unwilling to quarrel, because Rowland was the best hope for both Marborne and for revenge for Camilla, deepened her tones to sound more like Tom. "The singular help I need is to ensure that our family and the parish don't founder on the jagged rocks of mortgage and taxes."

"No, I mean…" Rowland clasped her hand, squeezing it. "I've been waiting for you to tell me. If I say it, you'll think that I seek to humiliate you. And I don't wish that at all. I deeply admire your fortitude and spirit."

She wiggled away, adding a mere inch between them. "Are you about to declare yourself, like Perry with Ned?"

"No. I shall declare that I'm hugely proud of you. You do better for your family than any hero in England. I shall trade you a secret. You preserve mine, and I shall never reveal yours."

"What's your secret?"

"I'm not, in truth, the best intelligencer. More a boastful Falstaff than a brilliant prince in disguise. My masters in Paris and Holland used me to prowl locked rooms, to bear messages between lords, to gamble with foolish lords. I was briefly an aide de camp in Monmouth's militia in Holland, because my secret master wanted to learn how those men were related to rebel supporters back in England. I've often relied more on my innocent face than my talents for subterfuge."

"But Uncle Absolom insisted that he had engaged the best intelligencer."

"He may have believed that, but I've learned that you are much better than me." He lifted her hand and kissed the back of it. "Tamsin."

You could hear those lace-web spiders spinning for all the time it took Tamsin to speak, while her pulse throbbed.

"Did you know yesterday?" She coughed out those words. The idea of Rowland knowing throughout the averil threatened to serve up pure humiliation.

"No, Tamsin. You are quite good. I learned doing what you told me not to do. Before dawn, I visited the invalid's room."

"Then Tom told you. He always does whatever you ask."

"No, Tom kept your secret. But he told a story that, much later, led me to realize you two had switched places. Like you did that time the bishop visited Mr. Gamlingay. Remember? When Tom curtsied, he tripped on his skirts and broke wind."

"All the while insisting that it was me who raised a ruckus and so must apologize to the bishop for being rude." She appreciated the brief levity, aware that Rowland was being kind. Helpful. "You put Tom and me up to that gambol, after Gamlingay complained to Absolom about the bishop wanting to bury his holy nose too deeply in ancient parish business."

"And Lizzie declared that we must do something for the dear old rector. You must admit, Tamsin, that all my ideas come from good, if not pure, motives."

"Aye, but..."

The leaves of the tree shook. The red-coated militia thundered past on the lane below, the sound echoing up for a long while. The presence of the soldiers interrupted the quiet meditation she needed, to know what to say to Rowland.

"Please don't tell Perry who I am. I shall do it myself at the appropriate moment."

"Perry's humor often intimidates. I've been made to know that myself. I shall leave the revelation to you."

"Let's go now, Rollo." Tamsin shimmied down the bough, leaping ten feet to land in a patch of bloomed-out bluebells.

"How do I..." Rowland hesitated.

"Come on. It's not as high as our old fleet in the oaks."

"But I'm not supposed to harm this suit or stockings." He edged down the boughs, then stopped ten feet from the ground. "I don't want Lizzie angry with me."

"Is that your highest wish for the life God has given you?"

"Perhaps. Yes, I believe it is."

"Jump," Tamsin said.

"I'll end up on my knees and stain this suit."

"God's bodkins! Jump. I'll keep you upright when you land."

She spread her feet to gain a sturdy stance, calling to him again to jump. When he leaped away from the tree, the sun flashed, blinding her, over the endless moments while he fell. She wrapped her arms around him before he landed. He caught his arms at her waist. They rocked for one tick, until he regained his balance and released her.

Tamsin felt his warmth recede. Like how Camilla embraced Tamsin when she was excited. The only moments when anyone held Tamsin close. Almost comforting. Except it wasn't Camilla.

— ROLLO —

"THANK YOU FOR your kind assistance," he said. "You preserved my clothes and hence my soul from the force of Lizzie's vexation."

Rowland stepped away, eyes on the ground, to avoid revealing how it startled him, being in a woman's arms, even though she dressed as a man. Startled, because one touch had rekindled the banked fire of his dreams about Lizzie.

He inspected his splendid suit for signs of tree dirt and twigs, and then finished the question he'd begun in the upper boughs.

"What does Tamsin win by pretending to be Tom?"

"I do it for our family, especially Lizzie. And for the parish. While we plead with the king, we need to preserve a path to return the earldom to a male heir of the Foxe family." She moved away, seemingly ready to change the subject. She pointed to the gap in the hedge. "Let's continue on our journey."

Rowland wasn't finished discussing her predicament. "Perry has already discovered that you and Lizzie go to London at the first of each month."

"Yes, we go begging for an audience with the king, to beseech him to restore the Marborne title, because—"

"Because the Princess Mary prefers that such titles not fall into James's Catholic hands." Rowland finished the thought. "That is not an immense secret."

"We carry pleas that Tom and Absolom have drafted. We shall go seeking an audience once more on the first of September. And October. And again in the chill winds and rain of November, until the king finally agrees to hear our plea."

"Or until Princess Mary has a better idea for Lizzie?" He coaxed his voice into a tease, hoping to hide the ridiculous pity he felt for his own case while trepidation nagged at his soul for what Lizzie might choose, or be forced by Mary, to do.

Not seeking a love match…and surely not with Heydon.

"You have forced me to see that truth, Rollo. I've been too happy to have Lizzie home again. I've been willfully blind to the obvious. Lizzie longs to return to court life."

He needed to change the subject, lest he reveal his own longings. "And what about Tamsin's future? How do you get on in the world if you must play Tom much longer? And how shall you emerge like a butterfly, when the parish learns that 'Thomasine' is not disfigured from pox, but as pretty as you ever were."

"What a kind thing to say, Rollo."

"Do you look in the mirror," Rowland said, "only to see a reflection of Tom? How do we get you out of this quandary?"

"One problem at a time." Tamsin brushed a bit of detritus from the hedges off Tom's good business suit. "That's what Absolom advised me, ever since all this hucker-mucker came home to Revelstone this winter."

"You are an excellent creature, Tamsin. If it will strengthen your trust in me as an ally, I shall promise on Absolom's bones to never underestimate you in this life."

"How kind. Perhaps I should promise the same." She glanced around as if to see whether they'd be interrupted. "But if you're not the best intelligencer on the Continent, why should we trust your wild gambol, Rollo?" No better options were at hand, but Tamsin needed to know where they really stood with Rowland.

"Ah. Our master in Amsterdam had a penchant for punishment. When we uncovered betrayals to the Crown among Englishmen living on the Continent, he liked to strip them of their wealth without invoking the king's name. Perry and I learned to run fantastical schemes under his instruction."

"Then you are wealthy from your time abroad?"

"Not at all. My masters never managed to find funds to pay me what they claimed I was worth to the Crown."

"Then you don't mind the short rations and lack of servants at Revelstone?"

"At least I'm not sleeping on straw in a barracks."

"Here's the Fairchild house," Tamsin said. "I beg that the secretive Viscount Orlando of Spain never forget that I'm Tom Foxe, Master of Revelstone."

"Catalonia, not Spain."

— NED —

HE BATTED AGAIN at bees that wandered from their nectar-feast to hover in front of his face. Ned waited behind a thicket of black-thorn and honeysuckle where the lane branched to the Fairchild house. He'd grown twitchy over the long wait, spying the militia in the distance.

Hearing the buzzing bees so close by.

Pondering the instructions for aiding Perry's planned theft.

Bearing the weight of Perry's hand on his shoulder.

Warm breath tickling his small neck hairs while Perry tutored him on the methods for prowling a house.

Ned now yielded to Perry's teasing questions, knowing he'd be exposing the sealed corners of his own soul. And…he…liked it. Perry had joined their cause. He was making everything…at least more interesting.

"To hear Rollo tell it, Ned, you all tumbled up together like a litter of abandoned puppies. Did no one sing and feed you hot milk with your buttered toast?"

"I suppose Mrs. Bell did when we were babies. However, Absolom was our caretaker. He didn't play baby's nurse."

"Would that I had met the man, for Rollo declares his uncle to be the fount of Wisdom and Honor, a preserver of Truth."

"Yes, that was our Uncle Absolom."

"Did he teach you Shakespeare too? Rollo never shuts up about the brilliance of his Bard."

"No, he bought brushes for me. My father taught painting."

"That does show honor. But Doctor Foxe was a scholar. What did he know of the wonders you are capable of? That you reveal the glory of God's creation in your work?"

Ned's ears burned from that compliment, uncooled by the soft breeze of Perry's whispers. A month ago, Absolom had said similar words, which Ned was too shy to repeat for Perry. ("We must ensure that you have every chance to manifest the glory of Creation in the way you do. You began as a good soul with nice hands, and you've grown to be a greatly talented man.")

Instead of repeating the cherished words from Absolom, Ned diminished his uncle's claim. "Absolom insisted I was talented. That I had nice hands.

"To be sure, Ned. You have exceedingly nice hands. And nice silvery Dutch eyes. Do people resent your Dutch ways?"

"I've only ever lived here. Though I can imitate my father's accent. What makes you think otherwise?"

"You walk like tall Dutchmen I have known."

"Lizzie says I walk like my father. I have no Dutch ways."

"Indeed? That is fantastic news."

"Why?"

"I shan't have to waste time battening down dour Protestant judgments that Dutch gentlemen are taught in their cradles. Still, we shall have to address your natural English reticence." Perry stirred suddenly, stepping away. "Here are Rollo and Tom."

"I'd best join them, if I'm to play the role you want."

"Aye. Though the moments without you shall distress me. Farewell, sweet chucking."

His ears still burning (perhaps not with joy, but near to that), he stepped out of the thicket and onto the narrow lane.

— TAMSIN —

ABSOLOM INSISTED THAT their corner of the shire would be heralded as an idyll in later ages: water-rails in the ditches, warblers and corn buntings in the lush green trees, and hares bounding into the undergrowth. Tamsin found this idyll marred by trepidations about the role she was to play in Rowland's wild gambol. And fears this rig might not secure Camilla's well-being.

Ned, sans Perry, joined Tamsin and Rowland where the lane branched, one lane leading northeast, the other northwest. They took the lesser branch, which ended at the sweeping drive in front of the Fairchild house. Built on the new model, more like new-built houses in London than the old style of Revelstone, the house opened its sleepy eyes on the sheep browsing its broad lower lawns.

The liveried man who opened the door wanted to refuse them before Tamsin could state her business, but she insisted.

"Good morning, Mr. Clopton. I hope you and your family are keeping well. I know Dr. Oakes is tending to Mrs. Leighton. Can you tell me, please, if she fared well over the night? I wonder if we might visit her."

"We haven't heard news from the doctor. And Mrs. Fairchild insists that Mrs. Leighton can have no visitors today."

Tamsin, seeing that Mrs. Fairchild had backfooted her without even coming to the door, began her request with respect, as Absolom had taught them.

"Thank you, Mr. Clopton. Our cousin, Viscount Orlando, has an invitation from Mr. Duncombe to meet with him here today."

As soon as Tamsin spoke that false name, Rowland bowed, Duncombe's invitation in his hand, the curls of his chestnut periwig bouncing and bright in the sunlight.

"Mr. Duncombe has gone riding with Mr. Leighton." Mr. Clopton was unsure what to do. (How distressing it must be to tread carefully with the elder Mrs. Fairchild ruling this house.) "Perhaps you might wait in the blue salon."

That pretentiously named room was no larger than a morning room, but had been stripped of any housewifery items. Rowland and Ned strolled along the edges of the room, studying the paintings on the wall, both with hands clasped behind them. Rowland glanced at Ned, a question in his eyes.

"Thank you, Mr. Clopton. Would you…" Tamsin paused. Tom, who should be an earl, would not beg from his solicitor's servant.

"Please give my regards to Mr. Fairchild and inquire whether he has time to wait on me. I should like to hear Doctor Foxe's will today."

When Mr. Clopton left them, Ned said, "Two of the paintings are signed by a Master. Genuine, I believe. Another two are mine, sold in London last autumn."

"Excellent." Rowland hissed the S sound. "We launch our gambol now, with Fairchild and Mr. Duncombe."

Tamsin said, "We also need Sir Isaiah and Hawksmoor."

"And Heydon. Our true target," Rowland said. "We might not be able to gather them all in until tomorrow."

Mr. Clopton returned to escort them to the solicitor's well-up-holstered, comfortable office. Tamsin mastered herself while dreading that she must now face the man who'd helped swindle Absolom and the Foxe family.

"May I offer you my deepest condolences, Mr. Foxe."

Mr. Fairchild rose from his chair to shake each visitor's hand, greeting Tamsin first, then Ned. His eyes rested on Rowland, not recognizing him, since the Fairchilds came to Cambridge after Rowland had gone into service.

"You are kind to say so," Tamsin said. In truth, she saw him as the father of a devil who'd hurt her friend. "This is Miss Foxe's cousin, Viscount Orlando de Flores of Catalonia. He and his sister are staying with us while they search for a home in London."

"Honored, sir. I am delighted to make your acquaintance." Rowland bowed too deeply to the untitled solicitor. "Miss Foxe says you have brought significant aid to her family's business."

"Pleased to know you, sir." The solicitor shook Rowland's hand, faint twitters of surprise around his eyes. "We meet under sad times. Shall I ring for refreshments?"

Tamsin declined hospitality for all of them. "Can Miss Foxe be summoned from Mrs. Leighton's room? That is, if you are prepared to read our uncle's will today."

Mr. Fairchild offered his visitors velvet-cushioned chairs. Tamsin thanked him, yet too aware that she'd just shaken the hand of one of Absolom's swindlers.

Tamsin cast a question to Rowland with a flick of her eyes, about whether he should be present for a private family matter. But Rowland took a seat behind her without acknowledging her glance. Ned edged his seat nearer to a window, crossing his legs when he sat, as if folding into a tight, narrow blade.

Lizzie appeared and took a seat beside Tamsin. Mr. Fairchild began to speak, allowing neither time nor space for Tamsin to inquire about Camilla.

30

The Fairchild House

"GOOD DAY, MISS Foxe," the solicitor said when Lizzie entered. "We can begin. Here is the traditional preamble."

Rowland felt the man had been dressed to portray a noble man of law and letters, with his white starched collar hinting at the old Puritan style, and his tailored blue velvet coat and vest as good as a London tailor might offer. He wore a fine periwig with curls to remind you of a judge, not a courtier. Everything a good country solicitor should be. Except...

Fairchild was a scrawny man. He had thin lips but a pudgy nose with a bulbous beak. Gin blossoms bloomed across his nose and cheeks. His hands shook as he held up the paper. He began reading, his trumpeting voice fading at the end of each sentence.

> I, Absolom Caius Foxe, a modest scholar at Trinity College, Cambridge, do make this testament from Revelstone House, Marborne Parish, Cambridgeshire.

Rowland, rigid in his chair, copying the demeanor of a Spaniard with whom he'd played *vingt-et-un* in Paris, the aide to the Grand Master of some military order. Though his pulse beat in his ears at the rustling of Lizzie's skirt, he did not turn his head.

Mr. Fairchild interrupted his reading. "When your uncle asked me to write this last month, I learned much about him that I never knew." He then fumbled to find his place, though he'd read a mere two lines.

I am the last surviving son of the thirteenth Earl of Marborne, Caius David Foxe, and his wife Sarah née Anglesey. With this testament, I complete my duties as executor of my father's estate, which I have performed faithfully for these past twenty-five years. I set the provisions in this testament for the future care of my father's descendants and his legacy.

Because he'd been introduced as Orlando, Rowland sat discreetly and observed the twitches and sighs that betrayed his cousins' grief. Ned peered at length out one window, then the next, his hand fingering an invisible something, likely with Perry on his mind. Tamsin, impatient to see her friend Camilla, shrugged within Tom's suit coat whenever the solicitor paused to pontificate, but she swiped at her eyes whenever Absolom's name was mentioned in the reading.

Lizzie kept glancing between Ned and Tamsin, her throat flushed, as if with emotion, her red-rimmed eyes brimming. She had her handkerchief out, the one from her mother. She touched it to one corner of her eyes. That sight had Rowland rubbing at his own eyes. All of them had barely begun to mourn their uncle.

Imprimis, upon my death, I beg that within the first day of my passing my soul be committed to God, if He will have me, and my body laid to rest in the Foxe family vault beneath Marborne church.

The solicitor said, "He must have advised you, Master Foxe, so that you were able to complete that first item. You did well. Here is the next request."

Item. My eldest brother Samuel, the designated heir of the Marborne title and land, perished while leading a Royalist militia in the conflagrations that began in 1642.

Fairchild said, "I insisted that Doctor Foxe confirm the correct date, so you may be assured this is accurate. And I advised your uncle that this next item did not seem appropriate. However, he insisted, disregarding my counsel."

Reading again:

> The Marborne title, declared extinct under the Common-wealth, should have been restored and returned to my father's heir. That legacy should now be conveyed to my father's next eligible heir. We await restoration of the title by His Majesty, James II, or his successor, who will also adjudicate the possession of Marborne holdings, which Charles II granted me only for my lifetime.

The pettifogging solicitor was a rabbity sort of fellow. Not like a quick-witted, rapid-fleeing hare in the copses. No, like the kind raised in cages for meat and fur, eyes too close, a pink and itchy nose. Fairchild held the will close in his two paws, either unblinking as he read or blinking too much when he spoke. He'd be the model of a country solicitor, except liver spots mottled his forehead. A web of red veins spread across his cheeks and nose, the kind of web spun by the spiders of wine or gin.

Rowland considered it remarkable that this solicitor might have helped Absolom's enemies, given that the man must be deep in his cups much of the time.

> Item. My other brothers, Walter Foxe and Josiah Foxe, together with their sons were also lost in the plague of 1665. As a consequence, I have enjoyed the blessing of caring for my brothers' grandchildren. All these Foxe family heirs have reached the age of majority. I hereby give them equal parts of the residue of my goods and chattel and my interest in the Marborne estate, with the command to preserve Marborne in its entirety, as long as they are able to do so. They shall know how this is best achieved. For each, I leave these particulars.

"These next items you will most regard." Mr. Fairchild wore small oval spectacles with wire rims. As he read, he often pushed the spectacles up his nose, so smudges clouded the lenses.

Item. From my own sparse possessions, I leave the following for those who might find better success than I did in setting the world right again:

> To Ysabel Flores Foxe, the ancient book of prayer given me to hold by her grandmother, also named Ysabel, and two paintings in the Dutch style that hang in my room.

"Miss Foxe, you know where to find this prayer book?" The solicitor peered over his cloudy spectacles. "Your uncle didn't direct me to record the location of these items."

Lizzie drew a handkerchief over her face before she nodded. Then she leaned over to whisper to Tamsin. The solicitor waited, Absolom's will shaking in his hands.

"Continue, sir." Tamsin's eyes were also red-rimmed.

"We shall pause if you need a moment." The solicitor rattled the paper.

"No, it's fine." Behind her kerchief, Lizzie sounded hollow.

> To Thomas Foxe, the antiquaries preserved in my room, to do with them whatever he chooses.

> To Thomasine Foxe, my horse called Thunder and my dog Caesar, together with the care of all creatures in the house, and all my books not consigned to others' care.

"Tom...uh, Mr. Foxe, you shall carry this request to your sister?"

"Yes, sir, I shall. Please continue." Tamsin pressed at her heart.

Rowland still hadn't perceived what that gesture meant. Not colic. A prayer? It was a wonder Tamsin's Protestant neighbors hadn't called her out as a secret Roman.

> To Rowland Foxe, my volumes of Shakespeare and all else he finds and cherishes in the place he knows to look. "Let me be that I am and seek not to alter me."

Mr. Fairchild glanced up, pushing down his spectacles while he addressed Tamsin. "I asked him to explain that, but Doctor Foxe said it was a quotation. Mr. Foxe, shall you be able to find your cousin, so that this item can be carried out?"

Rowland might have heard Tamsin's answer, except for a moment he wasn't the scheming, cosmopolitan Orlando, but instead a small boy begging to read a leather-bound volume, *Henry V* etched on its cover. Despite years of separation, Absolom knew what was to be found at the core of Rowland's heart.

— N E D —

WHAT MIGHT BE a bee bumped against a window. Ned, too, was anxious to escape from the stuffy, close confines of this room. He held his breath, waiting for a chance to perform the task Perry commanded. But then the sound of his own name pierced his anxious thoughts.

> To Eduard Wijck, the only son of Ysabel Foxe's mother, the remainder of paintings that hang in my room and elsewhere in Revelstone House, especially the ones he admired as a child.

Ned was unprepared for how the words struck him, as if he heard Absolom's own low-pitched voice again, the sound resonating from deep in the small man's body. Calm, sure of himself.

Tamsin had bowed her head, hiding her eyes.

Lizzie squeezed her eyes tight, one finger rubbing the thumb of her other hand.

Rowland turned his head, raised his arm as a cover, and sneezed. Perhaps only Ned saw him wipe at his eyes.

The solicitor read on, unaware of how undone the cousins were. "Master Foxe, you shall have to manage the next action." The solicitor paused to shake an admonishing finger.

Ned stirred, preparing himself. He too had to manage an action, when he could divert attention from the sentiments of the moment. How to do what Perry needed?

"Yes, sir, I shall. Please continue." Tamsin remained calm. The rest of them jittered.

> To my dear friend Theophilus Gamlingay, I give my amethyst ring, which he has long admired. I also leave him with the hope that the benefice of Marborne parish remain with him as long as he cares to hold it.

"My gracious Savior!" Ned exclaimed. "A wasp!"

He dashed for the tall window near a side table, jerked back the bolt, and thrust the window open. He tugged his kerchief from his pocket and waved it, hoping it worked. However, he didn't trust his eyes or his pattering heart, because he could not spy Perry anywhere in the landscape.

Returning to his seat, Ned made an excuse for his frantic act. "Excuse me, sir. My sister Ysabel reacts badly to wasp stings."

Ned believed everyone in that small, confining room must hear the thumping of his heart.

— ROLLO —

PEERING OUT THE window over Ned's shoulder, Rowland spied the outlines of a tall, gaunt man's face deep in the hedge, like the Green Man in tales. Perry, ready to prowl.

Assured that they'd succeed, this band of brothers, Rowland attended to the solicitor, who commenced reading again.

Item. I appoint Thomasine Foxe to serve as executor.

Mr. Fairchild paused. "I warned your uncle that he might be placing too large a burden on Miss Thomasine, since she has been ill. Yet he insisted you would all agree with his choice."

"Yes," Lizzie murmured. "We all agree."

"Please know that I will do whatever I can to assist her. And all of you." The solicitor began to read again.

Miss Foxe may name an Overseer if she sees such a need. I shall not presume to choose for her. She will know what best actions to take.

I make this, my last will and testament, on the first day of July in the Year of Our Lord, 1685.

Witnessed and sealed before Mister Barnaby Prickwillow, constable of Marborne parish, and Doctor Winwood Oakes, a physician.

As the solicitor finished reading the single page of the will, his hands shook more, like a man gripped by the tremor of age. But no, the fellow couldn't be more than fifty, perhaps younger. From Rowland's experience in French courts, a fading figure like this had an assistant close by, someone who did the real work that this soul could no longer manage on his own.

An assistant who'd helped the solicitor swindle Absolom.

"And, yes, young Tom." The solicitor was answering a question from Tamsin. "We shall prove this will before the magistrate. I shall seek an appointment for Monday next."

At the moment the reading concluded, the twin office doors opened—handsomely painted in the style popular in Paris for the past ten years—and Mrs. Fairchild entered, her grey silk skirts whispering as she crossed the room.

"My poor children, I haven't had a moment to condole with you today." Her voice offered all the musical pleasure of a hymn sung in an empty church. She offered a tender handshake, first to Lizzie, then Tom and Ned. "And Lord Orlando, I am honored you have come to visit."

Mrs. Fairchild mastered the room, ushering them away for refreshments in the blue salon. She spoke of the room in the French way. She was, Rowland surmised, Mr. Fairchild's keeper, perhaps even the one who assisted in swindling the Foxes. The doctor's visit had interfered with her minder duties.

Lizzie caught Rowland's arm, handkerchief still in her hand, and balanced on tiptoes to whisper in his ear. "Winwood can't wake Camilla. Too much poppy syrup, he says. Distract Fairchild and his witchy wife while we do what we must."

Viscount Orlando had to follow the others, not familiar with the house. After Mr. and Mrs. Fairchild passed through the door, the Foxe cousins stopped and condoled together for a moment, Tom and Ned offering comfort to Lizzie. Rowland listened to their whispers, which deepened his respect for Tamsin as the leader of the Foxe cousins. She had wept for Absolom during the reading of the will. Then she'd crafted a plan to remove Camilla from this house.

He stepped up to the task he'd been assigned, greeting Mrs. Fairchild with his best courtly manner, while his partners in this gambol deserted him, turning all their thoughts to Camilla.

"Madam, it is kind of you to welcome me, a stranger in this land. I see that you are possessed of the magical touch that turns a house into a beautiful home."

"Oh, sir." She trembled when he bowed lower than warranted and kissed her hand in the French way. "I'm unfamiliar with the modes of address in your country, sir. How shall I address you?"

"Please, madam, call me Lord Orlando. The rest is foolishness from ancient times. We who should be friends must overlook it."

"You are kind to say so, Lord Orlando. What can I offer to increase your comfort?"

Seeing that his cousins needed a moment to finish whispering with each other, Rowland said, "Mrs. Fairchild, may I beg you to tell me about these spectacular paintings in your salon? I was not prepared to encounter such exquisite taste in this bucolic setting."

31

Stealing a Thief

"Camilla is in her room?"

As soon as Tamsin rose from her chair, she whispered that question to Lizzie. Time to find the next action. Leaving the solicitor's office, she pulled the office door shut behind them. Lizzie leaned against the door, her face in her hands, her shoulders shaking, preserving her mourning as cover for their whispers.

"Yes. Winwood is with her. I shall divert the maid who's there."

"Ned." Tamsin tugged his sleeve until they both wrapped their arms around Lizzie. "There's a servants' passage past the last room at the north end of the upper floor. Take her down to the back door. We'll ask Mr. Frake to carry her away."

"To Revelstone?"

"No, Leighton will search there immediately. Take her to the rector's cottage." Tamsin pried the amethyst ring from her thumb. "Have Perry give this to Mr. Gamlingay and beg him to shelter Camilla in Absolom's name."

"I shall go with him," Ned said.

"No, Rollo needs all of us here. Lizzie, you too."

Lizzie said, "You must have ice in your veins, cousin. I thought you'd be frantic."

"But I am." Tamsin held Ned back, since he wanted to rush off. "Where's Perry now?"

"In a moment, he'll be in Mr. Fairchild's office."

"Lizzie, go direct Perry to the back of the house."

Certain he'd heard all, Tamsin caught Rowland's eye. He tapped his lip as if in thought, then he pursued Mrs. Fairchild to the archway that led to her best parlor. His voice carried. "Mrs. Fairchild. Madam. May I beg..."

The racket of company arriving in the yard carried into the anteroom where the cousins whispered together. The front doors were thrust open, banging into Ned. Leighton stomped in, followed by that London fellow, Mr. Duncombe.

"Gad's bobs! You here, Tom?" Leighton gazed past him. "Ned?"

While the sight of Leighton ignited a burning fury that threatened the icy calm Lizzie had commented on, Tamsin appreciated the distraction caused by his arrival.

"Lord Orlando." The London man bowed to Rowland, hat in his hand. "I'm happy you could join me. I wish you good morning, Miss Foxe." Mr. Duncombe bowed much lower to Lizzie, who reached out her hand in greeting, then drew back, clasping her hands to her breast.

"My kerchief! I've dropped it. It's all I have from my mother. Please excuse me a moment." Lizzie fled back to the solicitor's office, closing the door behind her.

Mrs. Fairchild busily coaxed her guests into her parlor, wanting each man to take a seat where she directed. A commanding wave of her hand consigned her son and husband to hard straight chairs near the door, though the two men remained standing, since Lizzie had not yet been seated.

With Camilla's removal underway, Tamsin tore her worries away from the upper room to focus on Rowland's gambol.

Duncombe behaved as a man at a loss for what to do when Lizzie departed. Unable to sit down before Lizzie did, he remained in the center of the room, his violet-and-yellow suit buttoned tight, like a Carlisle game rooster. Rowland came to the man's side and spoke intimately, as if they were friends.

"If I may ask your help, Mr. Duncombe," Rowland said, "how shall I address the Earl of Hawksmoor? We do not have earls in

Catalonia. Our grandees are princes, dukes, marquis, counts, viscounts, and barons. Miss Foxe assures me that her friends will help me understand the customs of your island."

"You are doing well, my honorable friend. I believe our English earls are similar to your Spanish counts."

"Ah. Then I am indeed humbled by the attention his lordship showed my dear sister. Did you hear of that adventure?"

Before Duncombe answered, Lizzie entered the salon. The gentlemen turned toward her, their faces brightening—including Rowland. Tamsin pitied him, since it was a hopeless case.

However, Lizzie didn't acknowledge any of them. Instead, she grasped Mrs. Fairchild's hand and begged for the assistance of her maid. "I had no idea you were entertaining such a crowd, Mrs. Fairchild. I don't mean to importune, but please give me a moment to refresh myself."

Lizzie pretended innocence and did not wait for her hostess's answer before mounting the stairs. Her gold-linen gown flashed in the panels of sunlight from a high window as she hurried to the upper floor, softly calling the maid's name, performing the next step in Tamsin's diversion.

Leighton's voice rose. He had hold of his father's sleeve. "The militia came here? To our house? Why did you not keep them until I returned?"

"They didn't ask for you," Mr. Fairchild said. "They came to inquire about quartering. Your mother explained that we have no room in such a small house."

That soft answer did not turn away Leighton's wrath. He jammed on his hat, the feathers along the rim jiggling in fury. "Which way did they ride? I shall find them."

"Do you mean the king's men?" Tamsin used Tom's most sensible voice. "They did not pass us on the lane. They must have taken the road to the Phoenix and Swan. Or perhaps toward Ely."

This reasonable answer, coming from "Tom," further infuriated Leighton. His coat tails swished as he passed Tamsin, the feather rim of his hat still dancing.

"I say, you fool! My horse!" Leighton shouted at the groom from the open door. He jerked the door closed, slamming it, causing Mrs. Fairchild to shudder as if struck by a blow.

Lizzie returned with a ribbon wrapped in her curls. The men hurried to offer Lizzie their greetings, and in that commotion, Ned disappeared up the stairs.

— NED —

"SEE, NED? THIS is the tincture I gave Mrs. Fairchild last night. It's a small flask, but it should be mostly full, not almost empty." Winwood ran his hands through his hair, agitated, which Ned had never seen in the uncannily calm doctor. "Camilla should have wakened long before now."

"Tamsin insists we move her to safety. Mr. Frake shall carry her away."

"He'll take her home? I mean, to Revelstone?"

"No, to the rector's cottage. You know how to find her there? Good. Lift her into my arms."

"Should we guess who did this to her?"

"Leighton and his witchy mother, I'm sure." Ned shifted his stance when Camilla was in his arms, though she wasn't a significant burden. Her pale ivory color and pulsing blue veins gave him a fright. This ghost was the woman who always found more reason to laugh than anyone else in the county. "Winwood, please keep the servants away while I traverse the back stairs. Then sit where you can't be blamed for this."

"Mrs. Fairchild said that I should find refreshment in the kitchen when I finish my work."

"How rude. Does she think you a servant? Still, it's a good place for you to take cover."

Ned tread the narrow, steep stairs, the weight of his burden causing him to take heavier steps than he wished. He had no idea what to do if he encountered anyone, but with the help of the blessed angels, he saw no one until he spied Perry in the shadows of the eves out back of the house.

"Odds bodkins!" Perry whispered as he took on Ned's burden. "Is she alive?"

"Drugged, the doctor thinks. Do you remember the path I showed you that leads to Mr. Gamlingay's house?"

"Indeed. That's to be her new hostel?"

"Aye. T–Tom says to give the rector this ring." Ned slipped the amethyst ring onto Perry's thumb, though he could only push it to above the first knuckle. "Beg him in Absolom's name to hide her from everyone. Except Winwood Oakes."

"Are we performing this rescue because your cousin Tom is in love with her?" Perry shifted her gently, as if she weighed nothing in his arms.

"We're doing it because she's been trapped in a vipers' nest since her father remarried. We should have removed her before today if we followed Absolom's rules for enlightened people. Go now."

Perry gazed at the pale, sparse figure in a scarlet shawl. "If I didn't already know you were a good man, Ned, I'd be on my knees to you. For the goodness you show your friends." He rubbed the thumb with the ring along Ned's jaw. "I hope I am one, too."

"We shall discuss that when there is a world large enough to accommodate our own needs. I must go play my part in Rollo's gambol." Ned said three more words before Perry was beyond the range of his whispers. "*Afscheid, mijn vriend.*"

Perry, strong enough to carry his burden with one hand, held the other up in farewell, then disappeared into a nearby hedge.

Ned adjusted his cravat and straightened his suit, the same brown wool he'd worn the day before. The black armband still declared mourning. As he walked around the house to the front door, he rubbed where the amethyst ring had scratched his jaw. He slipped into the crowded parlor as if he'd taken a moment to visit the jakes. No one noticed him come in; no one noticed that he'd been gone.

Except for Tamsin, who'd been waiting for him.

Ned nodded, the only reassurance he passed along to her. Tamsin steepled her hands as if offering thanks, her face as ashen as poor Camilla.

32

The Imposters

WHILE PRETENDING TO be Tom Foxe and standing stiff as a sentry, Tamsin worried about how Perry fared, carrying Camilla to safety on the narrow trail to the rector's cottage.

Then Rowland launched his appeal, and Tamsin fiercely governed her mind, listening and considering what must happen.

"My plans have a certain immediate focus, Mr. Duncombe. My cousin Miss Foxe asked me to join with her in a royal opportunity, which will take my attention for several days."

"Pray caution, my dear viscount!" Lizzie exclaimed. "The role of my mentor was to be a secret. Did you not understand?"

Time for the supposed Tom to intervene.

"I am not convinced this is the best action for you, Ysabel. However much your mentor encouraged you."

The allusion that invoked Princess Mary as that mentor sent a wave through the parlor, like a sudden wind on water. The solicitor and Mr. Duncombe tugged at their embroidered coats, glancing at each other as if not knowing who should speak first.

Mrs. Fairchild sought attention, tapping Duncombe's arm, begging but not obtaining a response. Instead, Duncombe said to Lizzie, "You must tell us what your mentor advises."

The lady of the house tried again with her husband, but he shuffled toward Lizzie, like the others, like bees drawn to nectar. Briefly, Mrs. Fairchild's too-white complexion flushed an angry pink. Tamsin saw that they must account for that lady's determination to control everyone. How to warn Rowland?

Lizzie raised her hand, seeking silence. "My friends, please."

"Miss Foxe, if I may." Mrs. Fairchild commanded attention, silk swishing around her. "Please, gentlemen. And Miss Foxe. May I offer refreshments? So that you can converse in comfort?"

"Thank you, Mrs. Fairchild. You are much too kind." Lizzie turned again to the buzzing gentlemen around her. "If I can trust you to be discreet, I should welcome your advice about the business I am planning with Lord Orlando."

Her declaration carried past where Tamsin remained at the archway leading into the parlor. Lizzie's words carried into the foyer, where Heydon was entering the house, trim and tailored in a dove-grey suit of even better quality than Rowland's liberated suit. Notions of snowy lace at his collar and cuffs fluttered when he moved. Heydon removed his immaculate, low-crowned black felted hat, revealing abundant, well-groomed hair, tied into place with a black ribbon.

"What is Miss Foxe asking, Tom?" Heydon spoke softly near Tamsin. He adjusted his cravat. The light reflected in a parlor mirror caught the diamond pin nestled in those folds. "Why are you letting your cousin appeal to these men for business advice?"

"I have no control over Ysabel." If Heydon was their enemy, Tamsin had to weigh each word she spoke. "She conceived of this idea, which she believes can help us with our debts. I hope these gentlemen steer her to safety."

"Yet a stranger has come among you who might not have your family's best interests at heart." A statement, not a question.

Tamsin sought to steer Heydon into Rowland's gambol. "Are you impugning his character? He's not a stranger. They were acquainted for years in Holland."

"No. I mean Mr. Duncombe. He seems eager to strike a mercenary friendship with Miss Foxe and Lord Orlando."

"You distrust him, sir?" If Rowland was wrong about who their enemies were, then perhaps Heydon meant to help. Or to steer them away from one who could reveal him. Still too much they didn't know.

Heydon had his arm on Tamsin's shoulder, drawing her close while he spoke in a low voice. "Remember last summer, when I advised you and your uncle not to consider any offers to buy Marborne land? That gentleman proposed just such a scheme to my brother. I am inclined to resist and distrust such proposals."

Good stars! Heydon had advised Tom once upon a time.

Tamsin felt Tom's suit bunch up around its padding, as if it possessed a spirit longing to betray her. She stood taller, stiffened her shoulders.

Heydon withdrew his arm from Tamsin's shoulder. "You've shaved. It looks well on you, Tom." He studied the scene in the salon with Lizzie, Duncombe, and Orlando. She endeavored to judge this man, though her attention shifted to Camilla's jeopardy every ten ticks of the longcase clock at the end of the room. Before Tamsin said more to Heydon, Mrs. Fairchild greeted him.

"Good morning, Mrs. Fairchild. I was in the neighborhood and stopped to ask after Mrs. Leighton Fairchild. What ghastly fiend attacked her?"

"You are kind to enquire, Lord Heydon. She mishandled a servant's hunting dag. A foolish accident. But she is mending. Won't you join us? I believe you have met all my guests."

Heydon took a moment to acknowledge Mrs. Fairchild's invitation. At last he answered. "You are gracious, madam. However, I shall not stress your household."

"Indeed, your lordship. My husband's friend, Mr. Duncombe, asked if he might invite guests for conversation this morning. And since we are all neighbors and friends, it is no burden." Mrs. Fairchild appeared to sense that Heydon was condescending to her, and therefore responded with more deference than in her initial welcome. "Please let me offer you a chair, your lordship."

Heydon took the seat that Mrs. Fairchild indicated, at Lizzie's right hand. He exchanged quiet words with Lizzie.

The lady of the house had observed proper etiquette for rank. Given that the Marborne title was in abeyance, she didn't offer Tom a seat at all. Therefore, Tamsin remained stiffly near where Heydon sat and near the door, her eyes often darting up the nearby stairs.

Rowland sat across from Lizzie, beside Mrs. Fairchild. A Foxe cousin would immediately identify the twitch at the corners of Rowland's mouth as a sign of satisfaction for launching a good gambol. Rowland didn't glance once at Tamsin, while she hoped he could read her mind:

Mrs. Fairchild needs to command them all.

Heydon suspects Duncombe. And he'd been giving advice to Tom and Absolom. Which Tamsin couldn't ask about until they were all back home.

Tamsin again dared to glance up the stairs, her hopes rising because no hue and cry came from the upper floor. Then Ned appeared at the front door, as if he'd been to the necessary. He caught Tamsin's eye and nodded before taking a seat on Lizzie's left side, where Duncombe had hovered but not yet claimed a place. The man looked about, surprised, then recovered and sat next to Rowland.

A single day had passed since that black-clad giant had emerged from Hawksmoor's carriage. Then, she'd been rooted to the spot, licking her lips in fear. Now, she'd entrusted Perry Frake with saving her most precious friend in this world…and the next, if there was one.

"Won't you have a seat, Mr. Foxe?" Mrs. Fairchild finally offered an invitation, waving her hand (in the same way she'd commanded her husband and son) to indicate the last chair in the room, which would leave none for her.

"Please, you must take that seat, madam." Tamsin imitated the bow Tom would offer this woman. "I am comfortable as I am. Let us hear Miss Foxe."

"Yes. My cousin Ysabel shall brighten your life, Mrs. Fairchild." Rowland leaned close to the woman in that irritating, beguiling way he had. "As surely as she has brightened mine."

HE'D EXPECTED TO engage Duncombe and the solicitor that morning. Then (joy!) Heydon arrived. Which meant the whole gambol could advance quickly. Perhaps Rowland might find an opportunity to lure Hawksmoor and Sir Isaiah that very afternoon.

First, he treated Mrs. Fairchild to flattering kindness. If her solicitor-husband was rabbity, she resembled a half-wolf herding dog, intent on control but also likely to turn and devour her charges. Even her dogged social smile was marred by two fang-like dogteeth. Like a good herder, Mrs. Fairchild directed her flock with a wave of her hand or by setting her nose in the direction to be followed.

Go there. Sit there. Speak. Quiet now.

Rather like Rowland's last master.

Meanwhile, Heydon had Lizzie trapped in an inquisition, asking about her cousin Orlando. She used the same small voice as when she began to beg these gentlemen for advice. "We met in Amsterdam—when exactly, dear Orlando?"

That called their nemesis's attention directly to Orlando. Heydon studied every inch of him. Heydon's suspicious eyes traced a triangle from Rowland to Tom to Duncombe, until his well-mannered attention returned to Lizzie.

Good work, nemesis! Heydon had learned that in a royal court, where one must always know who's coming up unseen.

"The summer of '82, if my memory serves." Rowland wished they'd created a deeper fiction, but Lizzie smoothly invented falsehoods as needed. He only had to remember each invention.

Lizzie became poetic. "My cousin Orlando's kindnesses recommend him to new acquaintances, but what I most admire is how he cherishes and protects his sister Taresa. The two of them won my friendship, and I'm delighted that they chose to make England their new home."

Their nemesis was not pleased. Heydon inspected Orlando sharply. His eyes might cut the viscount's curls and cravat to bits.

"When Miss Foxe and I first met," Rowland said, "she urged us to seek the green beauty of England. It's taken far too long to unravel our business on the Continent." He directed his attention to Mr. Duncombe, who hung onto each word Lizzie spoke. "Miss Foxe and I have discussed for many months how my sister Taresa and I can gain the best value for certain assets we possess."

"I hope," Mr. Duncombe left off making calf-eyes at Lizzie for a moment, "that I can be of service for such business."

"You are all kindness, sir." Rowland spooned out graciousness, thick as butter. He accepted the interruption, hoping Duncombe might drag others into Orlando's web.

Heydon's frown deepened through that friendly exchange. A shake of his head. He raised a cautioning finger, his eyes on Tamsin, though Jupiter grant he believed Tom stood there. Rowland had no idea what confidence passed between them when Heydon arrived. However, Heydon repeatedly flashed dagger-eyes when Duncombe spoke, so there seemed no chance that those two were joined in treachery.

However, Rowland intended that the two of them play in the same gambol, though he held different prejudices for each man about why punishment was required.

"Miss Foxe, may I share our story?" Rowland began to unspool the thread, intending to tie up the greedy. "My father has a collection of Italian and Spanish paintings I wish Louis Quatorze might purchase. That king is seeking to collect the best of the world's art, but I had not yet found an agent who can succeed with him. Then Miss Foxe wrote to me a fortnight ago about the opportunity that her, uh, *mentor* offered."

"Ah." Duncombe exhaled, his eyes brightening.

Again, Rowland insinuated the princess's name and drew attention from Duncombe and the difficult Mrs. Fairchild. Their nemesis's prying eyes shifted to Duncombe again. A respite for Rowland.

"What exactly has Princess Mary proposed?" Heydon asked what everyone in the room wanted to know.

Rowland had intended to merely allude to Mary's name, to pique interest. Heydon was driving people's interests too fast.

"I beg caution. I say *mentor*, because Miss Foxe urged me to be discreet about the specifics of her—"

A servant pushed open the salon door, dislodging Tamsin from her post. He carried a tray with glasses of...Rowland despaired...cold posset.

While the servant passed the tray, Lizzie began quizzing Mrs. Fairchild about her delicious posset. "We never had such nectar in Mary's court."

Lizzie was exquisitely talented and seemed ready to increase suspense and belief among her admirers.

"It's Mr. Fairchild's favorite," the woman said. She batted her lashes, silently refusing to answer Lizzie's request to learn the secret of the spices used to ruin good cream and wine. Rowland pretended to sip at the throat-clogging concoction while they all waited for the servant to leave. When Tamsin closed the doors again, Rowland used the distraction to set his glass on the little table behind Mrs. Fairchild.

Then Lizzie embroidered on Rowland's fiction. "I appreciate my cousin Orlando's discretion. But we are all friends here. You must know that Princess Mary has been my mentor since we were children. She provided me with an introduction to an agent in London who is allied with men commissioned to seek art for the king of France."

"Ysabel has shared that agent with me, which I consider a great kindness." Rowland used Lizzie's Christian name, intending that people perceive an intimate friendship between them. "I encourage Ysabel to use this agent to sell her collection, which is what Princess Mary intended with her introduction."

"A sound idea." Heydon again accelerated the pace Rowland had set for revelation, drawing people too rapidly in the direction Rowland intended. "I'd leap at such an opportunity."

Eagerness written on his face, Duncombe said, "Will you follow your mentor's advice, Miss Foxe?" He rubbed his hands along his pantaloons, as if grasping for a dangled profit. Exactly the man Rowland expected him to be.

Before Lizzie could answer, Tamsin struck a stern pose. "Without our Uncle Absolom to guide us, I wish my cousin Lizzie would not choose such a risky course. This opportunity calls for a quick decision. The agent requires a great deal of trust, plus an initial investment. And then, my cousin must trust in couriers to convey the artworks to Paris."

"An investment? A quick decision?" Heydon's frown deepened. He too had abandoned his posset to a side table.

Their nemesis was asking "Tom," which increased Rowland's apprehension about what was going on between them.

"The investment is minor." Rowland waved a dismissive hand. "Like most such agents, he requires his commission at the beginning. He asks a mere ten percent of the expected sale price. I've already placed my paintings in his care—and gained an immediate sale for one painting."

"The quick decision," Lizzie kept her small voice, "comes this week by way of letter from the princess. Our king is preparing to sell a royal collection of art. She urges me to sell my paintings now, before the king causes values to fall."

"Similar to what happened with Dutch paintings at the end of the last war." Rowland spoke as if Orlando were wise about the ways of the art world. "It's the key reason why I urge my cousin to seize this opportunity."

Each time Rowland invoked the princess (by name or allusion), people's eagerness rose. Especially in Mrs. Fairchild, who shifted in her chair, ready to plunge.

Duncombe yearned to be invited, rubbing his seam raw.

Heydon frowned…even more than the gambol's designated Doubting Thomas.

The solicitor sipped that revolting posset, missing how his wife signaled for his attention.

Ned, seated in Lizzie's shadow, spoke so softly that the other men leaned forward to hear. "Shouldn't we first do what Uncle Absalom advised? We must find an adept who can judge the worth of the antiquaries and paintings we inherited from him."

"You possess a spirit of genius, Mr. Wijck," Rowland said. "That's what I advised when my cousin Ysabel invited me here. I have engaged this agent to come to Cambridge. Miss Foxe shall have good information to determine what action to take."

Their nemesis tapped a long finger at his chin while staring at Tamsin. Those two seemed to play at blind man's bluff, with Rowland as the blindfolded fool.

Lizzie said, "I began to seriously consider this opportunity when Lord Orlando revealed what this agent offered for the sale of his father's collection."

Every head turned to Rowland. He opened his hands, to appear as the most honest man on God's green earth. "My father has a small painting by Jusepe de Ribera. It's rather like the one you have here, Mrs. Fairchild."

"That one?" Heydon pointed to a piece that hung above Ned's head. Everyone except Ned twisted to see.

"Aye. Small as my father's painting is," Rowland said, "the agent believes it will fetch a thousand Louis d'or coins."

"I'd guess," Heydon said, "that a small Ribera might fetch only in the low hundreds. How does this agent achieve what other agents I've known in London cannot?"

Rowland did not plan for Heydon to be an adept judge of art. That placed the gambol in jeopardy if Heydon doubted or disputed judgments.

"I'm intrigued," Heydon said.

33

The Anglers

— N E D —

WHEN ROWLAND CITED a number that he must have fished out of a horse pond, Ned hoped no one saw him flinch. For such a large number, Rollo should have said Velázquez instead of Ribera. No matter, for Rollo had angled with a promised pile of Louis d'or coins and caught each one of them on his baited hook.

Duncombe stopped mid-sip to keep from spilling his posset.

Mrs. Fairchild clutched the arm of her chair, flushing pink.

Heydon had agreed with "Tom's" doubts, but now listened closely to Rowland's fiction.

Rowland had everyone's attention except Mr. Fairchild, who reached for his posset glass on the table behind his wife. When it proved empty, he snatched Rowland's glass.

This gambol was proving to be as easy as Perry promised.

Ned gazed out the window, judging how much of the day was spent. Noon or later. By now, Perry had returned to Revelstone and claimed the horse he'd ride to London. Ned had described which horse and which tack to select, offering Duchess, their best horse, to carry Perry to his next prowling task.

Such a capable man. Likely he's an hour down the road. Now Ned had nothing more to contribute today, except to remember each gesture and exclamation among these people, so that he could recount it to Perry later.

Ned still didn't perceive Heydon behaving as their enemy. In fact, Ned chose the London man for a nemesis, because of the ridiculous way that man hankered after Lizzie. He now saw what Perry had whispered, that Mr. Duncombe spread his charm for Lizzie like honey on bread. Yet Lizzie saved her own smiles and nods for Heydon. If it was his choice, Ned would paint them as a triangle, with those clever visual puns that rich Londoners love, like a rose with dew-dropped petals, a worn pocketbook, and a conch shell from an exotic land.

Heydon listened to both Lizzie and the false Orlando, though his eyes often drifted to Tamsin, dressed as Tom and grave as a Puritan by the salon door. If Ned were to paint a portrait of Tamsin in that pose, he'd paint a solemn man reading a book of sermons, keeping his counsel about his own sins. How long until he could paint the real Tamsin?

It wasn't likely that Tamsin was pondering her sins right then; it was far more likely she worried about Camilla, though Ned trusted that Perry had achieved their goal.

— ROLLO —

HE CAME TO coax those he intended to gull and, therefore, Rowland was not prepared for his nemesis to become the leading enthusiast.

"I am tempted by this significant promise of ready money," Heydon said.

"Indeed, sir?" Mrs. Fairchild's brief words hung on the edge of her usual impertinence, barely restrained.

Heydon caught Mrs. Fairchild's gaze and pretended to sip at his posset, performing that act gracefully, like Rowland's favorite master in Paris, with perfect movements. Heydon's grace served to mark a line, a titled viscount on one side, and plain Lieutenant Foxe from the Cambridgeshire water-meadows on the other. However, Rowland felt he was as well-groomed in his liberated suit as Heydon, even after climbing a tree.

Rowland touched his ear, which meant it was time for Doubting Thomas to speak again.

"Not once in this century," Tamsin said, "has the Foxe family prospered from the doings of the Royal Family. It'd be better for us to sell land to meet our obligations than undertake such a risky investment."

Heydon sat up, a finger raised again, as if cautioning Tom.

Duncombe leaned forward, eager to seize on Tom's doubts. "I can help you, Mr. Foxe, if you seek to sell your land."

That proposal earned a blade-sharp glare from Heydon, who avidly disliked the man. Rowland needed to find a way to take advantage of that.

However, Duncombe's offer to help sell land was lost, because Ned quietly declared, "Miss Thomasine will never agree to sell one spoonful of Marborne dirt."

"Aye." Tamsin answered slowly, her head bent as if admitting defeat. "This morning Mr. Fairchild read our uncle's will. We must take whatever course my sister Thomasine determines is best. Which, as Ned says, shall never include selling our land."

Heydon offered an approving nod for Tom. (God blind me! What do they share?)

Lizzie said, "Thomasine has no governance over the treasures our uncle left each of us. It seems that I should make the best of what Uncle Absolom left me." She gave up using her small voice, lifted her chin, and spoke with bravado. "Princess Mary is my particular friend, who has my welfare at heart. I should like to put that advice to work for the sake of the Foxe family. Except…"

"Except?" Duncombe hung breathlessly on Lizzie's words.

"Except that, whatever this agent proposes," Lizzie said, "how can I find funds to advance his fee? It is beyond what my family can afford."

"Perhaps," Heydon said, "as your neighbor and friend, you'll allow me to advance you the agent's fee."

"You are kind to offer, your lordship." Rowland privately swore to abandon his career as a crimping fellow, if he could not perform better than Heydon. "But I can advance my cousin Ysabel the funds for this venture."

"But what of the risk of giving her paintings to an unknown agent? I do not like that part of this gamble," Tamsin said.

"The risk of using an agent introduced by Princess Mary?" Rowland exercised the sweet manner that won friends in Paris and Holland. "This isn't a gamble. I have paid the agent's fee and placed my paintings in his care. The agent uses the best conveyances for receipts and money exchanges." He paused to add sugar to the idea, to spin the audience. "When I described two of my father's paintings in Paris, the agent offered me gold on the spot. In advance."

"I wish," Lizzie altered her attention between Heydon and Duncombe, "that you gentlemen might advise me. If you had the opportunity to…to gamble in this way, would you take it?"

Heydon said, "Lord Orlando, I should like to observe this agent's evaluation. I might bring some of my paintings for this agent to assess. When will he be here?"

"Tomorrow." Rowland restrained from more extravagant posturing. Heydon didn't trust Orlando, likely because of that untrustworthy gold-douser Senora Taresa, who hadn't made friends with Hawksmoor's brother—even though she'd been invented specifically for the purpose of disarming enemies.

"My stars, your lordship! Would you join me?" Once more Lizzie hid within her small, delicate voice. "That is dashingly cavalier of you, in truth."

Heydon said, "It is what any of us should do as your friends. I shall persuade my brother to bring a few paintings of his own if you will allow, Miss Foxe. And I shall visit Sir Isaiah on my way home. His wife has a set of paintings in her parlor. I wager he'd enjoy this opportunity. Fairchild?" Heydon's voice elicited a surprised glance from the solicitor. "Will you join us, sir, in support of Miss Foxe's opportunity?"

Was ever man in this world so quickly wooed? Was any enemy so quickly ensnared? Rowland congratulated himself for being as talented a rogue as Richard III.

Mr. Fairchild looked to his wife, who assented, her chin jutting sharply, her eyes shining with bright interest.

"I'm pleased, sirs, that you shall all join us in the agent's valuation of our treasures." Lizzie sounded like a gratified child.

"And Lord Heydon, please encourage your brother and Sir Isaiah to bring their worthy wives tomorrow," Rowland added.

"Ysabel," Tamsin spoke in her best Doubting voice, "our house is in mourning. We cannot possibly entertain."

"Let us all meet at my house," Heydon said. "Cambridge is convenient to all of you, is it not? Mr. Duncombe, do you want to join in this affair? I remember a conversation last winter, when you described your own investments in Italian painting."

"I should like this agent to examine my treasures in London," Duncombe said. "But, Lord Orlando, might I suggest a further way that we gentlemen can protect Miss Foxe's venture?"

"Please, sir." (Oh, please reveal yourself, sir.)

"I suggest that those of us who seek to enter this venture join in a syndicate, where we, as gentlemen, agree to share equally to cover any losses Miss Foxe might suffer."

"How is that fair?" Mrs. Fairchild interrupted Rowland's silent celebration over luring Duncombe into his gambol.

Duncombe seemed unfazed by the Fairchild woman's challenge. "Fairness is achieved when members of the syndicate share in the profits, in direct proportion to the shares that we each contribute. The members enter into the risk, expecting greater pay off when the business succeeds. That likely success far out balances any risk in agreeing to offset any losses Miss Foxe might incur."

"I–I…" Lizzie bent her head as if humbled. "I scarcely know how to answer to such a generous proposition, Mr. Duncombe."

"Come, sirs." Mr. Duncombe swept his hand to encompass the men in the room. "Are we not gentlemen? Prepared to protect Miss Foxe?"

"Yes," Heydon said. "It's a good proposal. I shall willingly join such a syndicate."

"I can bring the appropriate agreements," Duncombe said, "tomorrow when Lord Orlando's expert examines the paintings to be offered."

"The expert recommended by the Princess Mary." After years of cold, ungenerous dealings, Fate chose this time to give Rowland what he wanted, but he couldn't resist dangling that line once again.

Lizzie said, "Mr. Duncombe, if you would be so kind as to carry the treasures to London that I entrust to the agent, I'd believe my future to be in safe hands."

"I'm honored by your request," he said.

"Perhaps," Rowland said, "you and I can travel to London together, Mr. Duncombe. We should also hire a strong guard. To avert any highwaymen's assault on our carriage."

While everyone agreed with the arrangements, Rowland basked in the sense of a trap well laid. His cousins had performed well. He appreciated Lizzie's beguiling ways more than ever.

> All shall be well, and all shall be well
> and all manner of things shall be well.

Wait! Not Shakespeare. An older poet Absolom often ridiculed. ("The civil wars proved that sentiment to be wrong.")

After confirming the next morning's appointment, Heydon rose. "I must depart in pursuit of my day's other business."

Heydon spoke to Tamsin when he passed, but Rowland again couldn't hear the words. Before Rowland reached Tamsin to ask about the dance those two led, Lizzie waylaid him. She tugged at his collar, until he bent his head, her whisper sending shivers down his spine. "I adore your magnificence, Rollo. This is the best fun we've had since—"

The maid shouted from upstairs.

"Help! Mrs. Leighton is gone."

34

Camilla, a Complication

HEYDON GRIPPED TAMSIN'S elbow when he passed, dragging her into the foyer.

"Is Miss Foxe's cousin a friend of Mr. Duncombe?"

"No. They first met—and briefly—at the averil." She had to resist shrugging out of his grip.

"That is good news for us both, Tom." He released Tamsin.

"What do you mean? Are you teasing me, sir?"

"Let's talk over supper. Come to my house after they've sung evensong at King's College. We shall have a fine repast and leave enough twilight for you to ride home."

"Yes, Lord Heydon."

"Lord? Now who is teasing?" Heydon clapped her shoulder again. "Come, Tom, it's me."

After Heydon bid Mrs. Fairchild a formal farewell and was out the door, Tamsin rubbed at her elbow, still astonished that he'd grabbed her that way. Amid the morning's gambol, she'd decided that Heydon didn't behave like an enemy. Still, she needed to know: How often did Tom let Heydon guide him firmly by the arm?

Blessedly, Heydon had disappeared down the lane before the maid upstairs began shouting. Tamsin needed all her wits for Camilla's sake.

Lizzie ran up the stairs behind Mrs. Fairchild. The maid began protesting innocence before either woman reached her. "Mrs. Leighton was asleep when I left her."

"Pity sake, Jane. You were supposed to stay in her room." Mrs. Fairchild didn't raise her voice, yet it was the venomous witch voice Camilla complained about in private moments.

"The doctor came, mistress. And I required the necessary."

"Fie. A new post is what is necessary, Jane," Mrs. Fairchild said, "if anything has happened to Mrs. Leighton."

Lizzie, behaving true to her nature, attempted to quell passions. "I'm sure Camilla must be in the house."

"Where is the doctor?" Mrs. Fairchild ignored Lizzie. "Dr. Oakes? Where are you?"

The maid opened and closed doors across the upper floors, out of sight from where Tamsin could observe. Mrs. Fairchild came down the stairs, Lizzie trailing, just as the doctor arrived from the kitchen.

"Here I am, madam," the doctor called. "You sent me to the kitchen."

"For shame. Your patient is missing."

"She can't have gone far," Winwood spoke with professional calm. "Not with that injury to her thorax. The tincture I prescribed may have lingered. Perhaps she's walking in her sleep and wandered to a familiar place on the grounds."

The doctor imparted more information than the impatient Mrs. Fairchild wanted to hear. The woman's hands hung now at her side like talons, prepared to attack.

"Revelstone! That's where she's gone!" Mrs. Fairchild seized on that idea, as Tamsin had predicted. "For shame."

Tamsin held up a hand, warning poor Jane to remain upstairs. She motioned for the footman to come to her. "Mr. Clopton, you and I should search in the yard and along the foot paths. Ned, you can help. Doctor, you too? We shall need your services when Mrs. Leighton is found."

Meanwhile, Lizzie had her hand on Mrs. Fairchild's silk sleeve, restraining her. "Madam, shall you and I take a carriage to Revelstone House? You have a good notion, since Camilla visits so often. Perhaps she's gone there."

Such a heroic sacrifice on Lizzie's part. Rowland, who had been singularly useless amid this tumult, refused Lizzie's offer of a ride back to Revelstone House. He said, "A pleasant day such as this? I shall enjoy the walk. I remember the way from our stroll this morning."

Lizzie was still organizing Mrs. Fairchild to get her out the door when Tamsin departed with the searchers.

— ROLLO —

HE PRACTICED PATIENCE, waiting an eternity until Lizzie drew Mrs. Fairchild out of the house, leaving Rowland to his next endeavor. Fortunately, some affair drew Mr. Duncombe from the room, so the solicitor was free to be preyed upon.

"I have a private query, Mr. Fairchild. Can you spare me a moment, sir?"

"At your service, your lordship." The solicitor's eyes darted, as confirming that he was off his wife's tether. "Shall we sit in my office, sir?"

Rowland followed him, shutting the office door and holding its handle so it couldn't be turned, his heel against the door to prevent anyone from entering.

"Sir, I have few acquaintances in England. There's no one to whom I can turn for advice. But first, tell me, is it true that an English solicitor holds his client's business in strict confidence?"

Mr. Fairchild glanced at the door, as if he wanted rescuing. "Why, yes, Lord Orlando."

"Are you under any obligation to the Foxe heirs?"

Fairchild's eyes raced wildly, finding nowhere to rest. "I must see Doctor Foxe's will proved with the magistrate. But I am not otherwise under any obligation to the heirs."

"No? Then I believe I should like to engage you."

"How can I help you, Lord Orlando?" Mr. Fairchild hesitated. "Is that how you are addressed in your country?"

"It will do, sir." Rowland sank into the chair where Tamsin sat while the will was read. "But first, have you a drop to share? Brandy? I need a dram before I am brave enough to speak."

"Dutch courage?" The solicitor winked.

Rowland needed nothing of the kind, but the solicitor obviously did. The fellow pointed to a side table, and Rowland went to pour two small glasses for them. Pretty crystal glasses, the Venetian kind, in style on the Continent for the past decade.

"*À votre santé*, as they say in France." Rowland toasted him. "They say *chinchín* in my country, but I like the sentiment better in French, don't you agree, Mr. Fairchild?"

"Indeed." But the fellow was too happy to sip the morning drink Rowland brought him. "What can I do for you, sir?"

"To begin, my sister Taresa and I have procured proof that our lineage has the clearest right to the Flores inheritances in England." Rowland paused. Mr. Fairchild gawped, forgetting his brandy for a moment, his mouth open like a startled bird. Rowland continued. "Which includes the Marborne title. And, though you might not have heard, our king means to offer vacant titles at open bidding."

"I returned last night from London, where I did hear a word or two like that." Mr. Fairchild peeked at Rowland over the edge of his crystal glass.

"The first thing we do…" Rowland paused. The first thing was to learn what the solicitor knew. Rowland was prepared to wager ten Louis d'or coins that Mr. Fairchild was working with others — Heydon, perhaps — on a bid to gain what formerly belonged to the Foxe family.

"With your help, sir, I should like to bid for Marborne. In addition to documents proving my rights, I possess significant wealth, such that — this must be confidential between us — I can offer His Majesty a significant garnishment. Can I purchase your services to draft an appropriate offer to present to the king?"

"You astonish me, Lord Orlando. I had no idea."

"As your protected client, I must ask you not to mention to my cousins about what I plan." As Rowland spoke, the solicitor's eyes widened. "When I claim the title, I shall take great joy in delivering my cousins from poverty and ensuring they can continue to live at Revelstone House."

"You mean to act as a kindness for them?"

"Yes. And I think you'll agree, there's no benefit in consulting them in this. They are like children in the face of business."

"Yes, yes." The solicitor became increasingly flustered. "But with Miss Thomasine named as executor—"

"You, sir, perceive that your king shall leave Doctor Foxe's executor with nothing to administer." Rowland ameliorated his stern tone. "But I intend to offer for Miss Thomasine. She shall be my own executor, once I have secured the title, with Revelstone and Marborne estates preserved for the Foxe family."

"But Miss Thomasine is dis...dis..." Mr. Fairchild likely meant to say disfigured, but was distracted by the wave washing across his crystal glass. As he swirled it, sun from the window caught in the crystal and flashed rainbows on the walls.

"I am not the kind of man who might prefer beauty or wealth over the brilliance of a woman such as Miss Thomasine. Shall we discuss the details later today, sir?"

Fairchild mused. "I feel compelled to help you. Yet other business keeps me today. Friday, perhaps?"

"Friday shall suit me well. Now, I should release you and apologize for taking so much of your time."

However, Lord Orlando will have disappeared from God's earth before Friday arrived.

Rowland followed the gentleman, briefly enjoying a breeze from the open window as he prepared to say farewell and return to Revelstone House. He'd stated his proposition clearly enough that the befuddled Mr. Fairchild should be capable of spreading that tale to his wife and Mr. Duncombe.

> When law can do no right,
> Let it be lawful that law bar no wrong...

A good day's work. Every man Rowland suspected had revealed himself. Perhaps, with Perry gone to prowl in London, Rowland could persuade Ned to share a jug of wine under the oak trees, to toast the promise of tomorrow's success.

35

A Rose-covered Cottage

ALONG WITH WINWOOD, Tamsin, and Mr. Clopton, Ned joined the pointless search for the escaped Camilla. The doctor told a running story about what he'd been doing in the kitchen.

Ned expected he should also speak up to exonerate himself from having helped to snatch Camilla. But not one person noted that he'd left the Fairchilds' morning room. What did that horrible woman call it? A salon? Meanwhile, Ned found Winwood's nattering a comfort. Someone had been doing honest work while the Foxe cousins ran that rig in the Fairchilds' salon.

"When Mrs. Fairchild consigned me to the kitchen, the housekeeper asked me into her room so that I might advise her on a personal problem. Then she invited the cook to visit on a matter that's plagued her since the birth of her last child."

Ned suggested that no one could accuse Dr. Oakes of inattention to his duties. Tamsin offered polite nothings. Mr. Clopton pointed to another trail from the house they should inspect. Winwood continued to share medical gossip.

"Then the cook called her son in from the stables, asking me to examine a cut that might putrefy. Caution is always best, but his case was not alarming. The boy, however, didn't like either the spirits for cleaning his cut or the sulfurous dressing."

"Could she have wandered down by that brook?" Tamsin prompted Mr. Clopton's attention. The footman patrolled the reeds and marsh grasses for signs anyone had passed there.

He called back, "No, Mr. Foxe. No one's walked through here."

"Let us explore the westward trail," Tamsin said.

Winwood continued his recitation. "Then the cook's father appeared, needing a liniment for the pain he suffers. His daughter complains that he's malingering, but I do not agree. He had no external symptom on his limbs, yet his knuckles were swollen. Likely his other joints and limbs pained him, even in this heat. I aver, we cannot underestimate how much pain accrues in our aged friends' bones over a lifetime of labor."

Ned did his erstwhile best to inspect bushes, bowers, and patches of bloomed-out bluebells, seeking a woman that he knew wasn't to be found.

When at last Mr. Clopton left them, deciding to search in another direction, Winwood whistled in relief.

"Free at last." Ned could finally share news with Tamsin. "Winwood thinks Camilla was drowned in poppy elixir."

"Indeed, nothing else could account for it," Winwood said. "When Camilla awakes, I shall be forced to treat her pain with only willow-bark tea. When shall we return Camilla to her own house? After she wakes?"

Tamsin said, "When Camilla is clear-headed, she can choose where she wants to go. When will that be, Winwood?"

"In a day. Perhaps two."

"Let's hurry to the rector's cottage," Tamsin said. That meant doubling back to an overgrown, overlooked trail. "I'm impatient to see her."

Winwood said, "While I was tending Camilla, with Lizzie there, Mrs. Fairchild stood like a gargoyle under the eaves of a Paris church."

"What did the lady say?" Tamsin wanted to know what had occurred from the moment when Camilla ran off during the restoration until she reappeared at the averil.

"Camilla still sleeps," Winwood said. "So, I don't know."

Tamsin shrugged within Tom's coat, which was a fraction too big for her. "Then tell me, Winwood, what did Mrs. Fairchild say while you tended to Camilla?"

"Only 'foolish, foolish girl.'" Winwood lifted a bramble cane for Tamsin to pass in front of him. "That woman bears a powerful hatred toward you. She didn't voice that in so many words, but I'd need a surgeon's knife to cut through her animosity for you."

"Does she hate Tom or Tamsin? And why?" Ned trailed behind them (seeking signs that confirmed Perry's belief: Winwood had a *tendre* for Tamsin). Winwood released the bramble after Tamsin passed. It sprung against Ned's thigh. "Neither Tom nor Tamsin has ever done that woman any harm."

"Either. Both," Winwood said. "Isn't it obvious? Tamsin holds a station in life that Mrs. Fairchild can never attain as a solicitor's wife. And Tom represents many generations of esteem in this community, which her wet-headed son Leighton will never attain."

"But Tom has no title," Tamsin protested. "I have no station. We hold land, but it's mortgaged beyond our reach. We hold power over nothing."

Winwood, once more leading on the trail, glanced back, smiling at her. "You, Miss Thomasine, have the power to rescue an entire village after a fire, to shelter each family, and to direct the work that must be done to restore people's lives."

"That's not power," Tamsin argued. "It's merely duty."

"Mrs. Fairchild has no idea of duty," Ned said. "Do you see how she treats her servants?"

"Yes," Tamsin said. "We shall have to ensure a home for poor Jane if she loses her place because we rescued Camilla."

"Why," Ned asked, "doesn't Mrs. Fairchild show any loathing for my sister Lizzie? The way she defers to Lizzie is outrageous, compared to how she treats Tamsin. Tom, I mean."

"Honestly, Ned." Tamsin glanced back up the trail where he followed. "Lizzie has magic woven all around her. Didn't you see it while Rowland was leading our gambol today?"

"What magic? She's pretty, but that's not a spell."

"Two magic words," Winwood said. "Though I didn't witness your conversation in the Fairchilds' salon, I can guess the words used to ensorcel Mrs. Fairchild and the others."

"I'm not stupid," Ned said, though he felt it, having to ask. Perry would have perceived it and coached Ned to do the same, without making him ask. "What magic words cause others to see something about my sister that I cannot?"

"Princess Mary," Winwood said. "The presumed Stuart heir to the Crown of England. Miss Foxe glows with the magic that comes from serving royalty."

"Here's Mr. Gamlingay's house," Tamsin said.

But before they could say hello, there was a half-dozen king's men also arriving in the rector's yard.

"God's bodkins!" She barely remembered to lower her voice, to sound like Tom.

—

A rambling rose grew up a woven willow trellis at one side of the cottage door. It crawled over the porch eaves, then dangled bee-pleasing pink blossoms above the portly rector as he greeted the red-coated riders.

Tamsin intended to greet the soldiers as fearlessly as the rector did, introducing herself, Ned, and Winwood as men from Revelstone House.

One of the riders was Captain Starbuck's sergeant, who reported that they were canvasing the countryside at Mr. Leighton Fairchild's request, seeking the highwaymen who'd made trouble in the parish.

After Ned and the others denied knowing robbers or hearing rumors, Tamsin proposed a better use of the riders' time, offering bold lies in front of the rector of her own parish.

"We've been searching for Mr. Fairchild's wife. It's likely he doesn't know yet that she's missing. She's ill but has wandered off from home. The entire neighborhood would be grateful if you helped with the search."

All the riders liked this idea better than their current mission. Ned advised them about the tangle of riding trails and footpaths, and soon they were gone.

Mr. Gamlingay beamed as he waved farewell to the soldiers, still not betraying any curiosity for everything his guests had brought to his door.

"Come in, friends! Miss Camilla has stirred, but is not awake."

Tamsin said, "Thank you, sir, for accepting the visitor we thrust upon you. We've brought the doctor to tend her."

"You'll find her in there." The rector pointed Winwood to his tiny bedroom, where Camilla lay under a linen cover.

Ned quietly explained why his good friend Perry Frake had asked Mr. Gamlingay to shelter Camilla. Meanwhile, in the bedroom, Tamsin knelt beside the bed while the doctor tended Camilla. Winwood quietly repeated his observations, as if he knew that Tamsin needed his reassurances.

"Carrying her here did not open the wound. That's what I've worried about. Mr. Frake must have been most gentle."

"She isn't as pale as last night." Tamsin heard hope in her voice. Yet those three thin scratches on Camilla's face glowed.

"Aye." Winwood agreed. "And I'm pleased that there's no sign of fever, which has been my other great worry. Now if she will only wake."

Tamsin drew a breath so shaky it whistled past her teeth.

"You want to be of help." Winwood often seemed to read her mind. "You can apply this salve to her face. Talk to her. Stroke her hand. I'll speak with Mr. Gamlingay about her care."

While Winwood, Ned, and the rector chatted under the roses, Tamsin quietly said aloud every worry she'd carried since the previous day's restoration.

"I failed you, Camilla. But you must wake up and tell us what's happened." As soon as Tamsin spoke, Camilla's eyes moved under her closed lids, like a dreaming sleeper. "My sweet nutting, Rowland has a plan. You must get well because you should not miss this lark for all the pearls in the sea." She stroked Camilla's cool hand, the blue veins stark under pale skin.

Men's voices drifted in, buzzing like the bees in that veil of roses, softened by Winwood's voice: "May I express sorrow for your loss, sir? I understand Doctor Foxe was your great friend, Mr. Gamlingay. How long did you know each other?"

Gamlingay said, "Ned has heard the tale too often, I'm sure. Absolom and I played as children, read at Cambridge the same years, learned to shift with the winds over the war years, and then we endured what they call the Restoration."

Camilla's hand twitched within Tamsin's grasp.

Sitting still as a cat stalking a bird, Tamsin hoped to sense movement again, to know she hadn't imagined it. She bent to speak close, knowing her breath must tickle her friend's ear. "Camilla, my cousin Rowland is home. You remember the awful scrapes he used to get us into? Absolom asked him to come learn how we've been cheated by Lord Hawksmoor. All this time, Rollo has been a king's intelligencer on the Continent. Which means he spies on people and steals their secrets."

A deep sigh, as if Camilla prepared to speak.

Tamsin waited, listened, hoped.

No sound but the buzzing bees and the chatting gentlemen.

First, Gamlingay: "In truth, my father was ousted from the parish by Charles when he returned to the throne. Absolom helped me claim a proper place."

"Ousted? Why?" Winwood asked. "T–Tom says the family and parish have long been Protestant and Royalist."

"Charles threw out a good two thousand parish ministers who, like my father, couldn't prove a proper Church of England ordination."

Tamsin squeezed Camilla's hand. "Now, my friend, it's as Mrs. Bell often says, it's all a moider. Lizzie's keeping secrets from us. And Rowland's in love with her—I swear it's true. But he can't hope for more than a broken heart. And his comrade Perry has convinced Ned to be in love with him, but…well, there's too much to tell you. Don't you see, my flitter-mouse? You must wake and join us. You shall curse your luck if you miss one day of our adventures, because I failed you. I'm sorry."

"Sorry?"

"Camilla! You're awake."

"Maybe. Where?"

"You're at Mr. Gamlingay's cottage."

"Why?"

"You weren't safe at…Leighton's house."

"Wanted to give him a fright. He grabbed my pistol. Didn't mean to shoot me."

Tamsin brushed the scratches on Camilla's cheek. "He hasn't expressed any sorrow."

"He didn't know."

"But you said—"

"Leighton didn't know his father wants to ruin Marborne. I wanted to shoot his father, but he wasn't home."

Tamsin hadn't shared with Camilla the secret story of the forged mortgages. Still, Camilla had set out with her sweet, brave soul to challenge Tamsin's enemies. And suffered for it.

"You were going to shoot Mr. Fairchild?"

"Just frighten him to his toes. Shouldn't have loaded my pistol. Like you always tell me." Camilla's eyes wandered around the little room, as if she couldn't focus on Tamsin. "Was so mad I could catch fire. And the man is always the worse for drink."

"Leighton?" Tamsin would be satisfied if he caught fire.

"Him too. He tried to grab my pistol—well, it's your pistol. I don't think he knows he shot me. He was still staring down at the gun when I ran away."

"It took you hours to come to me."

"It hurt, but I didn't know how bad it was. I sat to rest by a tree and fell asleep. Then there was so much blood when I woke."

"Why didn't Leighton find you?"

"Didn't he come looking where he knew I'd go? To you? To Revelstone? Honestly, that beetle-head."

Winwood reappeared then. Agnes Bell was with him, Mrs. Bell's stick-thin granddaughter.

"Mr. Frake asked my grandmother to send a female helper." Agnes's eyes widened at the sight of Camilla's pale figure.

"Ah, our patient is awake." Winwood checked Camilla's eyes, then put his hand on her chest. "How are you today, Mrs. Fairchild?"

"Call me Camilla. I don't want to be a Fairchild."

"How's the pain in your middle?" He touched where bandages covered her wound.

"Been better." Camilla pushed at the bed, trying to rise.

"No, Camilla." Winwood gently guided her back down. "Stay in bed and stay still. You need a few days of rest."

"Not at the Fairchild house."

"You shall stay here." Winwood tapped Tamsin's shoulder. "Please let me show Agnes how to help Camilla drink water."

Tamsin made way, so Agnes could learn what Tamsin had practiced months before about coaxing liquid into Tom when he couldn't rouse to drink on his own. In between sips of water, Camilla's voice grew faint.

"Hard to stay awake," she said.

"But you'll soon be well." Winwood said. "Agnes, please talk to Camilla and keep her awake as much as you can. Sing songs if you've a mind to it."

"Not a baby," Camilla murmured.

"Pretend, dear nutting." Tamsin promised to return, then left, to let Camilla rest.

Outside, Tamsin thanked the rector, perhaps too much. Mr. Gamlingay fingered Absolom's ring at his knuckle and said it was his duty to serve Camilla. "Mrs. Fairchild castigates her as a sauce-box, but doesn't this girl stop to say hello most every day on her way to your house, leaving me a fresh loaf and a jug of milk? Miss Camilla is, I avow it, the sweetest woman in this parish."

Tamsin agreed. She'd managed not to weep, and not just because the real Tom wouldn't weep to see Camilla this way. She became braver with the knowledge that Camilla had awakened.

And Camilla made sense when she spoke. Still, Tamsin owed her cousins more tasks that day. She departed the cottage, her heart caught up in the dangling rose thorns over its door.

As they headed down the trail to home, Winwood said, "The rector is a true original. I haven't met the like."

Ned said, "Uncle Absolom claimed that Gamlingay invents half the scripture he recites. Though no one in Marborne parish would care to challenge him."

"How did such a grand philosopher end up curing souls in this parish?"

Tamsin repeated a host of Absolom's claims about the situation in Marborne parish. Talking kept her from wanting to run back to the rector's cottage, to sit by Camilla's side.

"Every man, woman, and child suffered under the tides that have ripped through the fens and vales, from when Henry tore down the abbeys, through Mary hunting papists and the radicals' terrors, until the Stuarts restored a small dose of ecclesiastical peace. Don't you know this history, Winwood?"

"My family left England when turmoil arose around the first Charles," he said.

Tamsin discarded the question she was raised to never ask. (Then you're Catholic?)

Winwood continued. "I grew up in the third generation of exiles. I must be grateful that my parents and grandparents endeavored to preserve our English ways over those decades. Else, you'd know me for a Frenchman. But tell me more about the gentle rector."

Tamsin said, "Our Mr. Gamlingay, unlike his father, was ordained by a bishop of the Apostolic Succession, which removed the suspicion his father encountered under King Charles. Though the bishop sniffs around once or twice a year."

"The bishop? Why?" Winwood asked.

"To ensure the rector upholds the faith, that he's not a phanatic."

"Why would he be?"

Ned said, "Absolom claims...claimed that Mr. Gamlingay crossed his fingers through his entire ordination."

"Crossed his fingers?"

"Don't they do that in France when swearing to something you cannot uphold?" Tamsin asked. "If you'd ever heard Absolom and Mr. Gamlingay drinking wine on the lawn at sunset, then you'd understand."

"The two of them," Ned said, "had more questions and doubts than beliefs. My father sat with them and was as bad, while he lived."

Tamsin said, "As if their views of the world are indeed wrong."

As if there's a heaven.

Which was what Absolom often said of hoping for what seems unattainable.

36

An Ambidexter

BEFORE ROWLAND COULD break away from Danvers Duncombe and escape the Fairchild house, Sir Isaiah arrived in an open carriage, Lady Candecote at his side.

"I've come to visit my stricken daughter."

After Sir Isaiah learned his daughter Camilla had gone missing, he succumbed to Mr. Fairchild's invitation to wait in the salon with refreshments until Camilla was found.

"Mrs. Fairchild will find her." Rowland sought to assuage Sir Isaiah's fears. "She's gone in a carriage to fetch her at Revelstone."

Sir Isaiah, it seemed, had no such fears. "She always runs away. And it's always to Revelstone. It's an unnecessary kindness for Mrs. Fairchild to fetch her. I believe it serves best if Camilla is forced to return on foot from her fancies."

Rowland resolved then to stay out of it, to wing his way from the house amid the commotion, since he'd achieved more than he hoped and needed to prepare for the next day. But Duncombe practically hung onto Rowland's coat sleeve. That delay proved worthwhile. Once Sir Isaiah was settled in a chair, Duncombe ensnared Rowland into repeating the plan for selling art to the king of France. Poor Camilla was forgotten.

Duncombe said, "It's an opportunity recommended by Princess Mary." As if that might be profound business advice.

Rowland had been commanded to inspect this man's business for supporting rebels. Yet the man seemed overawed by royalty, any royalty. The overly groomed, thin-nosed Sir Isaiah proved to be thin-witted. He and his bird-like wife were quickly drawn to the gambol while Lord Orlando answered Duncombe's queries. Sir Isaiah's questions focused on why the evaluation and sales must happen so quickly.

Duncombe appeared to have been lured deep into the gambol, for he answered that question, sharing information which an hour before Lizzie had declared must be a secret.

"Miss Foxe has private advice from Princess Mary that the king intends to sell paintings out of the royal treasures. That flood of paintings will destroy the market in France. Hence, we must act quickly if we want good value for our collections."

"And," the mostly silent solicitor introjected, "Princess Mary introduced Miss Foxe to an agent who has direct connections with King Louis in France."

Rowland had doubted Mr. Fairchild's grasp of the particulars, and therefore was happy to hear that the solicitor understood certain details.

"Mrs. Fairchild," the solicitor continued, "is eager to participate. Such an immediate repayment of our investment," he lifted a shaking hand to indicate the works that hung on the salon walls, "will go a long way to our participation in other investments we have discussed, Mr. Duncombe."

Duncombe had one hesitation. "Do you think Miss Foxe will decide to participate? Her cousins were not enthused. Can we take advantage of this opportunity if Miss Foxe decides against it? We should not pressure her if she hesitates."

(*God blind me!* He seeks Lizzie's comfort, though I swear she cares not one whit for him, nor any of the rest of them.)

"I am confident," Rowland said, "that the doubts Mr. Tom Foxe and Mr. Wijck expressed will not win out. When the agent shall judge their paintings tomorrow, her cousins will be as enthusiastic as we are."

"Mr. Wijck?" Sir Isaiah puzzled over the name, as if he hadn't been the Foxes' neighbor all his life.

"Ned."

"Ned?" Duncombe also puzzled.

"Miss Foxe's brother."

"Ah, I forgot she had a brother. That sort of brother," Sir Isaiah said. Though the two gentlemen nodded to show their understanding, Lady Candecote bit her lip, confused, and so Rowland explained. "Mr. Wijck is a love child."

Her eyes opened wide. "Oh."

Sir Isaiah continued. "But Mr. Thomas Foxe is the expected heir. If they can manage to gain the king's attention."

"Yes, if the title is restored to them." His wife spoke her first words beyond colorless greetings and murmurs of assent to her husband's declarations. "Which is in grave doubt."

"Grave, grave doubt," Sir Isaiah murmured.

Fairchild's rabbity eyes dashed to Rowland. His hand shook, sloshing the brandy in the glass. Rowland wanted to grab that shaking hand to still it.

"It's sad what happened to that old line," Mr. Duncombe said, his eyes on Sir Isaiah.

Lady Candecote said, "Won't the man who marries Miss Ysabel Foxe be first in line if the king restores Marborne to the Foxe family?" She obviously did not understand inheritance, surmising that a man marrying Lizzie could become earl.

"Not for an earl," Sir Isaiah said. "What foolishness, my dear. An earl's title passes only through the male line. Now, if we continue as we are, with no sons, my girl Camilla will inherit my land and wealth. But no title."

He was too happy to correct his wife and too blind to see that he had hurt her.

Rowland spoke, bringing everyone's attention to him, as if they'd forgotten him. "They hope Thomas Foxe will inherit, as the oldest male with a straight line from Caius Foxe." He delighted in the sensation that none of these duplicitous people would want Marborne to go to the foreign Viscount Orlando, once Mr. Fairchild began to gossip. But then he recognized what his audience wondered.

(Has God indeed blinded *me*? Orlando shows too much familiarity with English laws of inheritance.)

"As Miss Foxe explained it to me."

Fairchild's footman came in to report that no trace had been found of Camilla on the trails near the house, and he would next take the dogs out on the Cambridge road.

Sir Isaiah huffed, indecisive, but decided to take his carriage to the Phoenix and Swan.

"An excellent idea!" Rowland enthused. "Perhaps offer a reward. Five pounds would go a long way toward stirring the parish to search for Mrs. Leighton."

"Five pounds! For Camilla?" Lady Candecote disdained the idea of that excessive sum.

Rowland offered his farewells, eager to hike back to Revelstone. He'd been considering how much attention he'd drawn to Orlando that day, while Ned drew no notice to himself. For instance, when Ned slipped into the empty seat beside Lizzie, it was a wonder Mr. Duncombe hadn't sat right on top of him, having taken no note of Ned's exit or his return to the salon. People turned to listen when Lizzie spoke and attempted to judge her reaction when others spoke. They didn't see how her brother held her hand, as if to reassure her.

Ned never showed any sign of resenting how these long-time neighbors ignored him. However, if Perry were to witness it, he'd catch fire. Rowland planned to take advantage of Ned's ghostly nature. Tomorrow, when they welcomed the agent from London and his adept wife, no one would recognize Ned as the agent.

Because no one saw Ned now.

Rowland hadn't left the front steps of the house before Lady Candecote's voice echoed out through an open window, the presiding grumbletonian protesting unfairness.

"But, Danvers, you promised we'd be rich. Must we also sell our paintings to have enough to do as we planned?"

Perhaps Mr. Duncombe had ruined the fortunes of more men than Hawksmoor. Rowland laughed until he reached the footpath, when he retrieved his gold angel from a pocket and began to roll it over his knuckles, satisfied with a day's work well done.

Veiled Ladies

SHE RAN THE last half-mile back to Revelstone House, wanting to pour a pitcher of cool well water over her body. With Revelstone House in sight, Tamsin halted her rapid pace, letting Ned catch up. Sweat from the hot day tingled on her scalp, wetted her neck and forehead, and trickled down her spine.

Rowland joined them where she and Ned halted in dismay. Mrs. Fairchild's carriage remained in the yard.

"Good stars, Rollo!" Tamsin said. "I thought you'd be home long before now. Poor Lizzie and Mrs. Bell are trapped inside with that woman."

"Danvers Duncombe detained me," Rowland said. "Then Sir Isaiah arrived to visit his injured daughter."

"Is he upset that Camilla is missing?" Tamsin asked.

Rowland said, "The solicitor claimed Mrs. Fairchild would fetch her from Revelstone. No one mentioned that Camilla had been shot. You'd think she merely had a summer cold."

"Have we created a bigger problem than we hoped to solve?" Ned said. "By taking her away, I mean."

"No." Tamsin insisted, despite her many trepidations. "She woke up. Winwood says she'll be fine. The rector will protect her. Is Sir Isaiah the uncaring father I believe him to be?"

"Aye," Rowland said. "Sir Isaiah was diverted from worry over his daughter as soon as Duncombe asked me to bring him into our plans for tomorrow. Like Duncombe, Sir Isaiah is so greedy he practically rubbed his hands in anticipation."

"Good work, Rollo," Ned said.

"Now," Tamsin said, "help us with the dreadful Mrs. Fairchild. Come charm her toes off, like you did at her house."

"Nay, I shall not," Rowland said. "I'm hagged. I must beg Mrs. Bell for a bite to stave off the wolf in my belly. I've already done more to quell Mrs. Fairchild for today than should be asked of any man."

"Selfish creature," Tamsin called after Rowland when he took the path to the kitchen.

"He's right, though," Ned said. "Our Fairchild problem isn't his to sort."

"Let us go inside and face Judgment," Tamsin said. "At least we can save Lizzie from that woman."

Inside the large oak front doors, they followed voices to the back parlor, which never received direct sun. Tamsin longed for its coolness despite the chore Mrs. Fairchild represented.

But it wasn't the chill of the room that made Tamsin quake. It was the two figures seated on the low bench that Lizzie declared should be called a "divan."

She saw that Rowland had managed to don his Senora Taresa clothes quickly, and now sat beside Lizzie in a black veil and silk skirts, taking advantage of the situation to hold Lizzie's hand.

"For shame, Mr. Foxe. You've given up the search so soon?" The malapert Mrs. Fairchild upbraided them, as was her way, instead of offering a civilized greeting.

"Good afternoon, Mrs. Fairchild. I hope Miss Foxe has seen to your comfort." Tamsin smiled, hoping her expression didn't resemble a wolf tending to the comfort of a lost hen.

"Miss Foxe walked with me through this house in search of my daughter. Now, I cannot be comfortable, since Camilla must be lost in the forest." Mrs. Fairchild swiped at her eyes with a kerchief. "Pity sake. Have you no heart? Wouldn't a real man keep searching?"

"We met a band of the king's men," Tamsin said, "who gave up their hunt for highwaymen to search for Camilla. They can search more effectively on horseback than we can on foot."

Mrs. Fairchild wanted to quarrel with that notion. She longed to. She opened her mouth, likely to pronounce the deficiencies of that solution, except Senora Taresa greeted Tamsin and Ned.

"Good afternoon, Mr. Foxe, Mr. Wijck. You must be fatigued in this heat. Mrs. Bell provided us with a chilled tisane. Please take a glass with us. Sit and enjoy these lovely sweet biscuits, or some bread and butter."

Now she saw that it was not Rowland.

Rather, Tom. Exercising his comical idea of a Spanish accent. Every inch the foreign lady, his hands in the cotton gloves that Winwood suggested, to keep him from scratching.

"Madam, you are kind." Ned seized the false senora's hand and bowed as if greeting a titled lady. "However, it's likely best if I leave you ladies with Mr. Foxe. I've a mind to search the burned cottages in the village, in hopes of discovering Mrs. Leighton."

Ned slipped out of the room, which Tamsin couldn't hate him for, because she saw the effort it took him to keep from doubling over with laughter.

"What a noble hombre is your brother, Ysabel." Tom clasped Lizzie's hand. "I am jealous of the lovely family that surrounds you. Me, myself, I have only my brother Orlando, who is often too entangled in business to be by my side." Tom turned to Mrs. Fairchild. "You enjoyed more of my brother's time this morning than did I, Senora Fairchild. How did you find dear Orlando? He's handsome, is he not? Yet you cannot know him as I do, as a kind-hearted and virtuous cavalier."

Tom enjoyed talking up Mrs. Fairchild, then getting Lizzie to describe the reading of the will. Making up for all the restorations he'd missed while ill. Imitating Lizzie (poorly).

Though inclined to let Tom have this lark, Tamsin sought signs of fatigue. When Ned returned from searching the village, Tamsin prepared to send Mrs. Fairchild back to her own lair.

"Don't you think, Mrs. Fairchild, it might be best to prepare to receive Camilla at home? You've seen to a search of the village and Revelstone House. There's no more that can be done. We must wait for the king's men to find her."

"I should like to see poor Miss Thomasine before I go." Mrs. Fairchild set her jaw, like a dog that could not be deterred from prey it had treed.

Lizzie's eyes flashed. She'd forestalled this search, helped by Tom dressed as Orlando's sister. Those eyes begged Tamsin to fix this quandary.

"Senora Taresa," Tamsin rose, "will you come with me to see whether Miss Thomasine is well enough to receive guests?"

"Happily, Mr. Foxe."

Yet Tamsin saw the trembling hand Tom held out, pretending to be a lady while fatigued beyond endurance. Mercifully, Winwood came in then, recognizing Tom more quickly than Tamsin had. He offered greetings to all the ladies and bent his head to take a scolding for negligence from Mrs. Fairchild. He took a seat beside the false Taresa on the divan.

"I hope I find you well, senora. After the fatigue from your adventures yesterday, I had prescribed a rest for all of today."

"I'm in fine spirits, doctor. The physick you prescribed has strong healing powers."

Tamsin escaped the room, climbing the stairs alone to where "Miss Thomasine" was nursed. She'd have to play herself, praying for enough time to become an invalid before Mrs. Fairchild charged past all keepers in search of Camilla.

But an invalid already lay in the bed, veiled, wrapped in linen bed clothes.

"Best not disturb the window coverings," the invalid said. "The light pains my eyes."

Rowland. Hoarse as a crow.

"You poor dear." Mrs. Fairchild pushed her way into the room, nearly treading on Tamsin's heels. "I've longed to wait on you, Miss Thomasine, since I first learned of your illness."

"You are kind, madam." A croak from Rowland, not clever enough to know that Thomasine would not address that woman as madam. "I am sad to hear of Camilla's illness."

"It's a pity. But the doctor promises that she shall be well," Mrs. Fairchild mused. She examined every corner of the room, obviously still believing she'd find Camilla at Revelstone. Her eyes rested where the door to the doctor's adjoining room stood partly open, drawing her attention like iron to a lodestone.

Winwood appeared in that doorway. "Mrs. Fairchild, let me give you a physick to take home with you, to administer to Camilla when she's found. Won't you come in?"

That did it for Mrs. Fairchild. She entered the doctor's room. Tamsin stayed in the doorway. As much as Mrs. Fairchild longed to find her daughter-in-law in the cupboards or under the bed, this last room in the house did not grant her wish. Instead, she received a flask of some concoction from the doctor. Then Ned led the woman to her carriage.

With Mrs. Fairchild gone, Tamsin bent over in relief, still in the doorway between the doctor's room and Tom's.

Which was when Tamsin spied that scrap under the doctor's bed. She retrieved what proved to be a folded letter, its seal broken. And it was smeared with blood that must be Camilla's.

38

The Purloined Letter

"HELP ME GET Tom back to his bed." Winwood had an arm under Tom's shoulder. "He's off his head with fatigue."

Ned lifted from the other side. "Or just off your head, Tom?"

"It's from laughing." Tom clutched Ned's shoulder, accepting Ned's help. "That termagant came sniffing around our house, seeking to dig for our transgressions, pretending she cares about Camilla." Halfway up the stairs, he said, "How *is* Camilla? She's not truly lost, is she?"

"She will be well," Winwood said. "She's at Mr. Gamlingay's cottage. Agnes Bell is spending the night nursing her."

In Tom's room, Rowland rose from the bed and cast off his invalid disguise, then fixed his cravat and cuffs.

"Wait!" Ned paused. "I am not slow witted, but I missed certain news. When did Rollo learn that it's Tom in bed and Tamsin wearing Tom's suit?"

"Early this morning," Rowland said.

"Because Tom is a terrible liar," Tamsin said.

"I promise to practice more." Tom held out his hands in protest, declining (as usual) to be guilty. "I shall improve with more exercise."

"You need to be in bed." Winwood kept him upright, but Tom was nearly off his feet.

"Does Perry know?" Ned asked because…what if Perry kept secrets after teasing him since the moment they met?

"I shall tell Mr. Frake myself," Tamsin said. "When he returns from London."

Ned and Rowland helped Tom into bed, a special chore that required peeling off Taresa's black silk gown. Winwood fussed over the real invalid the way Tom often complained about.

Ned, however, believed Tom secretly liked it.

"I truly am better. I have imbibed that rare concoction, Doctor Oakes' Astonishing Horse Pizz." Tom sat up in the bed. "A remedy for ague, female decline, and common belly aches."

Winwood pushed Tom back into the goose-feather pillows. "You are about to imbibe the doctor's famous sleep draught."

"Not Mrs. Bell's chicken soup! Can it please be brandy?" Tom laughed again. "I was good, wasn't I, Ned? I saw out the window when Mrs. Fairchild arrived and knew Lizzie needed my help."

"How did you know about Senora Taresa?" Rowland said. "Who fetched that gown for you?"

"Tamsin told me you'd been in disguise in Hawksmoor's carriage. I'm not deaf. I heard the boys drag your baggage upstairs. And I'm not paralyzed." Tom drew up his shoulders, indignant. "I can get out of the house if there's a fire, and I can rescue Lizzie if she's trapped in a monster's maw."

"You were magnificent, Tom." Ned had caught some of Tom's giddiness, happy to see Tom out of bed. All that worry, and those trips to London without Tom, had been a bore and a chore. "An inspiration."

"God blind me!" Rowland said. "I was watching from the hall. I've never seen the like, on the stages of London or Paris."

"Perhaps Taresa shall go to church, come Sunday." Tom basked in Rowland's praise. "I shall lean on Orlando's arm and flutter a lace kerchief."

"Can Tom join us now? We can use his help." Ned had held back fear and angst over Tom's predicament for so long.

Winwood looked stern. "You shall remain in bed, my friend. I shall pray over your desiccated remains in hope you haven't ruined our entire summer's work."

"But we are brothers in arms, and Lizzie needed to be rescued." Tom's eyes drifted past the doctor to Lizzie and Tamsin. "We were taught from the cradle what it means to be an enlightened person."

"I am grateful for your rescue," Lizzie said. "Though my ribs hurt from restraining my emotions."

Amid everyone's laughter, of course Tamsin alone was serious. "Let's leave Tom to sleep."

Whatever Winwood was pouring down Tom's throat prevented him from complaining about being left behind when Tamsin shepherded the others into the hall and closed the door.

"Ned, Lizzie, Rollo. Come talk in Absolom's room." Upstairs, Tamsin closed the door, though the summer heat left Absolom's room stuffy and hot. Ned opened the two windows, which gained a faint breeze.

Tamsin jerked off her coat and untied her cravat. Rowland and Ned did the same. Ned also unbuttoned his shirt, eager for the breeze after the heat and effort of the day's work.

A scratching at the door indicated that Caesar wanted to join them. Ned opened the door, then left it ajar to cool the room.

"I found this under Winwood's bed." Tamsin held out a red-stained rag of paper. "It must be what Camilla stole from Hawksmoor's carriage."

Ned said, "Read it to us."

Tamsin unfolded a single sheet of rag paper. "It's dated from four days ago, in London. It's from Mr. Fairchild." She unfolded it further. "Good stars!"

Ned said, "Get on with it, Tamsin. Tell us what it says." She read to them, the paper shaking in her hands.

> Everyone repeats what is no longer a secret, that King James needs money to expand his standing army. Therefore, the king intends to sell extinct and vacant titles left since the

wars and the Interregnum. He will sell to any rich man who can assume such an estate's debt and taxes, and who will offer the king a suitable garnishment.

Ned asked, "What's a garnishment? A present?"

"A bribe," Rowland said. "A big one. A fortune."

"Can we gather that much?" Lizzie was asking Tamsin, who only said, "Let me finish reading."

He shall deliver up vacant titles for bidding on the first day of September. The king hopes to be satisfied by then that he has found and executed all the men who helped Monmouth.

"Upon my soul!" Lizzie murmured. "We have only one month to do so much."

Ned glanced at his sister, whose lips were pressed into a thin line, as if to keep from saying more. And Tamsin flushed bright red. He shared her anger at the letter's words.

"Is there more?" Rowland asked, curious but not upset like the rest of them.

"Only the final words," Tamsin said. "'Give me your command, and I shall act for your family and mine. Yours, etc., Sheldrake Fairchild.'"

Ned said, "How could Mr. Fairchild betray us this way?"

"I wonder," Rowland said, "how Mrs. Fairchild could let the solicitor wander alone in London. And Heydon is the one man in the neighborhood with sufficient wealth to buy an earl's title. I wager he'd like to be an earl sooner rather than later."

Lizzie said, "That is too cold hearted, Rollo. I do not believe it's any sort of thing Heydon would do."

When Rowland reached for the letter, Tamsin handed it to him. He folded it back into its original shape. Then his face darkened, like when clouds suddenly dim a sunny sky.

"I was too eager to condemn our nemesis." Rowland pointed to the scrawled name across the front of the letter.

Ned nabbed it. He whistled, then handed it to Tamsin, who bit her lip, then read it aloud.

"'To My Lady Candecote.' God's bodkins!" Tamsin exclaimed. "No wonder Camilla stole it."

Ned searched his cousins to understand their feelings, the way Perry examined people. He guessed that neither Lizzie nor Rowland was shocked about the king selling empty titles. Lizzie showed emotion only when hearing Lady Candecote's name. Rowland kept petting Caesar, cool and calm, until he saw Lady Candecote's name.

"Why was Hawksmoor carrying this letter?" Ned asked.

"A favor for a friend? He'd have been home a day earlier, except his coachman fell ill." Rowland clapped his hands, having decided something. "Now we know for a certainty that Sir Isaiah and Fairchild must play in our gambol."

"And now," Lizzie said, "we know for a certainty that Mr. Fairchild assisted in cheating Uncle Absolom."

Tamsin sounded cold and angry. "He, as much as any of them, continues to work to steal Marborne from us."

Ned coughed, then spat into the tiny fireplace, which had not held a fire since May-day. If only Perry were here, since the man had a talent for cutting through to the bone to uncover people's secrets. Unable to guess, Ned had to ask.

"Did you know the king intends to sell titles, Rowland? But didn't tell us?"

"I heard rumors," Rowland said. "Nothing specific. Yesterday didn't seem the kind of day to share rumors about more doom and damnation for all of you."

Ned shook his sister's shoulder. "Lizzie? Did you know?"

"Mary mentioned it as a possibility."

"In her last letter to you?"

"When she sent me home."

While she read the letter, Tamsin's face showed disgust. Now her face was cold as stone, not roused by either Lizzie's or Rowland's confessions.

Ned felt he had to ask them all to agree on the next step. "Our neighbors are revolting fiends. We must agree to run your gambol tomorrow, Rollo. We can't wait."

"Yes," Tamsin said. "There's no more time for another solution. But will we earn enough gold to buy what should already belong to us?"

"It is to be hoped," Rowland said, his face as dark as when he'd spied Lady Candecote's name on that letter.

39

The Priest Hole

— TAMSIN —

HER WHOLE BEING burned again, thinking of how angry Camilla must have been over Mr. Fairchild's letter to her stepmother. Angry enough to point an ancient pistol at Leighton, primed to shoot a man for such a betrayal of Tamsin and the Foxe cousins. Of Absolom, whom they'd just lost.

And then Camilla's angry action had gone terribly wrong.

Tamsin couldn't act just then on the new knowledge about Camilla and the letter. She instead sought to calculate how they could amass a great deal more gold in just one month.

"How much gold will the king require as a garnishment?"

Lizzie answered Tamsin's whispered question. "A fortune. I shall guess five hundred pounds. Perhaps a thousand."

An unattainable fortune. ("I shall act for your family and mine.") Tamsin swallowed more questions that no one knew the answers to: Could Sir Isaiah raise such an amount? Could he and Mr. Fairchild persuade the king to grant a title to a man who'd never had one before?

It was a wonder that the impulsive Camilla had not attempted to shoot all her relatives.

"Now we know that both Fairchild and Sir Isaiah will leap into the gambol, eager for a chance at ready money." Rowland coughed. "Can we sip some of Absolom's brandy? I'm dry as beggars' husks."

Lizzie rummaged in the shelves, found a jug and four small glasses that she set on the table. Rowland held up a glass for her to pour brown liquor into, neither of them catching the other's eye. Tamsin wondered if Lizzie knew any secrets Rowland might have. However, Lizzie often denied that she'd ever had a secret of her own, since she'd only ever lived in a royal court, where all secrets are traded for coin or power.

Rowland asked, "Where are the things Absolom left you?"

Lizzie pointed to a bound volume on the walnut shelves. "The lists in my grandmother's prayer book trace her lineage back to the Crown of Aragón. But that won't help any of us."

Ned jerked his thumb to indicate the paintings above the shelves. "My father left these to Absolom, because the Foxe family rescued him when he was a prisoner in the Dutch fen-gangs. Those two at the end he meant for Lizzie."

"Absolom left me those books," Tamsin said. "And Caesar, who typically sleeps with Tom." Caesar recognized his name and nudged her hand, begging to be scratched. "And the horse Thunder is too old to ride farther than Cambridge."

Rowland examined the shelves. "These are the antiquaries he left for Tom? The shards we dug out of his Roman stones?"

"Yes." Tamsin had forgotten that Tom and Rollo had enjoyed that adventure. "We'll find a buyer in London. This collection can help us out of trouble."

"Sad to see them go."

Ned said, "Where's your Shakespeare, Rollo? Absolom's will said, 'To Rowland Foxe, my volumes of Shakespeare and all else he finds in the place he knows to look.' Where?"

"In the priest hole, surely," Rowland said. "Though last time I hid there, it held only spiders."

"What priest hole?" Lizzie voiced everyone's acute interest.

"Did Absolom never let you use it when we played hide-and-go-seek games? Is that why none of you ever found me? Absolom claimed Revelstone hadn't sheltered secret priests since Elizabeth was queen. A hundred years ago."

Tamsin mused what the house's secret meant. "Perhaps the Roundheads guessed it and that's why they plundered this house during the wars."

"Ned, move, please," Rowland said. "I need to open the floor-boards where you're resting your feet."

Rowland shoved the bed over a hand's breadth and groped along the dusty floorboards. He jammed one with the heel of his fist and grabbed at the rim that popped up. The board came out, with a creaking noise loud enough to frighten the devil. Rowland removed a second board.

"I'll go down," Ned said.

"No, you're too tall." Tamsin didn't, however, volunteer.

Lizzie said, "I'm the smallest, so I should go down."

"Don't be foolhardy," Rowland said. "Light a candle. I'll go. No, wait!" he exclaimed. "That dark-lanthorn still hangs here."

"Chuck off your shirt and pantaloons, Rollo," Lizzie said. "We can't afford to give that suit to the rag-and-bone man."

"I've been careful through heat and dust and trees," Rowland said. "And you don't want to send me naked into the spiders."

Without waiting for an answer, Rowland dangled his legs over the hole. He took the candle from Lizzie and fit it into the lantern, which he hung back on its hook below the lifted floorboards. Then he dropped down, like he used to drop into Marborne brook of a summer's day, crying for his cousins to join him in the cold water. ("It's fine!")

The sound of torn cloth echoed up into Absolom's room, and the odor of ancient dust wafted up as Rowland's boots hit the bottom of the dark passage.

"Guess I was smaller in those days," Rowland called. "I can barely turn around. The old-time Foxes hid tiny priests."

"Be careful," Lizzie admonished.

"What's there?" Ned called down.

"Old candle ends. The world's driest bread crust. Ah!" Rowland rumbled about in that tight space. "Seven bound quartos of Shakespeare and the First Folio. Let me pass them up."

Ned's long arms made that easier. He knelt by the hole and received books as Rowland handed them up.

Another sound of torn cloth. Rowland called up to them. "Never fear. It's nothing Lizzie cannot repair."

Most muffled sounds of his search.

"Got the last one!" he called. "Stopped the spiders from carrying it away. Let me climb up."

Rowland's hand appeared, holding up a small bundle wrapped in thick paper. The lace dripping from his wrist now carried a film of ancient dirt. Tamsin took the packet from his hand. Rowland clambered carefully out of the hole, covered in the dust of ages.

Lizzie sneezed.

"Bless you, dear coz." Rowland dusted off in the hallway, then sat at the table with them. "How'd that old elf manage to place these books down there? Was he spry to the end?"

"What's this one, Rollo?" Lizzie passed the package tied with red string.

"God blind me! Look, it says, 'For Absolom from Josiah the Younger, July 1665. I found an old Hamlet for you.' It must be the last thing Absolom had from my father." Rowland rested his hand on the packet, traced the string, turned it over. "I was too grubby in those days to be trusted with this treasure. Absolom never let me touch it."

"The wrapping is so old," Lizzie said. "Did Absolom ever open it?"

"I suspect not," Rowland said. "It was only a week later than this date that he learned his brothers and nephews were all dead in the plague. I think this was a thorn, a perpetual reminder of that tragedy."

A new commotion in the yard drew Tamsin to the window. "Good stars! The king's men have returned." She spun around, alarmed. "Lizzie, Ned. Hurry. Find out what they want."

"No groundling audience would ever believe this on any stage," Rowland said. "Neither in Paris nor London."

After Ned and Lizzie left, Tamsin said, "Rollo, use the priest hole for its original purpose while we dispose of our visitors."

"Blinking damnation! When will you believe they are not seeking me? Didn't you set them to search for Camilla? Or perhaps they're in search of your restoration treasures."

"Oh no!" Tamsin wasn't reassured. "Help hide the boxes from yesterday's restoration. I'll hand them to you."

"Fine. I shall endure a second dose of dust and spiders merely to hide that you stole boxes from Senora Taresa. Boxes that contain my linen." Rowland surrendered to Tamsin's command and dropped again into the priest hole.

She passed down the boxes, then peered into the hole, hands on her hips.

"Step back, Tamsin, so there's room to climb out."

"What if the same rumors we heard about you being a traitor have passed around this neighborhood? I think you should hide there until the militia goes away."

"I promise you, I'm not in jeopardy from the king's men."

"Can you do it, Rollo? To prevent misunderstandings."

"As you wish, cousin. But hand me the brandy flask. And do not forget to fetch me for supper."

40

Christian Names

— NED —

THE CAPTAIN SPEAKING with Lizzie and Mrs. Bell was the man who'd come with the militia before the averil. His name was— what? Starman? Starbrook?

"Mrs. Fairchild recommended your house as the largest in the parish." The handsome captain held his hat under his arm, quite courteous while making his request.

"We are fortunate," Lizzie said, "but we are full to the eaves with people who have no shelter since the village burned. We cannot quarter your men."

The captain said, "Your great barn could serve us. At least for tonight. We've been searching the parish all afternoon for a lost woman and must begin again at first light."

It'd be a poor idea, quartering the king's men in the great barn, since all their restoration trappings and pistols were stored there. Ned stepped up to argue the point, first introducing himself as Lizzie's brother.

"Captain, it shall not rain tonight," Ned said. "Perhaps you might camp in the unthatched cottages in the village."

"What a good idea, Ned," Lizzie said. "The cottages aren't ready for women and children, but your men should do fine."

"The cottage residents will approve?" the captain asked.

"I shall ask," Mrs. Bell said. "The women are here with their children and might very well agree."

The captain accepted a glass of well water and chatted with Lizzie and Ned while Mrs. Bell secured permissions. Ned was as calm and pleasant as Lizzie while entertaining the captain that Lord Hawksmoor wished would hang them.

Permission secured, Ned led the red-coated visitors to the village, showing them where their horses could join similar livestock on the commons. Ned drew the men's attention away from the barn. "The best water is from the well near the cemetery. I have no idea why that is."

"Perhaps an angel stirred the waters," one man said. The others laughed.

Ned recognized it, vaguely, as something Biblical, but his thoughts were bent on drawing them away from the barn. "We shall send boys with grain for your horses. But the sweetest summer grass is here, since our animals haven't been on this part of the commons since June."

"Good lord!" One of the soldiers stopped, apparently taken aback at the sight of the half-burned village. "How can you spare us your grain?"

"We can do no less for the Crown," Ned said. He left off saying more, for fear of saying too much.

When he left them and returned past the barn, Tamsin was preparing to mount Absolom's riding nag, in a hurry to be gone.

"I'm going to supper with Lord Heydon in Cambridge. If I don't leave now, I shall be tardy and impolite." She readjusted her gloves. "Ned, please take care of Rowland. I made him hide from the king's men."

"No!" He hesitated, wondering why he felt a need to protest so strongly. "Rollo wouldn't be enthused about you going alone to Heydon's house."

"It's not Rollo's business. Or yours." She had one boot in a stirrup and was not to be stopped. "I'm as safe in Heydon's house as I was at the Fairchilds."

"He might unmask you. Like Rollo did."

"Rollo only guessed because Tom gave away our ruse. If I can be Tom for that endless averil with every soul in the parish, I can safely eat supper in town."

"Fine, Tamsin." Ned didn't think it was fine, but knew better than to stop her. "Don't spend too much time at Gamlingay's cottage on your way home. We need to practice our part of the gambol."

Just after she disappeared down the lane that led to the Cambridge road, Perry Frake rode up the trail from the Phoenix and Swan, his horse in a heat.

The man could not have ridden as far as the first posting house in the time since they parted at the Fairchild house.

Ned hurried to welcome him back.

To help rub down Duchess.

To see how well Perry treated the horse he rode.

And to satisfy his curiosity about Perry's early return. (For which he was unreasonably happy.)

Perry already had a curry-comb in hand. Two barn cats twined around his boots, also begging for the big man's attention. Ned's fingers tingled, he so longed to paint that image, an impressive man with two calicos yearning for his touch, his strong hands gentling a tired horse. It'd take every shade of brown on his palette plus shades of vermillion to make the animals come alive, and for the man's perfect mouth. Chalk white for stray flashes of sunlight. A careful mixing of orpiment with a benign white to capture the streaks in Perry's straw-colored hair.

"Perry!"

When Ned called his name, Perry looked up from the horse and cats. He beamed as if delighted.

Ned's heart pummeled his ribs when that sunny attention turned on him. What blues to mix to capture ice-blue eyes?

"Aye, so you've escaped, my dear Ned. The *kattenkop* Fairchild woman did not get her catty claws in you?"

"We all escaped. But you're back so soon."

"That's a tale that wants telling." Perry began his currying chore. "Now, please satisfy my curiosity, my love. Did I give you sufficient time to miss me?"

Ned, on the other side of the horse, ran a hand over Duchess's damp, heated flank. He smelled the sweet odor of sweat. A muscle twitched at Ned's touch, then the horse relaxed, content to have the two men brushing her. "I'm happy you have enough sense not to work a horse too hard on a summer's day."

"You assuage my heart, dear man. That's one of the nicest things ever said of me."

— TAMSIN —

"GAD'S BOBS, TOM. Where have you hidden my wife?"

At the same moment that Tamsin knocked on Heydon's door, a screeching voice called from the street. Leighton Fairchild.

"Good afternoon. Rather, good evening, Leighton. What brings you to town?"

"I followed when they told me you were seen on the Cambridge road." He bounded onto the portico, standing uncomfortably close, attempting to tower over Tamsin, though they were about the same height. She recoiled at his closeness. All her anger over Camilla's injuries rolled up again. She choked out a decent response.

"I'm honored, Leighton, but I have an appointment. Perhaps tomorrow we can—"

Leighton, once more the worse for drink, grabbed Tamsin's sleeve. "Give me my wife. I know you have her."

"You are mistaken." Tamsin spoke the truth. Camilla was still at the rector's cottage. "Your wife is not here."

Leighton jerked her around to face him. The door opened behind her at the same moment that Leighton took a swing, his fist closed, his ring gleaming in the slanted light. Tamsin ducked, a disgraceful cowering, but she had no experience with boys' fisticuffs. The force of Leighton's swing carried him over her, until he stumbled, his knee bashing her thigh.

Another bruise.

When Leighton got himself back together, a figure at the door began castigating him.

"Mr. Fairchild, you may be the master of contumely, but I will not allow insults and ungentlemanly attacks at my door."

Heydon had a hand to his left cheek where Leighton had mistakenly struck him.

"I'm sorry, your lordship." Leighton had never cringed like that in Tamsin's presence. "It's a private matter."

"You cannot conduct your private affairs here." Heydon's voice dripped distain. "You will cease your glimflashy conduct and deport yourself peacefully. Else, I shall call the constable."

After Leighton finished his abject apologies and walked down the street, desultory as can be, Heydon led Tamsin inside. He called for a servant to bring linen and water.

"What did that fustilarian want, Tom?"

"His wife, Camilla, went missing. Leighton often blames me for problems with his wife."

"Are you the cause?"

"No. Leighton causes his own problems." Tamsin waited for Heydon to tell her where to sit, but he wasn't forthcoming.

The servant appeared with the basin and cloth. "Will that be all, your lordship? We are about to depart."

"Yes. You may leave for the night."

Tamsin said, "Can I assist you, your lordship? You've taken a hurt that was meant for me."

Heydon cast an inquiring glance over his shoulder. "No, thank you, Tom." He mopped the wound on his cheek, washing away a trickle of blood. "It's a scratch, but it's an ill-natured one. Why ever does that man wear such a vulgar signet ring? What is wrong with him?"

He examined the linen, checking that he'd mopped up the last of the blood. When he returned his attention to Tamsin, he had three thin scratches along the side of his face.

"Good lord!"

"What, Tom?"

Her shock surprised Heydon. However, she couldn't explain that Camilla, hidden in Mr. Gamlingay's cottage, also bore three thin lines scratched on her face by the points of the letter F on Leighton's outlandish ring. Camilla said he'd grabbed her pistol, not that he'd struck her. Tamsin had just seen how hard Leighton hit Heydon to leave such a mark.

As soon as possible, Tamsin intended to chastise Leighton, though it would require yet another scheme, after they finished with Rowland's gambol.

"There's a speck of blood on your cravat."

"Oh? Thank you." Heydon removed that small diamond pin he always wore, unwound his cravat, and tossed it away with the linen he'd used on his face.

"I'm sorry to have brought that to your door, your lordship."

"Come, Tom." Heydon motioned for his guest to follow into the next room. "You shall forgive me, but I must say it. Though it's been months since we've enjoyed supper together, are we not long-time friends, Tom? Won't you please still call me Poynter? We agreed between us to use our Christian names."

"Yes, Poynter." She'd never said his Christian name aloud. Why hadn't she taken half an hour to know more from Tom? "The past weeks at home have been a punishment. We've been isolated and grieving. I've been so wound up in my cousins' travails, and with my sister and Absolom both ill, I've abandoned my friends. You will forgive me, I hope?"

"It's not a serious trespass. I merely wanted to confirm that we remain friends." He gestured to a chair. "Please, let's sit and talk. I've let the servants have the night free. My cook left a collation for our supper."

Tamsin chose a corner of the narrow table in the darkest shadows. She slipped onto an intricately carved chair. The early summer evening meant that candles weren't required. Heydon pressed attention to the platter of cold meat and cheeses, urging his friend to begin while waiting his own turn. Tamsin, having to remove her gloves, used her left hand to make generous choices using a new-made fork with long, sharp tines and a crest stamped on the handle.

Heydon buttered bread with a silver-handled knife, then passed it to Tamsin on a trivet. She had no intention of being afraid of this man. If Rowland was correct, that Heydon had greedily impoverished Marborne, it made him an enemy but not a personal threat to her. He had, in fact, offered Lizzie kind support that morning. However, if Heydon had invited Tom Foxe for a conversation, he was slow to speak. She sought to break the silence.

"We appreciate that you honored us with a visit at our Uncle Absolom's averil."

"Averil is such a surprising word." Heydon said. "As if you imported the idea from York or Berwick-upon-Tweed. However, the Foxe family has been here since—when, Tom?"

"Absolom says...said Marborne appears in the Domesday Book." Tamsin took time chewing her first bite of supper. "It's Mrs. Bell, who had a Scots mother, who taught us to say averil."

"It's been a long time since the parish experienced such a funeral feast. It's not often we lose a man as important to so many people as was Doctor Foxe."

Again, Heydon spoke kindly, offering comforting words.

"It's been a long time since the Foxe family has lost anyone." Tamsin's mind flitted away from the loss of Absolom. "We were infants when our parents were lost in the London plague."

"I was but a boy, but I remember that sad time." Heydon shook his head. "There was no feast to honor those lost. Only a service in Marborne church on a dark, rainy day." He buttered another piece of bread, pushing it toward Tamsin on a trivet. "But let us not dwell this evening on those sad losses."

"I must confess," Tamsin said, "that I've been curious about your invitation to supper. What shall we discuss?"

"We shall do as everyone did at your averil." Heydon set down his fork and stretched his thin frame, leaning back from the table. "We shall gossip about our neighbors and agree on how to defend ourselves from them."

41

Quartering

— ROLLO —

As SOON AS he descended into that hole, Rowland baked like a salamander caught on the fire-dogs, yet he could do nothing more than put Shakespeare to use, cursing his weakness for assenting to Tamsin's fear of the king's men.

> You starveling, you eel-skin,
> you dried neat's-tongue,
> you bull's-pizzle, you stock-fish.
> O for breath to utter what is like thee!
> You tailor's-yard, you sheath, you bow-case.

He rolled his gold angel over his fingers, guessing how long it would take for his cousins to send the king's men away. The candle-lantern revealed ancient dust, which was likely ruining his clothes. He'd again be scolded by Lizzie.

At last, Rowland decided to remove himself from that hell-hole and not wait for his cousins to save him. After several attempts to get the proper angle, he braced on the ladder to shove the floorboards free. Yet when Rowland coiled and struck, the ladder step broke, and he again tore his borrowed pantaloons. The floorboards remained unmoved.

He placed a foot on the next higher step, which meant doubling up like a French acrobat. In his next attempt, he couldn't coil enough power to move the tight-fitting boards.

He took weak comfort from Caesar, who had been left behind and sniffed at the boards, whining.

"Good Caesar. Kind Caesar. Fetch someone. Find Ned. Oh blast, you're trapped too, aren't you? Well, dog, please bark."

Rowland tried it, barking, hoping that Caesar would join in a chorus. But that just evoked more whining.

"Yes, Caesar. They spent years saying, 'No barking.' Forget your manners for a moment. Scratch and howl at the door."

But then someone entered.

"My blessed Lord! Who left this poor critter here?" It was Mrs. Bell. Rowland prepared to pound on the boards, intent on release. She said, "I hope it will do for you, captain. I'll send boys to remove these boxes."

"Have no mind about it, Mrs. Bell. We shall beg quartering only for tonight." A nice Hereford accent. "And I'll break bread with my men, so please don't go to any bother for us."

"It's no bother to aid them that protect us. Here, help me move this bed back in place." The scraping meant that the heavy timber bed had been placed once more over the floorboards. "I shall take Caesar away and send someone with clean linen."

Caesar, however, scampered under the bed. More conversation, with Mrs. Bell coaxing the dog out.

"Take no mind, mistress. I like the company. We shall leave the door open, so the creature can depart when he's ready. His name is Caesar?"

Though the bed was heavy, it creaked when that captain sat on it after Mrs. Bell departed. Caesar scratched at the boards.

Rowland determined that he would accept being drawn-and-quartered before smothering in the heat and dust, which he'd do if he remained in that hole any longer. He beat on the boards. Caesar at last raised a voice above a whimper.

"What is it, little friend? Rats in the rafters? Here, come out of there." That captain moved the heavy bed again, which must be when he heard Rowland pounding.

"Ghosts?" An amused voice asked.

"Push the notched board," Rowland called. "Now pull up."

When Rowland rose from the dusty depth, he encountered the eager Caesar and also Valentine Starbuck, who'd won every round while shooting targets when they'd served together in Paris. Still as fresh-faced as when they'd last gambled in Paris a year ago (and Rowland again lost at target shooting), Starbuck's sole concession to the passage of time was a neat beard in the new English style.

"Rollo! I've been hoping to find you. And as I recollect, you owe me two Louis d'or coins." Starbuck held his arms wide, offering a soldier's embrace, no surprise on his beaming face.

"'Would I wert clean enough to spit upon,' as the Bard says. Don't get my filth on your lovely red wool." Rowland clutched Starbuck's hand, elated to see him, yet keeping his friend at arm's length. "I've been swimming in the dust of the ages. You, a captain! But then, I knew you'd meet your destiny."

"Was it always your destiny to emerge from a hole in the floor? Why were you entombed?"

"My cousin has a wild idea that you might think I'm one of Monmouth's rebels, and so might want to hang me. But please know that my Royalist cousins would never harbor a rebel."

"I shall not hang you before I get my two gold louis. Is this an old-time priest hole? You always have such surprises, Rollo."

When Starbuck stepped away to examine the hole, Rowland stripped off his filthy shirt, which sent dust twirling in the sunlight. Starbuck sneezed. Caesar sneezed.

"You cannot believe how ecstatic I am to find a gentleman here." Rowland found his other shirt on the shelf where Lizzie had left it, the one with its initials picked away. "And that the gentleman is you, Valentine."

Starbuck said, "How long have you been in England, Rollo? I came yesterday in search of you."

"Perry and I arrived in London six days ago. I'm fortunate to find you here, but not fortunate to have two spare gold coins."

"You're like hundreds of others that William sent home from Amsterdam? My colonel guessed you'd be returning to England."

Starbuck named as his colonel a fellow who'd gambled with them in Paris, a man who had a title and a fortune.

"Our old friend made colonel? Another war and he'll be a general, won't he? But he's a good man."

"Do you have an assignment in Cambridgeshire, Rollo? Shall we work together?"

"No, I'm here for certain family business, which I hope I can conclude quickly. Not sure where they'll send me next." He hadn't decided whether to share that he intended to solve his family's business and his task for the Crown in one gambol.

"I like this posting," Starbuck said. "I'm no scobberlotcher, but after battling rebels in early summer, it's a respite. And it's cozier than that snakes' nest of exiles and diplomats we endured in Paris. Here, you don't risk ten betrayals between breakfast and dinner among people out to sell each other's honor."

"Ah, Valentine. You blessed innocent," Rowland said. "The people here are as capable of betraying their neighbors as..."

Lady Candecote's weak-witted words struck him at last. ("We gave you our money, Danvers. You promised we'd be rich. Why must we sell our paintings to have enough to do as we planned?")

It had nagged at him since Tamsin shared details of Absolom's betrayal. It was unlikely—preposterous—that the famous and extraordinarily wealthy Sir Charles (or agents in his office) had forged liens and created a syndicate to perpetrate a fraud. Absolom had been deceived about that agent. Or misunderstood.

The infamous intelligencer Rowland Foxe, however, had just been a bennish beetle-head not to see from the moment he met Hawksmoor in London that Danvers Duncombe was at the center of the cheat played on Absolom.

"Rollo?"

"I'm weak from hunger, Valentine. Come with me to raid the kitchen before I perish."

42

Supper

— TAMSIN —

IN THE SHADOWS of Heydon's dining room in Cambridge, Tamsin bent to retrieve a dropped napkin, sneaking a moment to press at her Archangel pouch, hoping to capture and save her anger at Leighton for when she had the ability to act on that anger. Just then, she had to listen closely to Heydon, to identify whether he was their nemesis.

"You are wily, Tom, and likely have surmised from what I said yesterday and again today, that I intend to admonish you."

"I shall endeavor, like Ajax, to withstand your hectoring with bravery and admiration."

"Good man." Heydon clapped his hands as if in prayer, then tipped them in compliment for the jest. "May I pour you a glass of this excellent port I acquired in London?"

"A little." Tamsin made herself say his name. "A very little, Poynter. Yesterday's averil did damage to my head."

From where Tamsin studied him in the shadows, Heydon seemed magisterial, his narrow hand moving as he spoke, using many of the same gracious gestures as Lizzie. Likely from spending time at court in London. Likely from an inherited gentility that had missed Tamsin, who conceived herself to be a muddy farm-child sitting at Heydon's polished table.

"Indeed?" Heydon poured dark liquor into two glasses, watching that stream while he spoke. "I didn't see that you had time for so much as a mug of Revelstone's good ale yesterday."

"It was a working day, certainly. And I observed today that neither you nor I cared for Mrs. Fairchild's posset."

Heydon said, "Where do English women get such absurd notions? Ruining good sherry. Ruining cream that should be clobbered into butter."

He sipped port; she sipped one too-sweet drop, then decided that this was a good time to ask fearlessly about the mortgages.

But before she could begin, Heydon said, "It's Mrs. Fairchild that I want to talk to you about."

"The solicitor's wife?" The devil's own woman, whom the real Tom fooled earlier that day. "Whatever for?"

"You will think me a foul gossip, out to blacken your neighbors. Though you are at odds with her son. Perhaps you'll be inclined to lend me an ear." Heydon tipped his glass, moving it into the early evening light from the window, the watching the port crawl down the sides of the glass. "I've been asking questions. Let me share what I've learned. For your own protection."

"From Mrs. Fairchild? That's absurd, Poynter." Except that Camilla needed protection from that woman. But how could Heydon discover that? "She's stern. Judgmental. But she has no real power in the neighborhood."

"That's a notion of which I must disabuse you." Heydon supped his port. Tamsin set hers aside. "Remember last December when we talked, Tom? When I confessed that I planned to transgress against our neighbors, to uncover their private affairs? We haven't had a chance to speak since then. You brought your sister home, so desperately ill, and I was engaged at court all of the spring and much of the summer."

"I have been distracted and apologize again for abandoning our friendship." Had the invalid Tom forgotten everything when he took ill? He never mentioned such an encounter with Heydon.

"Understandable. But now I shall share with you what the intelligencer I hired has learned."

"An intelligencer?" (Good stars. Another besides Rowland?)

"It's a person who uncovers—"

"I know what an intelligencer is, Poynter. It wasn't a question, just a mark of my surprise. Why undertake such a venture?"

"As you and I talked at Twelfth Night, I discovered that my brother's business has turned desperate in the past year. And Marborne's affairs are caught along with his." Heydon swirled his port again, as if delaying what he'd say next, which sent a twinge of fearful anticipation through Tamsin. "I'm about to tell you this story, because you and I must act as partners to resolve certain...shall I say, awkward affairs?"

She reached for her glass, to sip port in anticipation, but she reached with her poorly healed right hand, so had to quickly draw that hand back into her lap. That hand, without its glove was not a pretty sight. She grasped the glass in her left hand, her body tense, not knowing whether the promised story might confirm or refute that this man was their nemesis.

"Tell your story, Poynter." The port was both bitter and sweet on her tongue when she took a sip.

"As you likely know, The Fairchilds arrived in the county three years ago. He inherited a law office and a house from an uncle." He waited for Tamsin to nod a confirmation. "With that law office, Mr. Fairchild inherited my brother's affairs."

"And Foxe family affairs."

"Yes. This is where your business and mine are entangled."

"And Mrs. Fairchild is involved?" Tamsin worried that she revealed her sense of Mrs. Fairchild as a personal nemesis.

"That woman," Heydon did not admire her, "quickly advanced in Cambridge society, introducing many of her connections to our neighbors. My brother and Sir Isaiah met their new wives through Mrs. Fairchild."

"Those three women who patrolled Absolom's averil as the enforcers of funeral manners?" Tamsin spoke her resentment, then repented. "I'm sorry. I was raised to speak better of my neighbors. Yet I remember our housekeeper, Mrs. Bell, gossiping about up-start brides more than once in recent years. But is that the story you want to tell me?"

"There's more. Be patient, Tom. Mr. Fairchild began to mis-manage my brother's affairs. When Monck complained—as politely as you can imagine—the solicitor passed all of Monck's affairs to a business man in London."

Tamsin's nervous sense rose again. This presented an oppor-tunity to ask Heydon about the mortgages.

"Sir Charles Duncombe?" Absolom had warned that one of the three men who tricked him was Sir Charles's agent. And it appears Hawksmoor was cheated too, while Mr. Fairchild proved to be the cheat Camilla had uncovered in that ill-fated restoration.

"No, it was Mr. Danvers Duncombe, whom you observed this morning. Since he turned his affairs over to Mr. Duncombe, all Monck's investments have fallen to losses. While most of London grows richer with each ship that arrives from the New World."

"That aroused your curiosity about Mr. Duncombe?" If Ab-solom had known this, would he have sent both Tamsin and Row-land in pursuit of Hawksmoor?

"I'm embarrassed at how long it took me to be aware of the problem." Heydon swished his port once more, which Tamsin now saw as a portent for another revelation. "I'd been away in Paris, and often in London at court. Hence, it's only recently—two years after my brother married that woman—that I was compelled to ask the help of an intelligencer."

"Poynter," Tamsin still wasn't comfortable with this familiar-ity, "if you wanted to tease my interest, please trust that you have all my attention."

"First, my brother's new wife is Mrs. Fairchild's half-sister."

"But there must be twenty years between them."

"Yes, just about the same span as between my brother and me. Lady Hawksmoor has a different father and was raised in a dif-ferent city."

"That's why they do not share an accent?"

"Yes. My brother and I are a generation apart, which shows in our tastes and experiences. But we claim each other. Do you not wonder why a woman would introduce a sister into the neighborhood, but never reveal their connection?"

"Are you about to tell me?"

"No, because I don't understand it. I'm about to tell you that Lady Candecote is another half-sister. Same mother. Yet another father. Raised by an aunt in Bath."

"Who is their mother?"

"An often-widowed merchant's wife, now also taken to heaven. Or so a charitable heart must believe."

"And her oldest daughter has married her sisters into the gentry of Cambridgeshire."

"And her son—who assaulted us tonight—also married Sir Isaiah's daughter. A worthy series of achievements for a merchant's daughter."

"What is her scheme?" Tamsin managed those few sensible words, while quelling her anger at what Leighton had done to Camilla, how Mrs. Fairchild made Camilla miserable. Then there was the revelation that afternoon, when Tamsin found the letter Camilla stole at the last restoration, proving that Mr. Fairchild and Lady Candecote schemed to steal Marborne.

"I can only surmise, Tom, because my intelligencer has not yet discovered the larger game the woman's brother plays."

"Brother?"

"Our new friend, Mr. Danvers Duncombe, the man who has mismanaged my brother's business in drastic ways, even from before he bought the Marborne mortgages."

Tamsin hoped the shadows hid the waves that twitched across her face while her mind tried to connect new ideas. First, the three judgmental queens of Cambridgeshire were sisters, who had dealt grief to Camilla. Second, Rowland was simply wrong about the viscount.

Heydon was not their nemesis.

"Mr. Duncombe?" Tamsin said it slowly, naming the man she'd considered a bit of a fool, but who was in fact their enemy. "Who has set his own sights high, believing he has a chance with my cousin Ysabel."

"You saw that too? At the averil, and at the Fairchilds? He has wooed other women who have court connections. And virtually all of his enterprises are buried in blind syndicates. Did you or Doctor Foxe learn more about his syndicates than my intelligencer has pierced?"

"No." How much would Perry uncover while he prowled in London? Since Tamsin had now discovered the error in Rowland's guesses about Heydon, she had to share what she knew, though it was as if Rowland still whispered cautions in her ear. "My uncle met in late June with the agent who brokered the sale of the Marborne mortgages to the syndicate. Absolom had papers proving the mortgage terms had been met, but the agent presented papers showing the terms ran another ten years. The agent insisted it was impossible to know who made up the blind syndicate. My uncle fell ill on the trip home and never recovered."

"Oh, poor gentleman. This is so very sad to hear."

"In the story Absolom told me, the agent worked in Sir Charles Duncombe's office. I see now he was mistaken."

"It's just our Mr. Duncombe, conniving in his own offices." Heydon checked the level of liquid in his glass. "What do you think now, Tom, after learning what I've shared?"

"I wish I'd known this at the averil when Mr. Duncombe presumed to shake my hand and offer condolences! But to take in all your insights—it's like a feast that needs to be digested."

She wasn't prepared to describe the turmoil in her belly, the fear in her veins. Heydon had diverted her perpetual worries about Camilla, but he'd doubled her worries for Marborne. Tamsin instead shared that day's other shock.

"Did you know, Poynter, that our king is selling empty titles? We've been to London every month, seeking an audience with the king, to beg the restoration of the Marborne title. Could it be that the wealthy Mr. Duncombe intends to bid for the title and turn us out as beggars?"

"That possibility has crossed my mind. More port, Tom?" He dangled the bottle in query.

"No, thank you. And I am grateful, Poynter, that you chose to share what you've learned. If nothing else, perhaps we shall be better prepared to defend ourselves from Mrs. Fairchild's blind syndicate of siblings."

"Clever. You are swift-witted." Heydon splashed a half portion of port into his glass. "You must imagine that I feel great trepidation, living among people unwilling to confess their relations." He stretched to reach Tamsin's hand where she clutched the carved arm of her chair. "It would, therefore, give me great joy if you'd trust me."

"But I do, Poynter." Tom and Lizzie were right, and Rowland was wrong about Heydon.

"I mean, please trust me to know your true self." Heydon held her hand lightly, tenderly. "Miss Thomasine."

43

Enlightened People

PERRY SNEEZED. NED SNEEZED.

They'd sneezed several times while leaning over Duchess's stall after they finished currying her. One of the orange barn cats again leaped up on Perry's shoulder, and he took it into his arms. Perry described his prowling business, but rather than an adventure, it was yet another lesson for Ned in how to run a rig instead of playing honest highwaymen.

They both petted the cat while Ned recounted the adventures at the Fairchild house, first with the reading of Absolom's will and then with Rowland's work to stir greed among their neighbors. He described how Mrs. Fairchild proved eager to join in Rowland's gambol while cruel to Camilla and her servants.

"And she's unspeakably rude to T–Tom," Ned said. "Then, when we came home, we found the letter Camilla stole during our restoration. It says Lady Candecote and Mr. Fairchild seek to run a diabolical trick to buy the Marborne title from the king."

"A specially bad way for men to strike at their neighbors."

"Aye, very black hearted," Ned said. "The Marborne title should be returned to the Foxe heirs."

In the dense accent he adopted when he teased, Perry asked, "Why do the Foxe cousins yearn to return to the nobility? English royalty has done nothing for the family in fifty years, except for making your sister the princess's charity case."

"I suppose that's true." What else seemed true: Perry could not resist plaguing Ned with outrageous ideas, even on a lazy summer afternoon like this.

"Now, proud serfs," Perry pointed with a thumb to his own chest, "we don't take it hard when yet another king appears. Though it gives pause when we wake up to find the king has stuck heads on pikes."

Ned said, "T–Tom insists that we can't repair the parish without the Marborne title being restored."

"You could choose another path." Perry's petting the cat caused it to purr so loudly that it rumbled under Ned's touch. "Plenty have gone to the New World to regain what they lost in the wars."

"They buy and sell people there." Ned repeated Lizzie's indignant words. "And earn their living off that execrable trade."

Perry said, "It is abominable."

"Then it's not strange," Ned said, "that we want to be here to protect and rebuild our parish. We can't trust that anyone else will take care of our friends."

"Likely true." Perry shifted the cat and then slapped Ned's shoulder, as if he had a sudden idea. "We need to extract coin from the ignoble rich, so we can wrangle the Marborne title back from the king." Perry stretched, his arm extending behind Ned's shoulders. "Now, shall we find Rollo? I needs must share what I learned from this day's work."

"Zooterkins!" Ned exclaimed. How had his mind emptied so completely? "T–Tom told me to fetch Rowland once the soldiers were settled."

"Soldiers?"

"They are quartering in the half-thatched cottages. Tom made Rollo hide when they appeared. I wonder what he's got up to."

Ned pounded through the back door into the winter kitchen, still guessing where Tamsin might have hidden Rowland.

But in that kitchen, usually deserted in summer, Rowland sat at the table with the doctor, wine cups in hand. And no sign of Mrs.

Bell, who didn't allow casual confraternity in any of the kitchens. Ned paused at the door, listening.

The cat brushed against Ned's leg. Perry came up behind and nudged him through the door. Ned had an argument to settle with Perry later, because the doctor proved to be the rational man Ned thought him to be. No one but Camilla had been allowed past the wall around Tamsin's innermost being.

"Oh, hello, Ned! You're dusty as scythe-men at harvest." Rowland smiled with pleasure at seeing them. Winwood seemed relieved. "Valentine has, as is his nature, charmed the housekeeper off her guard. He has gone off to fetch more wine with Mrs. Bell."

"Valentine?"

"Captain Starbuck." Then Rowland spied Perry lurking behind Ned. "Mr. Frake, have you magically transported your large carcass to London and back in an afternoon? Will Tamsin ever forgive you for abusing a horse in such a way?"

Perry took a seat on the bench near Rowland. Ned swung a leg over the bench to sit by Winwood, who pushed a plate of cheese and sliced cottage bread close to Ned's hand.

"I've been back some time." Perry had his hand over Ned's on the tin serving plate, coaxing Ned into serving him a slice of Mrs. Bell's best. "Before I was a furlong down the road, I had a notion—not for the first time—that our friend Duncombe would not leave his most precious papers behind while he's here on business. Therefore, I put my simple skills to work and examined his baggage."

"Good man." Rowland glanced over at the doctor, as if checking his reaction.

Perry said, "Did you guess in your midsummer dreams, Rollo, that Mr. Duncombe has corresponded with the Crown to learn what it might take to buy the Marborne title?"

That wasn't part of the "changed my mind about London" story Perry told while he chatted with Ned in the great barn.

"My thoughts drifted in that direction." Rowland passed his wine cup over to Perry, as if rewarding him. "Clever business."

"I'd best be going." Winwood rose.

Rowland touched his arm and motioned for him to sit down. "Captain Starbuck is not going to prosecute you for past sins, Mr. Surgeon. And you need no longer pretend ignorance about Foxe family business. My friend Starbuck isn't coming after me or any of my friends."

"Thank you, I suppose," Winwood said.

"Butter your bread, doctor. You'll miss a grand tale if you leave now." Perry pushed the tin plate over to him, then turned to Ned and spoke as if in confidence, but loudly. "This Starbuck is the fledgling who won at high-stakes shooting in Paris. Our master always liked him best."

"Oh?" Captain Starbuck appeared at the cellar door, Mrs. Bell behind him. "It's you, Perry Frake? You wagered they'd hang me before I came of age. You bet six francs that I'd fall into a deep scrape with no hope of rescue. Here I am. Time to pay up."

"It was merely a figure of speech," Perry protested. "Are ye still innocent and gullible as a lamb, Captain Starbuck?"

— TAMSIN —

"IT SEEMS YOUR hand took a grievous hurt." Heydon released Tamsin's hand and sat back in his chair. "And I should guess that it's Tom who is ill."

"Yes." As if she'd been stripped naked, Tamsin sought to cover herself, not knowing whether she was safe or if she'd been stupid in ignoring Ned's warnings.

"You are compelled to play Tom's part while begging our king to restore the Marborne title?"

"It's what my family and our villages need most."

Heydon said, "The...oddity was not apparent at first, though it was disconcerting to see you eat with your left hand. Then you barely sipped my excellent port. Tom loves port. Will you give him my best wishes for his recovery? I shall send the rest of this port home with you. He might find it a restorative."

"Tom wanted to come to supper, but he's not well enough. I hope I haven't injured your friendship."

"Never worry." Heydon sipped his port again. "Now, that we can be entirely frank with each other, I must say that the entire neighborhood knows how desperate Marborne affairs have become. Miss Foxe's plan to sell her paintings makes sense. But I wonder what more might the two of you intend?"

"Lizzie and I both seek to restore the earldom. I seek to protect the villages, and she seeks to do what she can for us before returning to Princess Mary's court."

"Have you conquered your misgivings about Lord Orlando's venture? Especially since he engaged Mr. Duncombe? Given what I just shared?"

Tamsin tried for diversion. "Lord Orlando assured us that our assets shall be safe, that there's no risk."

"Is his scheme genuine? Or a trick? I'm guessing he's the author of this idea, and not the Princess Mary."

Tamsin wasn't ready to answer. Had Rowland's gambol just been tossed to the winds?

"Trick then." Heydon waited scant moments for an answer. "Now, Miss Thomasine, I have my own plan to make Duncombe and his sisters accountable for cheating my brother. Can you and I please agree that we will not interfere with each other's plans?"

"I—I believe...yes." She could ponder it for days, but her heart said yes, right then.

"I cannot prove that Monck's wife is innocent, so if she begs to be admitted to Lord Orlando's plan, I will not object. But I ask that my brother Monck not be pulled into whatever you plan."

This was beyond confounding, and Tamsin had to call up all her courage as the bold leader of their restorations. "The day before he died, Doctor Foxe told me that Lord Hawksmoor and Mr. Fairchild together swindled him over those old mortgages. We are working to resolve that injustice."

"But Doctor Foxe was mistaken. My brother Monck is innocent. He has himself been cheated by Duncombe and his people. Can you please protect Monck from injury in whatever scheme Lord Orlando plans?"

Explaining this would mean a difficult conversation with her cousins. But they'd certainly see that she had to make this promise. "I owe you that, especially since I deceived you while enjoying your hospitality."

Heydon thought a moment. "And me? Am I on your list of those you believe perpetuated injustice?"

"Lizzie says no. Tom says no. And Uncle Absolom said you tried to make peace when he quarreled with your brother."

"Unhappy man! I am so sorry his last days were spent in turmoil and misery." Heydon reached out his hand. "However, my father first held your mortgages. I therefore inherited a responsibility for the Foxe family travails, and a duty to remove any resentments between our families. You do harbor hard feelings, don't you? Tell the truth."

Tamsin took a breath. "Uncle Absolom insisted that your father took advantage of his brothers during the famine years, giving those mortgages at usury terms."

"I was only a boy when my father died. I never knew him well enough to say whether he might have cheated his neighbors. As for Duncombe, we shall learn what more we can in the coming days." Heydon toasted her with his nearly empty port glass. "Miss Thomasine, you and Miss Foxe have noble goals, to save your people and your land. I salute you."

Tamsin tipped her glass to Heydon's but couldn't speak. Her ears burned at the compliment, but her head raced. She'd need an excellent disguise the next day, when she played the adept, so neither Heydon nor any neighbor might recognize her.

One ignoble thought could not be repressed. For Camilla's sake, tomorrow Tamsin intended to take revenge on the high-handed Mrs. Fairchild and her dishonest sisters.

Revenge is not the way of enlightened people.

Though Tamsin heard Absolom's voice, teaching his rules, her belly tense again, from anger and trepidation. Surely her uncle would also be in turmoil over Heydon's revelations.

University bells chimed the hour. She'd lost track of time.

"I must be off for home."

"Certainly. I have business to undertake also. Besides this port, you must also carry home my apologies to Senora Taresa. I was harsh with her at my brother's house yesterday."

"How so?"

"I accused her of fishing for my brother's gold. Now that I have met her brother Orlando—and you have recounted his worthy intention to help Miss Foxe—I see that I was foolish. Please carry my humble apology. Yet one thing remains true about what I said to Senora Taresa: I shall do whatever it takes to protect my brother and the Hawksmoor estates."

"I will. Good night, sir—Poynter."

"Travel safe. I shall see you tomorrow."

Not if Tamsin could prevent it, not while she judged paintings in the gambol. "No, sir. I am not available tomorrow."

"Then please give my greetings to Tom and my very best regards to your cousin Miss Ysabel Foxe. Be sure that she knows I am a servant to her cause."

44

In the Gloaming

— TAMSIN —

SHE URGED HER horse onward. Tamsin had hoped to be home by sunset, but supper lasted longer than she'd planned. She now rode with care in the gloaming, though she loved summer twilight, the pale blue skies turning pink. The peace of a warm day ready for sleep. She breathed the evening's odors, hoping to calm the turmoil of news and surprise mixing in her brain.

"What do you think, Thunder? More surprises than we're used to, don't you agree? And here, it's two days later and I still haven't explained to you that our Uncle Absolom is gone. How will we make our way now that life is changed forever?"

Horses are never good at philosophical discourse. Tamsin was about to choose a lane that passed near Gamlingay's cottage (and that bypassed the Fairchilds) when Thunder surprised a gaggle of geese browsing in a mint patch. The geese, annoyed, launched a virulent attack, swarming the horse, honking in fury. The horse stamped, not to attack the geese, but to find footing among the malicious birds nipping at its hooves.

By the time she'd calmed her horse, Tamsin chose another lane instead of braving her way through a mass of malevolent fowl. That called for a second decision: to return to Mr. Gamlingay's house later, after meeting with Ned to learn how to be an adept judge of paintings, which was her last task for that day.

"Come, Thunder, you'll be safe at home."

In the great barn, Duchess was already in her stall, fresh and happy, which meant that Perry had returned long before. Tamsin brushed Thunder and shared a carrot with each of the horses. Tired to the bone, she came into the house through the winter kitchen, on her way to find Ned.

But the kitchen had become a village pub, with scraps of supper still on tin plates and jugs of wine on the table.

Captain Starbuck smiled shyly when Tamsin came through the door, his cheeks rosy, his eyes poorly focused, one arm around Rowland, the other arm around Tom, who was enjoying himself as much as when he'd entertained Mrs. Fairchild.

Winwood moved a wine cup out of Tom's reach, then motioned to the empty stool beside him. "Please join us."

"Where's Lizzie?"

"She pleaded a headache," Ned said.

"After one infant's cup of wine," Tom added. "In fact, she left when I proposed dice, and Rollo argued that Perry must not take advantage of Valentine in our house."

"Valentine?"

"Captain Starbuck." Tom stood, swaying. "Valentine, allow me to introduce my sister, Thomasine Foxe. We call her Tamsin. She can run faster than any of us. However, I sit a horse far better than she manages, no matter what she claims."

Starbuck stood and bowed. "It is a pleasure to know you, Miss Foxe."

"Yes, Miss Foxe." Perry also stood and bowed. She tried to read his expression, but failed. "It is my extreme pleasure to finally meet you. Please allow me to I say how very much I admire the way in which you tie your cravat."

Tamsin slipped in beside Winwood, touching her Archangel pouch, seeking courage, waiting for the hordes in the kitchen to comment further on how she was to be addressed. Yet again, the world proved not to be as she believed.

No one commented on how she was dressed after Perry landed the first provocation. She kept glancing at Perry, to see if he meant to tease her with that greeting. Or, since she'd delayed the revelation too long, perhaps he felt insulted. She could not learn anything from his face. Perry wouldn't look her way. She could not mend this breach in the middle of this crowd.

Rowland nodded a brief hello, then turned back to the tale he was in the middle of telling, which Tamsin found maddening because she had so much news to share...and no idea, at first, what Rowland's story was about.

"To finish my story, our master in Amsterdam declared that, because Perry and I had failed our mission, his own royal master insisted we be dismissed. I attempted to explain the confusion, but we lost our positions, spying for the Crown in the Low Countries, in the same week we lost track of my cousin Lizzie."

Tom tapped his own nose. "It's right honorable of you to admit, Rollo, that the whole cockup in Rotterdam was down to you. I admire your perspi...pers...percacity. Your intelligence." He lifted his empty wine cup, admiring his own humor. "An intelligent intelligencer."

"What did you do?" Starbuck asked. "It's my own frequent nightmare, that one single failure might be taken as proof I have no ability to perform my duties."

Perry said, "If I'd had my druthers, we'd be in one of the warm colonies, sipping rum punch right now. However, Rollo falls seasick on any waters broader than a Dutch canal."

"Ginger is good for that," Winwood said. "Either a syrup or candied pieces."

Good stars! Both Tom and Winwood were drawn into that circle of comradery. And they should both know her well enough to see that she had something important to share.

Which, however, she couldn't share while Captain Starbuck was being entertained in the Revelstone kitchen, even though she'd ceased worrying that he'd arrest Rowland or sniff his way into the Foxes' restoration business.

"No, I'm not sailing to the colonies, the warm ones or otherwise." Rowland tipped his mug of wine to Perry. "We became personal guards for an English trader who likes to dine with titled exiles and diplomats."

"A step below the ambassadors' salons of our youth in Paris," Starbuck said.

"It did pay better," Perry said.

"Yes, we enjoyed that benefit," Rowland said. "However, every Sunday outside church, I begged our former master to reconsider. At last, he surrendered to my imprecations and sent us back to England, with commendations to the man he named who might take us on."

"Our new colonel offered temporary employment," Perry said, "declaring, 'You must prove yourself in England.'"

"Did you recite your gentleman's rules to persuade him?" Starbuck twitched his lips, as if remembering, then imitated Rowland. "It's, 'I do what I have promised.' And that one about 'Never fool an honest man,' which gives me great hope that I shall eventually see the two Louis d'or coins you owe me."

"I don't dispute that I owe you, Valentine," Rowland said, "but I cannot yet pay my debt. Soon, I hope."

Tom slurred while claiming Rowland had owed him four shillings for the past ten years. Clearly, Winwood should persuade him to return to bed.

Winwood, however, nodded when she caught his eye but made no move to remove Tom. And he kept smiling at her with an expression she could not interpret.

Perry, whenever he paused from smiling at Ned in a way that sent her cousin's hands shaking, offered Tamsin an eagle-like stare. Which she deserved, having vowed she trusted him that morning while still deceiving him.

She bit her lip, wishing Starbuck would leave so she could speak freely. And apologize to Perry first of all.

To her relief, Starbuck rose to go. "Shall we say good night before Mrs. Bell returns to castigate us as rakefires? I must see my lieutenant." He bowed to Tamsin. "Again, mademoiselle, I am pleased to know you. Kindly give my regards to Miss Ysabel Foxe.

And I pray that the influence of Revelstone's good ladies shall preserve Rollo from evil."

"SOAK YOUR HEAD, Valentine," Rowland said.

"Enlightened advice," Starbuck said. "As we learned in Paris, 'What shall it profit a man, if he shall gain the whole world,' without receiving crucial advice from Rowland Foxe?"

Rowland said, "I never float my friends into a bad current."

Starbuck stood at the kitchen door, his cheeks rosy from drinking, but a new serious expression on his face. "Don't let them make you captain, Rollo. You can't laugh when you're the captain. You can't have friends. Or gamble. Or tip a jug of wine with your men. Or enjoy nights like tonight."

As soon as the kitchen door closed behind Starbuck, Perry said, "Duncombe is Absolom's true nemesis."

At the same time, Tamsin said, "Duncombe is our nemesis. Not Heydon."

"I told you." Tom punched Rowland's shoulder.

Rowland didn't respond in kind, being impatient to hear what Perry knew that left him jittery as a young kitten.

"Give us your story, Miss Foxe." Perry intended the opposite from Rowland's wishes, a quiet torture on his part. Or else what he'd learned couldn't be divulged in company. "You've come straight from Heydon's lair."

"First, I regret deceiving you, Perry," Tamsin said. "And especially that, at the moment you asked me to call you by your Christian name, I didn't ask you to call me Tamsin."

"I'm not in the habit of calling any woman by her Christian name, Miss Foxe, except my own sister, of which I have none. My mother would cry for shame. Please tell us about your adventure with Lord Heydon in Cambridge."

She said, "Heydon paid an intelligencer to discover how his brother Hawksmoor's wealth disappeared. Can you guess what he learned? It seems that Mrs. Fairchild, Lady Candecote, and Lady Hawksmoor are—"

"Witches!" Tom exclaimed. "In an old-style coven, like in Shakespeare. The kind our first King James liked to burn."

"Perhaps." Tamsin laughed, which Tom had intended. "The three women are half-sisters. Duncombe is their brother. Danvers Duncombe bought the Marborne mortgages from Hawksmoor. It was not Sir Charles's agent, as Absolom believed."

The same detail it had taken until that afternoon for Rowland to recognize.

"Then," Ned frowned, "when Rollo overheard Hawksmoor talk about the Marborne mortgages and his 'brother,' it was about his brother-in-law?"

Tamsin nodded, her eyes afire.

Rowland should have seen Duncombe as the root of all evil before that day. He'd have to thank Tamsin for not chastising him for that failure.

"I wager," Rowland glanced at Perry, "the sisters are in the blind syndicate that bought those liens. And they are scheming with Duncombe to buy Marborne from the king."

Tamsin said, "Heydon didn't know that for a fact, but guessed it might be possible."

"That's why," Rowland said, "those people jumped quickly into our gambol. They need ready money to bribe the king. When I left the Fairchilds' house, Sir Isaiah's wife—"

"Lady Candecote, to whom Mr. Fairchild addressed that letter." Tamsin wasn't asking that as a question.

She clearly wanted to know why Rowland hadn't mentioned what he knew when they were reading Camilla's lost letter. But Rowland had a simple explanation: he was a blockhead who deserved to be left in that priest hole.

"I should have told this tale earlier," Rowland said, "but I didn't understand its meaning until later. After you left the Fairchilds, I cast bait for the solicitor, asking for his help to dangle an offer to the king for Marborne."

"Good stars!" Tamsin interrupted. "Why didn't you tell us that part of your plan?"

Because…because…he wanted to answer, that he'd been acting as an intelligencer and did not yet have all the information he sought.

"It was an impulse, not a plan," Rowland said. "Fairchild likely repeated my tale to Duncombe and the others as soon as I left the room, because Lady Candecote's voice came through an open window, piercing enough to stop birds from flying."

Perry said, "Give your story wings, Rollo. I am longing to know what the lady said."

"She cried, 'But we gave you our money, Danvers. You promised we'd be rich. Why must we sell our paintings to have enough to do as we planned?'"

"See? A witch!" Tom said.

"I still didn't understand," Rowland said, "until later that it was Danvers Duncombe, not his cousin Charles, who cheated Absolom. I'm still not sure whether those secret siblings share mutual intent or are in competition to snatch the Marborne title."

Tamsin touched her middle again, either praying or pressing back sickness.

"Are you well?" Ned asked.

"Of course, she is." Perry gripped Ned's shoulder. "And tomorrow we shall best serve Doctor Foxe by playing Captain Sharp and squeezing the oranges. For every last drop."

"What oranges?" Tamsin frowned.

"I mean that we shall take back from the traitors, vipers, and betrayers who cheated your family. Quickly and efficiently. We shall bilk the rattling liars on the morrow."

"But we shall have to break one of our restoration rules." Tamsin glanced at Perry. "I'm prepared to do it."

"Break which rule?" Ned seemed unsure.

"Tell us your rules," Rowland prompted. "I do long to know how highwaymen observe Uncle Absolom's rules for enlightened people."

"Since I'm supposed to represent the law," Tom said, "I demanded that one had to be, 'reap justice and shun revenge.' I also insisted on another: 'Our allies shall be innocent.' That's why we leave Winwood out of our schemes."

"Thank you for that," Winwood said. "Though it seems the time has come that I must forego innocence."

Rowland suspected that the doctor's loss of innocence happened long ago. Before he ever met Tom and the others.

"But we sail on the windy side of the law." Tom mangled the quotation from the Bard. "Because we keep a rule that says, 'Reave when sins are ripe.' However, it seems we shall have to transgress against one pesky rule, 'Never bilk a neighbor.'"

"We shall have to break Rule Two tomorrow," Tamsin said, "'Never trick a woman.'"

"And yet, you stole Senora Taresa's brooch." Perry's hand drifted from Ned's shoulder to instead cup his neck.

"And gave it back," Ned said. "Further, in that case, we ourselves were deceived by notorious behavior. I condemn myself for believing Rollo was a woman."

"We made that mistake yesterday," Tamsin said. "Tomorrow, we must keep only Rule One: 'No one dies.'"

Cursing silently, Rowland knew he couldn't promise to keep that one. Though Perry had begged for it, Rowland hadn't kept Benjie's name back from the list of rebels in Holland. He could have preserved Benjie Baird and his cousins from their fate in Bristol. Now, if Duncombe was more than a personal nemesis, if he had sponsored rebellion, then Rowland must be consistent and give that name and proof to his spymaster.

Rowland stood, which made the bench wobble. Winwood steadied Tom. "I need sleep. We have a full day's work ahead."

Tamsin said, "Since Captain Starbuck is in Uncle Absolom's room, you can take the divan in Lizzie's workshop."

"Tom?" Winwood nudged him.

"I spent six months in bed. Must I go now?"

"Yes," Tamsin said. "Oh, I'm supposed to tell you that Lord Heydon sends his best wishes and hopes to visit you soon. He sent this port as a restorative."

"Good lord!" Rowland threw up his hands. "Heydon knows you're not Tom? Is our gambol undone?"

"No." Tamsin seemed too calm, given her news. "He wants to help. He has no love for Duncombe and his syndicate of siblings. And he believes our family is owed justice for what happened with the mortgages."

"Heydon was our enemy this morning. Tonight he's your trusted friend?" Rowland lost all the soothing effects of wine and good company. "How so rapid a transformation?"

"It was only you," Tamsin said, "who insisted he was an enemy. I was never convinced. And if you'd been there, to talk as deeply and long as Heydon and I did tonight, then you'd trust him, too."

Perry said, "Do you assert, Miss Foxe, that a man who regards Mr. Duncombe as his enemy is half way to friendship?"

"More than half," Tamsin said. "If a man offers help for my family, I want to believe him. Now, did anyone leave a bite of food? I couldn't swallow my supper while listening to Heydon's tales."

"And someone," Tom gurgled a suppressed laugh, "finally twigged that you're not me. That must've gnawed your gizzard."

— NED —

TOM ARGUED THAT Tamsin must now wear a gown and re-enter civilized society. Ned, however, guessed that Tom pressed the argument merely to delay the end of the party.

While the others were all distracted, Perry spoke so low that only Ned heard. "Now that you shall be rich, Ned, will you marry and have children and a cozy home?"

What Ned wanted most at that moment could not be said in the winter kitchen. Instead, he reached for his oldest wish. "If the constable doesn't knock at our door and escort us to the gallows, there's a chance I'll gain my life's dream."

"You pluck at the strings of my heart. What is that dream?"

"The same as my father's. To...to paint," Ned stumbled over words. He could no longer say that he wanted only to be left alone to paint. Meeting Perry led him to want more in a way he'd never felt before. "But I shall not offer paintings like cheese and wool to be sold at market. Henceforth, I shall sign my own name, and let my agent do what he can."

"Here?" Perry asked.

"Mostly. But I should very much like to do portraits. I want to paint rich ladies' dresses. Such opportunities do not often arise in Cambridge. I'm tired of landscapes and flower vases that are easy to sell to the newly rich."

"I mean," Perry gazed from under his hooded brow, "will you stay at Revelstone House?"

"Where else would I go? The light in my workshop is quite good." Ned, unsure what Perry was asking, searched that intelligent face for clues. "What about you?"

Perry shrugged, as if he didn't have a care for the future. "Likely Rowland shall buy an officer's commission, a string of horses, and make me his aide de camp. Or his best sergeant."

"That's it?" Ned shrank inside, disappointed that Perry wasn't casting his lot in with Ned's. "Then what?"

"Then likely, the same as always. Hope for an assignment that doesn't risk my body or ruin my boots." Perry abruptly changed the subject. "Now, we must put an end to tonight's revels. Rowland and I have work to do tonight. You and Tamsin need to prepare for tomorrow."

—

Restoration Rules for Enlightened People
No one dies.
Never trick a woman.
Reave when sins are ripe.
Reap justice, shun revenge.
Never bilk a neighbor.
Our allies shall be innocent.

45

The Night Before

ONLY PERRY AND Rowland remained in the winter kitchen. Perry yawned. Rowland said, "I yearn, my friend, for the return of this evening's happiness. Tamsin's news complicates our plan. We must focus the scheme on Mr. Duncombe and that syndicate of siblings. Not Lord Heydon."

"I shall endeavor to offer consolation, Rollo. As it happens, I have happiness inside my vest. Here are the forged liens, which I liberated from Mr. Duncombe today."

"Truly? Truly?" Rowland sank down on the bench, ridiculously close to tears. "How did you manage it?"

"Sheer brilliance. A gift the gods delivered at my birth." Perry sat on the bench beside Rowland, proud of what he'd found.

"Yet I estimated Mr. Duncombe to be a man who never leaves precious papers far from his person."

"You judged correctly."

"Perry, pray tell me you didn't cold-cock him on the Cambridge road while playing highwayman."

"Rather than riding to London, I determined it might better profit my time to prowl his room at the Fairchild house. I chose the hour at which he undressed and took a wink in the afternoon's heat. These come from the inner pocket of his waistcoat." Perry handed more pilfered packets to Rowland.

"Will the servants suffer, being accused as thieves?"

"Not today or tonight. I replaced equal weights of paper in his inner pockets. Now, Rollo, you can give these forged liens to your cousins, to prove what a hero you are."

"No. It's you who should be called hero. Give these to Tamsin when you see her next. She'll be able to play more freely in our gambol if all her worries are lifted."

Perry said, "All her worries—except for the king selling the Marborne title to who knows what prideful malefactor. And her friend, the lady highwayman in blue velvet, whom I carried from that nest of vipers."

"If we succeed tomorrow, perhaps we'll earn enough that Tom can bribe the king to return the title. What else did you find, Perry? This whole evening, you have exhibited all the satisfaction of a weasel sucking eggs."

"You distress me, Lieutenant Foxe. Do you believe in your heart that I find pleasure in performing the Crown's business?"

"Yes, Mr. Frake. I do."

"Fine. I am transported to pure bliss, being able to provide you with these ledger pages for two syndics. Mayhap, we'll take these to our new colonel in London. Or perhaps you'll give these to Captain Starbuck, to settle your gambling debts."

Rowland unfolded the packet to read it. "It's in cypher."

"Aye. The simple cypher our first master taught when we were unfledged birds scurrying about to deliver notes between diplomats. Duncombe didn't even bother to give this list a clever title. It says plainly that it's the names of those who gave him funds to purvey for Monmouth's rebellion." Perry seized Rowland's shoulder, excited. "We journeyed into the dark fen shires and discovered gold."

"I bow to you for what you gained from one afternoon's labor. We have more than suspicions to report to our new colonel in London."

"We shall deliver to our new spymaster this condemning evidence only because your detour to Cambridge took us into Mr. Duncombe's path. If we'd stayed in London, we wouldn't have found this proof for the Crown."

"Could it be that Fate has smiled on us?"

"Mayhap," Perry said. "Rollo, I've been thinking. Whatever your gambol shall earn from gulling Mr. Duncombe and his sisters, I wager it won't be enough to pay the king a garnishment for Marborne."

"Aye. I should warn my cousins to temper their hopes."

"We, however, shall earn a significant gratuity for sending Duncombe to the Tower—especially if we help the Crown seize Duncombe's entire wealth. Are you thinking—"

"Yes. That the gratuity I earn from the Crown will be needed to ensure enough money for Marborne."

"Will there be enough left over to buy the officer's commission you've longed for?"

Rowland didn't answer, deeply considering a host of far-reaching implications.

"It distresses me, Rollo, to suggest that this quandary might lead us into the realm of what you call corruption. Should you and I raid Duncombe's offices, ahead of the king's men?"

Rowland said, "Our first master was explicit in his teachings, that it's not honest."

"And you think the Crown is honest?"

"I need to find a new occupation." Rowland let his thoughts drift again to the executions in Bristol of the naïve Benjamin Baird and his entire clan. "I was bred to serve the Crown. And yet here we are, holding evidence that will send people to the gallows."

"We can ponder that tomorrow, Rollo. Right now, I'm hoping you'll invent a clever way to lighten Mr. Duncombe's pockets before the Crown seizes everything." Perry rose. "I'll see you when Dawn lifts her skirts. We have many details come morning."

That left Rowland alone to worry about the restoration rule that pricked at his heart. *No one dies.*

He studied the cryptic ledger pages, translating names and amounts. Never in his career with Perry had they accomplished as much for the Crown as the delivery of Duncombe's papers would. Yet this work might hang a man and snare entire families.

And he still couldn't calculate how his private work and to-morrow's gambol might result in sufficient funds to preserve Marborne and make Tom the rightful earl.

— NED —

MUDDLED FROM THE evening's wine, Ned finished demonstrating how his agent's wife performed as an adept while judging paintings. He'd lit several candles and three hanging lanterns, so his workshop was nearly bright as day.

"Does she sniff them?" Tamsin said. "I hope not."

"Sometimes," Ned said. "Mostly she studies brush strokes like I showed you. She was niece and assistant to a great Master in Amsterdam. She's odd, but no one knows more about paintings in Europe."

Perry came in just then. "Do you need me to help teach a wee bit of Dutch?" He sat in the only chair.

Ned said, "The woman seldom speaks. She says 'houd je bek' when I ask a question. And she calls me eikel and ezel and lamzak. And then she calls a number to her husband, which will be the English pounds to be offered for the work."

"I can repeat numbers in Dutch. Your father taught me when we were little," Tamsin said.

"Then that might carry you through an hour of judging."

"The woman calls you donkey?" Perry asked. "Numb sack? She must be a terror. What a tremendously jocose time lies ahead for us, Miss Foxe."

Tamsin rose. "I'm off. I want to see Camilla again before the night is too far gone."

"One moment, Miss Foxe." Perry blocked her exit. "Rollo says you are to have this. To protect or destroy as you judge best."

Tamsin took the packet he held out for her. "What is it?"

"If I were an expert—oh, but indeed I am—these are the forged liens that Mr. Duncombe created to cheat Doctor Foxe."

"How in this world did you get them?"

"I took them from Duncombe's pocket. I hope this quiets some waves of your turmoil."

Ned felt his neck flush hot, secretly pleased that his new friend had done this, saved the property and their future.

Tamsin, who had scarcely smiled in the past year, seemed transported by joy. She grabbed Perry's big hand and kissed it, which seemed to embarrass the fellow.

"You are the savior of our world, Mr. Frake," Tamsin said.

"Not near so great. But it infuses my heart with peace to see you so jubilant."

As soon as Tamsin closed the door, Perry loomed over Ned. "Rollo has severely cautioned me not to bowl you over, since we're to return to London soon. He can be a worse scold than your sister Ysabel if he gets a notion."

"Bowl me—oh, like lawn bowls."

"But I'm not bowling on a Sunday after church, Ned."

His finger tickled along the back of Ned's hand, examining it in the bright candlelight, tracing the streaks of blue paint.

Foolishly nervous, Ned said, "I shall wear gloves tomorrow for the gambol."

Perry pressed Ned's hand to his chest, as if restoring it to his possession. "I admire your fine self and the life you have here, taking care of people. Living with hope."

"Hope?" Ned couldn't find words, either English or Dutch. Hope was a rare commodity for the past year. Now with the land safe and the gambol tomorrow, Ned didn't know how to ask for what he still wanted most. "I hope…to paint…to have enough to eat…to be warm in winter, and to…"

Perry kissed him, one hand cradling Ned's head and keeping him there, the other hand twining in Ned's fingers. The man tasted like honeyed wine, like the old gods must drink. His lips, which seemed so hard when he teased, became soft, first brushing over Ned's mouth, then his throat, then returning to coax a response. Ned did his best to return in kind.

This was the moment great painters caught, when they painted lovers befuddled by ecstasy, men whose souls were drunk on enticing lips, more intoxicating than wine or genever. Just when

Ned felt they could never stop, Perry released him, then circled the room to extinguish the lanterns and blow out the candles. Perry found him in the dark, like iron drawn to a magnetic stone. "You are the loveliest man."

The touch of Perry's lips caused bursts of light behind Ned's closed eyes, like the most exciting moments bent over a palette. First, remnants of points of candlelight, floating on rafts of midnight blue, in a sea of warm red. Then just the color and taste of ruby port, familiar and yet unique.

"I don't know how to do this," Ned whispered. Or at least not with someone he knew enough to care for.

"That does not distress me, sweeting. I have observed that you are a fast-witted student. It will come to you with practice."

When half a lifetime had passed, a rooster squawked in the distance. Imagination might cause one to believe dawn was near.

Caesar scratched at the door.

Perry sat up, alert, drawing on his boots. "Too many chores this morning to linger longer. But whatever Rollo and I must do next, you can be as sure as the sun rises in the east that I shall also endeavor to make the world a better place for you, Ned Wijck."

Alone, Ned considered, first, how his world had turned upside down and then found he rather liked the new orientation.

— TAMSIN —

AFTER RUNNING TO Mr. Gamlingay's cottage, Tamsin arrived breathless. The front door stood open. The old rector sat at his table, reading by a single candle, batting moths away from the flame.

"Oh, hullo, Miss Tamsin." He waved toward his tiny bedroom. "I don't think she's awake. At least, little Agnes sleeps."

Agnes lay on a pallet in front of the room's door, so Tamsin had to step over her to reach Camilla. The bright shadow from Mr. Gamlingay's candle reflected in Camilla's eyes.

"Stay with me, Tamsin. Through the night?"

"I will. Gladly."

She crawled in beside Camilla and lay with her back to the wall, atop the coverlet.

"In my dreams," Camilla whispered, "you said I don't have to go home if I don't want to."

"I did say that. I promised you."

"A dream."

"Dreams come true. For example, Mr. Frake liberated our mortgages today. I think it's possible that we can be happy."

"But Leighton…"

"Fie on that goose-cap. He shall not besiege you again."

"How will we make that more than a dream?" Camilla sighed. "I'm happy you're here."

Tamsin lay with one arm crooked over the top of her friend's head. "Are you better? Does it hurt?"

"Some. I must lie very still. Else, the pain pounds through my entire body."

"Oh, sweet nutting. How can I comfort you?"

"Tell me how it will be."

While endeavoring not to jar Camilla, Tamsin retrieved her Archangel pouch and pressed it under Camilla's hand. "This is the gold angel coin my mother gave me. It's supposed to make me wealthy. I think instead it brings me what I need."

"What do you need, Tamsin? I am always the needy person, depending on you to know what to do."

"My needs are as huge as all of Cambridgeshire. This week, I needed comfort when Absolom left us, and you were there."

"I'm so sorry he's gone. And you haven't had a moment to weep, because everyone makes you take care of them. Fixing things. And I'm one of your needy causes."

"Never, sweet one."

"Tell me your needs, Tamsin. I can count them along with my heartbeats, to not think of this throbbing in my middle."

"I needed Rollo to help us, though I didn't know at first. I needed Poynter, Lord Heydon to ask questions. And back, long ago, I needed you to come. I would be alone in the world if you were not with me."

"I'm always lonely," Camilla said. "Unless you are there. Can we stay together? How to make that possible?"

"I shall find a way, my precious dove."

Tamsin cuddled closer to Camilla.

"Your breath tickles my neck."

"I'm sorry, Camilla."

"I like it. That's like the breath of life, don't you think? I'd argue it before a judge. Before Parliament."

"If they allowed women to speak there." Tamsin lay listening to Camilla's quiet, regular breath. Then her friend's words touched a different part of her mind. "Before Parliament. That's what it shall take."

Camilla stirred but didn't speak.

"We'll be rich after our gambol tomorrow. That is, richer than we are now poor. I shall find a barrister to plead your case, to bring it to the consistory court and then to Parliament. It will take time, but we will free you."

"Ah, Tamsin. You dreamer. The blighting man swears he will never leave me. It would be unjust to find a woman whose father is richer than mine to tempt him. Unlike the eighth King Henry, but rather like every wife in England, I cannot divorce at will."

"We shall find a way. And trust that justice and common law will help us."

"You've never trusted English justice in your life, Tamsin. And please don't make promises you cannot keep. You always have to save everyone. Just be my comrade for the coming fight. Especially since I made the decisions that put me at Leighton's mercy."

Tamsin had to stop a dozen series of promises that formed on her tongue, not because she wanted to save Camilla, but because anxiety gnawed at her soul. She had to find a way to take action. Leighton was a simmering cesspool of spite and anger, and worse things would spill out if Camilla failed to find a safe escape.

"We'll find another kind of restoration," Tamsin said.

"Or perhaps highwaymen can roust Leighton on a dark lane and leave him for the crows and wolves."

"Good stars, Camilla! You don't think that. We have our rules for restorations. '*No one dies.*'"

"Of course, I won't do it, and not just because I could never persuade you. But please let me pretend."

"Fine. After all, it's Leighton who has hurt you."

"And tomorrow," Camilla said, "we must send word that I'm here with Mr. Gamlingay. I don't want my father to worry. And I don't want Leighton to harass the neighborhood on my account."

"You are brave, and I love you for it." Tamsin would not—ever—repeat what Rowland had reported. That Camilla's father wasn't worried, that he thought Camilla should be forced to submit to Leighton. "But we'll ask Winwood to insist that you are too delicate to be moved."

— ROLLO —

IN LIZZIE'S DESERTED workshop, her scent lingered, teasing Rowland's nose. Ignoring that, he stripped to his undershirt and linen, then lay on the workshop's divan, the night's vague breeze through an open window cooling everything but his thoughts.

The over-full house whispered late-night sounds, the pile of stone and timber groaning as it let go of the day's heat; thirty-five people sighed and turned in their dreams. He listened like he had as a child to voices seeping through the walls, drifting up and down the stairs, leaking out the open windows, while he strained to overhear what might be said.

Back then, in the room the three of them shared, Tom and Ned snuffled in their sleep, never hearing the danger coming.

They never heard the heavy footsteps, while Rowland hid under the quilt, not knowing whether comfort or danger loomed, though it always proved to be Absolom or Mrs. Bell checking on the sleepers.

Now, Rowland again heard murmurs through the wall, leaving him to speculate whether in conflict or agreement.

A child cried out, as if from a bad dream.

No one dies. One of his cousins' restoration rules.

He could let Duncombe's trespasses go unchecked. A reasonable man must admit that there were honest passions on both sides of the recent conflict, whether for a Catholic versus a Protestant ruler. And the rebels could not possibly rise again, with no Pretender, no arms. And massive redcoat resistance.

He could merely punish Duncombe for swindling Absolom, and not involve the Crown. Except this particular funder of rebels didn't act out of religious passion or loyalty. Duncombe had made a series of business decisions, wagering his hopes for good fortune, but backing the wrong candidate for king, gambling with others' funds.

It wasn't clear from the papers Perry had snatched whether all members of those blind syndics knew their investment was intended to fund a rebellion. Whether or not they knew about that, Duncombe's sisters and their husbands would be snatched up as rebels as soon as Duncombe was arrested. It fit Absolom's rules, and his cousins' restoration rules, to punish greedy neighbors by taking their ill-gotten assets. But it went against enlightened rules to send one's neighbors to the gallows.

Rowland turned on his side on the divan, cupping emptiness, nothing to offer comfort in the dark of night.

Yes, he'd surrender Duncombe to the king. But as for the others in that man's syndicates, the punishment the king would deal seemed excessive. Cruel and—

"Rollo." In the dark, Lizzie slipped onto the divan where he lay, silk skirts pressing against him. Her finger found his wrist in the dark and tapped it the way she often did. Except this time, neither of them wore gloves. Her bare fingers touched him. "You must help me."

"That's what I'm here for, Lizzie."

That's what an English summer smelled of, flowers in the hedge, rose water. Mint. She needed to sit still and stop wriggling against him.

"Mary insists that I marry before returning to her court."

"I've guessed as much, but Tom won't do for her purposes. And you cannot marry just any man who is able to buy you a title. Therefore—"

"Stop talking for one minute, Rollo." She tapped his wrist, her nail softly scratching him. "Please. Tomorrow I must undertake an adventure. I'm here to beg your help."

"Ah. 'I do love nothing in the world so well as you: is not that strange?'"

"From your Shakespeare, Rollo?"

"Yes. But I do love you, Lizzie. I'll do whatever you need."

"Yes, I love you too. But tomorrow—"

"No. Listen to me. I love you."

"Like in your Shakespeare plays? Like Romeo and Juliet?"

"We're older than that, Lizzie. Like Orsino and Viola."

"Don't tease, Rollo. That's just stories and songs."

"We have those stories and songs, because people give their hearts to each other."

"Other people. Not you and me. We can't be romantical." She shook her head in denial, which Rowland felt in the dark, able to see only her outline in deep shadows. "Only you understand me, Rollo. Because we are so alike—trained to serve the Crown, never meant for a peaceful life at home like Tamsin or Ned."

"Only," Rowland said, "you are much more devoted to your mistress than I am to any of my diplomatic spymasters."

"Even if that's true, you must agree that people like you and me aren't allowed romantic notions. We shall only ever be forced into alliances by the rulers we serve."

"Can we not indulge a feverish passion? Like your mother and Ned's father, burning for love?"

She went still. He couldn't even feel her breath rise and fall where she pressed against him. "If life were less precarious than it is for us now, if the world were different…"

"Are you dangling hope for me, Lizzie?"

"In a different world, there'd be no other man to think of. You are the best man I know. You make me laugh. You know me so well, yet you never scold. I have such tender feelings for you."

"I'm happy to be perfect, Lizzie." (I'll hold your tender feelings gently, forever.)

She laughed. "'Cease, tempter. None can chain my mind.'"

"Aye. I'm sensibly aware that if my protestations of love persuaded you to marry me, it'd destroy any possibility of the life you want to live."

"See? You know me best, and you chose the best for me. Which is also best for you." She nestled closer to him. "Because it would destroy your life, too. Don't you agree?"

"Yes." (And also no. The flame in my heart burns hot.) "What can I do to help?"

"You perceive what Mary sent me to do in England?"

"Aye. To help advance her support among the nobility. For you to do that, you must marry well, which requires restoration of the Marborne title. I shall help any way I can."

"There's more to it than you know." Silk rustled against his belly and chest. "I shall accept an offer tomorrow."

"Mr. Gamlingay doesn't have noble blood, so it can't be him."

"Clever, Rollo. I shall marry Poynter. Viscount Heydon."

(Go on, light the match on the Spanish grenade in my belly.)

"God blind me! He did not make an offer to you, Lizzie!"

"He did, and promised to help us —if my family agrees to the match." Her fingernail scratched the back of his hand again. Silk rustled against his burning belly. "And so, I beg you to be welcoming, Rollo."

"You cannot marry that man, Lizzie."

"He's not a monster. I've heard what Tamsin learned. Everything that you claimed about Heydon arose, in fact, from the doings of the earl's brother-in-law. Duncombe."

"But Heydon cannot possibly be a husband to you. He's—he's not the sort of man who marries. He'd rather entertain Perry than any wife."

"That is of no consequence," she said. "Either to him or to me. Like you and I do, we shall only play certain roles in service to the Crown. Heydon offers the quickest way for me to return to the work I've been trained to do."

(Marry me. I'll find a title for you. Or steal it. Or create an artful forgery.)

"You must help, Rollo." She lay back against him, as fully as the narrow divan allowed, trapping him against the wall. "Confess it. Your gambol won't return sufficient wealth to pay taxes, repair the house and village, and also buy the title back from the king. This is the only way I can help."

"The only way? After I've sworn to be your rescuing hero?"

"Promise you will help my plan, lambkin. You and I together must do whatever is possible to bring our cousins and Marborne out of miserable poverty."

"Lizzie, I am always prepared to do whatever you need. But please, give me through tomorrow to find solutions for you and for Marborne."

She cupped his jaw, turned his face to hers, and kissed him, a peck on the cheek, beside his mouth. He gently held her there, to linger longer than a cousinly peck.

She didn't withdraw.

And so, he kissed her, fumbling that first brush of his lips against hers, then possessing her mouth. She returned his kiss, deeper, eager, her tongue darting to pry into his mouth.

He let her devour him. Yet…

(This is so unfair, Lizzie.)

She tasted of lemon balm.

"You," she whispered. Her lips caressed his face. "You are forever and always my 'ever-fixed mark that looks on tempests and is never shaken.'"

(So unfair.)

While returning her kiss, Rowland removed his mind from what more he wanted. He enumerated everything he knew about lemon balm, determined to quiet his deeper arousal. Lemon balm tisane was a fad among wealthy women in Amsterdam a year ago.

(Please stop, Lizzie. Think what the Bard said: "Who shall be true to us, when we are so unsecret to ourselves?")

Lemon balm. A wonderful restorative for those who imbibe too much strong drink. Most men among couriers and diplomats, though, preferred to dose themselves with Carmelite water.

A lantern cast shadows across the workshop. "*Ssst!* Time to go, Rollo." Perry called to him, as they'd agreed. To attend to their early-morning details. "Oh, hello, Miss Foxe. Good morning. I hope this day finds you well in body and soul."

"Aye, thank you, Mr. Frake. I am well." She departed, taking the tattered remains of Rowland's soul with her. Before Perry could say a word, she came back. "I cleaned and repaired your copper-satin suit, Rollo. You shall appear royal if you wear it for our gambol today."

When she was gone, Perry hissed, "God's teeth, Rollo! You promised that it wouldn't be this way."

"It isn't any way at all. Let us go forth and do the terrible acts we have planned. I do not care if it sends my soul to hell."

"But, as you often proclaim, Rollo, as an enlightened gentleman you do not believe in heaven and hell."

"Experience has led me to reconsider my beliefs. I know now there is a hell."

Rowland tugged on pantaloons, stockings, boots. And he needed to pack everything, since they'd return to London that day. His long-headed wits having deserted him, he was forced to take care to do it all in proper order.

Why kiss like that and yet deny there's love in this world?

46

Aurora

AT THE PHOENIX and Swan, Rowland took Starbuck inside to share breakfast while Perry went in search of Mr. Warboys, to hire his carriage for a journey to London.

"If I understand your directions," Starbuck studied a small map Ned had drawn, showing the warren of trails in the neighborhood, "I shall have my two gold louis if I appear here at five o'clock, where you've marked an X."

"Yes."

"But I cannot have my gold right this moment."

"No, alas, you cannot," Rowland said. "In fact, Valentine, if you'd be so kind, please advance me silver to pay the fare for our breakfast."

The innkeeper appeared with steaming plates of ham, hens' eggs, and toasted bread. He promised them hot ale and invited Starbuck to assess which of his ales were the best in Cambridgeshire. Starbuck, obliged to judge, followed him to the taproom.

Dismayed to be badly affected by no sleep, Rowland condemned the hot and muggy English weather rather than the silk-clad visitor who'd kept him awake until dawn. But first, he set about to devour the first decent meal he'd been served since leaving London.

"Ah, good morning, sir. I'd thought I must travel all the way to Revelstone to see you." Heydon slipped into the chair beside Rowland. "You were quite young when I left for Oxford, and we were only briefly introduced when I was in Paris. Hence, I have no basis for begging familiarity. But I hope that now we can strike up a friendly if utilitarian relationship, Lieutenant Foxe."

Rowland refused to surrender to Heydon the satisfaction of showing his surprise. After all, Heydon only equaled Mr. Gamlingay by guessing.

"What do you want?" Rowland dreaded the answer. He again felt that grenade in his belly, ready to explode. Because, he'd do anything if only Heydon would give up Lizzie.

"It is my wish that you and I might conduct mutually beneficial business." Heydon leaned forward. The diamond pin in his cravat caught the morning light peeking through the window. "To begin, I shall offer what you need to gain that which you want most in the world."

"Isn't that the offer the devil makes when he comes to purchase your soul?" Rowland was too well trained to reveal any emotion that might interfere with business. "How can you have any idea what I might be seeking, your lordship?"

"Lieutenant Foxe, you and your cousins want the Marborne title restored. Would you not do anything in the world for that?"

No, Rowland wanted even more. And it was Heydon who'd obtained what Rowland wanted most. Rowland had no idea how to bargain for Lizzie's release.

"No, your lordship. I won't break my uncle Absolom's rules for enlightened people, which limits what I might do for any prize." Rowland recited the rules, like a catechism.

I keep my promises.
My family obligations are sacred.
I was born to help others.
The world improves from my toil.
I never fool an honest man.

Meanwhile, his heart begged transgression against the rules. He would indeed do anything to ensure Marborne belonged to his cousins.

"Inspiring, Lieutenant Foxe. Are there more?"

"My cousins have other rules, such as 'Reap justice, shun revenge.' It's admirable that they can keep such a rule, given the righteous grievances they have." Rowland did not agree with that rule about revenge. The sole restoration rule that weighed on him: *No one dies.*

"I think we should be able to work as comrades, Lieutenant Foxe, with mutual respect."

"What must I do?"

"I believe you intend to denounce Mr. Duncombe as a rebel one day soon. However, I do not want to see my brother Monck swept up in that business. Therefore, while I do not care what you might plan for Duncombe, but please do not include my brother, either through the courts or the militia."

"I do not denounce men. I'm not a Puritan out searching for witches in the hedges. I find the substantiated proof the Crown needs about men who are indeed traitors." Rowland repeated one side of the argument he'd had with himself all last night.

"Lieutenant Foxe, as enlightened gentlemen, let us not use morally freighted words such as traitor or betrayal or inquisition. Both of our families suffered for that in the past century. I want whatever you hold that is prejudiced against my brother. In exchange, I shall offer to give you any garnishment required to attain that which your family seeks."

"I do not accept special garnishments. I serve the Crown." And he'd learned years ago not to let trepidation trip his tongue or freeze his spine.

"Except, Lieutenant Foxe, don't you want the title restored to your family?"

"It's what anyone named Foxe wants." Yet it wasn't what he truly wanted most.

"That requires you *pay* a significant garnishment, which I am offering so that your family might gain the world." He smiled wryly. "and you shall still keep your soul."

Garnishment for the king, but passing through Rowland's hands. It was what Tom and Tamsin needed. Perhaps Lizzie might be gratified, that it'd be sufficient for her desires.

"Give me until later today to think about it." Rowland resisted touching his vest, which held the ledger pages Perry had purloined from Duncombe. "I must consider what I owe the Crown."

"Understandable. Consider my commitment to help with the king's garnishment as a promise and a testament to my good faith in your own honor, Lieutenant Foxe."

"You don't know me to guess at what honor I may possess."

"But your cousins trust you. Doctor Foxe spoke of you with great respect." Heydon offered his hand, which Rowland took, while silently wagering that Heydon was giving more than he'd get in this bargain. Hence, suspicions lingered. "Won't you call me Poynter and allow me to call you Rowland?"

"His friends call him Rollo, your lordship." Starbuck came in just then, bearing two tankards of ale. He sat down to tackle his breakfast. "Good morning, sir. If I'd known you were here, I'd have played pot-boy for you, too. I'll call the innkeeper."

"Good morning, Captain Starbuck," Heydon said. "No, I do not require anything. I must be on my way. Shall I invite you to Sunday supper again, Captain? Let us make it a tradition while you're billeted in Cambridge."

"Thank you, your lordship. That would be grand." Starbuck turned to Rowland. "Do you remember Viscount Heydon from that first winter we served in Paris?"

"Indeed." Remembered at last. Years ago, Rowland observed Heydon admiring the prettiest face in the room, Valentine's.

Heydon said, "Didn't we agree that we shall call each other Poynter and Valentine, if we're among friends?"

"Long ago. Now, Poynter, I must warn you. Rollo is notoriously slow to pay his gaming debts."

"I have faith in his noble nature," Heydon said. "For, 'What fates impose, that men must needs abide; it boots not to resist both wind and tide.'"

"*Henry the Sixth, Part Three,*" Rowland said. "Not so often played on the stage or quoted."

"Not a history England longs to remember," Heydon said. "A king more like a saint than any that the willful sinners in England have had in this modern age."

If Rowland said yes to Heydon's offer, he'd owe gratitude to the man whose heart he longed to rip out. Because Rowland could not have what he most wanted.

Yet if he said yes, Tom would be earl. Marborne would be saved. And Lizzie could find a way to return to Mary's court.

Rowland followed Heydon to the door.

"How did you guess?"

"You have the same quizzical brow as you did in childhood. The same as Doctor Foxe and your father. Tom and Miss Thomasine have that same brow. Only Miss Ysabel Foxe missed out on that family feature."

"No, how did you figure Mr. Duncombe's syndics were funding Monmouth? That he has endangered your brother?"

"I paid an intelligencer who works for the Crown—"

"A man with fewer scruples than me about taking payment for the Crown's information."

"Yes." Heydon wasn't embarrassed by Rollo's claim. "I paid him to discover what business Duncombe might be up to besides swindling my brother."

"Aye. Tamsin repeated your story about the flock of half-sister allies that man has in Cambridgeshire."

"Last night, my agent reported rumors that the Crown suspects Mr. Duncombe of funding rebels and sent intelligencers after him. It brought to mind how Lord Orlando sought to travel with Duncombe to London."

"I salute your perspicacity." Rowland chose the word that Tom mangled the night before.

"Ready to depart, gentlemen?" Perry came in through the Dutch door between the guestroom and taproom. "Mr. Warboys is at our service and—ah, good morning, your lordship."

Rowland got a fleeting glimpse of how Heydon smiled when he truly wanted to please someone.

But no, Perry now belonged to Ned. Heydon couldn't have him. It was bad enough that Heydon would have Lizzie.

Standing in the door, watching Heydon ride away, Rowland made the decision to save that syndicate of Duncombe's siblings from the gallows. Yet he still had to decide how to do it. He could destroy the ledger page from Duncombe that listed Hawksmoor. Or he could sell that page to Heydon.

One way seemed almost honorable—only Perry would ever know Rowland had kept information back from the king's brutal pursuit of rebels and their supporters.

On the other hand, if he agreed to Heydon's business offer, it meant the happy prospect of ensuring his cousins' future. He only had to break a key principle, that he performed his work only in service to the Crown, not to enrich himself.

No gratuities, no corruption. That's what his first master taught as a principle as strict as Absolom's rules for enlightened people.

"Rollo? Hello, moon calf!" Perry pummeled his shoulder. "We have a thousand tasks this morning. No fainéant idlers if we are to deal properly with your enemies before sunset."

47

The Adept and the Dealer

THAT MORNING, TAMSIN raided her mother's chest, finding a dark grey gown, the cut capacious enough to hide near-to-term twins, its twenty-five-year-old starched collar huge enough to hide the shape of Tamsin's face.

Lizzie's collection of liberated accoutrements included an ill-kempt, old-fashioned white wig. Tamsin wore Tom's working clothes under the dowdy gown, which was a punishment in the day's heat. The wretched white-lead maquillage Lizzie insisted on applying added nothing to Tamsin's comfort. She lodged the packet from Perry over her Archangel pouch. With all fears about the mortgages removed, Tamsin entered Lord Heydon's house free of trepidation.

The gambol players were carried to Cambridge in Mr. Warboys' carriage. Heydon welcomed them, more overtly friendly than Tamsin had ever seen him. As soon as Lizzie entered the house, she retreated to stand near a window, as if she longed to be out of reach from every person in the room.

Heydon said, "Lord Orlando, please introduce everyone."

"*Si*, your lordship. Lord Hawksmoor, Lord Heydon, Sir Isaiah, Mr. Fairchild, this is my agent, Meester Droochloot." Ned bowed low. "He has brought his wife, Mevrouw Droochloot, the famous adept who shall judge our paintings."

The introductions were brief, given that the gentlemen's wives had not yet arrived, having walked to the chemist's shop for a headache powder. And the Droochloot pair were too strange and dowdy for anyone's attention to linger.

"This blasted heat," Sir Isaiah said, making an excuse for the absent wives, "is too much, too much for any woman's constitution."

"Indeed." Rowland turned to Mr. Fairchild. "How is Mrs. Leighton faring? She *has* been found, I hope?"

"Yes, yes," Sir Isaiah answered. "Mr. Gamlingay sent word that he's given her shelter and fetched the doctor. Fairchild and I shall bring her home when this day's work is done."

Adding to the day's duties, Tamsin still had to find a way to keep Camilla away from the Fairchilds. Meanwhile, Mr. Fairchild remained absorbed with the mug of ale he'd received from a servant, not reacting to inquiries or news of Camilla. God could judge the man for all eternity if that was the way justice worked in the heavenly precincts, but on this day, the Foxe cousins would punish Mr. Fairchild.

"I hope, sir, the table my secretary set by the south window will be serviceable for your work." Heydon addressed Meester Droochloot, attired in bright orange velvet and a badly combed periwig. (Ned had also had his visage encased in white-lead face paint, but with rosebud cheeks and two black velvet patches.)

Heydon had his servants help the agent and his wife set up to do their work, and then ruptured the day's plans for the gambol by drawing Lizzie into the back garden to see his roses, saying, "my cook is growing Jerusalem artichokes."

Rowland kept his gregarious smile in place, but Tamsin saw embers glowing in his eyes, saw him grasp his hands at his back, twisted in agitation. Tamsin, too busy with her own worries, had neglected over several occasions to warn him about Lizzie, though his Bard said it: "The lady standeth steadfast in her heart, hath power over her own will, and hath so decreed..." Or perhaps she should repeat the verses in Corinthians intended for the kind of people whose hearts never burn. She should have given more weight to Rowland's hidden longings, given her own need to have Camilla close by.

When Heydon and Lizzie returned inside, the cousins launched the gambol. First, Rowland called for business arrangements to be made. "As we know, in order for Meester Droochloot to act for you, his fee is paid in advance."

"I advise each of you who has funds lodged with me," Duncombe said, "to write cheques for Meester Droochloot's fee." He held forth at length about using cheques as bills of exchange, which would be paid out of his London office as soon as the bearer presented them.

"Will a cheque on my bank do?" Heydon asked. "Both to cover my fee and my brother's?"

The notion of cheques settled, the next idea was to create a syndicate in protection of Miss Ysabel Foxe, which took considerable time. At last, Lord Orlando and Mr. Duncombe determined how receipts and cheques should be exchanged, with Rowland always conceding to Duncombe's suggestions. "You, sir, know best how business is done in England."

Duncombe turned into a task master with the role Rowland had yielded to him. "This situation calls for demand promissory notes written to the syndicate, to be paid by Mr. Droochloot."

Ned agreed, his periwig a jungle of bobbing curls. "Yes, yes. That is how business is done." Performing as the agent, Ned exaggerated his impatience. "And you, Lord Orlando, promised to bear these paintings to London. I cannot take that responsibility."

"Yes, Meester Droochloot." Rowland spoke to all in the room. "At Miss Foxe's request, I have hired my sister's guard, Mr. Frake, to accompany the paintings to London and then to Paris. He's good with both pistols and fists. He shall sit atop the carriage, which means there's room for one more to ride to London with Meester Droochloot and his wife. Who shall go with me to London? Miss Foxe?"

"No, but thank you ..." Lizzie pretended to hesitate. "Mr. Duncombe, do you still intend to accompany my cousin? We shall be in more secure hands with you protecting our treasures."

Preening at the compliment, Mr. Duncombe said, "I remain more than happy to oblige. I brought my baggage today, believing this was the plan."

"Dear Orlando," Lizzie said. "Did you hire Mr. Warboys, as I recommended? He knows the neighborhood and can find the fastest road to London."

"Your Mr. Warboys brought us to Cambridge, and now waits upon our departure for London." Rowland's face might crack, he smiled so hard for Lizzie.

Heydon's secretary appeared and set a table for the "scribes" who would write receipts for the paintings consigned into the agent's care. After seeing everyone supplied with quills, ink, and paper, the secretary disappeared into the back of the house. The earl took a seat on the left, Sir Isaiah in the center, and the solicitor on the right.

"Should have brought my own secretary," Sir Isaiah mused, and repeated himself as was his habit. "My secretary." He peered at the quill, ink, and papers as if these were oddities.

Tamsin judged him harshly. Sir Isaiah had let his daughter marry Leighton, an evil fool. And Camilla did it to get away from her father's new wife, who sought to steal the Marborne title. Therefore, because Sir Isaiah had not taken proper care of his child, he deserved to be punished. Punishing this transgressing neighbor by way of Rowland's gambol would not break Uncle Absolom's rules for enlightened people.

Mr. Fairchild fussed with the cup of coffee Heydon's servant had brought him. This man helped Duncombe with the swindle over Marborne mortgages. He'd plotted with Lady Candecote to buy the title. Tamsin didn't have to consider Mrs. Fairchild's cruelty to Camilla to feel that involving the Fairchilds in this gambol was fair and just.

And then Lord Hawksmoor. Perhaps less guilty about the last two years' swindle than Absolom had believed, he'd perpetuated the unfair mortgages his father had set twenty years before. The current earl could have negotiated more just terms at any time, but never did. While Tamsin was deciding how much accountability he owed, Rowland bent near where she sat at the work table and whispered, "All of Hawksmoor's paintings belong to his wife. Do not exclude them from our plan, whatever Heydon might have asked of you."

The wives appeared then, taking seats behind their husbands in a row of richly carved armchairs with dusky blue velvet cushions. Lizzie stood close to the window where the agent and his wife worked, where both Heydon and Rowland also hovered.

At a south window, which allowed all the bright light of a summer's day, Tamsin adopted a rapid routine to perform the pantomime Ned had taught her.

Turn it over to gaze closely at the threads of the canvas.

Flip it again and sniff it.

Study every inch, her nose nearly touching the canvas.

Call out any Dutch phrase learned in the previous night's lesson.

Then whisper in Ned's ear.

Most times, she whispered, "This restoration is for Absolom."

— NED —

IN A HEAVY Dutch accent, Ned barked exclamations in Dutch and then dictated Mevrouw Droochloot's judgments, to be inscribed by the gentleman-scribes. Ned's secret joy in the gambol was increased by how much Hawksmoor and Fairchild seemed embarrassed by the Droochloots' uncouth and mercantile behavior. Surely Tamsin was blessed with the same joy.

While Ned and Tamsin performed as the Dutch adepts, the gentleman-scribes said little, other than to request a number be repeated. Or a description be recounted. That sort of question roused the wives from where they sat fanning themselves in the midday heat.

"It hangs over our dining table, my dear lord. That one we got in London last year."

"Bless me, that's ten times what we paid!"

Then there were subtle remarks, seeking to lure Lizzie into their confabs.

"That blue satin is lovely, Miss Foxe."

"You have a London modiste? Will you share her name?"

"French, I suppose."

His sister Lizzie's voice sounded warm; she was good at pretending to be neighborly with those witches. "This thing? It's seasons and seasons old. I wore it because I believed that this would be a working day. But Lord Heydon has taken all the labor upon himself. We don't have to lift a finger."

Rowland sneezed, violently. Then he coughed so hard he had to leave the room for several moments. When he came back, he collided with Lizzie. Rowland recoiled, as if he'd hurt himself.

"Miss Foxe!" He glanced around, whispering, so that only Ned and Lizzie heard. "Give me another week. I need extra time to do what I can."

"The summer is gone soon. We don't have time." Lizzie, uncharacteristically, picked at her sleeve. "You promised."

"I keep my promises." Rowland's cheeks were crimson (perhaps with the heat), but Ned could not read his expression. "'My family obligations are sacred.'"

Rowland moved away from Lizzie, standing near Tamsin on the opposite side of the window. After Heydon had his own two paintings judged and rejected by the Droochloots, he turned his attention to entertain the women. Though busy with Tamsin whispering in his ear, Ned still overheard Heydon's conversation.

"Dear ladies, you must try this tea."

"Bless me, no thank you. My mother declared it vile." Lady Candecote sniffed.

"Ah. I learned the tea-drinking habit from Charles's queen, Catherine." Heydon sounded casually curious, while Ned appreciated the man's ability to backfoot these ladies. "You might enjoy it with milk and sugar, as do many in James's court."

"We shall be modern and try it." Mrs. Fairchild, her nose in the air, was persuaded by Catherine's and James's names.

"Bravo, madam," Heydon said. "I found this black tea in London. A Dutch trader ships it from Japan by way of Macao."

"Where's that, for heaven's sake?" Lady Hawksmoor asked, while Mrs. Fairchild was begging sugar and milk.

Heydon poured while answering. "It's a Portuguese colony, fallen on sad times now. I predict that the traders who can supply Europe with tea from China will rule the seas in the next century. The smart man would seek to invest in such ventures. Miss Foxe, will you take tea?"

"Upon my soul," Lizzie said, "it's what I've missed most about court life. But I prefer mine without sugar."

"And you, Lord Orlando?" Heydon held out the pot from which he'd been pouring. "Will you accept my offer?"

"I shall accept whatever you serve." Rowland turned to Heydon, offered a slight bow, pressed his hands as if in prayer. Rowland's dark gaze reminded Tamsin of his expression when he prepared to be punished for their childhood larks. "With all the sugar you choose to share. I say, Meester Droochloot, let me assist you with that canvas."

Heydon's lips twitched, as if suppressing a smile, the urn still in his hand. Then he bounced as if roused to action. He poured a cup of tea, added three spoonsful of sugar, and placed it on a side table almost within Rowland's reach.

Ned had a portion of his attention to lend to that exchange, which might have been freighted with meaning, like the clipped barbs Rowland and Perry often shared. Except that Heydon and Rowland didn't know each other. By the end of the Foxe cousins' charade, Rowland had not touched that tea. He remained overly active, helping the two adepts move paintings to be judged.

Each painting the adept (Tamsin) approved as genuine and worthy, and for which its owner accepted the (monstrously inflated) value, was carefully placed in one of several tin chests Ned had supplied, each painting separated by a thin, linen-wrapped board, and each full chest wrapped in waxed canvas and bound with cords, leaving handles on each side.

Ned carefully signed the receipt for each painting, as prepared by its owner. His spiky scrawl included the amount agreed as the agent's commission. He then filled in details on a pre-written billing (Lizzie had been writing these from supper time until late into the night) to the painting's owner, who signed it and then presented a cheque to Meester Droochloot for ten percent of that value.

"It's best if I write my name on the cheque," Ned said. "Englishmen find it a challenge to spell my name."

"*Zegene mij!*" Tamsin, as the adept, exclaimed *Bless me*, then pulled Ned down to whisper in his ear.

In an exaggerated Dutch accent, Ned claimed his wife demanded that he purchase this one painting of Miss Foxe's from their own funds. He opened a leather purse and counted out every piece of gold that had been saved for that quarter's taxes and mortgage dues. Then he set aside a small kitchen scene of Caesar sitting at Mrs. Bell's feet, a black kettle hanging over a winter fire.

Rowland leaned over his shoulder, as if for a closer look at the painting Ned held. He whispered, "Take every one from Hawksmoor. At your highest price." He stepped back. "I understand these homely scenes have become popular."

Tamsin muttered something in Dutch, having heard what Rowland whispered.

When they were valuing the Fairchilds' art, Ned cast a brief glance at two of his father's paintings. "We cannot accept these two. They are forgeries, of little value to anyone except perhaps an innkeeper who wants to decorate his walls. I shall offer ten pound each, to keep others from being cheated." He then praised one of the Fairchilds' paintings, a small rendering of blown-out roses in a vase atop an exotic carpet.

While Ned was making a radical offer, Heydon's modern pendulum clock toned the hour. Ned stopped, checking the clock. "I failed to track the time. We must depart for London now." He turned to Rowland. "Your coachman knows we want to travel through the night? We shall finish loading the chests now."

"We don't have enough chests for the art you have chosen," Rowland said. "There's no room for Miss Foxe's paintings! We invited you here to assess her paintings for sale."

Tamsin tugged at Ned and whispered in his ear. In response, he said to Rowland, "If you are coming to London with us today, perhaps you can transport Miss Foxe's paintings, Lord Orlando."

Rowland grimaced as if displeased, but nodded.

With a flourish, like a May-faire juggler, Ned stamped each chest with a wax seal—the one that Great-grandmother Sarah, Lady Marborne, used to seal her letters.

"Are we ready to depart?" Rowland called. His Orlando remained composed while orchestrating what they were about to do—if he didn't glance at Lizzie. Something more than teasing was going on between them, but Ned could neither see what it was nor ask what had happened between them.

Heydon took over the attention of the syndicate of neighbors. "You have all accepted my invitation to an afternoon repast. Miss Foxe, will you join us?"

"I should be delighted, Lord Heydon."

The merry band of imposters, together with Mr. Duncombe, left for Mr. Warboys' waiting carriage. On the street, Ned wanted to shout for joy. They'd done it. Only the easiest part of the plan remained. Tamsin seemed just as elated. She grabbed Rowland's sleeve and thanked him when he handed her into the carriage.

"*Merci*, Meester Orlando!"

Yet Rowland's face was so grim, his eyes dark with fury, you'd think a royal decree had just commanded the worst of fates.

—

"London bound, are ye, sir?" Mr. Warboys touched his nose and winked when he greeted the bewigged, disguised Ned. "It's a fine day for a journey."

"And shall be also a fine night, it is hoped," Ned said, glad that if only one person recognized him, it was Mr. Warboys.

The rest of the plan was child's play. They'd continue through the night to some lonely place outside London. Ned and Tamsin would request a necessary stop and then return as highwaymen to commandeer the carriage and leave Mr. Duncombe and Perry behind to walk into London. This plan ensured that Lord Orlando and the Droochloot pair were never recognized before disappearing forever. The paintings would be in the hands of Ned's art dealer before anyone knew the freight had gone astray.

Ready for a long night's ride, Mr. Warboys had brought out his best horses, huge Shire beasts whose great-times-six granddams and sires had arrived in England when the Dutch first came to drain the fens. Perry made significant business about guarding the freight and Mr. Duncombe's baggage with his life.

Inside the carriage, the agent and his adept sat facing the back, while Rowland and Duncombe rode facing the front. Rowland had the bag with Absolom's paintings in his lap, and his own smaller satchel, from which he produced one of the small Shakespeare books he'd fetched out of the priest hole.

"Do you mind if I read, Mr. Duncombe? It passes the time."

After that, Rowland was absorbed in his book, not answering Duncombe's repeated questions: How far to the London Road? Could the elderly Mr. Warboys really drive all night? Would the sweltering of this summer's day suffocate them all, even with the waxed-linen windows hooked open?

"Dreadfully muggy day." As should be expected, Duncombe was a chartered member of the grumbletonians. Perhaps Perry might be persuaded to dump Mr. Duncombe in a ditch sooner rather than later as they'd planned.

"*Paardereet.*" Tamsin grinned, repeating a word she'd learned from Ned, calling the man a horse's ass.

"My wife thinks," Ned exaggerated his Dutch accent, worse than his father's, "we shall have thunder today."

Rowland looked up from his book. "A good storm will clear the air. I do feel for the two riding atop in a storm."

Duncombe said, "Except they shall be washed clean while we cook inside like a Southwark eel pie."

The carriage shuddered over a rut in the road, tossing Tamsin out of her seat, across the coach, and into Rowland's lap. Gently, solicitously, he restored her to her seat.

"I'm thinking," Rowland addressed Duncombe, "of returning to Mr. Benson's lodging house in Covent Garden when we arrive in London. Or do you recommend better lodgings?"

"It's a pleasant and respectable place," Duncombe said. "Rebuilt after the Great Fire. I don't know whether I can confirm that it returns value for every shilling you might spend there."

"Cost is not a consideration." Lace floated around his hand when Rowland flicked his wrist. "I want a place where I can meet friends and execute my business in comfort."

Rowland stared at Mevrouw Droochloot, who blinked several times and dropped her head. After a moment, Tamsin squeezed Ned's hand. Then Ned finally understood that Rowland had signaled where they'd meet if happenstance separated them. Meanwhile, the rocking of the carriage became worse, Mr. Warboys having turned down a lane traveled only by farm carts. Everyone except Rowland braced when the carriage hit a large rut, juggling the carriage precariously.

"Is this the London Road?" Mr. Duncombe peered out the window, though nothing but thorn hedge and oak trees appeared.

Rowland said, "Must be what you Englishmen call a shortcut. Miss Foxe insisted that no one knows these country lanes better than Mr. Warboys."

Lower tree limbs and hedge-canes scratched the carriage. Duncombe spouted another curse. "This cannot be right."

"*Ezel. Lamzak.*" Tamsin grinned, her eyes twinkling.

Her Dutch expletives cheered Ned, who could be happy at whatever made Tamsin smile, since it happened so seldom.

Duncombe poked his head out the window, calling, "Mr. Warboys! Have we gone astray? This cannot—"

A hail of stones and clods fell on the carriage, one striking Duncombe's forehead.

"God blast them!" Duncombe swore. He pulled a small handgun from his capacious pockets.

"Gad's bodkins!" Tamsin cried, forgetting the Dutch oaths she'd learned.

Rowland pushed down Duncombe's pistol. "Give that to me. I was an army man for a season in the Low Countries. Mr. Frake will handle those ruffians."

Though Duncombe protested vociferously, Rowland had the pistol out of the man's hands. At the same moment, the carriage began to shake violently. A herd of boys shouted, "Heave!" on one side, and another batch of them called back, "Ho!" as they rocked the carriage.

"Blasted imps!" Duncombe shrieked. "We're being attacked by children. Where is your fearsome man, Lord Orlando?"

Tamsin was out the door first, likely impatient that others had undertaken a restoration without her. Ned followed. Rowland held Duncombe back, saying, "Let Mr. Frake handle it."

The hay cart from Revelstone blocked the way ahead.

The dog-cart, which had seen better days, blocked the lane behind them. Tom stood atop the cart, wearing a brown linen gown and a ruined bag-wig, with a velvet scarf tied over his face. He pointed a blunderbuss that had survived a much earlier war.

"Stand and deliver!"

The appearance of Marborne boys was surprising, but Tom roaring from behind a velvet mask gave Ned pause. Tamsin would never have allowed her brother out. However, Winwood, also masked, stood beside Tom. The carriage was thronged by every boy in the parish over the age of five. They'd swarmed over Perry and Mr. Warboys and were now arguing how to bind the two men.

Despite the surprise, Ned had no time to be distracted. Tamsin disappeared off the trail. He followed until they were out of sight. The boys' clamor could still be heard—likely as far as Cambridge.

"Did you know about this, Ned?"

"No. I guess we are to be highwaymen for a restoration now, rather than at dawn."

"I shall deal harshly with Rollo for inviting Tom to this juggle. And Perry, if he had a hand in this surprise."

Ned stripped off the wig and the velvet. Tamsin got rid of that immense grey gown and her own wig. From the gown's pockets,

Tamsin produced two wool caps, with slits for their eyes. When the two of them emerged from the hedgerow, the boys had already removed half the baggage from atop the carriage. A brigade passed tin chests to be loaded on the hay cart. Winwood offered pistols to Ned and Tamsin.

"Behold, the carriage!" Ned exclaimed, bent in his hunchback posture. "Out ye come, with your hands high!"

Ned relieved Rowland of the leather bag that held the paintings from Revelstone and carried it himself to stow it in the hay cart. Meanwhile, Tamsin took the pistol Rowland had seized from Duncombe and tossed it into a hedge. "Now, hands behind you, sir."

While Rowland protested the pain and rough handling, Tamsin bound his hands. When she fished inside his vest, he spoke to her, but all Ned heard was, "…only Lord Heydon in Cambridge."

Mr. Duncombe cursed and cried in pain when Ned tightened his fetters and then poked inside Duncombe's coat, having learned from Perry where the man lodged his papers. "And I wager a fine gentleman like you holds a purse with your ready and favorites."

Perry had warned Ned about the next part ("where that man keeps his valuables"), and it seemed so simple when described. Except Ned thought he'd be doing it in cool, predawn darkness outside London, not in the sweltering heat and dust of his own parish. He prodded Duncombe with his flintlock, then had to stick his hand in the fellow's disagreeably sweat-dampened drawers to fish out a small velvet purse.

Ned slapped his hand on his breeches, disgusted by the damp from the fellow's sweat. The small bag crunched in his hand, keys rattling. (Perry would rejoice, given what he'd said earlier: "It's my fondest wish, dear Ned, for what we might retrieve today.")

That gorgeous man, tied up like a Christmas roast, bawled at the boys, sounding caustically critical, while in fact instructing them on their task. Ned had sprung free of his surprise and now had to mask his amusement, as Perry called to the boys, "That's right! Carry it carefully, while you break the eighth of Our Father's commandments! What will your masters give you for such rude thievery?"

One boy shouted in answer. "A crown each and cake!"

The line of boys passing boxes began to shout, "Cake! Cake! We shall have cake!"

The boys loading the wagon cried back, "Pudding! Pudding! Steamed pudding and rum sauce!"

The boys handing boxes down from the carriage shouted, "Sweets! Sweets! Boiled sweets!"

This had to have been Perry's idea. All the Marborne kinder and Mr. Warboys seemed to believe they played out a jest on Lord Orlando. Mr. Warboys shook with laughter after the boys tied him up. Perhaps it'd pass as an old man weeping.

Tamsin whispered for Winwood to drive Tom home just as one of the larger boys called, "All done!"

The dog-cart departed, and the hay wagon lumbered around the turn into a lane that led directly to Revelstone. The creak of the wagon was lost in the distance before the boys' cries faded.

That was when thunder peeled, the skies flashed, and a summer rain began to pelt them, sending up the sweet smell of dry dirt. The plash on the oak leaves rang as loud as the thunder. Through the slit in Ned's mask, the hedgerow seemed to melt in the rain, like streaks across his palette when he washed it with spirits. Tamsin dove into the hedge. Ned followed.

"This is our best restoration! And what a surprise!" Tamsin gave Ned her pistol, then tore off her mask and used it to wipe away the face paint. "Now, Rollo says I must run to Cambridge for him. Be safe on the road, Ned. And in the city tomorrow!"

It was his role in the gambol to see the scheme as far as London, since he'd signed his own name on all those cheques now buttoned up in his pocket. He just hadn't expected this spirited change in plans. But then, Perry said as much the day they met. ("We shall have our frolics, Mr. Wijck.")

Ned retrieved that bright orange velvet suit, became Droochloot again, now thoroughly disheveled in that blasted wig.

"*Mijn vrouw!*" Ned cried. "My beloved has left me. I am bereft."

48

A Repast

— T A M S I N —

DRESSED AS A highwayman, hoping to pass as Tom in country work-ing clothes, Tamsin ran to Heydon's house. She ran as if borne by angels, her thoughts singing the whole way, of how she'd announce a catastrophic robbery.

Rowland and Perry threw a surprise into the plan, with the restoration occurring so close to Revelstone. But then Rowland sent her to Cambridge, which promised Tamsin an unplanned pleas-ure. She'd see the faces of their cheating neighbors when they learned that perfidious highwaymen had stolen all their paintings.

She also had a happy secret and no one in Cambridge to share it with except Lizzie. That is, everything they'd liberated was at Revelstone, where Tom was good at hiding liberated items. Even if the king's men quartered in Marborne village again that night, they'd never uncover treasures won in the gambol.

The Foxe cousins now had in hand all the elements of their most successful restoration.

They would not hang as thieves.

Nor lose Marborne because of poverty.

Nor allow their betraying neighbors to steal Marborne from its proper owners.

At a future safe day, Ned and the cousins would bring those paintings to London to sell via his genuine agent.

While still counting those blessings, having outrun the day's sudden storm, her clothes mostly dry, Tamsin slowed to a walk when the lane she traveled joined Lord Heydon's street.

Leighton Fairchild knocked on Heydon's door.

Fine. He'd be among the collective nemesis eating their repast at Heydon's table who'd soon learn their wealth had been reduced significantly by Fate.

Waiting until Leighton was inside, Tamsin walked up the street and knocked on the door, smiling at the servant who answered. "Please inform Lord Heydon that Tom Foxe has come with a message from Lord Orlando."

Heydon instantly appeared on the doorstep. "Then it's done?"

"Yes." Tamsin answered, not believing Heydon knew the full extent of what "done" meant. He didn't know Ned had been the agent and wrote his own name on those cheques. Or that "Lord Orlando" was about to disappear forever with all the paintings.

She passed Heydon the page Rowland had given her when she tied him up in the lane. "I couldn't read it. It's a cypher."

"I'm pleased he accepted my help. We shall now proceed with my plan for exposing the three sisters." Heydon clapped Tamsin on the back as sturdily as if she were Tom.

A grin spread over Heydon's face that he quickly hid with his hand, which Tamsin had never seen him do before. He took a breath, as if savoring deep satisfaction.

"Is Captain Starbuck taking Duncombe to London himself?"

"Duncombe? Starbuck?" She was as surprised as her horse had been when attacked by browsing geese.

"Aye. What other traitor needs to be in the Tower?"

"I—I left before they decided." Tamsin became again the successful highwayman at the core her being, and so managed not to reveal that she didn't know this part of Rowland's plan.

Heydon clapped his hands with glee. "Come, join us for a glass of wine. Please refrain from telling my guests about the arrest until I ask. And you—you are good at deception, so be creative if you are surprised. You and I are united, aren't we, in seeking to hold these miscreants accountable?"

"Aye, your lordship."

Deception? Duncombe arrested? Trepidation heated her veins. Tamsin did not enter Heydon's dining room with the same pure happiness she'd felt while running to Cambridge from the successful restoration. She did, however, continue to play a confident "Tom," despite Heydon's surprise.

Servants were removing the remains of the repast. Heydon asked, "Would you like a slice of pudding, Tom?"

Tamsin declined. Though her belly was empty, she was too full of news—and anxious curiosity—to eat. Heydon indicated an empty chair opposite Lizzie, and then took his place at the head of the table, with Lizzie at his right hand.

Lizzie gazed at Tamsin, her dark eyes brimming with questions. But Tamsin needed a very private moment before she could reveal all the good news she carried.

Tom was well enough to participate in a restoration again.

The paintings were safely hidden at Revelstone.

Perry had given Tamsin the forged liens, so Marborne was safe from Duncombe's evil fraud.

The only work that remained was to redeem the liberated paintings and Droochloot's agent fees, so they could pay the king's garnishment and reclaim the title.

For every moment while Heydon was seeing to each guest's wine glass and other desires, Tamsin endured a creeping certainty that she'd been sent to play in a scheme she didn't understand. Tamsin intended a word with Rowland later, for not trusting his comrades with all the details.

The syndicate of Absolom's betrayers were aligned along the table, Duncombe's three sisters by each other and opposite their husbands, Mr. Fairchild, Sir Isaiah, Lord Hawksmoor. Leighton sat at the far end of the table, accepting wine from a servant, glaring at Tamsin. His presence promised increased joy when she revealed how highwaymen had stolen their paintings.

"A glass of claret, Tom?" Heydon had already poured wine and set the glass down for Tamsin before she answered.

She sipped the wine, awaiting a cue from Heydon that she might reveal the news which should devastate the people here who had cheated Absolom and the Marborne estate. Lizzie, sober faced, locked her eyes on Lord Heydon, who stood at the head of the table, his arms open.

"I have a pair of surprising announcements."

Everyone but Mr. Fairchild and the sulking Leighton set down their wine glasses and waited on Heydon's words.

"First, Miss Foxe has done me the honor this afternoon of accepting my proposal of marriage. Please wish us happy."

Tamsin resisted showing surprise, her eyes on Lizzie, who gazed only at Heydon. A wave of sadness washed over Tamsin, because she did not understand Lizzie, who, since her return from Holland, had never opened her heart and thoughts. This was why Heydon offered not to interfere with the Foxe cousins' plans. This explained why Heydon forestalled the tragic news about Duncombe and the paintings. He wanted to bask in the joy of this news.

(But, oh, Lizzie, why didn't you tell me? Does Rowland know? Yes. That explained his black mood throughout a gambol that should have delighted him.)

Hawksmoor seemed as surprised as Tamsin felt. He lifted his wine glass high. "You astonish me, Poynter. You gave me no clue. Well, I thought this day would never come. May your life together be blessed."

"I thought she was marrying her cousin?" Lady Candecote's thin voice wheezed out a surprised and querulous question. The gentlemen all cut sideways glances at "Tom."

Therefore, Tamsin stood and lifted her glass, remembering the warning. ("Be creative if you are surprised.")

"I too heard those false rumors, my lady. Please know that I am content that my cousin Ysabel chose Poynter. He's a good and honorable man, and a friend. I wish them every happiness."

(Why, Lizzie? Did you not trust that our gambol will earn enough to buy back the Marborne title?)

Lizzie wouldn't look at Tamsin. She and Heydon accepted everyone's compliments with severe formality.

"When, when will the happy day come? Come?" Sir Isaiah asked, with his usual insipid, repetitive squeak.

Heydon said, "As soon as the king gives us permission to marry. Before summer is gone, we hope." A clamor of congratulations rose. Tamsin, however, knew that Lizzie didn't need permission from the king, only a blessing from Princess Mary. Had Lizzie already written to gain that blessing?

Hawksmoor said, "You have been persuasive with the king all year, Poynter. I don't imagine he'll make you wait."

"You said there were two announcements, sir." Lizzie spoke for the first time, drawing sober attention to her.

Heydon said, "Yes, though the second news will end this brief celebration. Tom, please tell us the sad news I made you hold back for the sake of my own happy tidings." Heydon gestured with two fingers for Tamsin to speak. "Mr. Foxe?"

This was the chance to announce what she'd rehearsed on her run to Cambridge. But as soon as she took a breath, she instead fabricated a different story, guessing what might have happened after she'd run from the restoration. She had to invent a story, because Rowland had not shared with her the "taking the traitor to London" part of the gambol.

She stood so she could see everyone's face clearly, though each time she glanced at Lizzie, her cousin's face showed the trepidation Tamsin felt. Not the face of a happily affianced bride.

"The militia has arrested Mr. Duncombe." Tamsin chose to omit the highwaymen in favor of a better story based on thin evidence from Heydon. "They seized everything from the carriage, because Mr. Duncombe claimed to have it all under his charge."

The syndicate of swindling siblings all gasped at once, like a long team of horses frightened by racing rabbits.

The moment felt as satisfying as when Perry gave Tamsin the forged mortgage liens, freeing Marborne.

—

"I was at the Phoenix and Swan," Tamsin said, "when Mr. Warboys returned there and reported the alarming news."

She repressed the day's thrills and worries, speaking solemnly while prevaricating wildly.

"Captain Starbuck declared Mr. Duncombe to be a traitor to the Crown," she hoped she guessed right, "and the militia is taking him to London, along with Lord Orlando."

She watched Lizzie for a sign that this might be true, more than a fiction Tamsin created by knowing that Perry and Rowland were intelligencers, and therefore had other professional work beyond the Foxe family gambol.

The men sighed; the sisters cried out, clutching each other.

"Fie, it cannot be!" Mrs. Fairchild exclaimed.

"They arrested Danvers as a traitor?" Lady Hawksmoor whined. "How could they know?"

Tamsin didn't see that anyone other than Heydon marked the admission in the last question. For the first question, Tamsin considered how Perry had purloined the forged liens from Duncombe, joined that with the paper Rowland asked her to carry to Heydon, and formed an answer.

"Mr. Warboys says the redcoats found incriminating papers on Mr. Duncombe."

"A pox on Danvers!" Lady Candecote exclaimed, wiping at tears. "He promised we'd all be safe. That he'd make us rich if we helped him to gain the—"

Mrs. Fairchild squeezed her sister's hand until the silly woman cried in pain, finally understanding not to speak.

"Did you know?" Hawksmoor glared at his wife. "Did you know what your infernal brother was up to?"

"I swear that I didn't know about the Duke of Monmouth." Lady Hawksmoor wrenched her hands as if praying to her husband. "Danvers only promised me the best return on our invested assets."

No one there had mentioned Monmouth, so for a second time, the lady admitted treason.

"If you declare a bed in the Tower and a cart-ride to the gallows to be your invested assets." Hawksmoor growled.

Lizzie murmured, "Upon my soul. They arrested my cousin Orlando? Why?" She twisted her mother's handkerchief around her fingers. Untwisting. Twisting again. "What happened to the agent and his wife?"

"I suppose we must go to London to learn what and why." For Tamsin, that now seemed obvious. Rowland and Perry had made a separate plan, perhaps while they caroused with Captain Starbuck in the winter kitchen—while both Lizzie and Tamsin were absent. "I only know from what Mr. Warboys reported, that everyone was taken by the militia."

Mrs. Fairchild said, "But Mr. Warboys will return all the chests of paintings to us? The agent will return the cheques that paid his fees?"

"Oh, no, Mrs. Fairchild." Tamsin assumed the same grim expression as when Camilla wandered in from the churchyard, nearly dead. Inside, though, she sang with the angels. "Did I not say? When they arrested Mr. Duncombe, the militia took everything. Captain Starbuck had a general writ of seizure. All your paintings shall go to the king. I expect the king will seize all of Mr. Duncombe's assets."

"We are ruined!" Lady Candecote shrieked.

"Perhaps your brother will be found innocent," Mr. Fairchild said, a mild attempt to calm her. But his own wife slapped at the solicitor's hand, as if he were being foolish.

This was the special moment that Rowland's change in plans offered Tamsin, to see everyone's ashen, frightened faces as they quarreled, those faces twisting with vitriol for each other. Each husband barked at his wife for having a traitorous brother; each wife insisted that she acted solely for her husband's interests.

"Are you calling me greedy?" one man shouted to a wife who cried, "You called me a fool."

Hawksmoor seemed to know little or nothing of his wife's dealings, while the other two husbands seemed to know and castigated their wives for having a bad brother.

Once during this turmoil, Lizzie stopped twisting her handkerchief and whispered, "Tell me they didn't arrest Rol—Lord Orlando. Did he do this?"

Tamsin held out an empty hand, to indicate she had no clear idea. Heydon, mistaking the motion, poured more wine in her glass while he watched the havoc. He only looked at Lizzie to see if her glass needed tending. The mêlée among his guests had all his attention.

Leighton at the far end of the table saved his attention alternately for his wine glass, for curled-lip glances of hatred in Tamsin's direction, and for comments that worsened the fracas between his parents.

"How, Mother, will you extract us from what my dulpickle of an uncle has wrought?"

Mrs. Fairchild again slapped away her husband's reassuring hand. "Fie. That den of Foxe kits stole our paintings."

This was perhaps the only truth spoken in fifteen minutes of vicious quarrelling. Lizzie, however, collected all her indignation, which saved Tamsin from interfering.

"Dear Mrs. Fairchild, Lord Orlando may have sought to help you sell your paintings, but no one in my family ever trusted their money to a traitor to the Crown. If the militia seized those paintings, I too have lost my only assets."

"I beg you, madam, not to cast aspersions on my affianced bride," Heydon also addressed Mrs. Fairchild. "Especially because I am about to save all of you, if you will let me."

"Get on with it, Poynter." Hawksmoor slapped the table in angry irritation. "Tell us what to do."

49

A Coincidence

— N E D —

A CLOT OF unnatural crimson streamed into the far end of the lane. The sight instantly replaced Ned's buoyant mood with fear and nervous apprehension.

Ned, again in orange velvet, rushed to Perry to unwind the braided leather that bound his friend's hands and feet.

"Take all the time you want," Perry murmured. "I like it when you take your time. Though that wig is not as alluring as your own bone-white locks."

"What?" Fear throbbed in Ned's head and hands. He could hardly hear for the pounding in his ears. "The militia is here. Our restoration is undone!"

"Sweeting, things aren't as they seem. But you will be safe." His hand free, Perry stroked Ned's jaw the way he had in the night. "Zeus's bolts shan't strike you. Prevaricate if you must."

"But last night, you said the plan was—"

"Dear Ned, I abstained from drawing you into that which might threaten your safety. Did you find the man's keys?"

"I–I...Yes." The militia thundered up the lane. He passed the jangling pouch to Perry. "Exactly where you said."

"I am comforted. You are a gift from the angels, as I divined when I first saw you."

"What is happening, Perry?"

"Ah. Well now, you must trust that I shall soon tell you the tale of how busy I've been today. But as it is, you and I cannot speak in this crowd."

Mr. Warboys called, "Blooming Hades! Release me too! This is the saddest jest I ever did see."

Ned untied Mr. Warboys' bonds. Perry helped Mr. Warboys out of the dirt of the lane, which was rapidly turning to mud. He slipped a packet to Mr. Warboys that must have contained coins.

"Thank ye, Mr. Frake. I take it we shall remain strangers."

"Aye, Mr. Warboys. Once the militia departs, please carry the freight from Revelstone to London as we agreed."

"Rain's not like to do a gun any good," the old driver said. "Let's fetch back our pistols from the hedges, Mr. Wijck."

While they hunted, Ned's heart still pounded to the beat of the militia riding up the lane, not reassured by Perry's words.

Duncombe castigated Perry while the big man worked to remove the business man's fetters. Perry seemed unfazed by the myriad chastisements for his failure as a guard.

"You shan't be paid! Lord Orlando, do not pay this incompetent fool. He failed us."

Duncombe charged at Perry as if to strike him.

Any innocent watching would only see Perry hold up his hand to fend off the charge, but Duncombe flew backward, landing in a mud-filled rut.

Just as the militia clattered up to join them, Ned emerged with Mr. Warboys from the hedges, loaded with firearms, which they laid down at the edge of the road.

Perry might claim safety, but Ned's insides twisted in knots.

Their entire gambol was undone.

They'd all hang.

"We've been robbed!" Duncombe screamed as he rose from the mud.

Ned scowled at Perry. It would have all gone better if they'd stuck to the plan and waited until pre-dawn to toss the clamorous Mr. Duncombe into a ditch. Perry returned only a beatific smile.

Duncombe continued to scream at the dismounting redcoats. "They stole a fortune! You must go recover it."

"Which way did they go?" A sergeant asked.

"Both ways! And through the hedges, too!" Duncombe paced, unable to contain his agitation over this catastrophe.

Captain Starbuck dismounted and came to Duncombe's side, not glancing at or greeting any of the men he'd been drinking with in the winter kitchen the night before. "We didn't encounter anyone in the lane. How many were they?"

"Two dozen or more shouting boys. And a half-dozen masters calling orders to the boys. And wagons!"

"Why would you carry a fortune in a hired carriage?" Starbuck turned to the driver. "It is you, isn't it, Mr. Warboys? From the Phoenix and Swan?"

Duncombe interrupted. "This old man was as useless as the guard we hired."

The color rose in Mr. Warboys' cheeks at the insult. But his attention was on Starbuck. "Aye, captain. But we was only badgered by some boys kicking up a lark."

"A lark? Are you in this with them, old man?" Duncombe might burst a vessel. His whole body wrenched up in anger. "Those fiends stole a carriage full of goods I'm responsible for. And my baggage and business papers." Duncombe touched his vest, from which pocket Ned, as the hunchback brigand, had removed a packet of papers.

That made Ned rub his hands on his orange velvet breeches again, thinking of retrieving the damp purse that held the keys Perry wanted. His hand came away no drier, for the sudden rain was drenching them all. Perry and all the militia men had their broad hats. Mr. Warboys had replaced his wonder of a felted hat on his grizzled head, and Rollo and the London man wore hats over their fancy wigs. Only Ned stood in an unkempt periwig, the skies pouring rain down his face, white-lead face paint melting into the lush neckcloth Lizzie had tied on him that morning.

Ned prayed that the overly friendly Captain Starbuck would go on his way. By now, the liberated freight had been safely hidden at Revelstone. If the militia would just leave, then Perry could toss Duncombe into a ditch farther from Cambridgeshire, with only that change in the original plan.

The red-coated riders scarcely hunched against the summer shower. Ned was beginning to recognize that only he and Mr. Duncombe were surprised at this meeting. Ned took a breath. Stepped back. Used all the clever wit that Perry insisted Ned possessed—and began to hope the sudden appearance of the militia might not lead to catastrophe. He tugged at his soggy neckcloth, trying not to think of the magistrate's noose. Then Perry, lovely even in the rain and mud, winked at him, and Ned was reminded of a promise made the night before to improve Ned's life. Perry would never break a promise, so Ned decided that they'd meet safely on the other side of whatever this new rig might be.

— ROLLO —

THE FIVE O'CLOCK bells in Cambridge echoed in the distance when the militia arrived.

That's Valentine Starbuck, always precise about time. The Revelstone boys—and Tamsin—had cleared off. Rowland had warned Starbuck over breakfast that they intended a masquerade with local boys, to trap Warboys' carriage where he'd promised that the militia would find it. It always felt good to keep Starbuck at least partly innocent.

Behind Captain Starbuck, out of Duncombe's sight, Perry winked at Ned, who seemed anxious when the militia appeared. Neither he nor Perry could say it aloud at that moment, to promise Ned that he'd be safe.

To be sure, Perry would harangue him later for not allowing Ned to know about this second gambol.

Rowland brushed at the mud on his copper-satin suit, but only smeared it. That suit might be beyond rescue. He swiped at his muddied boots with a kerchief, and then bent to inspect the patch of road where Duncombe had been bound. He picked from his own pocket the packet that Perry had purloined from Duncombe's vest, dropping it in the lane.

"I say, Mr. Duncombe! Is this yours? Did those miscreants drop your papers? What good fortune!"

Rowland offered the packet to Duncombe, but Starbuck pushed away Duncombe's hand and seized it. Holding the papers under the overhanging brim of his hat, Starbuck read while keeping the papers out of the rain.

"This is written in a cypher." Starbuck stated it, not asking (because Rowland had warned him over breakfast what they'd be taking from Duncombe). Then Starbuck once more denied Duncombe's reach, tucking it into his coat, away from the rain.

"I keep all my business records private," Duncombe said, "to protect my clients. You must return my papers."

Starbuck said, "It's a simple cypher I learned when I served the English ambassador in Paris. Not so clever that it requires a key to translate." He signaled his sergeant. "Place this man under arrest. Bind him to a horse so he can ride with us. We shall take him to the Tower in London."

Valentine performed his part perfectly in every way. With the short thread Rowland had given him over breakfast, he'd woven the entire story of Duncombe's treachery.

"What?" Duncombe sputtered. "Is this a jest? We have been robbed. Leave us be, captain, and pursue the highwaymen."

"You are Mr. Duncombe?" Starbuck, standing stiffly, formed the very picture of a commanding officer. "A Crown intelligencer warned me to watch for you in Cambridgeshire. I am arresting you for conspiring against the lawful king of England and for giving succor and aid to traitors."

"Will you not pursue the highwaymen, captain?" Rowland spoke for the first time since the militia arrived.

Starbuck turned from Duncombe. "You are Lord Orlando? The foreign visitor at Revelstone House? What are you doing with this gentleman?"

"I offered him a ride to London. I lent him my sister's guard, Mr. Frake, to protect his baggage."

"My baggage!" Duncombe exclaimed. "Those boys took every bag and case."

"I have mine." Rowland signaled the simple satchel slung over his shoulder.

Starbuck asked to see inside that satchel, then shook his head when he found only two volumes from Absolom's Shakespeare hoard and a clean kerchief.

"Mr. Warboys," Starbuck said, "are you included in the party with these gentlemen?"

"No, captain, sir. Just driving. Never saw them before today. Except that one," he pointed to Perry, "was in my carriage when the highwaymen took me by surprise on Tuesday. I remember me the very day, because it's when they carried Doctor Foxe to his Eternal Rest. The grandest averil it was, though sad."

"An astonishing coincidence." Starbuck's smirk flashed before he covered his mouth to hide it (but only if one knew him well enough to expect it).

"You must imagine my distress that day," Perry said, "my linen being pilfered by highwaymen carrying dags and daggers."

"My condolences," Starbuck said. "And today?"

"Nothing lost, no harm done," Perry said. "Just rowdy boys kicking up a lark. Your Mr. Duncombe took a fright, imagining things he feared when it was just lads on a tear."

Duncombe again let off a stream of protest, as if he'd agreed to play the part of lunatic. Starbuck's sergeant threatened him with a musket, quieting the man for a moment.

Starbuck turned back to the carriage driver. "If you please, Mr. Warboys, you may be off for home. Your passengers are all going to London. We shall ride too hard to be held back by a slow-going carriage."

"My carriage ain't slow." Warboys grumbled at the insult but went to check his Shire horses.

"Wait!" Duncombe cried. "Where is the Dutch fellow's wife? She ran into the hedges. She must be in league with the robbers. You must go after them."

"Your wife?" Starbuck stared at Ned as if astonished. He'd spent too much time in the kitchen the previous night, and so recognized Ned despite the wig and the outlandish orange velvet suit. "You don't look like a man who'd keep a wife."

"Sir?" Ned looked innocent. "Odsheartlings! What would I do with a wife?"

Starbuck accepted this with no comment, though Rowland had prepared him only to take "Lord Orlando and his sister's guard" with the militia to London. Duncombe shrieked in protest until a sergeant thumped his chest with the butt of his musket.

Rowland intended to congratulate Ned later for not showing fear when the militia appeared. For not spinning unnecessary falsehoods. And for glancing Perry's way only briefly. Rowland passed his own signal to Perry: all was well.

Starbuck, meanwhile, chose which of his men would travel to London and which would return to their posting in Cambridge. He'd agreed with the plan explained that morning, that Rowland must continue to play Orlando, to cover for both his and Perry's roles as intelligencers. For the entire ride to London, the militia and Mr. Duncombe would see only Lord Orlando and his friends. Once in London, the Viscount Orlando would disappear forever.

Though he was helping to send a traitorous fool to the gallows, Rowland no longer felt that, serving as an intelligencer, he met Absolom's rules for enlightened people. He was coming up short on at least one rule: *The world improves from my toil.*

Hence, Rowland Foxe must find a new way to live in a changed world. Where Marborne had been made safe, and where Lizzie had consigned her life to Heydon.

— NED —

NED UNDERSTOOD THAT he'd be traveling to London when, at Captain Starbuck's command, eight men on four horses rode back to Cambridge to inform the rest of the militia that their captain was going to London on Crown business.

That left four horses for the men that Starbuck was taking to London. His sergeant tied Mr. Duncombe in the saddle with practiced skill. When the sergeant prepared to tie Perry in place, Starbuck told him to desist.

"Let them ride unfettered. They have no money and do not know the countryside. Where else can they go but to London with us?"

"They must be part of this plot!" Duncombe exclaimed. "They have fabricated all of this!"

"Can you please gag him, sergeant?"

While that command was being carried out, Starbuck turned to Rowland. "And you? Do you have complaints about how the king's militia shall manage your transport to London?"

"None, sir. I understand your duty in service to the Crown of England. And so, it is 'but fortune. All is fortune.'"

"If I have to hear Shakespeare all the way to London, I shall have you gagged too, your honorable lordship." Starbuck again had to hide a smirk. "Is that how they say it in Spain?"

"Catalonia. But please, call me Lord Orlando."

The man riding closest to Ned claimed that their pace meant seventeen hours hard riding. Half to be taken in the dark. However, the rain had ceased, and only the first two hours of the ride involved mud and dripping trees. There was not one conversation in the saddle that Ned felt fit to participate in, even among the two redcoats surmising when their captain had met with a king's intelligencer.

"I expect," one fellow said, "we shall have to share the king's gratuity with whomever that spy proves to be."

The other said, "Even though it's us and our Captain Starbuck what done all the work, catching this traitor and bringing him to justice."

Later, in the dark part of the ride, Ned imagined how he'd paint mounted redcoats on an English country lane. Easy to set up a scarlet and green palette. But the scene had to be romantical, not a tribute to war. Perhaps a Cambridge spire in the distance?

50

The Bristol Road

— TAMSIN —

"I BRIBED AN officer of the Crown," Heydon said, "to sell me this page from your brother Duncombe's ledger." From his vest pocket, he produced the page Tamsin had carried to Cambridge.

Tamsin coughed, caught by surprise and needing to mask her dismay. Bribed an officer of the Crown? He must mean Rowland.

Lizzie bit her lip and wrenched at her handkerchief, and so must also have guessed it was Rowland. Tamsin wanted to caution her. ("It will prove to be like Rotterdam! There's more we don't know!") Instead, she waited anxiously. This must be the plan Heydon mentioned at supper, when he'd asked her not to interfere.

Heydon waved the page, but he didn't let anyone read it. "That great expense gives me joy, because this paper contains all your names as members of a syndicate supporting Monmouth."

"What are you saying?" Lady Candecote shrieked again.

"I'm saying, dear lady, that Danvers Duncombe has been arrested, but your names will not be delivered to the Crown today as his accomplices."

"Was it that ingratiating Captain Starbuck you bribed?" Hawksmoor asked. "The upstart who's sweeping the countryside for Monmouth's rebels?"

"No," Heydon said. "I must preserve the officer's secrets. All that matters is that I have preserved you from immediate prosecution by the Crown."

Tamsin, roused by this surprise, used all her practice playing Tom to keep the shock from her face, though her hand crept up to touch her Archangel pouch. However, the skills Lizzie learned in court about governing her emotions seemed to have deserted her; she sucked in a breath, hugged herself, each hand tightly gripping her arms. Then she recovered her stoniest expression.

While Tamsin and Lizzie quietly fretted over their shock, the sisters and their husbands bickered over the fateful news.

"Fie. What are you about, sir?" Mrs. Fairchild puffed up, offering her usual disdain.

"The king's men are bringing your brother to the Tower," Heydon said, "to be judged as one of Monmouth's conspirators. You know how harsh the king has been with rebels."

"Poynter! What is this?" Hawksmoor's fist hit the table.

"Your name is protected, brother. That is why I purchased this list at great personal cost."

"Why do you choose to cause us all of this trouble, Poynter?" Lady Hawksmoor said.

"Me?" Heydon paused, seeming confused by her accusation. "I'm not responsible for your predicament. Surely you see you are all in peril for your lives because of your brother."

"But you hold the list with our names." Lady Hawksmoor continued her plea. "The king won't know."

"I cannot protect you once the king's men search Duncombe's office. Or when the Crown's intelligencers question him. They tend to be persuasive."

"What shall we do?" Lady Candecote twisted the necklace at her throat. It popped and sent black beads everywhere.

"Let the servants attend to that." Heydon motioned for everyone to remain seated when the gentlemen began to rise. "I need you to please listen and understand. You see, I learned a week ago about your close connections with Duncombe. I also learned the Crown considers him to be a conspirator with the Duke of Monmouth. Hence, I've been busy with a plan to protect you. I put all elements in place in time, having learned this morning that your brother's arrest was imminent."

"High handed, Poynter." Hawksmoor growled. "You should have come to me."

"But I did," Heydon said. "I have repeatedly begged you not to put your property and people in jeopardy, not to use Duncombe as your man of business. Now your life is at risk, so I have done everything I can to save you."

"What do we do?" Lady Candecote tugged at the lace that lined the ends of her sleeves.

"You must take advantage of what I've done to save you." Heydon made a sweeping gesture. "I've paid your coachmen to take you to Bristol, where I have engaged a ship that will carry you to safety in Barbados. There, you shall have comfortable homes on my estates. I am reasonably sure that the Crown will not pursue you there."

"Pity sakes," Mrs. Fairchild frowned. "We shall not go."

"Dear Mrs. Fairchild, I've paid a considerable fortune for these arrangements, as well as for this list. Now, are you fully assured that your brother Danvers will be as discreet as I am? Will he remain silent once the Crown begins interrogating him?"

"Shame—" Mrs. Fairchild began.

"Hush, Dorcas." Mr. Fairchild seized her hand. "I warned you that Danvers's scheme might come to tragedy."

Hawksmoor glared at Mrs. Fairchild. "We can lay all this at your feet, can we not, madam? You've been busy scheming with your light-heeled brother."

Mrs. Fairchild had her nose where it always was, in the air. "*My* brother is loyal. It's your brother, Hawksmoor, who seeks to exile us."

"Ah," Heydon said. "Duncombe might be loyal, but not to the king who sits on the English throne. There lies the source of your grief. And I—well, I seek only to protect my brother's life while the king is busy seeking retribution. The rest of you are offered free passage only on his account."

Amid all the anger and fear roiling among Duncombe's syndicate, Tamsin could not tell what Lizzie was feeling, and she couldn't yet locate all her own feelings, except for a conflagration in her belly. Heydon had claimed over last night's supper that they shared mutual interests. Yet he'd said nothing about proposing to Lizzie or scheming with Rowland. Whatever Heydon had planned, Lizzie and Tamsin needed to hear from Ned and Rowland that all was well on the road to London.

And they both needed to hear from Rowland about the nature of his business with Heydon.

—

Enmired in the unhappy situation, which Perry had predicted, Tamsin was watching the death of souls. Duncombe's syndicate of siblings writhed as if in Hades while Heydon drove home the danger in which they now existed. Lizzie might destroy her mother's handkerchief, and Tamsin might rub her Archangel raw, before they were freed from watching the flames of fear and anger that consumed their enemies. Tamsin caught Lizzie's glance, sharing the regret that the two of them were condemned to listen to this family squabble. They had no place there—oh, except Lizzie had agreed to marry Heydon.

Ashen, angry faces around the table awaited the next word from Heydon, who fetched a leather wallet from a side table.

"I prepared in advance for whatever catastrophe might arise from your brother Duncombe's business. For that purpose, last night my secretary drew up these papers to protect you, not knowing how timely our efforts might be." He set the wallet on the table along with a brass inkwell and a silver cup of quills. "By signing these writs, you declare loyalty to the Crown and make me the agent for each and all of your properties and businesses."

"Outrageous!" Mrs. Fairchild would not be hushed.

Her sisters again set up their wailing protests.

Heydon continued as if he didn't hear their outburst. "These writs, among all the other commitments inscribed here, promise that I shall deliver your profits annually, with itemizations of what it costs me to administer each of your properties. These arrangements pre-suppose that I am able to prevent the Crown from seizing your property."

Shuffling papers from the wallet, he moved the inkwell close to Tamsin. She stared at that inkwell, a bowl cast in bronze with a tripod formed by robust roosters, while Lord Heydon presented papers for Sir Isaiah and Mr. Fairchild to be signed.

Heydon stopped his brother from reaching for the papers he'd laid in front of Lady Hawksmoor.

"For you, Monck, I have this writ which annuls your marriage. You shall be protected from any nefarious business your wife has conducted. You need not flee the country, though I cannot protect your wife unless she leaves England."

"I shall not sign it," Hawksmoor said. "I will not leave my wife's side."

"Then I have prepared this alternative, similar to what Sir Isaiah signed." Heydon presented another page from his capacious leather wallet.

Lord Hawksmoor read without comment. He set the paper down, his face like one of the grieving gargoyles above the Marborne church door. "Poynter! How can you?"

"Dear Monck, you put the Hawksmoor estate at grave risk. I have always said that I will do anything to protect the people and land of the estate. Everything I've done is to that end—and to save your life. Now, which shall you sign? Writ of annulment? Or refusing to use your title?"

Refuse to use the title? Tamsin glanced to see if Lizzie shared her shock, but her cousin sat stiffly, without expression.

"You do not have to do this, my lord!" Lady Hawksmoor's voice trembled. In fact, she was shaking in her chair. "You do not have to give up anything for me."

"Do you think I would abandon you, my dear?" Hawksmoor had been thundering thus far, but now his voice dropped to tender entreaty. "What kind of man do you think I am?"

"I–I...my dear lord, you cannot sacrifice everything for me."

"I can, sweetkin. I will. At this very moment." Hawksmoor picked up the quill and began to sign.

Lady Hawksmoor, her face mottled with rage, shrieked at Heydon. "We shall never speak to you again in this life!"

"I shall endeavor to bear that silence," Heydon said. "But I am comforted that your life will be longer than it might be if I did not act as I have."

"We won't sign—" Mrs. Fairchild began.

Her husband pulled the paper over. "We will. I have no desire to face the gallows."

"Father!" Leighton exclaimed. "You must not sign that. We will be ruined."

"You are already ruined." Heydon spoke solemnly, no trace of the delight he'd shown when Tamsin gave him that paper from Rowland. "When you all invested in Duncombe's syndics, and then when Monmouth was defeated, it was a matter of weeks until the Crown came to knock at your doors and carry you to the gallows."

Tamsin had studied the reactions of each of the angry members of the syndicate, not sure of her own feelings as Heydon unrolled his plan. Witnessing Leighton's discomfort, though, was a small pleasure amid the chaos.

"You immoral, duplicitous arsworm!" Leighton cursed Heydon. "This is the ambuscade of a poltroon."

"Me?" Heydon maintained his affability amid these repeated attacks. "My only questionable act was to bribe an officer of the Crown. But even that, I did it to save your lives."

Tamsin came closer to understanding her own feelings: bewilderment; disinclined to think Rowland had crossed his cousins; at a loss to understand why Heydon dragged her into his family scene. He'd claimed that he too wanted justice for Marborne, with no word about forcing his brother into a sort of exile.

"You can choose," Heydon was saying to Leighton, "whether to bring your wife. Or do you prefer to annul your marriage and leave her here?"

"Does Camilla want to go with Leighton?" Lizzie said. "I very much doubt that."

"You? Handmaiden to the Ice Princess in the Low Countries?" Leighton turned on Lizzie. "Mind your own business."

Tamsin bit back against revealing her soul. ("Camilla is my business. I love her. You don't.") She managed to choke out sensible words. "This predicament is not Camilla's doing. As her friend, I know she would not choose to go with him. She doesn't need that torture for one more moment."

"You, Tom Foxe, are a malicious black-mouth." Leighton railed at Tamsin, whose insides churned for fear of Camilla's fate. "Keep out of my business, nick-ninny."

Heydon replied calmly. "Enough bear-garden discourse. I would never coerce a woman into anything she doesn't want to do." Heydon sought to pacify Leighton. "However, if your wife wishes to join you, I shall send her to you in Barbados."

"A wife isn't supposed to choose." Leighton pouted.

"If she didn't choose to participate in your scheme with Duncombe, she shouldn't be forced to participate in the results." Heydon again handed Leighton a quill. "Then annulment it is, Mr. Leighton?"

"You chittifaced cur, Tom Foxe." Leighton jumped from his chair, fists out. "You always wanted to steal my wife."

"Oh, stop it," his mother scolded. "Sir Isaiah has signed away everything to Heydon. That hoyting girl isn't worth one whit to us without the barony and her inheritance. I'd as soon leave that saucebox rotting in the fens."

Leighton required more cossetting from his mother and more pleading from his father ("You'll be hung if you stay here!") before he left off barking at Tamsin and signed the papers Heydon presented him.

Camilla to be free of that punishing marriage! Tamsin now owed immense gratitude to Lord Heydon for all his foresight. Surely Camilla will see him as a hero. Tamsin watched Leighton as he signed a writ that freed Camilla. Relief flowed over her. How glorious it shall be to see Camilla present a writ of annulment to the Church courts! Perhaps Mr. Gamlingay can advise how—

Then Tamsin's rational mind woke and came back to work.

"But, Lord Heydon, what good are these papers for Church and Crown? These people can say they were forced to sign. Or that you forged these writs."

"Did you think I lack diligence, Tom? We have witnesses, better than my fiancée and her cousin. I have representatives of the Church of England and an officer of the Crown to witness your signatures." Heydon went to the door that led to his morning room. He brought in Mr. Gamlingay and a man in an officer's red coat that Tamsin didn't recognize. "They will require your sworn oath that you have not been coerced into signing these documents. But we are all agreed, are we not, that you sign out of your own personal free will?"

"Is this the Crown officer you bribed?" the foolish Lady Candecote asked.

"This officer is a man of great skill and integrity." Heydon enunciated the words carefully. "He is loyal to the Crown and also discreet. Do you need to know more about him?"

Lizzie said hello to the rector but did not greet or seem to know that officer, her face otherwise etched in dark misery. Tamsin felt sure this wasn't the officer who'd been bribed.

Heydon's secretary had appeared with the officer and the rector. After the witnesses finished signing, he collected all the papers. Heydon shook hands with those two men, offering each a basket with a bottle of port and, most likely, a gratuity for their service. When those men departed, Heydon gestured to the door.

"Now, gentlepersons, your coachmen await. Your servants packed for you this afternoon, but my men have not found any who'd choose to go with you to the New World. However, I promise, you will find good service on the road and while sailing. My people in Barbados will attend to all your needs."

Isaiah Candecote rose, no longer laying claim to the privileges of a baronet, and nodded as if he'd already reconciled himself to a new and sudden fate. "They say Barbados is warm and beautiful."

"What can be warm and beautiful," his wife sobbed, "when you are no longer a knight of the realm?"

"You mean, now that I shall be no better than my father?" He clutched his wife's wrist and led her away from the others, scolding her in the corner.

"The Bristol Road calls you," Heydon said. "In three days, you shall be on the open seas. You will like Barbados. I expect to see you there, the next Christmas but one."

"Gad's bobs, Tom Foxe. You villain!" Leighton stood before Tamsin, taking his last opportunity to strike out.

Mrs. Fairchild again interfered. "Come, Leighton. Those Foxe kits aren't worth bruising your fine hands."

Yet Tamsin saw, once more, the flash of his signet ring and his fist striking. She raised her wizened right hand to block it, receiving a painful, bruising blow. She seized that bronze inkwell with her other hand and struck him with more strength than she knew she possessed. Ink splashed over both of them and then onto the carpet. Leighton sank to the ink-splattered floor.

Mrs. Fairchild screamed and rushed forward. "He's dead! You've killed him, Tom Foxe."

Heydon held her back from attacking Tamsin. The ink that flecked Mrs. Fairchild's clothes spread to his coat.

"He's only cold-cocked, Mrs. Fairchild. Tom saved me from doing it myself." Then Heydon spoke quietly to his secretary. "Please ask the Fairchild's coachman to come assist Mr. Leighton to his carriage."

When Duncombe's syndicate had been escorted out, Heydon called after them, "Adieu. God grant you safe travels."

Still standing at the door, Heydon said under his breath, "Every crow-mother thinks her fledglings sing sweetly. Even a worthless hatchling like Leighton Fairchild. Barbados will suit his hot temper."

On the other side of the room, Lizzie and Tamsin regarded each other, as if each waited for the other to speak.

Lizzie murmured, "I hope Barbados is as hot as Hades."

"'Reap justice, shun revenge.'" Tamsin said it to calm her own battered thoughts, not to upbraid Lizzie. Too much had happened since she entered this house, and her greatest feeling was awe at the turmoil Heydon had created with his plan.

"Where is there justice for Absolom and Marborne in any of this?" Lizzie, gripped by a passion, whispered furiously. "Absolom's bones lie cold. For years those people cheated and lied to him. Now Heydon takes his personal wrath on them."

"Lizzie, our gambol succeeded. And Perry retrieved the mortgage papers. We might have enough wealth now to pay the king a garnishment."

Heydon asked his servants to clean up the spilt ink, and then joined the two women by the window to watch the syndicate's departure. His face was stiff with grief—and his first words when he joined them?

"I wish my brother loved me more than that creature."

—

Tamsin turned away from the window where she'd judged paintings that morning, still sorting her feelings about Heydon's plan and what it meant for those people; what it meant for Lizzie, who was to marry Heydon.

Heydon came behind Lizzie and rested his hands on her shoulders. "Now, Miss Foxe, you shall soon be Lady Heydon. That should please Princess Mary. Will you share another glass of wine with me? Miss Thomasine, you must be famished. Let me command a plate for you."

Lizzie neither shrugged off nor sank into his light embrace. "How could you do this, Poynter?"

"I have very capable people working for me," Heydon said. "We made all our plans in the last week, not knowing exactly when I might be forced to take action. Each man had his own tasks to complete, and—"

"No, I am asking how you could take your brother's title from him." Lizzie stiffened and stepped away. "I cannot marry you, Lord Heydon."

Tamsin shivered, despite the humidity, glad at Lizzie's refusal. Heydon's farrago that day was too....dangerous for Lizzie to be involved.

"He merely chose not to use his title and to go abroad. I took nothing away from him." Heydon seemed perplexed; not hurt, simply puzzled. "But it doesn't matter for your future. I hold my title in my own right. For your sake, our arrangement suits the needs of Princess Mary."

"I cannot marry you, sir."

"Surely our business arrangement does not so quickly come to nothing."

"You betrayed your brother, Poynter."

"His wife betrayed him. I saved his life," Heydon said. "And hers. And I saved her conniving relations. Should I have let them go to the gallows?"

Lizzie said, "And now you shall control Hawksmoor."

"You witnessed what happened, Miss Foxe. Monck chose to stay with his deceiving wench. If he'd chosen the path that I preferred, he'd still preside as earl."

"And now you govern Candecote's estate. And Fairchild's, too, for whatever that might be worth." Lizzie crossed her arms over her heart, the sternest posture she ever assumed, confronting him.

"It seems," Heydon folded his arms into his favorite lecturing pose, "a fair payback for saving them. Which I did at my own great effort and cost. Anyway, most of Candecote's estate is not entailed, and he consigned it to his daughter."

"But you used us to sort *your* relatives."

"Used you? I only asked Miss Thomasine not to involve my brother in your scheme." He turned to Tamsin. "Did you not tell all your cousins what you and I agreed?"

"Yes, but—"

"See, Miss Foxe? I neither interfered with nor took advantage of your cousins' wild scheme to gaining retribution from your cheating neighbors. Tamsin and I agreed not to interfere with each other's schemes in pursuit of justice."

"Justice?" Lizzie seemed ready to erupt, white lines of anger deepening near her mouth. "You perpetrated a disgusting corruption, bribing an officer for the Crown's secrets. That man should be driven from the service."

"It was your cousin Rowland," Heydon said.

Lizzie, undone by that surprise, grabbed the back of a chair, as if for support. That in turn surprised Tamsin, who had carried Rowland's page to Cambridge with no thought that what Rowland sent constituted corruption. The other surprise: Lizzie had endured the afternoon's chaos without recognizing that Rowland had helped.

Tamsin said, "Poynter, you didn't mention last night that you knew Lord Orlando was Rowland."

"I didn't guess until this morning." Heydon turned back to Lizzie. "Miss Foxe, I don't think either Lieutenant Foxe or myself perpetrated anything so dramatic as 'corruption.' Nothing we did rises to the level of everyday corruption in the royal court."

"But it is," Lizzie insisted. "You suborned Rowland Foxe to get that list of names. He never accepts so much as a gratuity for simple court favors."

"That accounts for his poverty." Heydon remained affable, but he could not be unaware of how furious Lizzie was. "We simply agreed on an exchange that allowed me to protect my brother. It was a gentlemanly kindness on his part."

"He didn't do it for whatever you paid him." Lizzie tapped a finger on Heydon's chest, an impertinence one could never imagine her taking. "He did it for...for...for Marborne."

"Isn't that also why you chose to marry me? A business arrangement for the sake of Marborne? I sought only to ensure you attained what you most desire."

Lizzie glanced out the window again, where the last carriage rolled onto the Cambridge cobbles. "I cannot marry you, sir."

"As you have declared. I shall never attempt to coerce a woman into what she does not want to do." Heydon moved to action. Whatever he might be suffering from Lizzie's refusal, it wasn't heartbreak. "I'll call for my carriage to take you home."

—

Tamsin respected Lizzie's silence until the carriage passed the last cottages at the edge of Cambridge. Then she asked, "Lizzie, why were you surprised where Heydon got that list? Rollo made me run to Cambridge to deliver it."

"You knew? You helped? Upon my soul!"

"I didn't know what I carried," Tamsin said.

"Aren't you furious with Heydon for stealing the earl's title?"

"You need not be so dramatic with me. The title will merely lay unused until Hawksmoor goes to heaven. We witnessed the earl making his choice, Lizzie. Those people would all be arrested without Heydon's interference."

"Don't you see?" Lizzie still wrenched her hands. "Rollo did it for me. He suborned himself, because I insisted there was no way to save Marborne without Heydon's aid. And I made Rollo promise to help me."

"Rollo must have been devastated." Tamsin had seen his bright, hopeful glances in the past days, and then the black-as-night expression when he left for London.

"But he knows I need a noble marriage before Mary will invite me back into service."

"Did you not see Rollo's dark looks while we ran the gambol this afternoon?"

"Yes, but that's because he knew the only way to save Marborne was for me to marry Heydon. He wanted to be the hero, but we don't have time to gamble, waiting for whatever he might invent."

"Who are you angry with, Lizzie? Heydon or Rollo? Both? Each tried to save what mattered most to them."

Lizzie's words were nearly lost when the carriage rocked on the rutted lane. "I'm angry because it was a surprise. Even you kept Heydon's plans from me."

Tamsin said, "No, it was a surprise to me too. I shall repeat, I didn't know what Rollo had me carry to Heydon. But amid those people's shock and anger, I enjoyed their unpleasant afternoon."

"Still, Heydon used us."

"Heydon's farrago doesn't have anything to do with us. Heydon's plans didn't interfere with our gambol. Which, I repeat, succeeded. I saw the carriages leave for Revelstone."

"Have we earned enough to pay the mortgage?"

"Lizzie, did you not hear me? Mr. Frake retrieved the mortgages from Mr. Duncombe yesterday. They were forged—and now we are free."

Lizzie sat utterly still. "Give me five more breaths to set aside my excess passion. Five breaths, and I promise to be myself."

"Truly, I've never seen you so impassioned."

"I learned better than to let my passions run free rein years ago. What has infected me?"

Rollo. Tamsin could think of no other source. By simply appearing at the averil, he'd made Tamsin nearly catch fire and burn. Though his effect on Lizzie on this day seemed different.

Lizzie said, "We have to go to London and free Rollo. And Perry and Ned, of course. You said the militia arrested them."

"It's a story I made up, Lizzie. I don't know what happened, but simply guessed that Rollo and Captain Starbuck made a plan to arrest Duncombe. And, yes, we must go to London. To sell those paintings as quickly as possible."

"Will we earn enough to pay the king's garnishment for restoring Marborne?"

"We shall continue to hope." Tamsin kept figuring the numbers, but couldn't be sure until they sold the paintings.

"You know what I think, now that you've helped me restore reason? I wager that Rollo sold that list to earn the king's garnishment. It's like our last restoration, when we sought to relieve Hawksmoor of money to pay the mortgage."

"If that's true, then it's Lord Heydon who will be paying the king's garnishment."

A sunbeam flashed through the carriage window. As if in answer, a star shone for a moment in Lizzie's hand.

"What are you holding, Lizzie?"

"This?" She held it up, inspected it. "It's the diamond pin Heydon wears on his cravat."

"Lizzie! You stole it?"

"He vexed me exceedingly, dragging me through this day's tears and tragedy."

"You can't steal his pin."

"But I did. I wanted him to endure as much anxious fear as he caused me today. I imagine by now that he's sent his men after the syndicate, to see if the people he saved from the hangman stole his pin."

"Lizzie, you can't—"

"I'll give it back. But I want to enjoy a day of imagining Lord Heydon in as much turmoil as he forced on me."

51

When the Hurly-burly's Done

— NED —

SEVENTEEN HOURS IN the saddle would have been an even greater punishment if Perry hadn't pulled Ned aside at the first stop to refresh the horses.

"Must I start over again, to once more earn your trust?" Perry searched Ned's face in the twilight. "Did our secrets break your heart, sweeting?"

"N–No. Though I remain bewildered." Ned, however, had been guessing about the unplanned events, and had to quell with each breath his resentment that he'd been excluded from secrets between Perry and Rowland.

"It distresses me that you've fretted since Starbuck arrived." Perry leaned closer and dropped his voice further. "But Rollo and I had to preserve secrets, to make it all happen."

"I suppose." Ned's voice tightened with the effort to repress how much he resented that secrecy.

"Nay, I am beyond distress." Perry cried out, then dropped his voice to a whisper again. "I am frantic, my dear man, hoping you perceive that I cannot share all the secrets of my work."

"You trusted me to come along." Ned had begun to understand. Perry waited for Ned's answer in what seemed to be great agitation. "Though Rollo sent Tamsin away."

"Aye, you do see? Will you give me a day, a week, a year to mend what I trampled in order to capture the traitor Duncombe? I shall beg on my knees if you require it of me."

At each stop where they changed horses at other militia posts, Ned grew less stiff and less resentful when Perry put his hand on Ned's shoulder and whispered more of what he and Rowland had done in secret. At midmorning when they arrived in London, Perry said, "Now you know it all."

In London, Starbuck left Perry, Rowland, and Ned outside a lodging house and claimed back the militia's horses.

"I trust the Crown can find you here if there are questions, Lord Orlando?" Starbuck asked, but did not wait for an answer, departing with his men to carry their prisoner to the Tower.

As soon as the militia was gone from sight, Perry said, "Duncombe's office is just around the corner. But I will leave that business to you. I shall trot over to meet our colonel, so he first hears this story from me. Here are Duncombe's office keys."

"Give them to our colonel," Rowland said. "Ned and I will only redeem the cheques we won in a fair jig."

"You don't want to inspect Duncombe's strong boxes before the king's men seize his property?"

"We've already redeemed what's due the Foxe family," Rowland said. "The king can take the rest."

That was as many words as Ned had heard Rowland speak since the militia arrived. His cousin had been unusually taciturn on the road, not even offering a yes or no to questions. As dark as Rowland's mood was, Ned felt his own lighten while they turned the corner and entered Mr. Danvers Duncombe's offices. In his pocket, Ned carried the cheques for agent's fees from the art-selling syndicate. He exchanged polite greetings with the clerks, made his request, and traded complaints about the wretched August weather during the seemingly endless wait, all without betraying his nervousness.

After redeeming the cheques, Ned and Rowland stopped at the corner when the crowd parted to allow a half dozen redcoats to pass. Everyone paused to watch the soldiers dismount and leave their horses with one man. A sergeant then pounded on the doors of Mr. Duncombe's business establishment.

Rowland spoke again. "God blind me, they got here quickly."

"Perry isn't with them." Ned swallowed disappointment.

"That, I hope is a good sign." Rowland clapped Ned's shoulder. "No more dallying. Let's make our funds safe. Somewhere that won't be raided by the king's men before day's end."

Ned agreed. Tension jangled in his fingers and toes, while they carried more gold through the rough streets of London than he'd ever imagined might be in his possession. Rowland pointed Ned down a lane that led to Sir Charles Duncombe's offices, one of the few locations Rowland claimed to know in London. Ned signed receipts for the funds they deposited with a business agent in Sir Charles's offices.

Relief cascaded off Ned like rainwater.

He no longer had to spend days in the workshop, furiously creating works to sell. Or spend Saturdays with Tamsin, anxiously reviewing accounts to see where they might scrimp even more in their bare-bones household. No more risky restorations. And he didn't have to worry about Lizzie and the unhappy haze she lived in, for she'd soon be returning to Mary's court. He'd paint whatever he wanted. In fact, he'd ask his agent that day how to obtain commissions for portraits. He'd—

A stray sunbeam caught him, occluded by clouds in the next moment, yet it evoked a memory that struck him so hard, Ned halted on the street. ("I shall return to you, Ned Wijck.")

He hurried to rejoin Rowland, who trudged up the street with little notice of anything around him.

Ned could not just repeat his long-time wishes for how it would be different if the family weren't fighting deprivation and tragedy. Two nights before, everything had changed, and he therefore already lived in a new world where he could wish for more than new paintbrushes and coin for canvas. The most gorgeous man he'd ever known promised to return to him. Nothing would again interrupt his joy or threaten his life.

But then, out of nowhere, a jolt of fear hit Ned again. He felt in his pocket for the receipts he'd just signed.

"My name! It's on the ledgers at Duncombe's office. Those red-coats will see—"

"No." Rowland had his hand on Ned's shoulder. He dangled the sheet from the ledger that Ned had signed. "I haven't worked with Perry this long without learning at least one thing from him. Now, I need food."

"It's two nights without sleep for me," Ned said. "I'd like a kip and a bath."

They came to Mr. Benson's lodging house in Covent Garden, more respectable than any inns they'd passed. Rowland arranged sleeping rooms, hired a private salon, and ordered breakfast and coffee—all of it exotic compared to how Ned and his cousins stayed at the cheapest inns, carried their own food, and knew nothing about service or privacy.

They'd just settled in the salon with their coffee, awaiting food from the kitchen, when Perry arrived, sans Starbuck.

"I salute your genius, Rollo." Perry sat by Ned, his thigh pressing against Ned's. That touch offered more comfort and a nicer thrill than anything that had happened since their journey began. "You found a better doss-house than when we were last in London. Can we afford to stay until business is done?"

"How long will that take?"

Perry shrugged. "Kings and their minions take as long over business as they choose."

"And Duncombe?"

"Lodged with a host of others in the Tower. The whole collection is to be tried by a panel of judges who'll convene a traveling court across England."

Rowland frowned, darkness encompassing his entire face. "The butchery in Bristol and London wasn't a sufficient lesson for His Majesty's enemies? Why can't he load all the traitors onto ships with their families and send them to the colonies?"

Perry didn't answer that complaint. "If I am to believe our new colonel's promises, there shall be officer's colors for you, Rollo, and a significant new assignment for both of us."

"Merely for what you stole from Duncombe's pockets?"

"Our former master has communicated details about our last few years of service. And our friend Starbuck proclaimed you to be a brilliant mind, a master intelligencer."

Rowland denied that. "Valentine just wants to see that we receive a decent gratuity for Duncombe's arrest. He intends that I pay my gambling debts."

"Our own colonel joined with Starbuck's colonel to arrange an appointment at Whitehall. At three o'clock this afternoon. He wants enough time for his men to seize Duncombe's business and home, and then he intends to present our findings to the king. With us present." Perry said it coolly enough, yet he shuffled his feet. Ned felt a thrum of excitement in his friend.

Rowland pulled at an ear, and twitched and wiggled in his chair, not as pleased or excited as Perry. "You may have all the pleasure of that meeting." He rumbled in an inside pocket of his coat, then handed Perry two gold coins that he'd saved back from their deposit. "Give Starbuck these, with my promise that I shall see him later. I'm not prepared to dress for court."

Perry took the two coins from Rollo and didn't beg for a better excuse. Rowland began to roll another gold coin silently over his knuckles.

It wasn't true about Rowland's clothes, though his copper-satin court suit suffered greatly from the ride to London. Ned couldn't understand Rowland's indifference about meeting the king. Yet, Ned's stomach churned at the idea of such a meeting, given that they'd just cheated their duplicitous neighbors, conducted highway robbery, and then enlisted the king's men to bring Absolom's nemesis to the Tower.

ROWLAND DID THE best he could, brushing his court suit and performing sufficient ablutions to restore the appearance of an enlightened gentleman. He rejoined the other two men.

They ate in the private salon, then ordered more coffee, taking a few peaceful moments before Perry went to Whitehall. Rowland wanted to read. Ned intended to sketch.

"I'll watch," Perry said.

"You can't watch because I intend to sketch you."

"May I say how I am comforted, my dearest sir, by your interest in me as a subject for your art?"

Rowland unwrapped one of the Shakespeare volumes that he'd carried in his satchel, the one with a wrapper inscribed from his father to Absolom. He carefully untied the ribbon and folded that wrapper, with the child-like notion of saving it because his father had written on it.

He traced letters on the first page of the volume before sharing it with the others. "Look at this."

Ned read that page.

The Tragicall Historie of Hamlet, Prince of Denmark
By William Shakespeare
As it hath been diverse times acted by his Highness servants
in the Cittie of London, and also in the two Universities
of Cambridge and Oxford and elsewhere.

"Look at the date." Rowland felt as if he were coming alive for the first time that day. "It was printed in 1604. This book is so old, Shakespeare himself could have touched it."

"But Absolom had it from your father," Ned said. "Your grandfather was a baby in 1604. Shakespeare could not have given your father this book."

"I'm not saying my father had it from Shakespeare. No matter how my father acquired it, he once held it in his hands. And it *might* have passed through the Bard's hands."

Rowland turned the yellowing pages with avid interest.

"I shall paint you," Ned said, "as an actor studying his lines. I know just the colors I'll mix to get that shiny copper."

When Rowland turned another page, a packet fell to the floor. Perry bent to retrieve it.

Ned complained. "Mr. Frake, you cannot move about while I sketch you."

"Oh, I believe in my heart that you, Mr. Wijck, have sufficient talent to do your work while I—God's teeth, Rollo! Look at this."

Rowland stared at the packet so long that Ned came and read over his shoulder.

"Relieve my troubled mind," Perry said. "Read the words." Ned complied.

Unto His Majesty, the King of England
The heirs of Marborne send greetings.

"Zooterkins!" Ned seemed to catch Rowland's excitement. "This is as old as we are. Is that your father's writing? Open it!"

"N–No." Rowland stammered, unable to name the feelings flooding over him. "It's addressed to the king. And the wax is stamped with the Marborne seal."

Just then, Tom, Lizzie, and Tamsin came in, offering noisy helloes and clearly exhausted from a long ride in Mr. Warboys' carriage. In the hubbub that arose, Rowland tucked the book and the packet back into his satchel.

"Hello, Rollo. Ned. Mr. Frake." Lizzie greeted them.

His mind and heart were still aroused by that ancient letter, but Lizzie's voice and her presence awoke new curiosity. (Lizzie in London, without her new inamorato? Please, be kind to me.)

"Tamsin in a dress! It's a new world," Ned declared. "It's Lizzie's grey silk. Perhaps I should paint you in it."

"It fits," Tamsin said, "because the sleeves are not attached."

Rowland said, "I'm surprised you are here." He meant it for Lizzie, but Tom answered.

"Mr. Warboys learned to drive from the devil himself. We made it in twenty hours, which is Mr. Warboys' best time."

Tamsin said, "And we paid good silver for four extra changes of the team. The horses weren't hurt by our speed."

Perry leaped up. "I shall get rooms for all of you. And order food. Ale?"

"Claret." Tom coughed the word. Despite long hours on the London Road, he exuded a great deal of bright energy. "The dust in my throat requires a curative cleansing."

Rowland looked for what Lizzie was feeling—and what she was doing in London. "So, you did it, Lizzie?"

"Yes, but—"

"Look!" Tom pointed behind Rowland to the salon door. "Here come more of us."

Winwood entered with Camilla, who offered a bright smile, no longer the ghostly waif who disrupted the averil. "Good afternoon, Rollo. I salute you as king of this gambol."

"Hello." Rowland took her hand, bowing over it. "You look well. I understand Dr. Oakes is a marvel with bullet wounds."

"Blessed Jove!" Tom cried. "at last Winwood has another case to practice his experiments. I'm relieved. That duty weighed upon me heavily."

Perry returned from his search for the innkeeper. "The ladies shall all be together. I'm with Ned. Tom, you and Winwood will have to kip with Rollo."

"Can Camilla be served in her room?" Winwood asked. "We've been tumbled about as if in a butter churn and then poured out on the streets of London. She needs a rest."

Camilla waved a hand to discount that idea, yet she trembled when she let go of Winwood's arm.

Lizzie stood apart, silent, and Rowland could not read a clue on her face about her thoughts or feelings. Though she seemed as exhausted as the others.

"I was surprised," Tamsin said, "by the addition of the king's men to our plan."

"Did ye not heed," Perry said, "that Rollo and I had Crown business to attend to?"

"Tamsin, you couldn't be as surprised as I was," Ned said. "When Captain Starbuck arrived, I was sure they'd brought a tumbrel to carry us all to the gallows."

"Why did you do it, Rollo?" Lizzie asked, her voice barely carrying through the noise of their crowd.

Rowland twitched. Guilt and regret pounded in his blood, knowing what she asked, yet he chose to pretend she was asking about Starbuck's involvement in the gambol. "Captain Starbuck didn't want to lose sight of me before I paid the two gold louis I owed him."

"Is that true?" Lizzie said.

No one answered until Perry, back from his brief errand, said, "I aver, Lieutenant Foxe often requires the blessings of Fate in order to pay his gambling debts."

52

A Farrago of Fallacies

— TAMSIN —

SHE WANTED NOTHING more at that moment than to escape, after spending twenty hours trapped in a carriage with too many nervous cousins and friends. Tamsin pressed the Archangel lodged above her breast bone, as if to pray for just twenty minutes alone. But that served only to awaken her own better angel. She needed to ensure everyone else was cared for.

Tom remained ebullient, seeming to have convinced Winwood that his long-time invalid was strong enough to carouse in the parlor while the doctor whisked Camilla away to rest.

Ned, too, seemed quite happy, his movements expansive when he spoke. Perry had his hand on Ned's shoulder, smiling broadly, which he didn't usually do unless he'd launched a tease.

Lizzie kept folding and unfolding her arms, immune to her brother's and cousin's rowdy joy, watching Rowland. Tamsin felt sure that Lizzie couldn't get the reassurance she wanted from Rowland in this crowded parlor.

"The paintings?" Rowland didn't look Lizzie's way a second time, his attention all on Tamsin. He'd lost the black demeanor of the previous day, but now seemed grey, his usual fiery spirits dampened into ash.

"The paintings are all in Mr. Warboys' carriage," Tamsin said. "He's ready to take you to visit your agent, Ned. Then he'll put up in his cousin's livery a few streets over."

"You distress me, Miss Foxe." Perry gripped the sides of his head. He did indeed seem distraught. "You carried a fortune in art down the London Road? Without guards?"

Tamsin said, "We couldn't leave those chests in the Revelstone barn. And Mr. Warboys recruited two hardy grandsons with their blunderbusses."

"And we all had pistols," Tom declared. "Except Camilla, who shouldn't be trusted with a penknife. And Winwood, who caught a pacifying disease from the Quakers and Seekers, though we shouldn't persecute him for being a radical."

"That's an enormous exaggeration," Tamsin said. "Winwood simply dislikes the violence that war afflicts on people."

"Then you agree that he's a radical." Tom turned to Ned. "Is it true? We are rich now?"

"Not rich as a French king," Ned said. "Or even a Dutch trader. But no longer impoverished. We'll know how rich after we sell the paintings."

A servant brought in a tray of cold meats, cheese, jellies, fresh bread. Lizzie took up the jug of wine to pour for everyone. As soon as the servant was gone, she said, "I'm relieved to see you all. You can answer the questions we've debated over the long ride from Cambridge."

"We likely have many answers," Perry said, "but I must depart soon to meet our new colonel at Whitehall. Our answers must thus be brief."

Tamsin said, "First, when we learned about Duncombe's arrest, I worried that they'd also arrested you three."

Rowland seemed surprised. "You left before the militia arrived, Tamsin. How did you know?"

"I guessed it," she said. "When I gave Heydon your message, he asked if Captain Starbuck was taking the traitor to London. He seemed to expect the news."

"I was excessively surprised when the militia appeared," Ned said, "until Perry had a private moment to explain."

Perry said, "Our work for the Crown uncovered proof that Mr. Duncombe had helped fund Monmouth's rebels. We could not, as gentlemen, engage any of you, who are merely innocent swindlers and robbers, in that rough business."

"Further, we needed Duncombe to continue to believe I'm Viscount Orlando," Rowland said. "When he's interviewed by the king's intelligencers, he'll have no notion that the Foxe family had anything to do with the day's events."

"We needed to meet our own colonel in London," Perry said, "so we had arranged earlier with Captain Starbuck to travel with his militia."

"You sent me to Heydon but kept Ned." Tamsin had her own adventure the previous afternoon, and got to travel with Camilla, so she resisted any jealousy over Ned's great adventure.

Perry shrugged. "I thought Ned might prove useful."

Ned sipped wine, seeming embarrassed to have attention drawn to him, and pleased at the same time. "It took me some time to understand why Mr. Warboys was laughing while I was sure we were all on the way to the gallows."

Perry said, "I persuaded Mr. Warboys and the Revelstone boys that I wanted to play a jest on Viscount Orlando."

"You can imagine my surprise—and Ned's—when we were attacked by those boys," Tamsin said.

Perry said, "Aye, mademoiselle. But you recovered very well and did an admirable job of playing highwayman."

"She had a couple of years of practice," Tom said. "Could any man take greater pride in his sister than I do with mine?"

"But you put the boys from the village at risk," Lizzie said. "And Tom and Winwood." She still hugged herself, standing away from her happy cousins, regarding Rowland, seeming stuffed with questions, even as the story unfolded.

"Perry's jest is all that Mr. Warboys saw," Rowland ignored Tom. "We had previously engaged Starbuck's assistance with arresting Duncombe."

"Starbuck also believed the boys' attack was a jest," Perry said, "a diversion to hold the carriage until the militia arrived where we had promised a rendezvous. The boys were always safe from the militia."

Tamsin had more to ask. "I overcame my surprise and surmised that you had other business. But did you know—especially you, Rollo—how much your Crown business would affect our neighbors?"

"They were equally upset," Lizzie said, "over the loss of their paintings and the arrest of their brother Duncombe."

"I wish I'd been there to see it." Tom spoke like a wistful romantic. "Wait until you hear Tamsin describe their faces and how they quarreled with each other. And with Heydon."

"Why did they quarrel with Lord Heydon?" Perry asked.

"Because," Lizzie said, "Heydon exiled his brother to Barbados, with his wife and all her sisters and their husbands."

"They all went to Barbados?" Ned beamed, happy with this news. "Then no one will raise a hue and cry for those paintings? That is good news."

"What." Neither asking a question nor expressing surprise, Rowland sat at the table, hands down on the covering linen cloth. "Why." He then slipped into what must have been another line from Shakespeare. "And, 'Wherefore; for they say, every why hath a wherefore.'"

Lizzie said, "It seems the intelligencer that Heydon paid to uncover the truth about Duncombe and his sisters also warned his lordship that Duncombe was about to be arrested. Heydon made a rather elaborate plan to deal with that."

Tamsin said, "Heydon worked to save his brother and Lady Hawksmoor's relatives from being arrested."

"Isn't it a cracking coincidence," Tom grinned, "that Heydon had to launch his plan the same day as our gambol? What grand shockers Absolom's nemesis had yesterday."

Lizzie said, "I was shocked too, thinking Heydon's plan might be nefarious, until Tamsin assured me that Heydon didn't take advantage of our own gambol."

Perry rose, preparing to leave. "Whoever wants to accompany me to Whitehall had best be ready. We must depart now."

Tamsin stepped forward, eager for the opportunity. Everyone seemed to be in fine spirits, except Lizzie and Rowland, and she'd given up any idea of helping them out of the blues. "Is Tom well enough to come? If he can gain an audience with the king, we shall finally succeed by paying whatever garnishment he asks."

"Lizzie and I intend to go," Tom said. "We have a plan to use our share of earnings from our gambol as the garnishment we offer the king."

"You can also have mine," Rowland said. "And whatever gratuity my colonel offers for my recent service to the Crown."

"Alas." Perry had his eyes on Ned. "You cannot bribe the king with my share of the gratuity. I need new boots and a coat come winter."

"Won't you join us, Rollo?" Lizzie tapped the back of his hand with a finger.

— ROLLO —

"YOU WILL ALL surely enjoy court." Rowland removed his hand from Lizzie's reach as he spoke. He could not express how much he did not want to meet the king who decided Benjie Baird's head should be on a pike and his family destroyed in Bristol. "Ned and I have paintings to sell. We need funds to pay for all your very midsummer dreams."

At the door, Rowland pulled Tom aside to give him that packet from the Shakespeare book. "This fell out of a book Absolom had from my father."

Tom glanced down at the address. He whistled.

"Take it with you, Tom. Perhaps you will find a chance to pass it on to the king."

"What does it say?"

"I have no idea. It's sealed."

"What if," Tom frowned, "it says to slay the bearer upon presentation? Like in one of your Shakespeare stories."

"You are not Hamlet." Rowland slapped Tom's shoulder. "Call for chairs to bear Tamsin and Lizzie to Whitehall. After all we've done this week, our cousins should not traipse through the streets of London."

Tom started off, but Rowland called one more bit of advice after him. "Do not forget that the first words you say to royalty must be a compliment."

With the others gone, Rowland led Ned to the street.

"Let's finish our business with the man who sells your art. Lizzie and Tamsin seem sure that your neighbors' attention has been diverted, but we don't know whether any of them might send an alarm to London that Mr. Warboys' coach was robbed."

— TAMSIN —

FROM PREVIOUS ATTEMPTS to gain a royal audience, Tamsin expected to be made to wait by the king's lords who served as gatekeepers. She'd endured the tedium of general audiences where the king undertook minor requests and presentations. Therefore, the pulsing heat of the court in summer, with flies buzzing and ladies wilting, did not disturb the peace that now nested in her belly and heart. She touched the Archangel pouch lodged under the beaded bodice of her dress. Her mother's wishes had come to fruition.

She and Lizzie were, of course, confined to the back ranks with other women, able to observe but not participate when Tom and Perry were presented to the king. Perry's spymaster had given him a red coat that almost fit, then called him sergeant and introduced him as such to the king. Perry answered questions so softly that Tamsin strained to hear.

Perry solemnly nodded while the king spoke. The spymaster beamed. "You are generous, your majesty."

"Your new men who came home from Holland," the king said, "have proved to be more adept than any you've recruited."

Despite that criticism, the red-coated officer kept his smile in place. Then a lord stepped forward and whispered to the king, the same lord who had, month after month, prevented the Foxe cousins from being granted a royal audience.

The king answered in a strong voice. "What does that have to do with rewarding these intelligencers?"

That lord's words were lost in the shuffling of courtiers, but the king's next question carried through the room. "He comes from a titled family?"

The gatekeeping lord beckoned Tom forward. Tom gave him a letter, which the lord then gave to the king, speaking about the letter while the king read it. Visibly annoyed, the king waved away the interruption.

"What is it?" Lizzie whispered.

"I don't know," Tamsin said. "Rowland must have more secrets he didn't share." She wondered how Absolom had known so certainly that Rowland would be their savior.

The king's voice carried through the hall. "You are Thomas Caius Foxe?"

Tom bowed again, looking very much like a lord in his black velvet suit. Lizzie had covered his splotched complexion with a tinted cream and tied his cravat, and he'd borrowed Rowland's elaborate court wig.

The king said, "These letters were addressed to my brother."

"You are kindness incarnate, your majesty, to give attention to our affairs." Tom didn't seem at all nervous. Perhaps Tamsin had enough anxious fear and hope for both of them. "These letters have been lost and only found yesterday. To my family's great misfortune."

The king tapped his nose, as if in thought. "If my brother had received them, he'd have set things right. Now I must do so." He pointed to that interfering lord. "We shall restore the title of the Earl of Marborne to the Foxe family with all the rights and perquisites due."

The king's voice dipped as he conferred with the advisors around him.

"Upon my soul!" Lizzie whispered. "How?"

Tamsin made too many guesses about how it happened but was unable to speak through her shock. She clutched Lizzie's hand.

The king's voice rose again. "And now, the angels must rejoice instead of weeping."

Tom bowed again and beamed, while that officious gatekeeping lord and the king discussed a date for consulting the Committee for Privileges and Conduct. While backing away from that audience with the king, Tom caught sight of Tamsin at the back of the crowd and winked.

If only Absolom were here for this moment!

When they met again outside Whitehall, Tamsin embraced him. Tom crowed, "We were not called upon to spend one farthing to reclaim the title."

"What did you give the king?" Lizzie asked.

"A letter Rowland found in one of his Shakespeare books," Tom said. "It seems the letter should have gone to the Crown twenty-five years ago. Among other notes, it included a letter from James, as Duke of York, claiming that the Foxe family served the Crown throughout the war between Parliament and Charles, and hence we should have our title restored."

"Why did Rowland give it to you?" Lizzie frowned. "*When* did he give it to you?"

"Just before we departed for Whitehall, just before he chided me about ordering chairs for the ladies."

"Lizzie, don't you want to celebrate?" Tamsin asked, bewildered by Lizzie's stern expression at such an exquisite moment.

"How did Poynter know who Orlando was?"

"Ask him." Tom pointed to where Heydon chatted in the courtyard with one of the court's minions. Heydon was handing over that leather wallet of papers signed and witnessed the previous afternoon.

Tom went over to shake Heydon's hand. "Hello, Poynter. Thank you for all your encouragement for so long. The king has just this moment restored Marborne to us."

Heydon clapped Tom's shoulder. "Congratulations, Tom. What did you have to offer him?"

"Just a letter from my uncle that had gone astray. Gad, but I wish deep in my soul," Tom turned sober suddenly, "that Uncle Absolom had lived to see this."

Heydon glanced past Tom. He bowed. "Good afternoon, Miss Foxe. Miss Thomasine. I hope I find you in good health. And good spirits. Though from your excessive good looks, both of you, I shouldn't have to ask."

"Indeed," Tamsin said, "we are this moment in the best of spirits. Thank you."

Lizzie, who'd departed from her usual blue haze, now blazed white hot. "Good afternoon, Lord Heydon. I trust your business fares well."

"You are kind to say so." He spoke the words, but clearly Lizzie meant no kindness. "Miss Thomasine, can you please bear this to Mrs. Camilla Fairchild? It's the writ Mr. Leighton Fairchild signed, and also the writ from Isaiah Candecote, devolving all his possessions to his daughter."

"Thank you, Lord Heydon." Tamsin didn't call him Poynter here in the courtyard. And because she was no longer Tom.

"You all came away from my house too quickly for me to give these writs over to you yesterday. Your friend needs a barrister to help her carry these through the Church courts and through Parliament."

"Thank you, sir."

"And this is your uncle's will, which I found in Fairchild's papers last night. It still needs to be proved before a magistrate. If you'll allow it, Miss Thomasine, I shall ask my secretary to send you recommendations of barristers and solicitors who can be trusted with such chores."

"Yes, your lordship. Please."

Heydon had done the most to gain the freedom that Tamsin had promised Camilla. That knowledge removed any lingering doubts about his good intentions, and she seized Heydon's hand in gratitude.

That was also the exact moment when hot joy flooded her veins. Tamsin had forgotten what it was to be happy until new joy infused her entire being with delight.

Lizzie at last came forward to shake Heydon's hand, one gloved hand holding his, the other clutching the deep fold of his sleeve. "I do wish you well, Lord Heydon. Thank you for lending us your carriage yesterday."

He murmured niceties in farewell and then crossed the courtyard, his hand up to greet Captain Starbuck, who was shaking Perry's hand.

Tamsin was looking only at Lizzie, who came to her side. "I gave the pin back. Don't judge me, Tamsin."

Perry walked around the edge the courtyard, coming to meet the Foxe cousins. "Congratulations to the honorable Foxe family of Marborne." He clapped Tom on the back.

"Is Starbuck joining us tonight?" Tom asked. "I think we should have champagne."

"He's promised to Lord Heydon for the evening," Perry said. "Miss Foxe, Miss Thomasine, shall I call for chairs to carry you to our lodgings?"

"Lizzie might like it. But I shall walk. In fact, you shall have your hands full, Mr. Frake, to prevent me from flying."

They all struck off for the lodging house, Lizzie's hand on Tom's arm, Tamsin's tucked in Perry's elbow.

Lizzie said, "What do you know, Mr. Frake, about this day's doings at the king's court?"

"Less than nothing, Miss Foxe. Or I should say, as much as I heard in the court at Whitehall."

"Truly?" Lizzie sniffed. "Because I continue to worry that Rowland might have sold his soul for thirty pieces of silver."

"Do you now, Miss Foxe?" Perry answered mildly. "It distresses me to hear that. He'd do so only if he believed that those thirty pieces of silver would buy your heart's delight."

"We shall ask him," Tamsin said. "We can trust that he'll tell us the truth."

53

A Man for the Moment

DOING HIS BEST to hide his unease, Rowland bargained with the art dealer's adept. Ned had deserted him, huddling in a conversation with the dealer about other business.

"I am loath to part with even one of these." Rowland had introduced himself as Orlando, Viscount de Flores. "But necessity breaks my heart. I am in need of ready money."

"Gambling debts, Lord Orlando?" Mistress Hildegonda tapped her chin thoughtfully, proving to be extraordinarily judgmental and intrusively curious, and seeming determined to examine his soul as closely as she had examined the paintings.

Taller than Rowland and half again as wide, she asked Rowland to call her by her Christian name, because she didn't like her husband Simon Touchstone's surname.

"I shall not be addressed with a clown's name from your great poet."

For all her Dutch curses murmured while examining the paintings, she had a refined English accent learned in London. While complimenting each painting Rowland presented, she probed the life story of Lord Orlando, which meant Rowland had to repeat every falsehood he'd told in the last week.

"My father is a diplomat and has lived in many large cities on the Continent. He has long considered art an investment, but we have agreed that now is the time, when we must move to a new country, to take advantage of his life-long investment."

Throughout all of that, Ned huddled with his dealer to discuss how he might find commissions for portraits. At last, Mistress Hildegonda's inquisition and judgments ended, and Mr. Touchstone gave Rowland a cheque, an advance on what he'd pay after each of the paintings were sold.

"Is your agent entirely honest?" Rowland asked Ned as they departed the art dealer's warehouse. "His wife never questioned a single provenance I presented."

"How would I know?" Ned said "I sell him forgeries that he never disputes. But today, we had the excellent records that our neighbors brought to our gambol." Ned had lost all the tension he'd carried, beginning when they began to unload paintings from the carriage into his agent's warehouse.

"Look at the size of the cheque he gave us." Rowland felt gratified that his gambol would eventually return much more than the amount Absolom had been defrauded over those mortgages. "You don't mind that I asked him to pay Lord Orlando? I'm intending that none of this ever comes back around to create a predicament for you, Ned."

"Aye. It's a good idea. Have we now passed every reasonable chance for our gambol to be fouled?"

"We're safe," Rowland said. "Your dealer promised to forward future funds to Sir Charles's office. That's the last the world shall see of Lord Orlando in the flesh. Let's redeem this cheque now. Then we will have passed every threshold of danger. And be free, the way we hoped that gambol might free us."

Rowland and Ned made their way to Sir Charles's offices for a second visit, intending to deposit most of the agent's advance. Ned, it seemed, couldn't stop smiling, growing gleeful now that all danger had passed.

"Wait!" Ned halted in front of a haberdasher's shop, tugging Rowland to stop, too. "I cannot continue in this orange suit any longer. It smells of horse, and so does your court suit, Rollo. This shop must have ready-made for us."

It took Ned a long time to find a suit, being taller and thinner than most men. And he was a good deal fussier than Rowland expected him to be. Rowland's new ready-made was not as grand as what Lizzie had lent him. He was satisfied to wear his own boots out of the shop. Ned took more time with the bootmaker, making a series of decisions about new boots for himself.

When they set out for Sir Charles's offices, a sudden dousing rain sent them under eaves in an alley just off the main fare. Rowland turned up his collar, his new suit instantly damp and losing its shape.

"Let's just run for it," Ned said. "Better than—"

"Ho, hardies!" Sharp, cold metal pricked at Rowland's neck, sending a shiver down his whole frame.

"Ye shall stand!" A second man had a knife at Ned's throat.

In an endless moment, rain gushed down Rowland's face and neck, bounced up from the cobbles and drenched his boots. A stinking footpad threatened to leave him bleeding in a squalid gutter. Rowland prepared to step back, his elbow ready to jam his attacker.

But a rough hand grabbed his elbow and pulled. Pain ran up and down Rowland's arm. The blade jabbed at his neck.

"You lovely gentleman shall empty your pockets now."

"No," Ned said.

"Ned, no." Rowland pitched his voice with all the authority of a captain of men. "Let my friend go. He's empty-pocketed. You only want me. Best to—"

The growl at Rowland's ear. "Best to turn out your pockets and live another day. Both of you."

Another voice, brighter, harsher, rang in the alley.

"Stand down."

Yet one more voice called, loud, intending a threat. "Let these gentlemen go. If you want to live."

The fellow behind Rowland twisted his arm harder and barked, "This is not your patch!"

"Back away, you bird-witted blackguard." A youthful voice strained to sound dangerous. "Give it up."

"My dag and bodkin rule this alley." The man gave Rowland's arm a hard wrench, sending more pain with each challenge from the interlopers.

The youth who would be their hero called, "But I'm the better footpad. I've robbed lords of England and Spain. And my own dag is pointed at your head. It's a fat target."

Rowland was prepared to beg: *Don't leave us bleeding in this stinking alley.*

He had too much left to do. He had to secure Marborne and his cousins' future. And do what Absolom expected of him in this world. And profess his honor and love to Lizzie, at least one more time.

A deeper voice thundered. "Aye, Captain Queernobs. I advise you to grab your pratts and run. I cannot restrain these pistoleers from shooting your gingamobs."

Was it too much to hope that it was Perry who called out?

"Don't shoot!" Rowland called, believing Ned most likely to be hit. The rain, like a veil, made it impossible to see who sought to rescue them, hindering the interlopers from seeing who's attacked and who's the attacker.

"You destroy all joy, sir." It must be Perry! "I aver, We shall—"

A pistol fired.

The shot hit the nearby brick wall. Shards struck Rowland and his attacker. The knife pricking at his neck and the pistol shot both sent tremors of fear through him. Yet Rowland elbowed his captor, then twisted his arm free.

The attackers ran, lost in the rain-drenched alley's shadows.

"A hex on you bleeding hedge-birds!" Rollo shouted, though he wanted to scream.

"Zooterkins!" Ned croaked out the word. "I thought we were done for. I wasn't emptying my pockets for those nithing cheats."

"Should have done," Rowland said. "Should have—"

"Now, 'The wheel is come full circle. I am here.'" At the top of the alley, Tamsin still pointed a just-fired pistol. Beside her, Lizzie held her pistol with two hands. Neither woman flinched from the lashing rain. "That's Shakespeare, am I right?"

"We saved you," Lizzie said.

"And we've about drowned doing it." Tom stood behind his sister, and Perry stood behind Tamsin, both men with their hands folded under their arms. Amused.

Lizzie was not with Heydon. Rowland's heart might still burst, just from an overload of hope.

"Rollo, how dreadful!" Tom exclaimed. "A man like you cannot go about dressed as a shipping clerk. Why did those miscreants think to rob a fellow wearing such low clothes?"

—

Rowland repeatedly offered to call a chair for Tamsin and Lizzie, but they refused. While he endeavored to clear his head of the sound of the pistol-shot striking a wall too near him, the whole sodden crew walked two streets over to Sir Charles's offices and waited in the foyer while Ned and Rowland finished the day's second visit, safely storing the Foxe cousins' new wealth with a trustworthy banker.

The downpour ceased, leaving them all wet through, the women's gowns in particular having sponged up the rain.

He'd wanted to be a hero, to rescue his cousins. And Lizzie. Then he took one turn in the rain and almost lost everything. Rowland listened to his soggy boots making squelching sounds, as if that would help him forget the feeling of a cold blade against his neck. Rowland grew increasingly glum, thinking that what Lizzie heard as they walked together was the squishy boots of the man who'd promised to save her. And only partly succeeded.

Until they left Sir Charles's offices, there was no ability in the pelting rain to hear about Whitehall, though Tom kept saying, "Don't you want to know?" He and Tamsin seemed especially buoyant. One might guess what happened, given that Tamsin floated, or at least walked on her toes, her fingers lightly resting on Rowland's arm.

At last, Rowland said, "Yes, I do want to know. Tell me before I'm forced to drown you in a horse trough, Tom."

"Your packet of letters worked better than a hedge-witch's charm, Rollo." Tom punched his shoulder. "The king is restoring the Marborne title."

Rowland longed to catch Tom's joy. "Then everyone has their heart's desire? Do you, Lizzie?"

Lizzie started, as if Rowland trod on her toes.

"You promised to help me, Rollo." She clutched Perry's elbow. "When you left for London, you said you weren't ready. Therefore, I had to accept that proposal."

"I asked for another week. And I promised that I'd do what I could. But please, I don't judge you for—"

"Caution!" Perry called out. "Watch your step, ladies. The muck is bad here."

Rowland continued. "I confess, I am not utterly joyous that you chose to marry Lord Heydon. But I'm sure you did what you thought best."

"What? No, Lizzie!" Ned snapped at her in surprise.

"Of course, I'm not going to marry Heydon, you booberkin." Lizzie was indignant.

"Not going to—"

Rowland felt Perry grab his collar, holding him back while again calling for caution, stopping them from stepping into a street where a dung cart was passing, the clappers and bells ringing their noisy caution.

"Marry Heydon? Lizzie? Truly?" Ned said.

"It is neither wonderful that I said yes, nor remarkable that I have now said no." Lizzie let go of Perry's elbow and stood with arms akimbo while she scolded Ned for scolding her.

Trying to puzzle out which answer Lizzie gave last, Rowland almost forgot that cold blade.

Except he couldn't forget. Fear still tingled in the small hairs on his neck.

"Why?" Ned saved Rowland from having to ask. "Why say yes? And why say no?"

"Heydon promised to help regain the Marborne title. So that I could return to Mary's court." Lizzie sulked while Ned pestered her. "I didn't believe Rollo could find sufficient fortune to pay the king's garnishment."

"But we didn't have to pay a garnishment." Tom rubbed his hands like a gleeful lawn bowler knocking down pins on a Sunday. "You never had to marry Heydon to save us."

Bless his heart. Tom did not understand Lizzie.

"I didn't know that yesterday," she said. "Because I thought we had no more time for any other solution."

"And so, you said no?" Rowland forgot the threat of that knife as his breath caught on hope.

"I said yes," Lizzie said.

That long-carried grenade in Rowland's belly threatened to explode. "But you said Heydon wanted your family to approve."

Ned gripped her elbow. "Dear sister, I, as one close family member, do not approve."

"I said yes," Lizzie tugged her elbow free, "but then I said no. Because I thought Heydon suborned you, lambkin, by buying your list of traitors so that he'd be the Earl of Hawksmoor."

"Selling your list?" Perry stopped abruptly in the road. "You distress me, Lieutenant Foxe. In fact, you twist me to the core."

—

Rowland couldn't sort how he'd forgotten, for even a heartbeat, that he had two friends to pacify when he explained his unannounced change in plans. He pleaded with Perry, hoping the others might understand. "I gave Heydon a single page from Duncombe's papers, the page that listed Hawksmoor's name. Because Heydon asked me to protect his brother."

Lizzie begged his attention. "Rollo, please tell me you didn't seek to help Heydon steal the title from his brother — and that you didn't do it for my sake."

Tamsin interrupted before Rowland could answer. "We went over this many times on the way to London. Heydon didn't seek to take his brother's title."

Tom said, "It's not possible for Hawksmoor, nor any lord, to give away his title. He can choose to not use it, but that title is not going anywhere until the blind ferryman brings the earl across the River Styx. And that's assuming Hawksmoor has three coins to pay—"

Rowland interrupted, to answer what was demanded of him. "I did not come to Cambridge to do all this for *you*, Lizzie."

"You often claim that," Perry said. "Jove smite me, but I remain less than convinced."

"I gave Heydon that list for my own purposes." Rowland looked to Perry, intending that his comrade understand. As for Lizzie, he couldn't even glance her way, fearing how she'd judge him for cheating the Crown of more traitors. "I didn't want to condemn Duncombe's entire family. Even you, Perry, see that our king is exceedingly bloodthirsty."

Tom said, "Then join us in lauding Heydon for sending them all to Barbados. And we must thank you for saving us from sitting in church with those chuffing cheaters any more Sundays."

"Barbados?" Rowland, completely surprised, forgot the turmoil in his belly.

Tamsin said, "The earl refused to leave his wife. To protect his brother, Heydon made Hawksmoor confess in a writ to the king, begging forgiveness of his wife's errors. Then he exiled all of them to his plantations in the colonies."

"Except Camilla," Tom said. "She won an annulment out of Heydon's game."

Perry snapped his fingers for attention. "For years, Rollo, you denied any emolument to avoid corruption. When did you turn selfish? And what did you earn for cheating the Crown out of all those betrayers' names?"

"Heydon promised to pay the garnishment, to convince the king to return the Marborne title." Rowland said it, still believing that was also what Heydon had offered Lizzie.

"How selfish of you," Tom said. "Though I'd do the same if I had the chance."

"Selfish? Selfish?" Lizzie missed that Tom obviously spoke in jest. "He did it for me, Tom. To make it possible for me to return to Mary's court."

"Then it's you who is selfish," Tom said, still teasing her.

"No, I came to Revelstone because Absolom commanded me." Rowland persisted with his plea. He seemed to have persuaded everyone but Perry and Lizzie that he'd done the best possible in all that chaos. "By working together, Perry and I made Marborne safe, which has long been Tamsin's deepest desire. And yours, Tom. Is it not your desire also, Lizzie?"

"If there is no moral dilemma ..." Lizzie began, but couldn't seem to decide how to continue.

"Lieutenant Foxe has convinced me. We shall chalk the entire victory in this gambol to Rollo's careful planning." Perry's words lifted a great burden from Rowland's soul. He dropped his voice. "Except the robber-boys were my idea."

Tom said, "Lizzie, the only moral dilemma was your feather-brained notion to marry for a title."

"Whatever Rollo's intent," Tamsin said, "Heydon need never pay for that list, because Fate finally delivered our fathers' letters to the king. We regained the title without Heydon's help."

The party reached their lodgings in Covent Garden. While Tom held the door open for everyone to pass, he said, "Let's have peace now. The title Absolom wanted restored will surely bear as great a weight as poverty. Let us now drink champagne to celebrate Marborne."

Once inside, Tom pulled off his soaking felted hat and then the wig he wore, stuffing it into the wet hat.

"That's my best court wig." Rowland complained, though he could now afford another.

"Oh, right. I'll ask a servant to carry it to a barber."

"It's late Friday. Will you find a barber of quality tomorrow?"

"No matter. You don't want to wear that mop tonight, Rollo, because we shall be busy making merry. Hello, Jack." Tom then engaged the porter in an elaborate order for dinner that began: "First, champagne. Today's the day for all my cousins to learn what it tastes like. And I'm hungry enough to eat the entire cow roasting on your kitchen fires."

"It's a pig that's carbonadoed for tonight, sir."

"Excellent. I'll trust you to the fixings. Can we have a tansy cake at the end? And port, please?"

"Our cook prepares a fine tansy with a rosewater sauce and primrose leaves. And also, the first of the season's pears."

"I shall leave it all to you and your kitchen, good man."

Tom rubbed his hands. Absent wig and hat, his hair roamed freely. Formerly clipped short, it was now growing out and stood on end, alternately rigid and wild after an afternoon at court.

He shared a confidence with the porter.

"Please let the entire household know that this is an occasion of great importance. We are cousins who have come to London for the Earl of Marborne's restoration. Tonight's dinner shall be a celebration like none we've known before."

When the two women went to change for dinner, Tom said, "Ned, Rollo. Come upstairs. Lizzie packed clothes for you."

Ned took up the offer immediately, with Perry at his side.

"Thank you, no," Rowland said. "I just need to tie my cravat properly so that Lizzie thinks me civilized. And I have a hankering to sit in our private parlor in my shirtsleeves, at least until the ladies return."

———

After Tom bounded away to change out of wet velvet, Rowland begged a servant for a small beer, and then sought solitude in the private salon they'd hired. Perhaps he should just run away, after being castigated through the streets of London with the Bard's words burning his heart: "I burn, I pine, I perish."

But he couldn't be alone, because Winwood paced the salon, not noticing Rowland's entrance. The doctor stopped near the window to read a letter clutched in his hand.

"Good evening, doctor."

Rowland tugged off his new and already damp coat, which Tom had disparaged. He draped it over the back of a chair and unwound his cravat, hoping it might dry before dinner. He resigned himself to spending the evening in sopping boots, there being no solution for that.

Winwood looked up, worry etched deep in his smooth, handsome face. He brightened seeing that Rowland hailed him.

"Mr. Foxe. You might be the very man for the moment."

"If you require a man drenched and dirtied by a London downpour."

"I've just had this." Winwood held out the letter, not to share it but to indicate the source of his affliction. "I sent a message to my cousin to say that I was in London. She forwarded a letter from my father, who warns that if I do not return to my studies in Switzerland, he can no longer support my lark in England. But I do not want to leave Cambridge."

"Perhaps I can help. I destroy mortgages, save estates, and gratify kings. With no special effort, I can also part women from their bad husbands. What can I do for you, Dr. Oakes?"

"May I beg you to call me Winwood? I need your advice, not your heroics. Miss Thomasine was at sixes and sevens for what to do about the house and the villages. Then you came and —"

Rowland had his hand up for silence. A servant entered with his small beer. Words and signals passed, the servant seeking the doctor's comfort, accepting Winwood's refusal, until the two men were alone again.

Sipping his beer, Rowland realized he was parched and famished. He set the mug on the table to keep from draining it. "Before you ask anything of me, Winwood, please satisfy my curiosity. I am grateful for what you did for Tom and Camilla. For how you helped bring everyone to London."

"Thank you, sir."

"Sir? Call me Rollo, please. Now, tell me your secret. Are you a deserted field-surgeon? Or a gambler hiding from debts on the Continent? I've guessed both, but cannot decide which."

Despite his distress over the letter he clutched, Winwood laughed. "Yes, I was a field-surgeon. The last place I saw action was at the Battle of Saint-Denis, more than ten years ago."

"With King Louis's French army?"

"No, I was with Dutch and Spanish forces. What a field-surgeon sees—well, perhaps it was just as bad two hundred years ago with arrows and swords, but now, battle injuries from gun blasts make up my nightmares. I left…"

"Deserted?"

"Yes. I ran from nightmares and gambling debts. My family lent me funds to study medicine under a famous doctor in Switzerland. I haven't completed those studies, but I'm better educated than a field-surgeon. And the sole person I gamble with is Tom, for straws and half-pennies."

"That's your secret?"

"It's no secret. I just don't want others to condemn me, either for being in that fight or for leaving the army."

"I won't condemn you, Winwood. I am also in shaded territory, rendering traitors to the Crown for judgment. Did you know that's what I do?"

"I heard the Miss Foxes talk about it on our journey here."

"Our iniquities on the Continent should be forgotten here in England."

"Then this is what I seek to ask you. Do you approve of me seeking a position with Tom so that I can remain in Cambridge? Not as a physician, since I haven't completed my studies. But perhaps as his clerk?"

"Yes, but…" Rowland raised a finger of caution.

"Pray tell me. The others will arrive soon."

"It appears, doctor, that you have a *tendre* for my cousin Tamsin." Rowland steepled his fingers. "And now she has a fortune that I am obliged to protect."

"A *tendre*? No, I admire her as a great hero. To her family, her friends, the villages." Mild-mannered Winwood didn't rise to Rowland's accusation of fortune hunting.

"You protest, doctor. But I did see the familiar marks of a man who loves in secret, without hope."

"Familiar? Because of your own *tendre* for Miss Foxe?"

"Is it that obvious?" That casual remark struck Rowland to the core.

"Yes, Rollo, it is." Winwood shook his head. "For my part, I am a student of the natural world, the world as it is. Not unattainable dreams in the night. Have you not observed that Tamsin has given her heart to Camilla? When Camilla comes to live at Revelstone, you'll see it too, sir."

"Camilla at Revelstone?" Rowland, caught in his own mulligrubs, had failed to see that Tamsin's happiness rose from more than the previous day's successful restoration.

"Yes," Winwood said. "Miss Thomasine is effervescent with delight. You must have noticed, since you are so observant. It is gratifying to see her so—"

Tom burst in, bouncing across the room in excitement, claiming a place beside Winwood. Ned and Perry trailed more peacefully behind.

"It will be breakfast before we can talk, Winwood." Rowland reached for his nearly dry coat and cravat, since the women would not be far behind. "For all that the Foxe family owes you, let's discuss your business then."

As his next business, Rowland intended to coax himself out from under his mopes, to join the celebration. After all, the title was restored. The family's financial yoke was lifted. And Lizzie was not marrying Heydon.

54

Fortune's Fool

TAKING A SEAT beside Camilla at the round table in the hired salon at their lodgings, Tamsin felt again the quiet thrill of Camilla safely at her side. It'd be far into the future before Tamsin became accustomed to the sensation of happy peace. She'd thought it impossible a week ago.

Winwood sat between Camilla and Tom. Ned and Perry sat close by each other. That left just one empty seat, beside Rowland, which Lizzie took. Though Rowland seemed to seek but did not receive Lizzie's attention, Tamsin thought each of that pair seemed to be lifting their own spirits in celebration. She rested her hand on Camilla's forearm, glad for that comfort.

Rowland addressed everyone at the table. "We have agreed, then, that I'm not Judas Iscariot? I simply did not want to condemn your neighbors as traitors."

"We understand now," Ned said. "And Duncombe's syndicate shall likely be happy in Barbados. Waited on by people forced into slavery." He called to Lizzie. "Did you know that Heydon owns people? In truth, dear sister, I wish you'd spoken to me before agreeing to marry him."

Rowland sat back in his chair, a smile in place as if he'd joined the celebration, even though he repeatedly failed to catch Lizzie's attention. Only a few days before, Tamsin had also misunderstood

Rowland's actions. How could she now rake the two of them out of the ashes of that recent misunderstanding?

"You are not required to rescue everyone," Camilla whispered, folding her hand over Tamsin's. "Some people have to save themselves."

"Are you reading my mind?" Tamsin whispered back.

"Often times."

Meanwhile, Tom grew gregarious, and Tamsin glanced at Winwood to see if she should worry. But the doctor seemed as happy as Tom.

"Speaking of Heydon," Tom said, "why do you think he came to court today, riding so hard he was covered in trail dirt?"

"You saw him?" Rowland said. "Likely he came to offer the king the garnishment he'd promised, for Marborne."

"He didn't say so to me when I said hello," Tom said.

"No." Lizzie tapped Rowland's hand, which seemed to startle him. "I'm sure Heydon came to present all the writs the Duncombe syndicate signed yesterday, abandoning use of their titles and leaving their property in Heydon's care."

"And also," Tamsin said, "Camilla's writ for an annulment, which protects her from Leighton being in the syndicate."

"Yes," Camilla said. "Thank you for what you did, Rollo. It leads the way to my freedom."

"Moreover," Perry said, "I am comforted beyond reason to be saved from the heartbreak of witnessing Lieutenant Foxe sink into a mire of corrupt emoluments."

"Mr. Frake, you have never cared about the corruption from emoluments, one way or the other," Rowland said.

"No, Rollo. However, I remain rather in love with your sense of honor. What's your Shakespeare for this? 'Some rise by sin, and some by virtue fall'?"

"No, that's not the best—"

The serving door opened. One man came in bearing a bottle of champagne and another with a tray with glasses. Two more servants carried trays of food.

"The champagne has arrived!" Tom jumped up, jerking the table in his abrupt excitement. Tom's blooming health cheered Tamsin as much as all the good things that had happened that day. "Have a glass, Winwood. It's as much a healing restorative as your horse-pee tincture."

"Are we now done castigating Rollo?" Perry asked while Tom poured fizzy wine in everyone's glass. "Because I should like to offer a toast. May you now all live free, with no more need for either the rules or the dangers of restorations."

Tamsin raised her glass. "However, our rules served us well over many hard seasons. Then yesterday, we broke nearly every rule."

"But in an enlightened way," Tom said.

"I think it's fine to break the rule, 'Never trick a woman,'" Lizzie said, "since those women tried to steal from us first. The same for trespassing on the rule, 'Never bilk a neighbor.'"

"Our fair redistribution, made possible by our restorations," Tom said, "does not break the Eighth Commandment. Though I don't have the verse to quote at hand."

Ned said, "One rule fell into a fen-ditch and was lost. 'Our allies shall be innocent.' Instead, we are here toasting with Winwood and Camilla and Perry."

Tamsin said, "We managed to keep one rule: 'No one dies.'"

"Except perhaps for Mr. Duncombe," Perry said, "and anyone he might name as his conspirators."

"That's down to him," Tom said when people remained quiet for several uncomfortable heartbeats. "Nothing we did caused Danvers Duncombe to betray the Crown."

"It's also down to King James," Lizzie said, "who panicked and began executing people, because he doesn't know how best to rule this country."

"Perhaps Duncombe shall only be transported." Rowland sounded hopeful.

Tamsin agreed, pitying Duncombe's fate, though the man had brought it on himself. She also found it gratifying that Rowland, as an enlightened gentleman, hadn't wanted to hand over anyone else to the Crown, that he hoped for a better outcome than heads on pikes.

Tom splashed more fizzy wine into each glass. "Come, Rollo. A man in your position should be merry. Happy as a lord, as they say. What more can we do to spark joy?"

"Oh, this will bring everyone good cheer." Tamsin knew what to do as suddenly as she'd known they must rob Hawksmoor's carriage. She snatched the empty tin tray from the sideboard, then pushed aside her dining plate. Thrilled with her grand idea, she dipped into the bodice of her dress and jerked free the pouch that always hung there. "We shall have our own Lammas-tide bonfire."

Reaching to the candelabra on the table, she lit the papers from her pouch and dropped them to burn on the tray.

"The mortgages that crimped our lives are gone. Shall we toast our freedom?"

"And," Camilla said, "let's toast to Rollo and Tom being here with us once more."

Tamsin lifted her glass, happy for each of them and delighted to see Perry hold his glass up to hers, his other hand on Ned's shoulder. Ned stared rather dreamily at Perry and didn't seem to notice the tiny bonfire. Tamsin had to swipe at tears, since happiness seemed about to overcome her. But then, the acrid smoke stung her nose and made her cough.

"To love without fear and life without care." Tom raised his glass. So did Winwood, but he tipped his glass to douse the smoking mess on the tin tray. Tom chided the doctor for wasting champagne, then said, "'God send everyone their heart's desire!' Did I remember that quote properly, Rollo?"

Camilla touched her glass to Tamsin's, leaning close. "You are my heart's root. Nothing shall divide us."

Tamsin felt bubbles from the glass tickle her nose. "Camilla, 'I do not wish any companion in the world but you.'"

She felt mostly sure that she'd got that quote right, but was not about to ask Rowland to confirm it or correct her. Camilla nudged her, indicating with her chin how Lizzie's little finger rested on Rowland's hand. Camilla slipped her hand over Tamsin's once more.

"God save my giddy cat!" Camilla whispered. "What will happen to us next?"

— NED —

HE TWITCHED WHEN Perry traced the faint remnant of paint (from costly lapis lazuli) on Ned's fingers.

Perry leaned closer, tipping his glass against Ned's as if toasting, his whisper warm in Ned's ear.

"You have captured my heart. My soul. My very being."

Ned felt the champagne sparkle in his head, just behind his eyebrows. His blood burned so hot, his shirt might catch fire. "Then don't find another spymaster. Stay here with us. With me."

"Aye, sweet chucking. But what shall I do at Marborne?"

Ned turned to Tamsin. "Absolom said you could name an overseer. Why not Perry?"

It took Tamsin a moment to hear her name and tear her attention from Camilla. Ned had to repeat the request.

"I'm sure he's fit for the work," Ned said. "And the barn cats like him."

"Mr. Frake, I'd be honored," Tamsin said. "No one else could do as well."

"You bring peace to my heart, mistress," Perry said. "That tender organ has been besieged by storms this past week. I shall do whatever you command me, Miss Thomasine."

She smiled warmly while saying, "I rather doubt that, sir."

Lizzie said, "Does this mean that Tamsin doesn't have to do every bedeviled thing to keep Marborne and Revelstone alive and well?"

"Surely you didn't think I'd return to being master?" Tom asked, aping astonishment. "I shall have my own burden of work to take up, practicing law for the villagers and cottagers as Uncle Absolom predicted. Better for everyone if Perry manages foresters and thatchers and disputations on the commons."

Ned sat quietly, taking his last bite of carbonadoed meat, contented beyond all reason. It seemed that he had his heart's desire, though a week ago he didn't know what he desired, except to paint his own work instead of forgeries.

"Will you like it if I'm at Revelstone?" Perry spoke low, for only Ned to hear in the chaos of the parlor. "You have all your village ways, and I have only the ways of a soldier. How shall I fit in your world?"

"There's an enormous hole that's been waiting for you," Ned said. Within the bone cage that held his heart and belly, a heat glowed that was more than the remains of a summer's eve. "I just didn't know."

"And now you can paint portraits of titled and rich ladies." Perry rubbed that trace of blue on Ned's fingers. "Shall you first paint the new Earl of Marborne, to serve as your calling card?"

"No." Ned glanced at Tom, who seemed to be bargaining with Winwood about pouring another glass of champagne. "I shall paint the heirs of Marborne in their finest clothes. Though first I'll gild the great hall's fireplace, to serve as background."

"With real gold?" Perry purred in his ear, his voice as soft as a barn cat. "Are you that rich now, sweetkin?"

"Nay. My father left me a recipe that uses copper and zinc and rabbit-skin glue." Ned leaned back to where Perry's arm draped over his chair. "But in other ways, I might as well claim to be the richest man in England."

— ROLLO —

"I TOO PROPOSE a toast." Rowland stood.

"Dash it, more Shakespeare?" Tom groaned. "I feel it in my bones, like an old man feels the coming of rheumy weather."

"Aye, coz." Rowland lifted his glass. "Let us salute Absolom Foxe and everything he did for us. 'So we'll live, and pray, and sing, and tell old tales, and laugh at gilded butterflies, and hear poor rogues talk of court news.'"

"To Absolom Foxe." Tamsin chimed in first, then the others followed. Perry, the last to raise his glass, murmured, "I wish I'd met the old gentleman who taught and enlightened you all."

Tamsin and Lizzie began serving food, the house's servants having been sent away. Giddy after the king's court, now that the champagne flowed, they all seemed chirping-merry. Rowland smiled so broadly his face hurt, but champagne or not, he felt everyone's happiness wrap around him, buoying him up.

"Congratulations, Tom." Rollo swatted his cousin's arm, in place of embracing him. "I didn't have a chance to felicitate you when we met in that alley."

"That grand moment shall echo through the ages." Laughing, Tom nudged Ned, which almost dislodged Ned from his deep whispers with Perry. "Say, coz, shall you paint it like a famous classical tableau? Rowland Foxe of Marborne in dire straits, saved by women. My good luck in witnessing that made up for every single restoration I missed this last half year."

"I'm happy that my distress gives you joy." Rowland expected his cousin to torture him for the next half year, over a scene as embarrassing as it had been frightful. "But I do mean to congratulate you. Though you claimed to never like the idea of bearing the title, I wager you'll do us proud."

Tom tilted his head. He cleared his throat three times before he spoke. "Rollo, that letter you handed me, from our fathers and grandfathers? Did you read it?"

"No. As I told you, I didn't want to break the seal, since it was addressed to the king."

"Aye, correct protocol," Tom said. "I didn't open it either."

"You bennish feather-head," Perry said.

Tamsin said, "That's rather harsh. Tom doesn't deserve it."

"Not Tom," Perry said. "Rollo, this is the first time since I've known you that a sealed letter kept you from peeking inside. I am bewildered at your choice now. Do you not wonder, seeing Tom as befuddled as I am?"

Before Rowland could answer, Lizzie again moved closer to him, which left him unable to voice words, feeling her heat so nearby.

"That packet of letters," Tom said, "described how our grandparents and parents died in the plague, painting a gruesome picture of them mourning another loss, day after day. Each new page was written by a surviving brother or son or nephew, informing the king who must next inherit Marborne."

"God blind me! I'm sorry I inflicted that on you, Tom. I never imagined it contained a grim tale."

Perry said, "Those gruesome letters disturbed the king."

"And me!" Tom exclaimed. "But I have since recovered my spirits. By the time the king finished reading, I felt my right ear itching. You know what that means, don't you?" Tom folded his arms, his expression unreadable.

Worse, Perry copied him. "My granddam claimed it means the angels are bringing you good luck."

Laughing, Perry and Tom reached behind Ned to slap each other's palms.

"I don't understand," Lizzie said.

Perry glanced at Lizzie, then Tamsin. "But you heard what the king said at Whitehall."

"That he restored the title, yes," Tamsin said. "Then we heard only his last words to you, that the angels must now rejoice instead of weeping."

"I personally was gratified that the last letter in the packet," Tom said, "was written by Josiah Foxe, the Younger, the last survivor among them. For my own part, the angels did indeed carry good news."

"Rollo's father? How sad and—oh, I see." Tamsin choked, coughing, then covered her mouth. She grasped that pouch that had held the mortgages. "My lucky Archangel might even be laughing. Can you hear it, Rollo?"

She flipped a gold coin across the table to him. Rowland caught it but still didn't catch the humor, distracted by the idea that it was his father who wrote the last sad letter.

"Stop laughing, Tom. You should have told us all plainly before now." Lizzie stabbed her finger at Tom but then dropped her hand to caress Rowland's. "Did you also not know until this moment, lambkin?"

"Know what?"

"That you are Marborne's fourteenth earl?"

"God blind me! No!" Rowland's voice cracked. He felt the same jolt as when that pistol sent shards of plaster and stone flying through the alley. "'O, I am fortune's fool!'"

While Rowland tried to speak sensibly, each person at the table watched him. They beamed with happiness—and kindly waited for him to find his feelings and regain his thoughts.

Tom grinned. "It's true, my lord."

"Lord? No, it's—it's...unbelievable."

"You made everyone at Revelstone believe you were Viscount Orlando," Tom said. "I wager most people will believe it when you are introduced as the Earl of Marborne."

"It's as Absolom always claimed," Tamsin said. "Rollo shall be the one to serve the king."

Rowland found what he wanted to say. "Rather than being your lord, it is I who must be a servant to all of you. How shall I be the lord of Marborne without you as my comrades?"

Meanwhile, Tom seemed to have few sentiments, busy counting facts on his fingers. "Besides relieving me of the burden of the title, that packet contained proof for the chain of title back to the first earl. Whose name was Rolland, a Norman. I'd forgotten that, if I ever knew. The king commanded Lord W— to persuade the Committee for Privileges and Conduct to resolve the title on Friday next. Which will give us time to acquire better clothes."

"We are free from jeopardy." Tamsin exulted, her face as free from care as Rowland remembered it from childhood. "And Rollo's gambol makes it possible for us to restore the villages."

While she smiled at Rowland, Tamsin grasped Camilla's hand. For both women, the world had just come safely together in unexpected ways, not upended like Rowland's. He gulped the wine in his glass, his throat still filled with sand.

Lizzie tapped Rowland's hand, like she used to, except the tap on his middle knuckle sent a shiver up his arm. "And now, Lord Marborne—"

He laughed out loud, hearing the title as if it were real for the first time. "You, Miss Foxe, may call me Rollo."

"Perhaps now the times have become less precarious. Now that we all have most everything we wanted in the world." She'd become softer, even wistful, repeating words from the sleepless night in her workshop. Or perhaps it was the champagne that softened her.

Tom said, "By all logic, Lizzie, the king should allow Rollo to court you. And then—"

"Court?" Rowland coughed, choking on his own breath. He turned to Lizzie, but she leaned so close that they knocked heads, painfully.

"Yes," Tom said. "Otherwise, the king shall choose a stranger for you to marry, my lord cousin."

"There's no other woman in England who can appreciate you like I do, Rollo." Lizzie rubbed her forehead where they'd knocked heads, then rested her hand on Rowland's. "Or who shall know how to work at your side, as comrades in arms."

Perry intruded. "Yes, Lord Marborne. You must ask the king's permission to court Miss Foxe when you see him next."

"Court Lizzie?" Rowland repeated the words, like a dulpickle.

"Yes, your lordship. I hope the king agrees." Lizzie smiled warmly, the kind of smile he hadn't seen since they'd whispered gossip in Holland.

"I wager," Tom said, "she'll allow your courtship before the king forces it upon her."

"Force Lizzie?" The champagne kept Rowland from quickly becoming wise again. "No one can force Lizzie."

"See, you do understand me, Rollo." As Lizzie looped her little finger around his hand, she spoke tenderly, losing the cool practicality with which she claimed that sentiment two nights before. He felt his heart pound again, but not with fear this time. "Perhaps we can return to Mary's court together, after the harvest. What laughs we shall have then."

411

"You will allow me to court you? With a view to…" It took that many heartbeats for Rowland to see that she was serious, and he couldn't speak the final thought aloud.

"I keep my promises," she whispered, "the way Absolom taught me. Just like you do."

Awash in warm sensations—Lizzie whispering a promise, the king restoring the title, his friends happier than he'd ever dared to dream—Rowland knocked over his empty wine glass. He set the glass aright and fetched his gold coin with his other hand, running it across his knuckles. Though Fate had inundated him with good luck in the past two days, he needed even more luck, because he couldn't find a trace of confidence among his many brighter feelings.

Tom said, "Yes. It's best if the king declares that you must take the earldom and then chase after Lizzie."

"Everything is better," Tamsin said. "Everything in the whole world is better." Beside her, Camilla exclaimed over the tansy cake that a servant set before her.

Wistful, Tom said, "I hope there's enough tansy cake for two servings. And brandy. I forgot to order brandy."

Winwood kept Tom from rising. "Modern science has proved that brandy and champagne combine like a French grenade. The port is surely enough. I suggest we have an evening of lanterloo."

"We can wager real coin now," Tom declared.

"In Amsterdam, they simply call it loo." Rowland managed to voice a casual nothing. The sensations that filled him outdid the joy he felt when the gambol worked, when Starbuck appeared to take Duncombe off his hands. He suddenly felt hopeful. Eager. Curious about what might happen next. Ready for whatever might be on the next horizon.

Perry said, "Now you have tasted champagne, Mr. Wijck, mayhap we shall learn whether you can sing. Perhaps tonight is the night to discover the truth."

Rowland bent his head to whisper to Lizzie. "And still, 'I do love nothing in the world so well as you.' Please let me teach you how it is that people give their hearts to each other."

"You may instruct me." She gave him a sly look. "Because you are my 'ever-fixed mark that looks on tempests and is never shaken.'"

He was shaking, though, in his still damp boots. "It's not as if I have half a notion how to play at being a lord without you to guide me."

Tamsin, who had become gentle and dreamy with champagne and success, stood. "We swore a solemn oath, on our ancestors' bones, like a band of brothers. 'Until either angels or demons take us from this green land.' Let us swear again." She held up her glass.

"'…If it be a sin to covet honor,'" Rowland spoke, still caught by Lizzie's mischievous smile, "and love, 'I am the most offending soul alive.'"

"That's not the line as Shakespeare wrote it," Tom said. "I'm sure of it."

"'We few, we happy few.' Is that correct, Rollo?" Lizzie wound her fingers around Rowland's, forcing his gold angel to drop onto the table, fall to the floor, and roll across the room, clattering on the floorboards.

His gold angel lay face up, sparkling in the bright light of so very many candles.

"Yes," he said. "A thousand times yes."

THE END … OF THIS GAMBOL

Glossary

Afscheid, mijn vriend: Farewell, my friend.

Ajax and Hector: In *The Iliad,* these warriors fought to a standstill, each admiring the other's skill and courage.

ambuscade: An ambush.

amoretto: An amorous man.

ambidexter: A lawyer who takes fees from both sides.

angel: A gold coin worth approximately eleven shillings in this era.

angler: A cheat; a thief dangling to draw people in.

arsworm: A diminutive fellow.

averil: A funeral repast.

bagonet: A dagger.

bantling: A child.

Bard: William Shakespeare.

bear-garden discourse: Common, filthy talk.

beau coc: A handsome rooster.

bennish: Foolish.

beetle-head: Blockhead.

black-mouth: Railing, malicious.

bodkin: A dagger.

booberkin: A dull fellow.

boomken: A dumpy person.

borachio: Drunkard, called so after the wine-skin.

bravo: A merciless mercenary.

buttery: A pantry.

caballero: Here, a rough allusion to Perry serving as a Spanish lady's knight.

Captain Queernobs: A shabby fellow.

Captain Sharp: A big cheat.

carbonadoed: Grilled meat.

Carmelite water: A cordial made with lemon balm and other herbs soaked in wine or alcohol.

chirping-merry: Feeling pleasant over good liquor.

chittifaced: Puny child.

chuck; chucking: Dialect for chick, as a term of endearment.

chuffing: A euphemism for a taboo expletive.

cobweb cheat: Easily uncovered.

cockish: Wanton.

cock-robin: An easy and arrogant fellow.

cold-cock: Deliver a blow to the head.

contumely: Insulting language or behavior.

cove: A man.

coz: A diminutive for cousin.

cozen: To deceive or trick.

crimping fellow: A duplicitous dog.

crinkum-crankum: Elaborate decoration.

crufty-beau: A man who paints his face.

dag: A gun.

Dark Lady: A woman described in Shakespeare's sonnets. She has black hair and dark skin.

dark-lanthorn: A shaded candle lantern. Rowland is quoting from *A Midsummer Night's Dream*.

devil drawer: A painter of forgeries.

ducky: Dear.

dulpickle: A dim-witted, foolish fellow.

Dutch courage: Bravery gained from drinking alcohol, a phrase from the seventeenth-century Dutch-Anglo wars. Now, an ethnic slur.

eikel: Acorn, a word from the Latin for the male member; dickhead is perhaps the equivalent English insult.

ensorcel: To enchant.

eternity box: A casket.

ezel: Donkey, a mild insult condemning stubborn, unintelligent behavior.

fainéant: An idle, ineffective person.

farrago: A muddle; a confused mixture (of anything).

fen-gangs: Dutch prisoners of war used as laborers in projects to drain the fens.

Fen Tigers: People who live in the fenlands of East Anglia; in this case, locals who vandalized the early seventeenth century efforts to drain the fens.

fiddler's pay: Thanked with a drink, but not paid for work.

firkin: A hooped wooden barrel holding about nine gallons.

flitter-mouse: A term of endearment.

footpad: A highwayman on foot rather than on horseback.

forfend: Protect with precautionary measures.

froward: A contrary person.

fuddle-cap: A drunkard; as adjective, inebriated.

fustilarian: A lowly scoundrel who uses a cudgel rather than a sword (from Shakespeare).

gadding: Flitting around.

gamester-sharp: A cheating gambler.

genever: Holland gin.

gilflurt: A posh and vain woman.

gingamobs: Testicles.

glimflashy: In an angry passion.

God's bodkins: A minced oath; "God's body!"

gold-douser: Here, a fortune hunter. In other uses, someone who douses for gold (like a water douser); historically, many who represented themselves as gold-dousers were charlatans.

gold-never-brass: Ned assumes that Duncombe would wear real gold buttons and look down on brass buttons.

goose-cap: A fool.

grumbletonian: A malcontent.

gudgeon: A gullible person.

gull: An easily deceived person.

gutfoundered: Extraordinarily hungry.

habiliment: Clothing.

hackbut: Two-foot long handgun.

hagged: Half starved.

harridan: A bossy woman.

hedge-bird: A scoundrel.

houd je bek: Shut your mouth.

hoyting girl: A tomboy.

hucker-mucker: A confusion or muddle, with concealment.

intelligencer: An informer, spy, or secret agent.

jakes: An outdoor lavatory.

jerrycummumble: To shake and tumble.

jumble-gutted: A bumpy road.

kattenkop: Dutch for cat's head, an insult; similar to catty in English.

King's Company: The theatre group with exclusive play-staging rights, called a royal patent, from Charles II.

kip: 1) A bed; 2) a nap.

ladette: A tomboy.

lambkin: An endearment; someone who's sweet and innocent.

lamzak: Numb sack, an insult for a person who drinks too much.

lanterloo: A trick-taking card game that likely came to England from France at the beginning of the Restoration.

lashing: Rain falling so hard it bounces off the ground.

long-headed: Showing wisdom.

Louis d'or; louis: A French coin introduced in the seventeenth century; named for the face of King Louis on the coin.

mafting: Hot and humid.

malapert: Impertinent and supercilious.

mayhap: Perhaps.

mazed: Bewildered.

Medici porcelain: Early European imitations of Chinese porcelain, beginning in the sixteenth century.

milk the pigeon: Attempting the impossible.

miting: Little mite, an endearment.

moider: Throw into disorder.

mon trésor: My treasure.

moon calf: A foolish person.

muddled: Half drunk.

mulligrubs: An exaggerated bad mood.

natheless: Nevertheless.

Nederlandse: A Dutchman.

nestlings: Birds raised by hand.

nick-ninny: An empty, simple fellow.

nithing: A despicable person.

nuncheon: A midmorning snack, often of bread and cheese.

nutting: Term of endearment; "source of delight."

odds bodkins: A euphemistic or minced oath, substituting for God's body.

oddsfish: God's flesh.

odium: Hatred combined with loathing.

odsheartlings: God's heart.

orpiment: A pigment used (until the 19th century) for bright yellow, made by grinding down an arsenic sulfide mineral.

paardereet: Horse's ass.

pettifogging: Quibbling over petty points.

phanatic: A dissenter from the Church of England.

phisnomy: A medieval term for physiognomy; judging a person's character by his features.

picaroon: A scoundrel who behaves like a pirate.

pickthank: A gossip who's spreading malicious rumors.

piked off: Ran away.

pistoleer: A soldier who is armed with a pistol.

poltroon: A complete coward.

posset: A spiced wine-and-cream drink.

pother: A commotion.

pratts: Buttocks.

rakefire: A fellow who lingers as a guest until the fire has burned down, outstaying his welcome.

rampallian: An insult from Shakespeare; a mean wretch.

Ravenscroft's crystal: A lead glass created by the Englishman George Ravenscroft that was less breakable than Murano *cristallo.*

recusant: Someone who refuses to submit to an authority.

Roundheads: The rebel army aligned with Cromwell against the Royalists in the English civil wars.

royal progress: Summer travels by Elizabeth I and her court through the English countryside.

saucebox: An impudent person.

scaramouch: A boastful yet cowardly fellow, from a standard character in Italian comedies of this period.

scobberlotcher: One who never works hard.

scullion: An insult from Shakespeare; a base person.

scurvy: Contemptible; worthless.

Seekers: A dissenting Christian sect that rose during the English Civil War, first led by George Fox. "Quaker" was used to ridicule Fox's nonconformists, but then they adopted it themselves.

skulk: A group of foxes or any animal considered vermin.

squeezing the orange: To take all conceivable profit when undertaking an enterprise. A seventeenth century expression.

subaltern: A second lieutenant.

sweeting, sweetkin: An endearment, like darling.

syndic, blind syndicate: A committee of individuals or companies formed to advance a specific investment. In a blind syndicate, members are not known to each other or to outsiders, only to the managing agent.

tatterdemallion: A man with tattered clothes.

tendre: Tender feelings; a crush.

termagant: A harsh-tempered woman.

thunder-mug: A large, ceramic mug with a lid that fits under a bed, for nighttime use when it's inconvenient to use the jakes.

tickle pitcher: A randy seducer.

tincture of opium: Laudanum.

toss pot: A drunkard.

tumbrel: An open two-wheeled cart.

water-rail: A bird species found in wetlands.

weskit: A sleeveless waistcoat.

zooterkins: An embellished form of gadzooks; an exclamation.

Zounds: God's wounds.

About the Author

ANNIE PEARSON lives and writes in Seattle. In addition to the *Restoration Rules* and *Rain City* series, she also writes the *Accidental Heretics* adventure series (as E.A. Stewart). She posts about eclectic project planning at www.anniepearson.com.

By Annie Pearson:

Chaos House

RESTORATION RULES SERIES

No One Dies

Reap Justice

Call the Reavers

RAIN CITY INCIDENTS SERIES

The Grrrl of Limberlost

Artemis in the Desert

Nine Volt Heart

The Pirate King

Writing as E.A. Stewart:

LEGENDS OF VALERÓS SERIES

Wheel and Serpent: 1

Traitor: 2

Hero: 3

ACCIDENTAL HERETICS SERIES

1: *Bone-mend and Salt*

2: *Trebuchets in the Garden*

3: *Crux Lunata*

4: *Song of Valerós*

The Mad Woman of La Catalane: A Novella

The Blue Door… and More Accidental Heretics Tales

at www.eastewartauthor.com

Author's Notes

Historical Overview: This story is not intended to supplement the much-documented history of the Restoration era, but only to explore possibilities for imaginary individuals. My goal is to entertain, not to help you pass AP 17thC History.

If your secondary education was in the U.S. (and even if you passed AP World History), it's unlikely you read more than three pages about this period, most of which focused on the Great Fire, Samuel Pepys, and the extravagances of Charles II after everyone had had quite enough of Oliver Cromwell and his Commonwealth.

The events alluded to in *No One Dies* correspond with "Milestones: The Foxes of Marborne Parish":

1642–51	Civil wars in England
1649	Execution of Charles I, the second Stuart king; Commonwealth and Interregnum
1660	Restoration of Charles II
1665	London plague and Great Fire
1673	Test Act, enforced on all persons holding office, "preventing dangers...from popish recusants"
1677	Marriage of Mary Stuart, niece of Charles II and presumed royal heir, to William of Orange, governor of The Low Countries
1685	Death of Charles II; Coronation of James II, third Stuart king; Monmouth Rebellion, led by James Fitzroy, Duke of Monmouth, Pretender to the Crown

You can find a bit more about these events through popular history sources such as:

Peter Ackroyd: *Rebellion: The History of England from James I to the Glorious Revolution*

Ian Mortimer: *The Time Traveler's Guide to Restoration Britain*

The bibliographies in those references will lead you to deeper details about the Restoration and related historical periods.

History versus Fiction: The parish and village of Marborne are fictional. The Hawksmoor and Foxe families are fictional, as are Danvers Duncombe and his sisters.

The historic figure Sir Charles Duncombe was not knighted until a year after this story's events. However, I wanted readers to easily differentiate one Duncombe from another, so I knighted him posthumously at an earlier date.

Some have speculated that the Duke of Monmouth believed that his mother married Charles Stuart (when he was Prince of Wales). However, Monmouth lost his claim in a dramatic way that also brought harm to his supporters. Many characters in this story do not care whether Monmouth had a legitimate claim as King Charles's heir; they seek peace—or power—after decades of chaos.

After I invested hours of research to determine whether or not James II was in London during August 1685, it turned out that he was in the city and holding court *because* this story needed him to be in London.

What You Might Think: First, the obsessive mourning rituals adopted in the Victorian era were not yet in fashion. Wearing black to funerals wasn't required, only avoiding shiny clothes.

Next, despite the name of Ian Mortimer's book cited earlier, the kingdom was not "Great Britain" until 1707. Earlier efforts to unite England, Scotland, and Ireland were not successful.

Enclosure of the commons was already happening, but didn't pick up steam until the eighteenth century.

Literary References: Rowland endeavors to quote Shakespeare with precision, but alters the Bard's lines when he must. Lizzie's witticisms are twisted from the epigrams of Aphra Behn, John Dryden, Andrew Marvel, and Robert Herrick.

Acknowledgments: My profound thanks to Jacyn Stewart, Susan Urban, Laura Knapp, Jane Dow, Laurie Cropp, and Martin Fossum for critical and editorial reading. Special thanks to Ajax Bell for close reading.

And my eternal thanks to Waverly Fitzgerald for insight and for Monday through Thursday writing sessions at Liberty on Fifteenth Avenue East. *Orffwys mewn heddwch,* my friend.

All the errors here? Those I managed to make without any assistance.

From Jugum Press

HISTORICAL AND CONTEMPORARY FICTION
Nzinga, African Warrior Queen by Moses L. Howard

Nzinga is a brilliant leader during a time of violent upheaval. This fictional biography brings to life the 17th century flourishing African kingdom, now lost, where early explorers' maps of West Africa call out: "Here reigned the celebrated Queen Nzinga!"

Wheel and Serpent (Legends of Valerós series) by E.A. Stewart

To earn a place as a knight, Taresa of Valerós must get a message to the king of France. But crossing the Languedoc proves treacherous when Taresa and her friends are hunted as rebels after a murder at a Templar house. Amid the chaos and cruelty of the Cathar crusade, Taresa, armed with wit, loyalty, and her lover's third-best sword, sets forth to save herself and her friends.

This Charming Man by Ajax Bell

A chance encounter with an intriguing older man inspires Steven Frazier with visions of a more rewarding life. A vibrant snapshot of Seattle in the early 1990s, this story captures the drama of coming into one's own as an adult.

A Summer in Peach Creek by Michele Malo

Teenaged Faith travels to Peach Creek, West Virginia for a visit with relatives in 1932. When a scandalous murder occurs, Faith discovers the corrupt underbelly of Logan County. As summer progresses and peaches grow, Faith finds her moral center.

PERSONAL VOICES IN HISTORY SERIES
Journey into Gold Country: Memories of a Forty-Niner
by Ralph Buckingham; foreword by Charles Barker
The California Gold Rush, remembered sixty years later by a New England younger son who went to seek his fortune.

We Were Walimu Once and Young, edited by Brooks E. Goddard
True stories from the Teachers for East Africa and Teacher Education for East Africa experience in the 1960s.

www.jugumpress.net

www.ingramcontent.com/pod-product-compliance
Lightning Source LLC
Chambersburg PA
CBHW021123260626
47169CB00005B/1418